A VERY SPECIAL BOOK
TO SOMEONE THAT I
BELIEVE IS A VERY
SPECIAL PERSON. I KNOW
YOU WILL ENJOY IT
AS MUCH AS I DID

Ralph

Victoria at Nine

Books by Don Robertson

THE THREE DAYS (1959)
BY ANTIETAM CREEK (1960)
THE RIVER AND THE WILDERNESS (1962)
A FLAG FULL OF STARS (1964)
THE GREATEST THING SINCE SLICED BREAD (1965)
THE SUM AND TOTAL OF NOW (1966)
PARADISE FALLS (1968)
THE GREATEST THING THAT ALMOST HAPPENED (1970)
PRAISE THE HUMAN SEASON (1974)
MISS MARGARET RIDPATH AND THE DISMANTLING OF THE UNIVERSE (1977)
MAKE A WISH (1978)
MYSTICAL UNION (1978)
VICTORIA AT NINE (1979)

Victoria at Nine

Don Robertson

BALLANTINE BOOKS • NEW YORK

Manufactured in the United States of America

First Edition: February 1979
1 2 3 4 5 6 7 8 9 10

Library of Congress Cataloging in Publication Data
Robertson, Don, 1929-
   Victoria at nine.
   I. Title.
PZ4.R649Vi   [PS3568.0248]   813'.5'4   78-19630
ISBN 0-345-28097-0

For VANESSA HAMLIN *and her mother*

↬ Contents

1	Bear	1
2	Birthday	6
3	Sleep	9
4	Bed	11
5	Family	13
6	Bonnie	14
7	Sequins	16
8	Dyeing	18
9	Morale	21
10	Baths	23
11	Eavesdrop	26
12	Cat	32
13	Scolding	33
14	Principal	38
15	Ezra	51
16	Alone	53
17	Ago	59
18	Bleep	69

19	Doctrine	70
20	Homily	71
21	Dispute	75
22	Reconciliation	80
23	Veritas	84
24	Mischief	94
25	Stripes	112
26	Grandpa	116
27	Analysis	170
28	Owls	174
29	Chicken	177
30	Comfort	178
31	Disturbance	180
32	Concern	198
33	Wishes	204
34	Interrogation	205
35	Exile	211
36	Surrender	216
37	Grief	229
38	Farewell	232
39	Dirt	259
40	Hurt	263
41	Sunday	265

42 *Teddy*   310

43 *Tears*   315

44 *Speed*   321

45 *Safety*   325

46 *Escort*   328

47 *Exhumation*   330

48 *Resurrection*   332

49 *Comments*   335

50 *So*   337

1 ⚬ Bear

HERE WAS a Saturday in early June. Victoria's teacher had scolded her in school yesterday. Victoria did not understand why. It was a vague and misted six o'clock in the morning, and her window was open, and she sat in bed and listened to new leaves. (You should *join in* more, Miss Platt had said. You spend too much time forming words no one hears.)

"That's not so," Victoria said aloud.

Bear was sitting on her lap, and his head moved up and down.

One of Victoria's hands was curled around the back of Bear's head, making it move up and down. "I'm glad you agree," she said.

One of bear's eyes was loose, and just the other day Victoria's mother had sewn shut a tear in his belly. With me, you join in fine, said Bear.

"Just because I didn't want to run in that race," said Victoria.

Ridiculous, said Bear.

"Miss Platt said I was *too good*. Miss Platt said I was *too la de da*."

Miss Platt is a turkey, said Bear.

"Thank you," said Victoria. She brushed lint from Bear's ears. One of them was frayed. She hadn't had a really good conversation with him in she didn't know how long. These days she seemed to spend more time with Marybeth and Bonnie, who were dolls, and Rabbit, who was pink and white, and Cat, who was made

I

of wood and had orange stripes and black stripes and
red wheels and a string that was connected to a metal
loop at the end of his nose.
It's nice to talk to you again, said Bear.
"Were you jealous?" said Victoria.
Afraid so, said Bear.
"Lonely?" said Victoria.
Yes, said Bear.
Victoria kissed the top of Bear's head. More lint
was there, and so she brushed it away. "We were all
supposed to run back and forth between the fire
escape and the fence in the schoolyard," she said, "but
I thought it was silly. They call it physical education.
What's *physical* education? How does a person go
about educating a *bone?*"
Or a rag, said Bear. Or a hank of hair.
"Pardon?" said Victoria.
Nothing, said Bear.
"How come you know so much?" said Victoria.
I, um, I used to be president of Harvard University,
said Bear.
"Really," said Victoria, "you shouldn't fib like that."
Veritas, said Bear.
"Pardon?" said Victoria.
That is Latin for *truth*, said Bear. It is the Harvard
motto. Before I was Bear, I was a seeker of truth. I
believe it is easier to be Bear. But you should have
seen me with my books. I was impressive. I had a
splendid beard, and I wore Benjamin Franklin eye-
glasses, and I took tea with most of the distinguished
men and women of my day.
"Did you ever find truth?" said Victoria.
Every day, said Bear. And everywhere.
"Did it comfort you?" said Victoria.
A little, said Bear.
Victoria hugged Bear to her chest. She was wearing
a flannel nightgown. It was beige, and it was decorated
with canaries that were so yellow they were yellow

beyond yellow. She had celebrated her ninth birthday last month. She had spent it alone with her mother and father, and there had been a small white cake with butterscotch icing, and her father had insisted on calling her a gift of God. Now, smiling, Victoria whispered into one of Bear's ears: "You are a gift of God."

Thank you very much, I'm sure, said Bear, and perhaps he was smiling.

2 🔊 Birthday

THE ICING WAS the best part, and Victoria scooped it up with her fork. She wore a birthday dress her mother had sewn for her. It was blue with pink flowers. Victoria was careful with her fork. She did not want to spill any of the icing on the dress. Each time she lifted the fork, she sort of kept her tongue under it. That way, her tongue would catch any icing that might leak.

Her father and mother sat with her at the table in the diningroom. Her father smiled at her and said: That's my Victoria.

"Pardon?" said Victoria. The flavor of the butterscotch was a little sandy, and she moistened it by pressing her tongue against the roof of her mouth.

The way you are always so careful, said her father.

Such a little *lady*, said Victoria's mother.

"Thank you," said Victoria.

She really doesn't mind, said Victoria's father to her mother.

Not a bit, said Victoria's mother.

"Mind what?" said Victoria.

Being here with us like this, said her mother.

Being such a little *lady*, said her father. Choosing to be on your own the way you do.

Victoria frowned. She thought of Marybeth and Rabbit and Cat and Bear. She thought of her books. She thought of flavors, warmth, good smells. "I'm not

6

on my own so much," she said. "Things take up my time, you know?"

Her father cleared his throat.

Her mother blinked at her.

"People walk around," said Victoria.

People? said her father.

"In my head," said Victoria. "And anybody I want. Ladies with jewels and pretty faces. Kings. And more than people. Sometimes even talking frogs. *All* the time."

Victoria's father and mother were silent.

She looked at them. She smiled.

Her mother looked away.

All the time? said Victoria's father.

"Yes," said Victoria.

And they walk around? said her father.

"And they talk," said Victoria. "And they laugh. And they like me because I am so calm. I always make sure they are carefully dressed."

Victoria's mother looked at her and said: You *do* like your new birthday doll, don't you?

The doll lay on the table next to Victoria's plate. The doll was enormous, and it wore a pink dress, and its hair was dark. "I like her very much," said Victoria. "I've already introduced myself to her, and she's very friendly. She wants me to help her comb her hair every morning. Her name is Bonnie."

Bonnie? said Victoria's father.

"She comes from West Virginia," said Victoria.

Oh, said Victoria's father.

"I thank you for her," said Victoria. "And I thank you for the butterscotch icing. And I thank you that I am warm."

Victoria's father started to reach for her.

She smiled.

He scooped her into his lap, and he kissed her eyes. She reached for Bonnie, and then he also had Bonnie, and he hugged Bonnie, and he smiled, and Victoria's mother smiled, and Victoria heard the clear distant sound of a bell from a Rapid Transit car. It carried quick and clean. It was perhaps like a fingernail against fine crystal.

3 ~ Sleep

IN HER NIGHTMARES she often encountered trolls, but
they usually lost heart and repented. She did not plead
with them, and she was not afraid of them. Instead she
frowned at them, and some of the color went out of
her lips, and she told them they should be ashamed
of themselves. And they rubbed their eyes with great
remorseful troll fists, and they told her they would
try to be better. She rewarded them with readings
from *Five Little Peppers and How They Grew*. She
sometimes awakened in the middle of the night. She
had named her nightlight Bugs. It was in the shape of
a smiling rabbit. Bugs did not like it when people confused him with Rabbit. I don't want the world to
think I'm that square, said Bugs. Then, cackling a little, he told Victoria he was cool, and these days it
was good to be cool. Victoria supposed she agreed,
but she wasn't positive. She did not dream too terribly
much. Instead she was aware of colors, and sometimes
she would cup her hands over her face and inhale
bathsalts. Or what remained of the *odor* of bathsalts.
A crisp and puckery odor, safe and warm. Sometimes
she would whisper in the dark to Marybeth or Rabbit
or Bear or Bonnie, the newcomer. There were other
dolls and animals in the room, but they could be
standoffish, and they did not always comfort Victoria
when she was asleep. When occasionally an unre-
pentant troll came along. Or when the walls of her
sleep turned all spiky and harsh, and she became afraid.
She did not appreciate being afraid.

4 🐿 Bed

HER HAIR was in pigtails that Saturday morning in
June. The year was 1978, and Victoria's mother had
tacked a Hobbit calendar to the wall. Victoria was
not so certain she liked gnomes very much, but she
had said nothing to her mother. She did not want to
hurt her mother's feelings. Now, hugging Bear, she
kept her eyes off the Hobbit calendar. She thought
back on yesterday, on the scolding she had received
from Miss Platt. There are times, Miss Platt had said,
when we have to give of ourselves whether we want
to or not. You may not see the sense in running a race,
but believe me, there is a great deal of sense in such a
thing. It prepares a person for the way life is.

"Is that true?" said Victoria to Bear. She rested him
on her lap. She stroked his ears.

Not necessarily, said Bear.

"Pardon?" said Victoria.

If all you want is to be left alone, said Bear, then
there's no need for you to run a race.

"Is alone the same as lonely?" said Victoria.

Depends on the person, said Bear.

"That's not much of an answer," said Victoria.

Sorry, said Bear.

Victoria looked around the room. "Does anyone
else here have a better answer?" she said.

None of the dolls and animals said a word. Perhaps
they all were still asleep.

Victoria sighed. She shook her head at Bear, and

11

then she made an impatient clucking noise. She stretched, and Bear toppled off her lap. He evidently needed more sleep. Victoria scrunchd down under the covers. She listened to the leaves. Perhaps she would hear a bell from an early Rapid Transit car. She loved her bed. It had a canopy, and sometimes she was ready to believe it could be drawn by horses or reindeer. And sometimes she was ready to believe it could be lifted onto flanged wheels and pulled along tracks by a Rapid Transit car. And sometimes, in winter, which was of course a time of blankets, she was ready to believe her bed was a dogsled, and she was an Eskimo princess, and she was being taken to a ball in the royal igloo. And a great handsome furhatted prince would await. (Bed was grand. You could scrunch and wriggle, and you could pull up the covers, and you were safe.)

5 ᴀ Family

HER FULL NAME was Victoria Anne Tabor, and she
had been born on May 6, 1969. Her father, Carl John
Tabor, had the word *Reverend* in front of his name,
and he was pastor of Wrexford Methodist Church, in
Shaker Heights, Ohio, which is a suburb of Cleveland.
Victoria's mother was named Sandra Bird Tabor. Victoria was an only child. Her father was fifty in 1978,
and her mother was forty. Her father had two
brothers, Uncle Frank, who was a chemist and lived
in Chicago, and Uncle Mark, who sold farm imple-
ments and lived in Grand Island, Nebraska. Both of
her father's parents were dead, but her mother's father,
who was called Grandpa Bird, was still moving around
and taking nourishment. He made his home in what
was known as a retirement village, near Chagrin Falls,
another suburb of Cleveland. Grandpa Bird had an
artificial foot and a deep voice, and in his younger
days he had been an announcer on radio and then
television. Now, though, his deep voice was slurred,
and his words nudged one another too closely, and he
usually had an odor that was too ripe . . . especially
in the breath department, which too often put Victoria in mind of peaches and grapes. Still, he always
seemed happy to see her when she and her parents
visited him at the retirement village, and he always
told her the world still had a future, if the young
people would only stop to think about it. His words
rumbled, and they were like a heavy smear of she did
not know what.

6 🐿 Bonnie

BONNIE WAS having trouble fitting in with the others, and this worried Victoria. She had conferred several times about the situation with Marybeth and Cat and Rabbit and dear old Bear, and their consensus was that Bonnie was a little *tacky*.

After all, she *is* from *West Virginia*, said Marybeth.

And all she wants to talk about is Dolly Parton, said Cat.

She even told me she wished you would make her a sequined dress, said Rabbit.

And a pants suit, said Marybeth.

I don't think we should be so hard on her, said Bear.

Oh? said Cat.

If Victoria thinks she is valuable, said Bear, then we should give her a chance. I mean, look at Bonnie now, the way she is over there on the dresser. It's not right that her forehead should rest against her knee like that. What is she doing? Crying? Do we have a right to be responsible for that?

"She wants me to get a Dolly Parton record—she doesn't like my *Star Wars* album," said Victoria.

Myself, your *Star Wars* album makes me want to howl, said Cat.

Ah, I detest it as well, but there are different strokes for different folks, said Bear.

Victoria went to Bonnie and straightened her up. "The adjustment will take awhile," said Victoria to

Bonnie. Then, after glaring briefly at the others, Victoria said: "You shouldn't slump. You shouldn't let them know how you feel." She adjusted Bonnie's skirt, smoothed Bonnie's hair, kissed Bonnie's forehead.

7 🐿 Sequins

VICTORIA WENT to her mother and said: "Bonnie is very sad."

Bonnie? said Mrs Tabor. Bonnie who?

"Bonnie my birthday doll," said Victoria. "She would like to have a sequined dress. She is from West Virginia, and she is a Dolly Parton fan."

A *sequined dress?* said Mrs Tabor.

"I'd do it myself," said Victoria, "but I don't know how."

Mrs Tabor was blond and fragile, and Victoria believed her to be very pretty, and so did Victoria's father. But right now Mrs Tabor was frowning, and she was not as pretty as she could be. Do you think this is really very wise? she said to Victoria.

"Wise?" said Victoria.

The way you make up so many identities, said Mrs Tabor.

"Pardon?" said Victoria.

Well, said Mrs Tabor, what I *mean* is, Bonnie is only a *doll.* She *says* nothing.

"That's not true," said Victoria, speaking quickly.

Mrs Tabor's frown fled. All right, she said, shrugging. I suppose maybe I was this way when *I* was a little girl, too.

"It has nothing to do with being a little girl," said Victoria. "Bonnie wants a sequined dress. *That's* all it has anything to do with."

Mrs Tabor was sitting on the sofa in the front

16

room, and Victoria was tucked against her. She squeezed Victoria's hands, both of them. She kissed Victoria's hair. Then she said: And when would it be most convenient for Bonnie to be measured?

Victoria pressed her face against her mother's chest.

8 ❧ Dyeing

MRS TABOR wasn't really all that blond. She touched up her hair with Clairol from time to time, and she allowed Victoria to stand in the bathroom and watch. There should be a lesson in this, she said to Victoria as she carefully soaked the Clairol into her roots.

Victoria said nothing. She breathed the Clairol.

A lot of things are not what they seem, said Mrs Tabor.

"That's what Daddy says in church," said Victoria.

Well, he knows what he's talking about, said Mrs Tabor.

"I was wondering about something," said Victoria.

And what might that be? said Mrs Tabor.

Victoria looked away.

Now, now, said Mrs Tabor. Out with it.

"I was thinking about your hair," said Victoria.

What about it? said Mrs Tabor.

"How blond it is," said Victoria. "I was thinking . . . well, maybe Bonnie's hair should be the way yours is."

Blond? said Mrs Tabor.

Victoria looked at her mother and said: "I had more in mind a wig than, um, dyeing her hair . . . a nice blond wig."

For *Bonnie*? said Mrs Tabor.

"Yes," said Victoria. "I mean, now that Bonnie has her sequined dress, a blonde wig would make her look

perfect, and hardly anybody in the world would be able to tell her from Dolly Parton."

Mrs Tabor briefly rubbed her mouth.

Victoria stood on one foot and then on the other.

The next day Mrs Tabor took Victoria shopping for a doll wig. Victoria carried Bonnie along, and she spoke to Bonnie, and she said: "You will be just as glamorous as anything." But Mrs Tabor and Victoria could not find a place that sold doll wigs. So that night Mrs Tabor dyed Bonnie's hair with Clairol. Victoria was concerned that the chemicals would damage Bonnie's scalp, but apparently they did not. Mrs Tabor was careful, and Bonnie's hair did not streak.

9 🌊 Morale

VICTORIA TOOK Bonnie to bed with her that night, and she said: "Do you feel better now?"

Well, I feel prettier, said Bonnie.

Victoria cuddled Bonnie and kissed Bonnie's glistening hair.

I thank you kindly, said Bonnie. This surely beats waiting table.

"Did you wait table?" said Victoria. "Where?"

In Wheeling, West Virginia, said Bonnie, and there was truckers who pinched me, and they said to me: Hi there, Bonnie—where's Clyde? And I got so I couldn't stand the smell of bacon and eggs, you know? Which is why I answered the ad in the newspaper, the one that said: *Wanted—One birthday present, guaranteed to be treated decent, for Miss Victoria Tabor, of Shaker Heights, Ohio.* And I figured, well, maybe I would take a chance on you . . . and maybe you would take a chance on me.

"Do you think it's working out?" said Victoria.

Bonnie inclined her head toward Marybeth and Cat and Rabbit and Bear and the rest of them. They were scattered on the dresser and on the floor and on top of a trunk. Guided by Victoria's fingers, Bonnie's head moved in such a way that she was able to see absolutely *all* of them . . . even Bugs, the nightlight. And then, after giving the matter some thought, Bonnie said: It's probably too early to tell, but Bear *did* say I was a sight for sore eyes. And that one eye of his, the loose one, it sort of *rolled*, if you know what I mean. And myself, I feel better.

"That's good," said Victoria.

All they got to do is give me a chance, said Bonnie.

"I know that," said Victoria.

And I mean, if they was ever to get hungry, I could wait on them, said Bonnie.

"And would you even serve them bacon and eggs?" said Victoria.

You bet your sweet patootie, said Bonnie.

"I guess your morale *is* better," said Victoria.

I guess *so*, said Bonnie.

10 ～ Baths

IT SOMETIMES SEEMED to Victoria that she had been
born on a day when the snow had been flying and the
temperature had been below zero. But that was *dumb*.
She had been born in *May*, and May was a *warm*
month. Or at least it wasn't a very *cold* month. It
was just good old May, and it changed from year to
year, but it did not include blizzards, and its tempera-
tures never came close to zero—certainly not in Shaker
Heights, Ohio. So why, then, was it so important to
Victoria that she always be warm? She had discussed
this with her mother, and Mrs Tabor had allowed as
how perhaps Victoria's blood was a trifle thin. Victoria also had discussed this with her friends in the
bedroom. And Marybeth had said: It makes sense to
want to be warm. And Cat said: Myself, I understand
perfectly. Am I not a replica of a creature that sleeps
so close to an open fire it forever is in danger of
scorching itself? And Rabbit said: You do not have as
much fur as we do, and so *of course* you are afraid
of the cold. And Bear said: There is a fine comfort
to be achieved when one is warm and safe while winds
howl and snort. And even Bonnie, the newcomer, had
offered an opinion, saying: Look, honey, life is tough
enough without having to freeze your toes off. Or
your sweet patootie. And Victoria thanked her friends
for their expressions of support. And every evening
she looked forward to her bath. Her mother drew it,
and her mother scattered the bathsalts and the bubble-

23

bath. The bathsalts were green and red specks. The hot water ran, and the bathroom came all aswirl with steam and puckery fragrances, and Mrs Tabor laid out a nightgown and told Victoria to be sure to dry herself thoroughly. Then, after making sure everything was all right, Mrs Tabor went out of the bathroom, and Victoria carefully undressed. Then, holding her breath and perhaps gnawing on her tongue, Victoria lowered herself into the hot thick foaming water. And Victoria winced, but then Victoria sighed. The water gathered itself around her. The water was an immense cupped palm. Victoria's arms and hands trailed languidly, and she allowed them buoyancy, and she plucked handfuls of soapsuds, and she stuck out her tongue, and she blew at them, and she smiled. There were times, though, when briefly she would think of newspapers, and she would remember photographs of hungry children and dead people, of football players hitting one another, of people with guns. But these times always were brief. They could not stand up to the warmth and the fragrance. Victoria sometimes was afraid, but never when she was in the bathtub. Before her bath, she felt as though her bones had all been tightly lumped and clotted, but then the soap and the water and the bubbles and the steam combined to loosen the lumps and clots and finally do away with them. And this was all right. As Bear once had said to her: You have hurt no one. You did not ask for or demand any of this. You did not take it away from anyone else. Do what you can, but always remember to be what you are. If you were born to be a solitary princess waiting to attend the ball in the royal igloo, don't hit yourself on the head about it. After all, are you making anyone else suffer? (And so Victoria quietly plashed and hummed. And once she had a bar of soap that was in the shape of a green fish. She was unable to use the bar, since she did not want to destroy it. And so she took it to her room, and she named it Henry. Henry the soap fish. And now Henry was on her dresser. He didn't say much, but then, after all, the world wasn't exactly full to the brim with fish that had terribly much to say.)

11 ⟡ Eavesdrop

VICTORIA HAD excellently soft bunnyslippers, and she was able to walk without being heard. She seldom awakened at night, since she was not afraid of the trolls that crawled across her bad dreams and since she was able to soften most of them and get most of them to say they were sorry. Every so often, though (perhaps because she was too cold), she would awaken and find herself unable to return to sleep. Occasionally, then, she would put on her robe and her bunnyslippers and creep into the hallway and listen to conversations between her mother and father. Sometimes the conversations came from their bedroom; sometimes the conversations came from downstairs. In either case, Victoria was able to hear them quite easily. She would sit crosslegged on the warm burgundy upstairs carpeting, and she would back herself against a wall, and the words would carry distinctly, and perhaps she would pick at the skin on her fingers, and one night she heard her parents talk like this:

Sandra, I'm as fully aware of the dignity of the individual as you are, said Victoria's father, but one of these days Victoria will have to put away all her . . . her, um, *gossamer imaginings* . . . and come to grips with the world as it really exists.

Gossamer imaginings? said Victoria's mother.

Sorry, said the Rev Mr Tabor. That's pretty tattered rhetoric, I know, but never mind my imagery. Try to concentrate on the meaning.

When Morris and I were little, we played games.
We would count the cars that went past the house.
He would take Fords and give me Plymouths. I al-
ways lost. I don't really believe I was seriously dam-
aged by the experience, though.
But at least *you* had *Morris.*
What?
Victoria has *nobody.* No brother. Nobody.
What's that supposed to mean?
Nothing. Nothing at all. But an only child is, well,
you know . . . vulnerable.
Vulnerable to *what,* Carl? To imagination? To re-
sourcefulness? What do you want us to *do*—propose
her for membership in Rotary International?
No. That's silly. But we should encourage her to
. . . oh, I don't know . . . get *out* more . . . find little
girls and play with them . . . what do they play?
jacks? tag?
Look, this is 1978, and for all I know they play
napalm.
That's not funny.
Well, then, don't ask me such a stupid question.
Listen, Sandra, the universe is complicated enough,
and we don't want Victoria growing up unpre—
Leave the universe out of this, said Victoria's mother.
It's not Sunday.
All right. I apologize. I have a tendency toward
the fustian, don't I?
Do little brown bears have a tendency to drool
after honey?
But I am right about Victoria, said the Rev Mr
Tabor.
I've told you about Stanley Chaloupka, haven't I?
Yes. Many times.
He carried breadcrusts in his pocket, and he wore
vests. *Vests.* It was 1944, and boys wore *knickers,* but
they did *not* wear *vests.* And everyone thought he

was weird. But my brother didn't think Stanley was weird. My brother appreciated Stanley Chaloupka.

I know all about all this.

Carl, look: Victoria isn't weird. I dress her well, and she's pretty. So what if she wants to stay alone and talk with stuffed things? Isn't she entitled?

Entitled?

Whom is she harming?

Herself, said the Rev Mr Tabor.

Why? Has there been some *trauma?* There hasn't been, and you know it. She's an *only child.* So *big deal.* Why can't everybody just leave her alone? If it isn't you, it's her teacher, that Platt woman. Here we're supposed to be living in a day and age when people read Thoreau and do their own thing, but you don't even want our daughter to talk to dolls and stuffed animals . . .

But I don't want her to be hurt.

This is ridiculous.

How so? said the Rev Mr Tabor.

You want to *protect* her by *exposing* her. That doesn't make any sense at all.

But what do *you* want to do? Wrap her in cellophane and cut her out along the dotted line when she's sixteen or so? She'll become a . . . oh, I don't know what . . . some sort of rebellious, um, *monster* . . . who'll hate us because we overprotected her.

You miss the point, Carl.

Explain it to me.

We are doing nothing. She is doing it all herself. She may be the last child left in the world.

What?

How many children these days read *Five Little Peppers and How They Grew?* How many have the wit and the sensitivity to create identities for their dolls and their animals? This is an age of *facts,* of *mathematics,* of *physical laws.* What do you want

us to do? Preside over the removal of the world's last child?

Well, if she is damaged by what she is . . .

Who is to say she will be?

You read the newspapers, said the Rev Mr Tabor. And they report what is real?

For the most part.

And we all are bound and determined to learn everything that is real, aren't we? It's become a new catchword, hasn't it? *Reality*. It goes right along with *relationship*. And *space*. And *Jungian*. Whenever I serve tea and sherry to you and our friends, I have to wade through those words as though they're stuck on my feet. And I say to myself: Ick.

I could talk with some of the neighbors. A great many of them have nice little daughters who I'm sure would be happy to come here and play with Victoria.

I don't believe this, said Victoria's mother.

All I'm trying to do is make sure she survives.

Make *sure*? How can you make *sure*? Are you *that* familiar with the Almighty?

Sandra, please stop twisting what I say to suit your own—

She wears dresses. She does not wear Levi's. She bathes. She does not shower. She walks slowly and easily. She does not run. She speaks softly. She does not screech. Sundays, when she sits with me in church and you lead the prayers, she follows along with them, and she means what she is saying. The words represent truth to her. I can tell from the expression on her face. Have you ever known her to lie? Of course not. So she constructs imaginary identities for her dolls and animals. She has never hidden those imaginary identities, has she? Why, then, is she such a threat to your precious universe? You and your *reality*.

Sandra, please. We shouldn't argue this way.

Well, what way *should* we argue? Draw up the ground rules for me so I know.

And here Victoria decided to stop picking at the skin on her fingers. She placed her hands over her ears, and suddenly her parents' voices got to sounding like mumblewump and wallarahl and bloomerbop. She edged away from the sound, and the burgundy carpeting was warm against her robe and her nightgown and her buttocks. She retreated into her room, and she took off her robe and her bunnyslippers, and she gathered up all her friends (even Henry the soap fish, taciturn as he was), and she took them to bed with her and she said to them: "If I went away, they wouldn't argue, would they? Or if *you* went away." And something came down with a block and tackle, and the bed was lifted onto flanged wheels, and Victoria and her friends were borne away, and the tracks clicked and wobbled, and a benevolent conductor came along, and maybe he was Captain Kangaroo, and he promised warmth, bathsalts, a cupped palm. He had a fine smile, and his teeth inspired confidence.

12 ᘓᙎ Cat

CAT'S WHEELS squeaked when Victoria pulled him, so mostly she just hugged him. He appreciated this, since his squeaky wheels were a source of some embarrassment to him. Also, he enjoyed being hugged. *Also*, it was no fun to be pulled around by a string attached to your nose. It put a great deal of pressure on the nostrils. And there was something degrading about it. I do have pride, he said.

"Yes," said Victoria. "I can tell by the expression on your face."

It is a characteristic of cats, said Cat.

"You're not afraid of being lonely, are you?" said Victoria.

Of course not, said Cat. My nature has given me selfreliance.

"Even though you are pulled around at the end of a string?" said Victoria.

Could we discuss some other subject? said Cat.

13 &ear; Scolding

VICTORIA ONCE had heard it said that Miss Platt's grandmother sucked canal water through a leaky straw. This piece of information had come from a boy named Ezra Levine, and Victoria supposed it was accurate. Ezra Levine had curls, and his hair was a brilliant red, and his bones were sharp and went in every which direction, and he walked Victoria home that Friday after she refused to take part in the race.

The girls and boys were supposed to run from the fire escape to the fence to the fire escape to the fence to the fire escape, and Miss Platt had said: This will be much more fun than exercises and tag, won't it? And the winning girl will receive a prize. And the winning boy will receive a prize. It's all optional, which means you don't have to run if you don't want to—but I'm sure we all *do* want to, don't we?

The children were clustered at the foot of the fire escape. Miss Platt was short and thin, and her knees were pointed, and she was fond of wearing pleated miniskirts. According to Ezra Levine, even the other teachers thought she was the pits, and they laughed over her pleated miniskirts. (Mrs Rappaport, who taught sixth grade, was a first cousin of Ezra Levine's mother, and Mrs Rappaport sometimes would take Ezra aside in the schoolyard, and they would talk and laugh.) Now Miss Platt began to shout and gesticulate. The boys and girls were separated. Victoria was shooed into the girls' group, and Miss Platt pushed her with the flat of a palm, and it was then that Victoria decided she would not run. She didn't *have* to, and so she *wouldn't*.

Miss Platt held up a hand and motioned for silence. Just so all this is perfectly clear, she said to the children (all twentyseven of her thirdgraders, fifteen girls and twelve boys), I think you are now at an age where you must understand the nature of competitiveness.

The children looked at one another. Several of them giggled. Victoria's eyes were warm.

Miss Platt pressed on: We have spent a great deal of this year in the discussion of great persons. Abraham Lincoln. John Fitzgerald Kennedy. Thomas Alva Edison. Wernher von Braun. Each of these great persons, and all the other great persons the world has ever known, has had to run his or her personal race. That race never is easy. That race carries considerable pain. But I can talk and I can talk and I can *talk*, can't I? My *words* are not all that effective, and they certainly are less effective than a *demonstration* is. So today, then, you will run. You will perhaps feel what they felt . . . and at the same time you will fulfill your physical education requirement for today.

Victoria glanced down at her shoes.

Miss Platt persisted: The idea came to me in a dream one night years ago. The idea for the race, that is. I was dreaming of John Fitzgerald Kennedy, and he spoke to me of his bad back, and then he spoke of the pursuit of excellence. He spoke of Camelot. He spoke of impossible dreams. Like Don Quixote. And he told me yes, a race would be a good idea.

Some of the children frowned.

Miss Platt dabbed with a thumb at a corner of her mouth. She smiled at the girls. You will run first, she said. Spread out, and remember—fire escape to fence to fire escape to fence to fire escape.

Giggling, the girls spread out. Victoria did not join them.

Miss Platt blinked at Victoria.

Victoria stood to one side and folded her arms over her belly.

Didn't you hear me? said Miss Platt.

"Yes, Miss Platt," said Victoria, "I heard you."

Then please line up with the others, said Miss Platt.

"No," said Victoria.

What? said Miss Platt.

"You said we don't have to if we don't want to," said Victoria. "Well, I don't want to."

No, said Miss Platt, and her head jerked from side to side.

"Yes," said Victoria, and *her* head slowly moved up and down.

Miss Platt smiled. Some of her teeth were crooked. Others appeared to have caved in. She pressed one of her hands against the front of her pleated miniskirt. She said: Victoria, you did the best book report on President Kennedy I've ever read. You are a fine pupil, and I am sure your father is very proud of you . . . perhaps as proud of you as you must be proud of him, considering the spiritual leadership and guidance he provides at Wrexford Methodist. But do you think he will be proud of you if he learns you refused to take part in a silly *race?*

"If the race is silly," said Victoria, "then what difference does it make whether I take part?"

Now you listen, young lady, said Miss Platt, I will not tolerate smart remarks. I don't care if your father *is* the pastor of Wrexford Methodist.

Victoria shapped words with her mouth, but no sounds emerged.

Miss Platt took a step toward her.

A sound came from the clustered boys. It was a

cackling sound, and Ezra Levine was responsible for it.

Most of the girls giggled.

Miss Platt glared at Ezra Levine, and then she glared at the girls.

Ezra Levine rubbed his elbows and embraced himself.

Miss Platt spread her arms in Victoria's direction. You'll enjoy it, said Miss Platt. You'll enjoy it just fine. There is something about the *joy* of *competition*, you know? The *pursuit* of *excellence*.

Ezra Levine made noises into his chest.

Miss Platt ignored him. It came to me in a *dream*, she said to Victoria. A *dream*. And dreams mean a great deal.

Victoria looked away from Miss Platt. She looked toward Ezra Levine, and he quickly jerked a thumb upward.

Miss Platt looked toward Ezra Levine, and he tucked his hands behind his back.

Syllables came to Victoria's lips. She formed them. Still, though, no sounds emerged.

Miss Platt's attention again turned to Victoria, and she saw the trouble Victoria was having. She moved another step toward Victoria, and then she said: You should *join in* more. She was speaking briskly now, and she said: You spend too much time forming words no one hears. You are *too good*. You are *too la de da*.

Victoria moistened her lips.

Miss Platt moved forward in a sort of lurch. She seized Victoria by a shoulder and said: There are times when we have to give of ourselves whether we want to or not. You may not see the sense in running a race, but believe me, there is a great deal of sense in such a thing. It prepares a person for the way life is.

Victoria pulled her shoulder free of Miss Platt's grasp. She rubbed the shoulder.

So you'll do it, won't you? said Miss Platt.

"No," said Victoria. The word came out reluctantly. There was something else she wanted to say, and it was a whole lot more important.

You are *impossible,* said Miss Platt, and her voice sounded as though someone had filled her throat with rock salt and bottle caps.

"So are you," said Victoria.

What? said Miss Platt.

And now Victoria was able to give sound to the formed words, and she said: "Your grandmother sucks canal water through a leaky straw."

14 🦋 Principal

THE LAUGHTER CAME in a flabbergasted eruption. Some of the children even bent over double. Ezra Levine embraced a boy named Wesley Kiplinger, who was very fat. Most of the girls squealed, but one of them, Rose Stickney, who was one of seven black children attending the Wrexford Elementary School, actually brayed and howled, and at one point she nearly choked. Victoria went to her and clapped her on the back. Rose Stickney nodded, but she could not speak. All she could do was snort. As this was happening, some of the boys were jumping up and down and pummeling one another. And Miss Platt stood perfectly still, and now both her hands were pressed against her precious pleated miniskirt, and her mouth was open, and her belly moved in what seemed to be quick, tight spasms. Finally she turned away from Victoria. She turned away from everyone. She placed her hands on her hips, and she appeared to be drawing deep breaths. Victoria watched her closely, and Victoria was sorry for her. It wasn't that she hated Miss Platt, but Miss Platt had given them a *choice*, correct? And Victoria had *chosen* not to run in the race. If the other children *chose* to run in the race, that was their business. But Victoria had *chosen* to abstain, which was Victoria's right, according to the ground rules Miss Platt herself had established. So why, then, had Victoria been scolded? Why had she been forced to string together the unformed words and make the

accusation against Miss Platt's grandmother, who anyway probably was dead and buried now? Victoria
did not understand. Perhaps she never would understand. Perhaps she was too stupid. Perhaps it was the
absolute pits to take a teacher's word on anything.
(Victoria hated the word *pits*. It was an ugly word,
and she knew little ladies really should not employ
it in their vocabularies. Especially since it reminded
Victoria of *prunes*, which she probably hated even
more than she hated *pits*.) Victoria supposed she would
get it good and proper for accusing Miss Platt's
grandmother of sucking canal water through a leaky
straw. Still, she didn't believe she cared. She narrowed
her eyes when Miss Platt finally turned to face the
laughing children. Miss Platt's hands were still on her
hips, and she had planted her feet widely apart. She
exhaled, and then she shouted to everyone to be quiet.
She drew her lips into a thin grimace, and the laughter
gradually went away. She went to Victoria and stood
over Victoria and told her to stay out of the way;
the race would still be run. Or, more accurately, two
races would still be run—one for the boys, one for
girls. And she said to Victoria: When this is finished,
you and I will be paying a little call on Mrs Bee, and
perhaps you can explain to *her* why all of a sudden
you have become such a comedienne. Do you understand what I am saying to you? And Victoria nodded.
"Yes," she said.

Mrs Bee was the principal of the Wrexford Elementary School. She had been the principal of the
Wrexford Elementary School for seven hundred
years. She was tall and broad, and she had hair that
was streaked red and gray, and she almost always wore
dresses that had horizontal stripes, and sometimes the
horizontal stripes were in a sort of zigzag and caused
her to resemble an Easter egg. Victoria knew little
about Mrs Bee other than that perhaps she was expected to be afraid of Mrs Bee. She stood to one

side and watched the races. She breathed slowly, and she tried not to think of Mrs Bee. She thought instead of Bear and Cat and Bonnie and the rest of them. She even thought of Bugs. She even thought of Henry the soap fish. And she thought of angels in the snow. Last winter she and several other girls had lain in the snow here in this schoolyard and had vigorously moved their arms up and down and had made angels. Her mother had been upset with her for getting her snowsuit all cold and wet, but her mother also had smiled, saying: What sort of world would it be without snow angels? And then her mother had embraced Victoria and had taken her off to the bathroom and a fine warm tub. But now there was more in store for Victoria than a fine warm tub, and it wouldn't be fine (unless you counted fear as being fine), and it wouldn't be warm (unless you counted anger as being warm). Victoria picked at her fingers and tried to concentrate on the races. The girls raced first, and the winner was Martha Vandevoort, who was tall and skinny and whose voice was so salivary she talked as though her mouth were full of live flopping fish. And maybe turtles and seaweed. She won easily, and she was the only girl who neither giggled nor shrieked. (Leaving out Victoria, of course.) The winner of the boys' race was Bruce Doubleday, and he had enormous teeth, and his shirt was moist at the armpits, and he laughed. Miss Platt congratulated Martha Vandevoort and Bruce Doubleday, and she marched the children back to their room, and she took the prizes out of her desk, and they consisted of identical small bags of Fritos Corn Chips.

It was an hour or so later, when school was dismissed for the day, that Miss Platt escorted Victoria to Mrs Bee's office. Victoria had to go to the bathroom, but she said nothing. Miss Platt *steered* Victoria up the hallway to the school office, and the hallway smelled of chalk and paste and old raincoats. Victoria

was aware of drawings, of gold stars, of bulletin
boards, of a display case. The drawings had something to do with astronauts and bald eagles and the
Declaration of Independence and the Cleveland
Cavaliers. Victoria thought for a moment of the races.
Most of the girls and boys had seemed to enjoy themselves, and they had made a lot of noise, laughing and
shrieking. And they had elbowed one another. And
they had shoved. And their clothing had flapped. And
some of them had even clutched at the air. And it
appeared that none of them remembered what Victoria had said about Miss Platt's grandmother. They
had forgotten their flabbergasted eruption of laughter.
Now it was *the races* that mattered, *the challenge*,
and even Victoria's friend Ezra Levine had taken
part. What had it been with all of them? Scaredness?
Why was Victoria the only one who'd refused? Was
she crazy? Was she spoiled, contrary, numb, stupid?
Oh, dear, it was too bad she felt such a convulsion of
fear right now. If she didn't perhaps she would be
able to get Mrs Bee to explain, or at least get Mrs Bee
to get Miss Platt to explain. But that probably was
out of the question. There was no moisture in Victoria's mouth. Now more than anything she wanted
to press her face against a warm benevolent lap.

The door to the office said OFFICE, and the door
to the principal's office said PRINCIPAL. Both doors
were open, and Miss Platt marched Victoria straight
into the principal's office, and Mrs Bee looked up from
her desk and said: Wellnow, Winifred, what might
all this be?

Miss Platt steered Victoria until they both were
standing directly in front of Mrs Bee's desk. We
have a problem here, said Miss Platt to Mrs Bee.

I rather thought so, said Mrs Bee to Miss Platt.
I mean, you don't normally burst in here with a child
in tow because you want to tell me he or she received
a perfect score on a spelling test.

"I did," said Victoria. "Just last week."

Hush, said Miss Platt to Victoria.

Congratulations, said Mrs Bee to Victoria.

Please don't encourage her, said Miss Platt to Mrs Bee.

Mrs Bee's dress was white with pink horizontal stripes. She leaned forward, and her elbows smacked the edge of the desk. Ow, she said. Then she rubbed her left elbow with her right hand, and she rubbed her right elbow with her left hand, and she said to Miss Platt: I beg your pardon?

She needs to be disciplined, said Miss Platt to Mrs Bee.

Why so? said Mrs Bee to Miss Platt.

Right out in front of the entire class she told me my grandmother sucked canal water through a leaky straw, said Miss Platt to Mrs Bee.

Mrs Bee had been frowning over her elbows. She hesitated, then unfolded her arms and looked up. I didn't know that, she said to Miss Platt. I do hope she doesn't damage her, um, digestive tract.

Nadine! said Miss Platt to Mrs Bee.

Yes? said Mrs Bee to Miss Platt.

This is *serious*, said Miss Platt to Mrs Bee.

Victoria cleared her throat, and a sort of rusted noise came from her nostrils.

Mrs Bee leaned back. If it is serious, she said to Miss Platt, then you'll have to give me all the specifics.

Well, isn't it enough that she *said* what she *said?* said Miss Platt to Mrs Bee. Isn't it enough that she *insulted* me? I mean, what sort of world is this when a *child* can say such a rudely pejorative thing to a *teacher?* We forever talk of discipline. Hardly a faculty meeting goes by without talk of discipline. And *parents* talk of discipline. Every survey a person comes across, the findings are that most people favor firmness.

Please, Winifred, said Mrs Bee, leave *the world* and

surveys out of this. I am simply trying to get at the
specifics of this infamous affair.

Victoria nudged at a nostril with a knuckle.

It's not *funny!* said Miss Platt to Mrs Bee.

Well, you could have fooled *me*, said Mrs Bee
to Miss Platt.

Miss Platt sighed. Your famous wit is at work
again, isn't it? she said to Mrs Bee. I've known you
how long? twenty years? Well, it's too bad I've never
been able to appreciate it.

Yes, said Mrs Bee to Miss Platt. It is.

Victoria briefly closed her eyes. For some reason,
she no longer particularly needed to go to the bathroom.

You shouldn't talk this way in front of *her*, said
Miss Platt to Mrs Bee.

Victoria opened her eyes.

Mrs Bee ignored what Miss Platt had said. She
smiled at Victoria. You're not afraid, are you? she
said.

"I don't think so," said Victoria. She spoke quickly
and easily, and she surprised herself, at least a little.

Mrs Bee patted some of her hair that was red,
and then she patted some of it that was gray. You're
Mr Tabor's little girl, aren't you? she said.

"Yes," said Victoria.

Does your father teach you to say bizarre things
to your teacher? said Mrs Bee.

"No," said Victoria.

Your mother? said Mrs Bee.

"No," said Victoria.

Jesus Christ? said Mrs Bee.

"Pardon?" said Victoria.

I expect you go to church every Sunday, said
Mrs Bee, seeing as how your father does what he
does for a living. And I was just wondering . . . well,
perhaps somewhere Jesus Christ suggests that little
girls say bizarre things to their teachers.

It was more than *bizarre*, said Miss Platt to Mrs Bee. It was *insulting*.

Victoria's lips began to move, but no sounds came from her.

Again Mrs Bee ignored what Miss Platt had said. What really happened? she said to Victoria.

Miss Platt broke in. It was the *races*, she said to Mrs Bee. Today was the day for the *races*. You know the races I'm talking about . . . the ones I've been holding for years . . .

Oh, said Mrs Bee to Miss Platt. Your *races*. I remember them now.

But Victoria here would not participate, said Miss Platt to Mrs Bee. And when I remonstrated with her, she told me my grandmother sucked canal water through a leaky straw.

Is that true? said Mrs Bee to Victoria.

Victoria nodded.

But why didn't you want to participate? said Mrs Bee to Victoria.

I've been holding those races for years and *years*, said Miss Platt to Mrs Bee. And never once has a child refused to participate.

Until today, said Mrs Bee to Miss Platt.

All right, said Miss Platt to Mrs Bee.

Victoria's mouth formed an *o*. She moistened her lips and grimaced.

Go ahead, said Mrs Bee to Victoria.

Victoria coughed. She could not speak.

She does well in her classwork, doesn't she? said Mrs Bee to Miss Platt.

Miss Platt nodded.

Does she behave herself? said Mrs Bee to Miss Platt.

Well, she keeps *to* herself, said Miss Platt to Mrs Bee. And do you see her mouth now? Do you see the way it is working? She does a lot of *that*. It is as though she is whispering to invisible friends who perhaps, um, *counsel* her.

Oh, said Mrs Bee to Miss Platt. She rose. She went around the desk to Victoria. She stroked Victoria's hair for a moment, and then she pressed Victoria's face against her belly. It was a warm belly, and Victoria rejoiced in its warmth. I think I know all about it, said Mrs Bee to Victoria. Mrs Bee's voice was thin, and perhaps it was perforated at the edges, and she said to Victoria: I think *you* don't think it's necessary—the race, I mean. I think you would rather be left alone.

Victoria's head moved up and down against Mrs Bee's belly.

I was a little bit that way when *I* was a little girl, said Mrs Bee to Victoria. I was too fat, you see, and I didn't want people to watch me. I wanted to be invisible. So I . . . well, I stayed out of the way. Which meant I wasn't ridiculed as much as perhaps I would have been. *You*, though, you're not too fat. You're really very pretty, as a matter of fact.

And she knows it, said Miss Platt to Mrs Bee.

Please, Winifred, said Mrs Bee to Miss Platt.

Oh, said Miss Platt to Mrs Bee.

So why didn't you want to run? said Mrs Bee to Victoria.

"I . . . I thought that was my . . . right," said Victoria into Mrs Bee's belly.

Mrs Bee took Victoria by the shoulders and pushed her away a little. But was it your *right* to tell Miss Platt her grandmother sucked canal water through a dirty straw? said Mrs Bee to Victoria.

"A *leaky* straw," said Victoria to Mrs Bee.

Oh, said Mrs Bee to Victoria, I beg your pardon. If you can, though, please answer my question.

"I just . . . she wouldn't let up on me," said Victoria to Mrs Bee.

So you think that means it was all right for you to be disrespectful? said Mrs Bee to Victoria.

"Maybe," said Victoria to Mrs Bee.

But there are standards of conduct, said Mrs Bee to Victoria.

"Only for me?" said Victoria to Mrs Bee. "How about everybody else? How come Miss Platt tells us we don't *have* to run if we don't *want* to run, and so I don't want to run, and so she yells at me?"

Did you *yell?* said Mrs Bee to Miss Platt.

I, ah, I was *firm,* said Miss Platt to Mrs Bee.

Victoria looked at Miss Platt. "Please, Miss Platt, I don't hate you. I don't hate anybody. But I . . ."

Miss Platt was unable to look directly at Victoria. Her eyes were brown and dull, and they moved loosely, and they would not focus on Victoria.

"Don't think I hate you," said Victoria to Miss Platt. "Please don't think that."

Miss Platt poked at a corner of her mouth with a thumb.

Winifred, for heaven's sake, set the child's mind at ease, said Mrs Bee to Miss Platt. It seems to me we're permitting this entire situation to get out of hand.

In all the years I've conducted the races, said Miss Platt to Mrs Bee, not a one of them has refused. So how can I honestly set her mind at ease? *I* have feelings, too. Just because I'm a *teacher,* that doesn't mean I'm a *stone.* I mean, not *necessarily.* I mean, I have nightmares. I mean, I go to the bathroom. Scratch me, and I bleed. Rob me, and I starve. Attack me, and I scream.

"I scream for ice cream," said Victoria.

Mrs Bee and Miss Platt looked at her.

"That's what I always say when my parents buy me a cone," said Victoria.

I scream for ice cream, said Mrs Bee to Victoria. You scream for ice cream. We all scream for ice cream. That's how it goes, isn't it?

"Yes," said Victoria to Mrs Bee.

I don't believe we have much of a problem here, do we? said Mrs Bee to Victoria.

Victoria shrugged. She wished her face were still pressed against Mrs Bee's belly.

All you have to do is apologize to Miss Platt for your remark, said Mrs Bee to Victoria. I understand the principle you are trying to uphold, and I sympathize with it, but it does not excuse rudeness. Nothing excuses rudeness.

Victoria's mouth opened and closed. She said nothing.

Mrs Bee patted one of Victoria's shoulders.

Victoria looked up at Mrs Bee.

Please, said Mrs Bee to Victoria.

Victoria made an *o*.

Now you listen to me, said Mrs Bee to Victoria. Mrs Bee's voice was steady, and she did not appear to be angry. She actually was smiling a little. Her lips were moist. They were vaguely purple. Now, as she spoke to Victoria, she curled herself into a sort of crouch, and her moist and vaguely purple lips enunciated all her words with a scissored precision, and she said: Sometimes we have to cooperate whether we want to or not. Sometimes we have to put up with injustice whether we want to or not. You see, this is a *school*, and all you youngsters are supposed to *learn*, and so there must be at least some discipline at all times, even when it makes no sense. The world is very complicated, and we must have order. Oh, yes, I know what you want to say. You want to say you don't understand why there has to be order when it's wrong. Well, I'm sorry. I wish I could answer that question, but I can't. If Miss Platt was wrong in going back on her word that the running of the race was optional, then you were just as wrong when you said what you said about her grandmother and the canal water and the rusty straw.

"*Leaky* straw," said Victoria to Mrs Bee.

I beg your pardon, said Mrs Bee to Victoria.

I don't believe any of this, said Miss Platt to no one in particular.

Please apologize, said Mrs Bee to Victoria.

Another *o*.

Please, said Mrs Bee to Victoria.

Victoria's tongue pressed against the insides of her upper teeth. "No," she said, and the word sneaked through the *o*, barely emerging.

Mrs Bee looked at Miss Platt and said: Veronica here apparently does not believe in the principle that two wrongs make a right.

"*Victoria*," said Victoria to Mrs Bee.

Sorry, said Mrs Bee to Victoria.

That's the second time *you've* apologized to *her*, said Miss Platt to Mrs Bee.

That's true, said Mrs Bee to Miss Platt.

A good principal supports his faculty, said Miss Platt to Mrs Bee.

I am not a *his*, said Mrs Bee to Miss Platt. I am a *her*.

Please, said Miss Platt to Mrs Bee, haven't we known each other long enough so we don't have to . . . ah, wallow in semantics and complicate what is essentially a simple situation?

Mrs Bee was still in the crouch. She straightened. She leaned toward Miss Platt and said: It may be simple to you, but it's not simple to me, and it's not simple to this child. It seems to me that perhaps your behavior cancels out what she said.

Pardon? said Miss Platt, pressing a palm against her throat.

It would be refreshing if someday before you died you stopped being ~o officious, said Mrs Bee to Miss Platt.

Vicious? said Miss Platt to Mrs Bee.

Mrs Bee shook her head and said: The word was

officious, not *vicious.* You and that race, your *symbolism.* I mean, suppose you *do* inspire one of them to be another John F. Kennedy? Why should all the others pay for it? And, then, you remember what happened to Kennedy, don't you?

Miss Platt frowned toward Victoria.

Are you afraid she understands? said Mrs Bee to Miss Platt. Then, smiling at Victoria, Mrs Bee said: Do you understand?

"I . . . um, I think so," said Victoria to Mrs Bee.

Mrs Bee sighed. She went back behind her desk and seated herself. She folded her hands on the desk blotter. She sucked on her lower lip for a moment. Then she smiled at Victoria and said: I do believe you do understand.

We shouldn't talk this way in front of one of the children, said Miss Platt to Mrs Bee.

You are absolutely correct, said Mrs Bee to Miss Platt. Then, still smiling, Mrs Bee said to Victoria: Everything is canceled out.

What? said Miss Platt to Mrs Bee.

You heard me correctly, said Mrs Bee to Miss Platt.

Well, I don't believe it, said Miss Platt to Mrs Bee.

You may leave now, said Mrs Bee to Victoria.

I don't believe it *at all,* said Miss Platt to Mrs Bee.

But I'd like *you* to stay, said Mrs Bee to Miss Platt.

Miss Platt made a sound that perhaps came from her chest.

Victoria did not move.

Really, said Mrs Bee to Victoria, it's *all right.* You may leave now. As far as I am concerned, the books are balanced.

Victoria nodded. She really wanted to leave, but somehow her feet were stuck to the floor. It was as though globs of chewing gum had been slapped on the soles of her shoes. Finally, though, she was able to lift a foot. She wondered what Cat and Bear and

the rest of them would think of her when she told
them about this day. Miss Platt was saying something
angry to Mrs Bee, but Victoria was unable to concentrate on the words. Now she was able to lift both
of her feet, and she was moving nicely toward the
door that said PRINCIPAL. Mrs Bee said something
to Miss Platt having to do with who was the teacher
and who was the principal, who was the Indian and
who was the chief. Or who wasn't boss and who was.
Mrs Bee shouted to Victoria to close the door behind
her. Nodding, Victoria went out. She closed the door
firmly. The need to go to the bathroom had returned
to her. She hoped Mrs Bee wouldn't yell too much
at Miss Platt. She really didn't hate Miss Platt, even
though Miss Platt was silly, and even though Miss
Platt's grandmother unquestionably *did* suck canal
water through a leaky dirty rusty straw.

15 ❧ Ezra

EZRA LEVINE was waiting for Victoria when she emerged from the school after visiting the bathroom. Ezra lived on Shaker Boulevard—less than a block away from Victoria's home. He often walked with her. He was perhaps her only real friend in the whole world—or at least her only real friend at the Wrexford Elementary School. He grinned at her, and he scuffed along next to her, and he said: I waited for you.

"I was able to figure that out," said Victoria.

Did Mrs Bee yell at you? said Ezra.

"No," said Victoria.

Not at all? said Ezra.

"Not at all," said Victoria. "She was very nice."

She and Miss Platt *live together*, said Ezra. Didn't you know that?

Victoria made a face at Ezra.

I'm not putting you on, said Ezra.

Victoria kicked at a twig.

Mrs Bee is a widow, said Ezra, and she and Miss Platt have been living together since maybe the Civil War.

"The what?" said Victoria.

The *Civil War*, you dummy, said Ezra. I mean, they're *old* . . .

"What's the Civil War?" said Victoria.

It was fought back in I don't know when, said

Ezra. The time of George Washington, whenever that was.

"Oh?" said Victoria.

You sure did give us a good laugh today, said Ezra.

"Oh?" said Victoria.

The canal water thing, said Ezra.

"Oh," said Victoria.

I thought old Platt was going to swallow her ears, said Ezra. Everybody was real proud of you.

"But you all ran in the races anyway, didn't you?" said Victoria.

Yes, said Ezra, clearing his throat.

"How does a person swallow her ears?" said Victoria.

Ezra looked around for a twig of his own. He found it. He kicked at it. His cheeks were moist and pink. Then he said: I waited for you. I like you.

"So?" said Victoria.

I didn't *want* to run, said Ezra. And I came real close to speaking up.

"Real close," said Victoria.

Don't be mad at me, said Ezra.

Victoria stopped. She placed her hands on her hips. Ezra also stopped. His arms hung loosely. He was wearing moccasins, jeans, a plaid shirt. He sometimes wore a T-shirt that said DARTH VADER, but this day he was wearing a plaid shirt. Most of the colors were reds. He said: You're not like anybody in the world. Please don't be mad at me.

Victoria squeezed her hips.

I don't care if you're Protestant or *what* you are, said Ezra.

16 ᘓᕝ Alone

NEARLY ALL the girls in Miss Platt's room usually
wore jeans and T-shirts to school. Victoria always
wore a dress, or a skirt and blouse, or a jumper and
blouse. This was by her own choice. "Maybe my
name should have been something besides Victoria,"
she once said to her mother. She hated no one. She
became impatient now and then, and she became
disturbed when people broke their word, but she
hated not a soul. There once had been a time when
she had held solemn and important conversations with
her mother's comb. She had been fond of plucking at
its teeth with a thumb. If she did this just right, the
teeth actually sort of sang. But then several of the
teeth came loose, and her mother bought a new comb
and threw out the old comb one day while Victoria
was in school. Victoria wept a little for the old comb.
She lay in bed, and she pressed fists against her eyes,
and she made hardly any noise. Her dolls and animals
were crowded around her, and they told her they
were very, very sorry. They told her they understood. Victoria made pinched sounds in the back of
her throat. She was not angry with her mother,
though. That wouldn't have made a bit of sense. After
all, how could her mother have known? Oh, yes,
there were many days when it was no fun to be
Victoria Anne Tabor, days when even a warm bath
every ten muintes wouldn't have helped. She had
come to believe that she never would know why she

was the way she was. Sometimes she would squeeze her eyes tightly shut and try to bring back what it must have felt like to have been born. A cupped palm may have been involved, and her body probably had been all puckered and sweet. But all she really could summon was a sort of damp silence, a desire to be wrapped in a towel, to curl, to gulp, to sleep. And maybe it was silence that she felt more than anything . . . and maybe it was silence that provided the warmest cupped palm. Certainly she *knew* silence better than she knew spelling or arithmetic or history or whatever else a person would care to name. She was the daughter of a man who had the word *Reverend* in front of his name, and she had always known she could not run and giggle. And anyway, who was there to run and giggle *with?* So she summoned her dolls and her animals, and she held the solemn and important conversations with her mother's old singing comb. And now, at nine, in June of 1978, she only wanted to be left alone, to muse alone, to confide in companions *she* chose . . . for whatever reasons. If there were races to be run, let others run them. If there were cold places to explore, let others explore them. To Victoria Anne Tabor, silence perhaps was not golden, but at the same time it probably was necessary. It defeated cold winds, didn't it? On account of cold winds made noise, correct? Which meant silence was warm, correct?

So why, then, had she created a disturbance—of laughter—by accusing Miss Platt's grandmother of sucking canal water through a leaky straw? Lying in bed the next morning, remembering the laughter, she asked this question of Bear, who said: Well, there are limits.

"Limits to what?" said Victoria.

To patience, said Bear.

"But the words brought a whole lot of loud noise

with them," said Victoria. "The way the other kids laughed, I mean. If I hadn't said anything, I could have . . . um, protected the silence. The silence inside *me*, I mean."

The noise was proper, said Bear.

"It *hurt* my *ears*," said Victoria.

But you made your point, said Bear.

Victoria shrugged. She patted Bear's frayed ear. She supposed it hurt as much as hers had. She kissed the frayed ear.

Thank you, said Bear.

"You are very welcome," said Victoria.

Bear nodded. His head had been assisted by one of Victoria's hands. Or perhaps not. She could not remember. She did not really believe Bear had once been president of Harvard University, but then a person just never could tell. She always tried to listen with care to whatever it was that passed for his wisdom, his examination of what he called *Veritas*. But now he was being a little sentimental. He said: I appreciate our conversations, Victoria. You see, I love you. A little while ago, when you called me a gift of God, I was polite enough, and I thanked you, and I even smiled a little, but the *real* truth is: I wanted to cry. And my bad eye, the loose one . . . well, it almost fell out.

"Hush," said Victoria.

I *mean* it, said Bear.

"All right," said Victoria. "Fine."

I'm not saying it because I'm trying to be nice, said Bear. I'm saying it because I *mean* it.

Victoria hugged Bear, and there was a quick little patter and clack of applause from the dolls and the other animals. Even Henry the soap fish applauded, and even Bugs.

She smiled. She decided there was no real reason she had to get out of bed yet. She closed her eyes and tried to go back to sleep. Perhaps she would be able to disarm another troll and make it change its ways. She had heard her father speak of Bornagain Christians. Well, if there were Bornagain Christians, why could not there be Bornagain Trolls? She could see them now, tents full of them, Bornagain Trolls, singing, praying, clapping their claws. And Bornagain Dragons, quenching their fiery breath in the name of the Lord. Bornagain Porcupines, surrendering their quills. Bornagain Bulls, renouncing red flags. Bornagain Tigers, wrapping their fangs in cotton. Occasionally, in a sermon, her father would refer to something called The Peaceable Kingdom, which was a land where the lion lay down with the lamb and silent farmers tilled warm and heavy earth and children mused in the shade of plump green trees. And once she had seen a painting of The Peaceable Kingdom reproduced in a book. And she had shown The Peaceable Kingdom to all her dolls and animals, and she had said to them: "If we found this place, nobody would holler at us, right?"

And her dolls and animals had said: *Right.*

And then Victoria had said: "And the whole world would be baths and smiles and chocolate, right?"

And her dolls and animals had said: *Right.*

And then Victoria had said: "And we wouldn't have to prove a thing, right?"

And her dolls and animals had said: *Right.*

Now, as she tried to go back to sleep, Victoria embraced herself and attempted to set The Peaceable Kingdom clearly in her mind. And she listened to the new leaves outside her window. And they were quiet, which meant they did not offend her. And she tried to remember the precise pitch of the singing sound her mother's old comb had made. And she supposed she was as alone as anyone in the world, and the damp grassy odors of Shaker Heights, Ohio (here, now, as they came to her almost as a curl of steam), probably really were being tasted by *her* and no one else, and the secret of Bear's former presidency of Harvard University probably was known by *her* and no one else, and Bonnie's beauty probably was appreciated by *her* and no one else, and Victoria supposed this all meant she enjoyed being alone, even though she was more alone than anybody. And she supposed she would always leave the races and the explorations to others. And she supposed this was her *Veritas*. And at the same time she decided now was no time to be asking herself why she forever conferred with her dolls and her animals. Why she had made a comb sing. Why she had wept for it after it had been thrown out. And why she even had saved all her burntout nightlights. Before Bugs, there had been a mouse she had named Pluto, and a dog she had named Mickey, and a genuine Kermit the Frog from the Muppet television program. They lay on the dresser along with Henry the soap fish. And even though they no longer worked, they were not dead. They simply were retired, and retired things talked just as well as did things that were not retired. This was especially true in the case of Kermit the Frog, who was forever kidding Pluto and Mickey, telling them: She names the mouse Pluto, and she names the dog Mickey, and who says she doesn't have a sense of humor? And Victoria almost always smiled when she listened to the chatter of Kermit the Retired Frog. She appreciated it as long as it was quiet. She did not want the silence threatened. She did not want the cupped palm to be pushed away. Which was why this time . . . and most times . . . she would not ask herself why she had summoned the magic that had given voice to plastic and cotton and wood and glass and even soap, that had made an old frayed teddybear insist he once had been president of Harvard University. If she really questioned herself too often about all this, she might have taken to thinking she really was not alone after all, that she had surrounded herself with murmurous and benevolent multitudes. Perhaps her Peaceable Kingdom was a Peaceable Fortress. She pressed her face against her pillow. She frowned. She heard birds and bells, and then for a time she slept. She was alone. She did not dream. It was not so bad.

17 ❧ Ago

VICTORIA OFTEN helped her mother with the wash, at least to the extent of sorting the whites from the coloreds. And her mother appreciated the help, and one day she said to Victoria: I become tired, too, do you know?

Victoria nodded. She was folding pillowcases.

Very tired, said Sandra Tabor.

Another nod from Victoria, and she folded another pillowcase. The laundry room had an insistent and sterile odor of bleach, detergent, fabric softener, the steam from an iron.

Your Grandma Bird died when I was fourteen, said Victoria's mother.

"Yes," said Victoria.

Which was twentysix years ago, said Victoria's mother.

"Yes," said Victoria.

And since that time I have had all sorts of responsibilities, said Victoria's mother. We lived on Edmunds Avenue in those days, and I was only fourteen, but I *ran* the *household*. There wasn't too much money, but I saved whatever I could, and I kept the house dusted and cleaned, and I did the laundry, and I cooked the meals and washed the dishes, and at the same time I was going to school. Which meant I never exactly was able to rest for more than it seemed to be about five minutes at a time. There was myself, and there was your Grandpa Bird, and there was my brother, Morris. Your Uncle Morris. We visited his grave and your Grandma Bird's grave once when we went to Paradise Falls, do you remember?

"Yes," said Victoria.

It all was such a world ago, said Sandra Tabor, sighing.

Victoria nodded. There were only two more pillowcases to go, and then perhaps she would go upstairs and talk with Marybeth about makeup and hats and etiquette. Or tapioca. African violets. Whatever.

Victoria's mother was ironing one of Victoria's dresses. It was white, decorated with embroidered forgetmenots. This is one of the prettiest of your dresses, don't you think? said Sandra Tabor.

"I like it very much," said Victoria.

Do you get hassled very much in school? said Victoria's mother. I mean, do you *still* get hassled?

"Not as much like before," said Victoria.

You mean you're being allowed to hear your own drum? said Victoria's mother.

"Pardon?" said Victoria, folding the last of the pillowcases.

Listen, the dresses are one of the reasons you've been hassled, said Victoria's mother. You *do* know that, don't you? I mean, you refuse to wear the uniform of the day—the jeans and the T-shirts. You keep insisting on being like something out of an old book.

Victoria frowned at her mother.

Sandra Tabor spoke quickly. She pushed several strands of hair back from her forehead. Please don't misunderstand, she said. I'm not *criticizing*. As a matter of fact, I have *defended* you. And I'll defend you again if I have to. But what I want to know is, if you don't have friends, how much does it bother you?

Victoria shrugged.

You're prettier than any of them, do you know that? said Sandra Tabor. It's the way you look, and

it's the way you dress . . . it's the old book thing,
an illustration, I mean. Perhaps a drawing from *Alice
in Wonderland*. But are you sure there's nothing being
left out?

Victoria nodded.

Everybody asks you that, correct? said Sandra
Tabor, smiling a little.

"Just about," said Victoria, nodding.

Do you think you have friends? said Sandra Tabor.

"Yes," said Victoria.

The ones upstairs in your bedroom? said Sandra
Tabor.

"Yes," said Victoria. She wished her mother would
stop picking at the subject. She was grateful that her
mother had defended her, but why was it necessary
that the thing be beaten to death?

And they are sufficient? said Sandra Tabor.

"*Yes,*" said Victoria.

There are little girls who would be happy to play
with you, said Victoria's mother. *Real* little girls, I
mean. And I don't think they would want to look
like Dolly Parton.

"What's wrong with wanting to look like Dolly
Parton?" said Victoria.

Her mother shrugged and hung the dress on a
line.

"Do I hurt anybody?" said Victoria.

Of course not, said Victoria's mother, spreading
another dress on the ironing board. This dress was
a plain light blue.

"I'd rather play with Bonnie than anybody I know,"
said Victoria. "Except maybe Marybeth. Or both of
them together."

Fine, said Sandra Tabor. I can understand that. It's
one of the reasons I loved your Uncle Morris so much.

"Pardon?" said Victoria.

Everything I remember about him, said Sandra
Tabor, has a sort of *freedom* to it. He, um, you see

. . . he did have an independence to him, and back
in those days, those days that were so long *ago* . . .
well, in the '40s and the '50s his sort of independence
wasn't so very highly thought of. He was awfully,
um, *skeptical.*
"What's skepical mean?" said Victoria.
Skep*t*ical, said Sandra Tabor, means taking everything with a grain of salt. Not going along with the
crowd until a belief is, um, *proved out.* Which is, I
think, the way you are. There was a boy named
Stanley Chaloupka, for instance. He was an outcast,
and your Uncle Morris and I watched him die. He
carried breadcrusts in his pockets, and he wore vests,
and he had his own railroad in his basement, and he
ran his railroad the way you organize your dolls and
animals and nightlights, you know?
"You watched him *die?*" said Victoria.
Yes, said Sandra Tabor, and later I watched your
Uncle Morris die.
"Yes," said Victoria. "I know about *that.* But tell
me about the boy who carried the breadcrusts in his
pockets. Please?"
I've never said anything to you about him? said
Sandra Tabor.
"I don't think so," said Victoria.
And how he blew up? said Sandra Tabor.
"*Blew up?*" said Victoria. "No. Never. I would
have remembered *that.*"
Sandra Tabor shook her head and made a clucking
noise that came dryly from the roof of her mouth.
She was ironing the sleeves of the blue dress. Well,
she said, it was 1944, and your Uncle Morris had been
Stanley Chaloupka's friend, and I think probably Stan-
ley's only friend. Everybody laughed at Stanley
Chaloupka, but your Uncle Morris was *skeptical* of
the laughter. He wanted to make up his own mind
about Stanley Chaloupka. Which he did. And he liked
Stanley. And he liked playing with Stanley's trains.

And I don't believe he cared what anybody else
thought. He was a good brother, and my God, if he
were alive today, he would be *fortythree years old.*
Oh, my goodness. How fast the time flies when
you're having fun, right?

"Pardon?" said Victoria.

Nothing, said Sandra Tabor. She was finished with
the blue dress. She hung it up. She set the iron aside
and leaned on the ironing board. It's not important
that a long time has passed, she said. Goodness doesn't
change; it doesn't wear out. Not if it's the real article.
And your Uncle Morris had that sort of goodness.
It was 1944, as I said, and he and I went to see Stanley
Chaloupka, whose family had moved up by St Clair
Avenue. The reason I went along was I blackmailed
my brother. I was six years old, and I wanted to be
in on the adventure. You see, he was planning on
walking the entire distance to Stanley's new home,
and that distance was a good three miles. I told Morris I would yell and carry on if he didn't take me
with him, and so he didn't have much choice. He
rented a wagon from a friend of his, and he dragged
that wagon along, and I sat in it, and I do have a
vague memory that I gave him trouble, even though
I can't recall what the *nature* of the trouble was.
Well, anyway, we were on our way up the street
toward Stanley's house, and it was a day in October,
and I seem to remember that Stanley was waving at
us. I think he was standing on his porch, or maybe
in the front yard, when it seemed that the entire
world gave a sort of shuddery whoosh, and Stanley
vanished, and my brother and I were caught smack
in the middle of a . . . a conflagration. We behaved
well, or at least *Morris* did. I think he loaded a couple
of people into the wagon and dragged them away
from all the fires that were burning. It turned out
some East Ohio Gas tanks had exploded. And a lot
of people were killed. I don't know how many, but

it was a *lot*. But Morris never talked much about
what he had done. He did talk about Stanley, though,
and I distinctly remember that on more than one
occasion he told me there'd been nothing wrong
with Stanley. He told me Stanley had been a good
friend. I seem to remember that manholes were blown
away that day. And I seem to remember that a fire
engine fell into a crater in a street. But I was just
six, and the impression the thing made on me wasn't
that strong. It was too long *ago,* do you understand?
But I do remember the goodness. My brother's goodness, I mean. The goodness of your Uncle Morris.
Whom you never knew. Who was dead more than
sixteen years when you were born. But I think you
would have liked him. He might even have been
your friend, if you had permitted him entrance. And,
you see, when he died of leukemia just after Christmas, in '52 . . . and oh, dear, it's all been *so* long ago
. . . ah, anyhow, when he died, I *saw* him die, and I
wet my—never mind. Never mind *that.* When he died,
he died, and he was unconscious, but *when* he died
. . . at that precise moment . . . when he died . . .
when he died . . . well, when I thought back on the
quick and sassy way he had about him, when I thought
back on how he had befriended Stanley Chaloupka,
how he would hear out just about anyone, how he
had the strength and wisdom to reserve judgment
until all the precincts had reported . . . at that moment I knew something had been peeled out of my
life, and it never would be regained. And I was right.
He always had a sort of, ah, gentle *bounce* to him,
and he was generous, and he would make long in-
coherent speeches to me sometimes when he felt
people weren't being fair, but more times than not
he would write down something or carry the problem
out to the back steps and sit down and sift it through
his mind. And he would say to me: *Sandra, we can't
let the bleeps get us down.*

"The who?" said Victoria. "What are *bleeps?*"

People whose mothers aren't necessarily married to their fathers, said Sandra Tabor.

Victoria frowned. Her mouth moved, and a succession of *o*'s passed across it, and finally she was able to say: "Oh."

The bleeps are everywhere, said Sandra Tabor to her daughter. Some of them try to hit us over the head, and some of them try to sweettalk us into voting for them, and some of them even say they love us. There is a more specific name for them, but I really don't believe it's necessary that I expose you to—

"You mean bastards?" said Victoria.

Sandra Tabor moistened her lips.

"Ezra says it every so often," said Victoria. "And some of the other kids, too. Most of them are boys, but they aren't all boys."

Sandra Tabor covered her mouth and coughed. She rummaged in a washbasket and came up with another of Victoria's dresses. This one had a red top and blue skirt. She spread it on the board and began ironing it. She said: I really don't want to talk about *that.* I was trying to tell you a few things about your Uncle Morris. You know he played basketball at East High, and you know he was just seventeen when the leukemia took him, but what you *don't* know is that in his own way he was just as alone as anyone. He was not a recluse. I don't mean to imply such a thing. But he never seemed to mind operating independently, if such a thing was necessary. I think that's why he pulled me in that wagon all the way up to St Clair Avenue, which was the end of the world away from *our* neighborhood, believe you *me.* I only wish I could remember more of the specifics, but I do remember enough to tell you he behaved well—and on his own initiative, helping those people the way he did. And I seem to remember that *some-*

one, maybe a policeman, called him the greatest thing since sliced bread. Which was a way we had in those days of expressing admiration. Myself, I've always enjoyed hearing people use the expression. I think it is colorful. I have nothing against colorful words and phrases, you see. I mean, as long as they display imagination, then I am all for them. But I don't like triteness. Which is why I say *bleep* from time to time. It is my way of calling attention to the triteness.

Victoria didn't know what *triteness* meant, but she said nothing. When her mother became wound up this way, it was better to say nothing. It was better to let her wind herself down.

Sandra Tabor paused for breath. She made a moist noise, and her throat contracted for a moment. Then she said: Victoria, I'd really be happy if you never used that bad *bleep* word again.

"You mean *bastards?*" said Victoria.

Yes, said Sandra Tabor.

"All right," said Victoria.

Thank you, said Sandra Tabor. She reached across the ironing board and patted one of Victoria's shoulders. That sort of word really doesn't go with the sort of person you are, said Sandra Tabor. Oh, my brother Morris swore a lot, and your Grandpa Bird has been known to utter a cussword now and then, but *you* are *different*. And anyway, for Morris swearing was a safety valve. You see, he felt things so very deeply. Not that *you* don't, but you *are* a *girl*. I suppose I am as much a feminist as the next woman, but I have to draw the line at that sort of language. It doesn't solve anything, does it? Of course not.

Victoria shrugged.

It really *doesn't*, said Sandra Tabor. Please take my word for it.

"All right," said Victoria.

Not that *any* sort of language solves much of *any-*

thing, said Sandra Tabor (and she smiled), but at least we can be decent. The language is enormous. I mean, there are so *many* words, and who is ever going to miss the few of them that are obscene or naughty?

"Hardly anybody, I guess," said Victoria. "Are *obscene* and *naughty* like, um, *dirty?*"

Yes, said Sandra Tabor. Now she was hanging up the red and blue dress. She shook her head. I don't know why I have bought so many dresses that need to be ironed, she said. I could just as well have bought wash and wear dresses, the kind that come straight from the dryer and you can put on right away. But somehow *these* dresses are a little *finer,* aren't they? I don't really know why they should be, but they *are.* Or at least I think they are. Hah. I just had a question pop into my mind. How does a person put on a dress? Does a person tell the dress its shoelaces are untied?

"*Dresses* don't have *shoelaces,*" said Victoria, frowning.

Victoria's mother shook her head. I do believe I have just gone scampering around the bend, she said (and again she smiled). But at least I don't think I harm anyone. Ah, but we've strayed a little afield from talking about the past, the days that are so long ago. Long ago and far away. I believe there used to be a song with that phrase as a title. Dum de dum and far away; I hear the angels play. Something like that. Or maybe I hear the music play. I can't remember.

"Um, does it make you feel good?" said Victoria.

Yes, said Sandra Tabor.

"I'm glad," said Victoria.

I know that, said Sandra Tabor.

"Will I get so someday my *Star Wars* music will make me feel that way, too?" said Victoria.

I think so, said Sandra Tabor. Most people do get that way—over one thing or another, after they grow up. And you have to remember, your mother is getting up there in years. The *ago* thing keeps growing.

Victoria went around the ironing board and took one of her mother's hands and pressed it against her cheek. "I love you," she said. "I always have, and I always will, and I don't want you to worry."

You're not what you seem, are you? said Sandra Tabor, blinking.

"Pardon?" said Victoria. She pressed her mother's hand more tightly against her cheek. It was warm from the iron, and it was a little scratchy, maybe with a trace or two of moisture.

Victoria's mother's head abruptly moved from side to side. No, she said. I take that back. You are *exactly* what you seem. Just because you choose to be alone so much, that doesn't mean you don't love.

"I love a whole lot," said Victoria.

Yes, said Victoria's mother.

"And I don't mind when you talk about the *ago* thing," said Victoria.

Thank you, said Sandra Tabor.

"Whatever you want to talk about, you talk about it," said Victoria.

You are beautiful, said Sandra Tabor. It is what you *seem*, and it is what you *are*. I don't know why your father and I are so lucky.

Victoria rubbed one of her eyes.

Stanley Chaloupka was beautiful, and so are you, said Sandra Tabor. And never mind about his breadcrusts. And I'm only sorry I threw away that old comb. But I'm glad you told me about it. Next time perhaps I'll be more thoughtful. And are you sure I can talk to you about the *ago* thing?

Victoria nodded. Her nostrils held an odor of starch.

Remarkable, said Sandra Tabor.

Victoria kissed her mother's warm palm.

18 ॐ Bleep

LATER THAT AFTERNOON, while carrying an immense basket of wash upstairs from the basement, Sandra Tabor tripped over one of her husband's galoshes. Victoria stood at the top of the stairs and watched her mother fall back. The basket flew, and its contents rained down on Sandra Tabor, who bounced against a stair railing, banging an elbow. She landed on her coccyx at the foot of the stairs. She rubbed the elbow, and she leaned forward and rubbed her coccyx, and then Victoria distinctly heard her mother utter a very naughty *bleep*. Enunciating carefully, making the word all sibilant and soppy, exposing her teeth and fastidiously pressing her tongue against the roof of her mouth, Mrs Sandra Bird Tabor (wife of the Rev Carl J. Tabor, pastor of Wrexford Methodist Church) clearly and soberly and devoutly said: Shit.

19 ᘓ Doctrine

NOBODY IS PERFECT. Not even mothers are perfect.
If you stay alert, you learn something new every
day. And not all fish have to swim. And not all birds
have to fly.

What do fish and birds have to do with perfection
and mothers and alertness?

All fish are *supposed* to swim. All birds are *supposed* to fly. And all little girls are *supposed* to have
heads like leaky beanbags.

But Victoria Anne Tabor is different. As no doubt
are some fish and birds.

She remembers what is said to her. She remembers
what is said to her about naughty words. And she is
urged to avoid them.

But then the urger says: Shit.

Which proves nobody is perfect, correct?

And Victoria Anne Tabor understands this.

Which means there is no leaky beanbag.

Correct?

20 ᕍᕊ Homily

VICTORIA'S FATHER usually devoted two or three eve-
nings a week to the writing of his sermon. She was
not permitted to enter his study when he was working on his sermon, typing it in short bursts and now
and then talking right along with the short bursts.
Oh, there were times when she heard him talking.
There were times when she and Cat sat on the floor
in front of the door to her father's study, and occasionally she would pull Cat back and forth, and
Cat's wheels would squeak. But the squeaking of Cat's
wheels did not overcome the sounds of the typewriter
and Victoria's father's voice. And she would hear:
God. And she would hear: *Redemption.* And she
would hear: *Fellowship.* And she would hear: *Love.*
And occasionally she would hear phrases. Such as:
Goodness and mercy. And: *The miracle of Creation.*
And: *Salvation cannot be denied those who truly.*
And: *Praise the benevolent and magisterial power
of.* And: *Each breath, each leaf, each petal, each humble beast, is somehow touched by.* And sometimes Victoria brought along a little notebook and wrote down
the words and the phrases. And she supposed her
father was a great man. Or at least he was a greater
man than Ezra Levine's father, who was in the scrap
metal business. Or Colleen Foote's father, who directed
funerals. Or Vanessa Brickhouse's father, who was a
paving contractor. Or Kevin Riordan's father, who
owned a stationery store in the Richmond Mall. And

Victoria always paid attention when her father delivered his sermon, and no matter what he said. She sat primly, rigidly, and her mouth was pressed tightly shut, and she made sure her stockings were adjusted just so (she really could not abide tackiness), and she made sure she went to the bathroom just before the service began (that way, she would be comfortable, and she would be able to concentrate), and from time to time she caught her mother smiling down at her, and she always returned the smile, and her pride rose as though her belly were full of balloons and happily repentant trolls and a multitude of energetic optimistic frogs, all jumping this way and that. And one day, with his voice rolling and tumbling and echoing, one great spangled and blinding Sunday morning all awash with motes, a Sunday morning in April of 1978, when Victoria still was a puny *eight years old* and lacked the wisdom that she possessed in June of 1978 (since by then she was *nine years old*), that particular morning her father stood behind the pulpit in a sort of heavily cheerful straddle, with his shoes poking around the edges of the pulpit, and he rested his weight evenly on his feet that were so widely spaced, and he said: *We must not be budged when our minds and our thoughts turn to love of God. We must TAKE UP A POSITION and NOT BETRAY IT. At the same time, though, we must pause to reflect, and we must summon and reaffirm our awareness that the complexities of our age, not to mention the demonstrable fact that the sum total of humanity's RAW KNOWLEDGE has more than DOUBLED in the LESS THAN THREE DECADES that have passed since the century's midpoint, have crowded upon us, making simple explanations—explanations perhaps of faith—less and less easy to grasp, let alone accept. So, then, what does this mean? That complexity is causing us to lose our souls? That the prospect of cloning, of DNA, of a breed that will*

*produce breastless women, not to mention the promise
—or threat—of artificial food, plastic perhaps, that
these dangers will turn us into a race of robots as
envisioned by such as Capek and Orwell and Elmer
Rice? The planet abounds with Cassandras who not
only PREDICT this sort of soullessness but who say
it ALREADY EXISTS. If they are correct, is there
anything we really can do about the situation? I say
yes, there is. I say yes, in thunder. I say that, with the
loving guidance of a Merciful Providence, we can
join in generous fellowship to retain the humanity of
the human race. The word here, the key word, is
FELLOWSHIP. While granting and accepting and
rejoicing in the sanctity of the individual spirit, which
is of course the final ultimate distillation of the Holy
Spirit, we must also come to terms with our increasing
awareness that only through a firm and courageous
BONDING can we meet the CHALLENGE of the
FUTURE. The clasping of a hand is no longer simply
a social gesture. It is a commitment to survival. It is
an admission on our part that the problems of race,
of economics, of religion, of politics, of hunger, of
nationalism, even of philosophical doctrine, can be
solved only through a UNIFIED EFFORT, through
a POOLING OF OUR STRENGTHS AND OUR
RESOURCES. Then, and only then, will we be able
to extend ourselves as individuals and once again pro-
claim the glory and the miracle that is the human
soul, so alone, so beautiful, so lovingly vulnerable.
Until then, however, we must restructure our priorities and battle our common enemies with a sort of
joyful strength of numbers. What is needed, then, is
an army with banners—benevolent banners, of course,
signifying FELLOWSHIP and proudly announcing
yes, in the most contrapuntally righteous thunder
ever sounded. For we are not alone. We cannot be
alone. Not in these times. Not when the issue is
nothing less than survival. In short, then, the lines*

have been drawn, and we must place sweet dreams on the back burner. And here Victoria's father paused. He rubbed his mouth with the back of a hand. He smiled briefly in the direction of his wife and his daughter, and then the choir rose, and the congregation rose, and everyone sang *Onward, Christian Soldiers.* And Victoria blinked at the motes, and some of the motes were so close she wanted to stick out her tongue and lick at them, and some of them were rolling in a golden swirl around her father's head, and she supposed he had been talking about Bear and Cat and even Henry the soap fish and Kermit the Retired Frog, and she loved her father, she did, she *did* . . . but what was she supposed to do? Bury her days in the backyard by the pussywillows? run out into the street and hug the man who drove the big machine with the whirling brooms that cleaned the pavement and had CITY OF SHAKER HEIGHTS printed on its sides? join the Army? tear apart all her precious silence? push away all cupped hands? Slowly Victoria shook her head. Her mother looked down and tried to take Victoria by the hand. But Victoria turned away, and she folded her hands in front of herself, and the Christian soldiers marched on, and on, in thunder, and she cleared her throat, and she felt her mother pat her on the head, but she did not look up.

21 ~ Dispute

THAT NIGHT Victoria again scrootched herself against a hallway wall and listened to her mother's and father's voices. They came from downstairs, the front room. She crouched on the burgundy carpeting, and her bunnyslippers had made not a sound. So she knew she was safe, and she was able to concentrate on the words.

Carl, you are a remarkable man, said Victoria's mother.

Oh? How so? said the Rev Mr Tabor.

To write a sermon especially for our little girl, said Victoria's mother. All that talk about *fellowship*. You don't think you were fooling *me*, do you? All that sanctimonious calling to arms. My *Lord*. And in thunder yet. May heaven preserve us all.

Now, Sandra, you know me better than that, said the Rev Mr Tabor.

It's because I *know* you that I know what you *did*, said Sandra Tabor. Victoria listens to every word you say, and she always has. At the end, after the last of your magnificent pearshaped tones had thrilled and galvanized the assembled multitude, I tried to take her by the hand, but she made sure she did not see me. She was angry, Carl. Is that getting through to you? She was *angry*. There is a certain way she sets her mouth so that all the color goes out of it, and then sometimes she will form silent little words that

75

only she hears—and sometimes maybe they're only syllables.

Yes, said the Rev Mr Tabor, I am aware of what she's like when she's angry.

But you went ahead and goaded her anyway, didn't you? said Sandra Tabor.

I was goading *everyone*, said the Rev Mr Tabor. I was trying to tell them that we *all* must get involved.

Involved in *what?* said Sandra Tabor. Reforestation? The training of retarded children so that they can make extruded widgets for polifery machines? The saving of the yellowbellied Bulgarian skunk from extinction at the hands of evil fur trappers? My God, what *is* it any more? We live in a world where even the *causes* seem to have causes. The thing is, what ever happened to good old selfishness and privacy?

Now you're being irresponsible, said the Rev Mr Tabor.

I certainly *hope* so, said Sandra Tabor.

The Rev Mr Tabor said nothing, but he did let go a sort of snort. (And Victoria heard it clearly.)

Well, in any case, I've never heard such manipulative baloney in all my life, said Victoria's mother.

Did you say *manipulative baloney?* said the Rev Mr Tabor.

That I did, said Victoria's mother.

My sermons have no doubt been described in many pejorative ways, said the Rev Mr Tabor, but I don't imagine they've ever before been called manipulative baloney.

Well, there's a first time for everything, said Victoria's mother.

I suppose, said the Rev Mr Tabor.

Now I know a little of what Columbus must have felt, said Victoria's mother.

Pardon? said the Rev Mr Tabor.

The joy of discovery, said Victoria's mother.

Another snort from the Rev Mr Tabor.

Oh, we have to stop this, said Victoria's mother, giggling.

But why? said Victoria's father.

Because it's a serious subject, said Victoria's mother, and we're joking about it when we should be confronting it. Carl, look, I wish you'd stop hassling her because she is the way she is.

But a person can't be that way in this day and age, said the Rev Mr Tabor.

Now you sound like your sermon, said Victoria's mother.

So? said the Rev Mr Tabor. Has it ever crossed your mind that maybe I *mean* some of the things I say?

But did you have to *focus* all your sincerity or whatever on a *little girl* in *church* on *Sunday* with *three hundred people sitting there?* said Victoria's mother.

I wasn't focusing anything on Victoria, said the Rev Mr Tabor. Yes, I'll admit that her aloneness gave me the idea for the sermon, and I'll also admit that her silences and her imaginings do trouble me a lot of the time . . . the way she talks to her dolls and animals as though she is addressing a joint session of Congress. But none of this means I am some sort of monster that would deliver a verbal spanking in front of a crowd. She is my daughter, and I love her.

(Upstairs, crouching, Victoria hugged herself.)

The Rev Mr Tabor hesitated for a moment, then said: I mean that.

Of course you mean it, said Victoria's mother. I know *that.* You don't have to underscore the obvious with me. But maybe *subconsciously* you were spanking her today in your sermon. Isn't that at least a possibility?

No, said Victoria's father. I've thought it all

through, and I say *no,* and I'd appreciate it if we discussed something else.

Such as? said Victoria's mother.

Cheese and crackers, said Victoria's father.

Say again? said Victoria's mother.

Cheese and *crackers,* said Victoria's father.

That's what I thought you said, said Victoria's mother.

That cheese assortment you bought at Tassi's the other day, said Victoria's father. Well, it's been preying on my mind since early this afternoon. I think I'd like some, with perhaps a few Triscuits and a touch of sherry . . .

If I weren't hearing it, I wouldn't believe it, said Victoria's mother.

A little relaxation, and then perhaps bed, said the Rev Mr Tabor.

Certainly does beat sleeping on the floor or in the linen closet, said Sandra Tabor.

That is a fact, said the Rev Mr Tabor. But when I said *bed,* I did not, um, particularly mean bed in the sense to which you just made reference.

Oh, you meant it in some other sense? said Victoria's mother.

Yes, said the Rev Mr Tabor. There was a brief scuffling noise that was punctuated by a quick breathy squeal from Victoria's mother, and then he said: Cheese and Triscuits and sherry . . . followed by, um, a leisurely dessert.

Leisurely? said Victoria's mother, giggling.

I am fifty years of age, said the Rev Mr Tabor.

Shame on you, said Victoria's mother, and she giggled some more.

On second thought, perhaps we don't have to bother with the cheese and the Triscuits and the sherry, said the Rev Mr Tabor. Perhaps it would be enough for us to settle on dessert. I mean, I wouldn't want you to run around telling the world I am a glutton.

At fifty years of age? said Victoria's mother.

Shame on *you*, said the Rev Mr Tabor.

22 ❧ Reconciliation

So VICTORIA'S MOTHER and father came upstairs, and she had to scurry into her room and softly close the door. She crawled into bed, and she heard her mother and father laughing in their room next to hers. She pressed her hands over her face, and she was able to smell bathsalts. Briefly she thought of *FELLOWSHIP* and the *CHALLENGE* of the *FUTURE*. She breathed the warm odor of the bathsalts. She wondered if maybe she was being unpatriotic. A flapping noise came from her parents' room. A sort of grunt came from her parents' room. Then there were no words. Her dolls and animals called to her, and they asked her if they could be of any help. She opened her fingers and peeked through them at Bugs, the nightlight. She was able to make out the silhouettes of some of her dolls and animals. Bear's plump outline was clear, and Cat was recognizable because of his wheels. There were dolls and animals on the floor. There were dolls and animals on the dresser. Another grunt came from Victoria's parents' room, and then she heard her father's voice, and it was distinct, and it said: Sandra, I thank you very much. And then Victoria's mother spoke in a voice that was just as distinct, saying: Don't thank me. I was not doing you a favor. I enjoy it as much as you do. And Victoria's father said: There's no one in the world I love more than I love you. And Victoria's mother said: Careful. And Victoria's father said: About what?

And Victoria's mother said: Our daughter might hear you. We *do* have a daughter, remember? And Victoria's father said: Well, I love her, too, but it's different. And Victoria's mother said: Praise be to God. And then Victoria's mother giggled, and there were more flapping and grunting noises, and after a time Victoria's mother said: Carl, what's gotten into you? And Victoria's father said: I believe the question is, what's gotten into *you?* And Victoria's mother giggled and said: Now, now, don't be vulgar. And Victoria's father said: Awww, *shucks.* And Victoria seized a pillow and pressed it over one ear. And she seized another pillow and pressed it over the other ear. Her mother and father continued to chat, but now their words were indistinct, and it was as though their mouths were all abulge with feathers and cotton. But her dolls and animals still spoke clearly. Here we are, said Bear. We are truth, said Kermit the Retired Frog. We live for you, said Marybeth. That is our function, said Cat. Why would we lie to you? said Rabbit. If it wasn't for you, we'd be thrown out with the trash, said Pluto. I wouldn't be a bit surprised if we have a programmed obsolescence, said Bear. Which surely is true if you happen to be a nightlight, said Mickey, barking a little. And Victoria, her ears still covered by the pillows, nodded. And Victoria felt her eyes give way and turn warm and wet. And the pillows came away from her ears. Now the outlines of the dolls and animals were fuzzy and blotched. She squirmed out of bed. Her mother and father were still talking in the next room, but she did not permit their words to register. Instead she concentrated on the happy sounds the dolls and animals made as she scooped them up—all of them— and took them to bed with her. She even took the retired nightlights to bed with her. She even took the taciturn Henry the soap fish. Everyone went to bed with her except Bugs, who gleamed and grinned and

told her it was okay; somebody had to stand watch. So then, while the dolls and animals made murmurous soothing sounds, Victoria wiped the moisture from her eyes, and she sucked the moisture from her fingers, and its saltiness rolled across her tongue, and after a time she slept, and perhaps she beat away a troll or two with her high strong silent benevolence. And the dolls and animals slept. And the next morning, when she awakened, she looked around at the dolls and animals, and she said aloud: "Fellowship."

23 ❧ Veritas

VICTORA'S FATHER had taken his undergraduate degree
at Harvard. He had originally come from Hanover,
New Hampshire, and he insisted he had relatives back
there who still were peeved with him for not attending Dartmouth. He had been ordained in 1954, and
he had served as an associate pastor of churches in
Paducah, Kentucky; Cairo, Illinois, and Ishpeming,
Michigan, before coming to Wrexford Methodist as
associate pastor in 1961. He married Victoria's mother
in 1964, which was the year he was chosen to replace
the church's elderly incumbent pastor, a man named
G. Lewis Plumb, a widower who had six cats and four
dogs. The venerable Rev Mr Plumb packed the cats
and the dogs in his car and moved to Bradenton,
Florida, where he had a serene retirement that was
abruptly cut short in 1972, when his heart fatally
gave out at the bridge table while he was exclaiming
delightedly over a doubled contract of seven spades
he had just made because he had caught one opponent
with a trumpable ace and the other opponent with a
doubleton trump queen. This story made its way back
to Shaker Heights, and Victoria's father was con-
vinced there was a moral to it. He now and then
spoke of the moral, and one evening at dinner he
said to Victoria: If Mr Plumb hadn't been so involved in a *game*, perhaps he would still be alive today.

84

Victoria had been pushing peas and carrots around her plate. She looked up at her father.

Too much serious attention is paid to trivia, said the Rev Mr Tabor to his daughter.

Victoria supposed he was trying to get at the subject of her dolls and her animals. She looked back down at her peas and carrots. She poked them.

Seriousness should be reserved for serious things, said the Rev Mr Tabor to his daughter. Truth, for instance. Truth and honesty. Love.

Victoria's mother had stepped into the kitchen to fetch more boiled potatoes for her husband. Now she returned, and she set a bowl of potatoes in front of him, and she said to him: Are you talking about poor old Mr Plumb and that *bridge game* again?

I am, said the Rev Mr Tabor, scooping potatoes onto his plate.

Victoria's mother seated herself. She snorted and shook her head. But he died happy, she said. What was he supposed to *do?* Grapple with the stars every waking minute of every day? He was an *old man*, and it was time for other people to grapple with the stars. You know, sometimes I really think that if you had your way, hopscotch and marbles would be criminal offenses. Aggravated superficiality. Something like that.

The Rev Mr Tabor looked up from his potatoes and smiled at Victoria. See how I'm picked on? he said.

If you ever bothered to learn to play the game, said Victoria's mother to her husband, then you'd *know* how delighted he must have been. A seven contract doubled and made . . . there's not a bridge player in the world who wouldn't have been excited.

The Rev Mr Tabor's smile drifted away, and his mouth became tight, and he looked at Victoria's mother and said: Worth dying for?

Maybe, said Victoria's mother.

What?
Just as much as Nixon.
Now don't be—
Just as much as Vietnam.
Vietnam? We were talking about an old man dying
at a bridge table, and you bring Vietnam into it.
Vietnam and Nixon. Look, I voted for McGovern,
too, and you have no right to drag up some sort of
pacifist *non sequitur* that doesn't—
  Carl, I know you voted for McGovern. And I
know you marched at Selma. *I* was there, too, remember? And I know you led those memorial services at
Kent State. You are *concerned*, and you are *earnest*,
and you are *involved*, and you are the most relentless
liberal I know this side of Ramsey Clark, but my God,
when was the last time you were *silly?* And I don't
mean deliberately silly, as though you were going
through some sort of ritual silliness because you'd
made an intellectual determination to show the world
what a regular fellow you were. But I mean *really*
silly, without thinking about it, and without filing
it away because you think it might come in handy
for a sermon some dull Sunday morning. I mean,
like . . . oh, I don't know . . . pinching someone.
Singing one of those dirty songs about Popeye and
Olive Oyl. Flying a kite. Pitching pennies. Dancing to
a Jerry Lee Lewis record. Blowing bubbles from a
bubblepipe. Getting drunk on bad sangría that doesn't
have enough fruit. I mean, you say poor old Mr
Plumb died because of something that was trivial. All
right, then, *I* say good for him. Maybe the best thing
that could happen to all of us would be to die of,
um, trivial causes. I mean, how long do we have to be
pursued by great events?
  What? said the Rev Mr Tabor.
  Wars, said Victoria's mother. Race riots. Assassi-
nations. Hasn't it ever occurred to you that the day
we all keel over because of bridge . . . or maybe

bowling, or tennis, or backgammon, or, um, ah, sex
. . . will be that ultimate day of, um, *peace* in the
valley you and all the rest of your kind keep taking
about?

My *kind?*

You know what I mean.

The Rev Mr Tabor stabbed one of his boiled potatoes. He popped it whole into his mouth. Speaking
mushily, he said: Well, it won't be in my lifetime . . .
or yours . . . and thass a trufe you, um, know is a
trufe . . .

Nicely put, said Sandra Tabor.

The Rev Mr Tabor swallowed and blinked at his
wife. That's easy for *you* to say, he told her.

Victoria's mother shook her head.

So the argument was not resolved. Victoria had the
feeling that sometimes her father and her mother
argued for the sake of arguing, that sometimes they
had to prove to themselves they still had ginger. She
supposed most grownups valued ginger very highly.
Most of them talked so *loudly*, and most of them were
so *hearty*. And she supposed the resolution of the
argument really wasn't that important, just as long
as the argument took place. But she loved her father
and mother. Oh, she didn't know what the word
trump meant, and she didn't know what the word
backgammon meant (she would have to ask Bear
about them), and she didn't understand what a *Selma*
was, or a *Kent State*, and sometimes she became a
little irked when her father and mother tossed around
all those words she'd never heard of (especially since
there were *so* many of them), but who else provided
the warm water and the puckery soap and the cupped
palms? Who else provided the bed that could if necessary be placed on flanged wheels? Who else fussed
over her when she had a cold? Who else fed her
cake on her birthday? At nine, Victoria knew the
truth and the significance of these things. So she was

not reluctant to hug and kiss her father and her
mother. She figured she owed them that much . . .
and a whole lot more. And besides, she could not
help hugging and kissing them. Could she help
breathing? being thirsty? laughing at the ticklings in-
flicted by urgent benevolent fingers? savoring chocolate and licorice? Could she help smiling as she
sleepily inhaled the warm and comforting fume of
Vick's Vap-O-Rub as it was being spread on her
chest because she had a cold and she was confined
to her bed, where she was served cocoa and butter
cookies and given a paper napkin so she would not
scatter crumbs on the sheets and blankets? Oh, there
were too many quiet pleasures, too many murmurously warm times of delight, and only a wicked little
girl would not have loved the people who stood
with her inside those times and pleasures. And this
was a large truth of Victoria's days, and she knew
she never would want to damage those people. She
always moved softly when she was with them. Oh,
yes, there were occasions when mischief got the better of her, but it never was what anyone would have
called a *destructive* mischief, and it really didn't happen all that often. Perhaps once a year she was a
genuinely bad girl, but the rest of the time she tried
to show respect, since she believed respect was one
of the ways she kept her love flourishing. And she
was *interested* in her father and her mother. There
were times when she would sit in the kitchen with
her mother, and perhaps she would have a glass of
milk while her mother drank black coffee and smoked
cigarettes, and the kitchen was all white and coppery,
and the kitchen table was heavy and pitted (Victoria's
mother had found it in an antique store out in Middle-
field, where a lot of Amish people lived), and Victoria would ask her mother about the *ago* thing.
"Is it sad to look back?" said Victoria. "Does it
make you feel bad?"

No, said Sandra Tabor, inhaling. Not really.

"But I mean, Grandma Bird and Uncle Morris . . . them being dead so many years and all."

No, said Sandra Tabor, exhaling. It's *all right.*

"Mama, try not to think of the sad things."

Victoria's mother nodded. Oh, I do try, she said. All the time.

"They look very nice in their pictures," said Victoria. "I mean, Uncle Morris in his baseball uniform, the way he—"

Basketball uniform, said Sandra Tabor.

"Oh," said Victoria. "Excuse me. *Anyway,* I like the way he is grinning. Makes him look like he knows what he's doing. Did he know what he was doing?"

Most of the time. Or at least I think so.

"Mama, you shouldn't smoke."

I know.

"They show us pictures in school. Real icky pictures."

I can imagine, said Sandra Tabor, inhaling.

Victoria's hands were folded in her lap, and her knees were pressed together. She wore a skirt and blouse, and the blouse had a pattern of beanstalks, and a grinning Jack was climbing them. It was the same Jack climbing all of them. "I don't want to be like that," she said.

What? said Victoria's mother. Like what?

"*Nervous,*" said Victoria. "*Smoking* and all."

Oh, said Sandra Tabor, exhaling.

"Why are you nervous?"

I'm not nervous.

"But I thought that's why people smoked," said Victoria.

There are lots of reasons people smoke, said Sandra Tabor. Nervousness is just one of them. They smoke because they are getting old. They smoke because it's an excuse to sit with a cup of coffee and think back on a dead brother who played basketball, because the world crowds around them too closely, beating on them with little fists that nick and gouge. And, Victoria, believe me, when a person gets older, those fists sometimes are able to draw blood, and sometimes it's as though flesh is being laid back. I'm sorry. I shouldn't talk this way to you.

"Mama, do you *hurt?*"

Never mind.

"I love you," said Victoria.

Victoria's mother snubbed out her cigarette. She rose, came around the table, pressed Victoria's face against her belly. She said nothing, and neither did Victoria. Her fingers curled for a moment around the back of Victoria's neck, and then she stroked Victoria's hair. Victoria inhaled. The refrigerator hummed, clicked, was silent. Her mother's hands were easy and soft. This was as good as a bath, maybe better. Victoria's eye were closed, and she smiled into her interior darkness, and her arms encircled her mother's legs, and slowly she rocked, and a sort of comfortable heat formed behind her eyes and her throat. It didn't matter that her mother smoked. It didn't matter that her mother maybe was nervous. It didn't even matter that her mother maybe hurt. All that *really* mattered, right *here* and right *now*, was the love, the gentle rocking, the comfortable heat. Everything else was pushed away. So Victoria figured she had a right to smile into her interior darkness. And finally, the sound coming as though it had been crammed inside a wool sock, she wept a little. And her mother kissed the top of her head. And Victoria continued to smile, even though she wept. And her mother finally said: Thank you. I thank you very much.

There were many times, quiet times, when Victoria's mother was attending to housework and her father was out making a pastoral call, that she quietly entered her father's study and walked to his desk and thoughtfully touched the typewriter on which he wrote all his sermons. She softly pressed fingers, and sometimes a thumb, against the typewriter's keys. It was an old Royal portable, and the *e* key had been rubbed clean, and the *g* key, and the *s*. And Victoria looked at photographs of herself, taken when she was very small, hardly more than a baby. And in the photographs she was grinning at the camera, and her teeth were soft. She barely was able to recognize herself. The photographs were in color, but somehow the color seemed to be off. It was not clear enough; it was too smeary and indistinct, as though the camera were looking back down a long imprecise tunnel of sentimental years. Victoria always frowned at these photographs, and she wondered *who* on *earth* had posed her that way. Surely her mother and her father would have had more sense. And so she always turned away from the photographs. And she fingered her father's volume of Holy Scripture, his Bartlett's, his Hymnal. Sometimes she would open one of these books and breathe its pages, and a dryness would tickle her nose and adhere to the roof of her mouth. But she never sneezed, since sneezing would have created too much noise and would have damaged the silence. Sometimes she would squat and rub the nap of the purple rug that was behind her father's desk. It was thick, and it had a design of zigzags that she often traced with a finger. She enjoyed squatting. She enjoyed hearing her knees pop. And she would inspect the spines of the books that were in the bookcase next to the desk. The books were behind glass doors, and the authors were named Merton, Wesley, Hemingway, Mann, Tolstoy, Aquinas, Homer, Shakespeare, Baldwin, Darwin, Hardy, Melville. The glass doors were locked, and atop the bookcase was a large beer mug with the word HARVARD on it.

There also was a red badge on the beer mug, and the letters

VE RI
TAS

were superimposed on the badge, and they appeared to be written in three tiny opened books. One day Victoria dragged a chair to the bookcase and climbed up so she could examine the beer mug more closely. It was dusty, and so was the top of the bookcase, and she had to thumb a nostril in order to keep herself from sneezing. She quickly hopped down and returned the chair to its place. Her mother was in the basement, and the dryer was setting up a racket. Victoria ran across the room to her father's typewriter. She hugged it. She fell over it, and she hugged it and hugged it until the keys made peremptory little clicking sounds. She flopped on the rug, and she rolled on the rug, and she made her nose follow along one of the zigzagging lines. She spoke to the rug, and she told it to keep her father's feet warm in case he ever decided to go barefoot while composing a sermon. "You mind my words," she said to the rug, and then she smoothed it and gracefully scrambled to her feet, not making a sound. Her panties had twisted themselves, and so she reached up her skirt and straightened them. She wriggled her rear end back and forth, and she bit her tongue, and she grimaced. Then, when everything was in order again, she tapped a toe against the rug, and she said: "I mean what I say." And she heard the rug assure her it would cooperate to the fullest. And she nodded. And here was her truth. And she smiled at chairs, photographs. And here indeed would be forever her truth. Laced with love, of course, and sweet hallucinatory visions, fragile breath, a clamor of plastic and metal and stuffing and wheels and cloth, the wisdom of dear friends, the concern of a tiny relentless army that sought only peace and the truth of silent days and silent games and puckery baths and the nearness of a forever necessary cupped palm.

24 ᧞ Mischief

IN 1974, when she was five, Victoria decided her father's best umbrella would make a fine horsie. So she stole it from the front closet and hid it in the rose bushes next to the garage. The reason she thought it would make a fine horsie had to do with its handle, which was in the shape of a horsie's head. Her father and mother were mightily puzzled by the umbrella's disappearance, and her father finally decided he'd probably mislaid it somewhere in the church—even though he just about could have *sworn* the last time he had seen the thing it had been in the front closet. Victoria crept into the rose bushes whenever no one was looking, and she stroked the horsie's head, which was knobbed. The horsie had rigid ears and a sort of pointed jaw. "Good old horsie," said Victoria. And she shuddered a little, and the horsie's ears and jaw were perhaps too belligerent for her, and so she said: "Good old *scary* horsie." And the horse said to her: It's just that I'm always on my guard—and, ah, ready to go. And Victoria said: "Ready to go where?" And the horsie said: Anyplace you want me to go. And Victoria thought about this for a number of days. And finally one warm afternoon, while her mother was upstairs lying down because of a headache, Victoria removed the horsie from the rose bushes and took a wild ride on him. She galloped him into the house, and he bumped along the floor down the hall from the kitchen to the diningroom, and he bumped

94

too hard, and so he tore the rug, and then he became caught in the rug, and Victoria bumped into a chair, and this hurt her head, which caused her to weep, and the chair fell into the table, and somehow one of Victoria's mother's most fragile crystal water goblets was knocked to the floor, where it broke, and Victoria tripped and fell atop the shards, cutting an elbow, and so she wept some more, and her mother came running, and that night, after a great deal of discussion, her father spanked her with a soft reluctant hand, and her mother said: Well, Carl, it's not much, but it's more than I could do. And then, sighing, Victoria's mother gave Victoria a splendid bath, and she let Victoria have a cup of cocoa in bed. But the horsie thence and forever remained unmolested in the front closet.

In 1975, when she was six, Victoria eavesdropped one night on her parents while they were discussing something called streaking. Said her father: It may have been trivial, but at the same time it was symptomatic of something a great deal more significant. Said her mother: Yes, *sir*, Professor. Said Victoria's father: Well, all right, so sometimes I am polysyllabic, but I still believe you have the capability to keep up with me. Said Victoria's mother (laughing a little): Thank you, I'm *sure*. But we *are* only talking about *streaking*. I mean, the subject at hand is *not* the pillars of the universe. We're talking about people who run naked at public gatherings, who disrupt Epworth League covered dish suppers and college commencements and retirement banquets, people who in a sort of, um, *personal* way seek to call attention to themselves. Said Victoria's father: But there are social implications. Said Victoria's mother: Let's leave the social implications out of the conversation. That way, I can enjoy my Cointreau without giving myself heartburn. Let them who wants to be naked in public be naked in public, I say. Let them run. I only hope they have good muscle tone. On account of the esthetics of the thing, you know? I drink to them. Long may they wave. Or dangle. Or whatever. And then Victoria's mother laughed, and Victoria's father also laughed, and he said: Blessed be the incorrigible. And Victoria's mother said: For they shall inherit eternal exasperation. And Victoria's father said: Amen. Praise the Lord. Then there was more laughter, and Victoria's father said: I drink to you, my love. And Victoria's mother said: Thank you, kind sir. And there was a sound of glasses being touched. And there was silence. And finally Victoria's father said: Shall we streak upstairs and commune with our basic emotions? And Victoria's mother said: Yes indeed. Then was a sound of footsteps, and Victoria's father and mother came careening up the stairs, and she barely was able to duck back into her bedroom.

She took Marybeth to bed with her that night, and she carefully whispered to Marybeth of streaking and laughter and love, and Marybeth said: Well, I don't *know* about *that*. And Victoria said: "It will be *fun*. I mean, you should have heard the way they *laughed*." And Marybeth said: Well you're the one who's in charge, and whatever you want, you get. Correct? And Victoria said: "But I don't want to hurt your feelings." And Marybeth said: Never mind about my feelings. Everything's fine. And Victoria said: "Word of honor?" And Marybeth said: Word of honor. And Victoria embraced Marybeth, but she took care not to wrinkle Marybeth's dress, which was white, lacy, with a blue sash that matched Marybeth's great blank gleaming blue eyes. Victoria waited until the following afternoon before she prepared Marybeth for her (Marybeth's) surprise appearance at supper. Victoria had a tote bag that was gray and brown, and the words MY TOTE BAG were printed on the tote bag, all in capital letters. Clucking at Marybeth, reminding her that she had to be silent, Victoria carefully slid Marybeth into the MY TOTE BAG tote bag. Then, squinting, Victoria peered inside the MY TOTE BAG tote bag and said: "Are you all right in there?" And Marybeth said: I'm fine. I'm a little cold, and I don't really think this is doing an awful lot for my dignity, but otherwise I am just fine and dandy, thank you very much. And Victoria said: "Oh, but think of the *fun.*" And Marybeth said: Big deal. Smiling, Victoria closed the tote bag, but not so tightly that Marybeth wouldn't have any air to breathe.

There was rice pudding with raisins and heavy cream for dessert that night. Rice pudding with raisins and heavy cream was maybe Victoria's favorite dessert in the whole world. She had brought the tote bag down with her from her room, and her parents had asked her what was inside, and she said: "That's for me to know and you to find out." And she had smiled at her parents, and her father had cast his eyes heavenward, and he had said: Why hast Thou forsaken us and presented us with such a snippy child? And everyone had listened for a Reply, but none had been forthcoming, even though everyone had drawn in his and her breath and had listened for that Reply with urgent and searching ears. And supper passed, and Victoria ate all her rice pudding with raisins and heavy cream, using her spoon to scrape up the last precious smears of sweet gumminess, and her mother and father were discussing Mrs Betty Ford's breast operation, and they did not see her bend over, and they did not see her open the bag, and they did not see her remove a nude and shivering Marybeth from it, and they did not really notice until Victoria began running around the table, and her mother's face was a blur, and her father's face was a larger blur, and the lights and the silverware and the dishes spun in front of her immense demented eyes, and she banged the nude Marybeth against the surface of the

table, which meant Marybeth was in effect herself running around the surface of the table, and Victoria lifted Marybeth and kept her away from the reaching hands of her mother and father, and Victoria said: "Streak streak streak." And Victoria said: "See the streaker. See the streaker streak." And Marybeth bounced helplessly. And Marybeth's great blank gleaming blue eyes rolled. And Victoria said: "Streak streak streak." And Victoria ran from the room. She held the nude Marybeth aloft. She ran through the kitchen. "Streak streak streak," she said. She ran through the family room and the front room. She ran upstairs, and she ran through her parents' bedroom, and she ran through her own bedroom, and her other dolls and animals laughed and applauded (and some of them perhaps blushed). "Streak streak streak," said Victoria, and laughter also came from downstairs. Later, though, she had to take Marybeth to bed with her and cuddle her. And Marybeth said: I could have *died*. And Victoria said: "Hush now. Everyone enjoyed it." And Marybeth said: Hush now yourself. *You* weren't the one who was *exposed*. And Victoria said: "Now, now. It's not like you have *warts*. You're very pretty, and you ought to be proud of yourself." And Marybeth said: I don't care *what* you say. *I* say I could have *died*. And Victoria cuddled Marybeth closer, and she hummed, and she stroked Marybeth's hair, and after awhile Marybeth slept. And Victoria thought back on her parents' laughter. And she thought back on what her father had said to her a little later. I never realized you had so much get up and go, the Rev Mr Tabor had said. And Victoria had said: "But it wasn't *me*. It was *Marybeth*." And the Rev Mr Tabor had said: Oh, yes. Marybeth. She's quite a little devil, isn't she? And Victoria had said: "Oh, yes, indeed, Papa. That is a fact."

In 1976, when she was seven, Victoria sat with her

parents in the Milwaukee, Wisconsin, airport, which was named after a man named William Mitchell. They had been on their way to visit her Uncle Frank, the chemist who lived in Chicago, but that city's O'Hare Field had been closed by a snowstorm, and their plane had been diverted to Milwaukee. It was early December, and the airport was crowded, and Victoria and her mother and perhaps a hundred other persons were waiting for a bus that would take them the rest of the way to Chicago. She had chosen to have Bear accompany them on this journey. She sat quietly on a plastic chair, and her legs did not touch the floor, and she bounced Bear first on one knee and then on the other, and occasionally she whispered with him. They discussed a fat man who had a beard and carried a flight bag that said HEINE-KEN. They smiled at a little towheaded boy who crawled on the floor and pushed a wooden locomotive that had a bright yellow snout. He made choochoo noises, and now and then he tried to whistle through the openings between his teeth. Victoria patted Bear's ears and his head and his belly, and she overheard her father say to her mother: I bet Frank is having a fit. You know how compulsive he is about punctuality. He's probably pacing around O'Hare like your proverbial caged lion, and I feel sorry for Martha and their kids if he brought them. Oh, she married a rare one, she did. A classic Type A. And Victoria's mother said: But I think she loves him. And, grinning, Victoria's father said: She'd have to. Back in Hanover, when he and Mark and I were growing up, he always was early, and it didn't matter where he was going or what he was doing. He'd make a date with a girl, and then he'd show up half an hour early, and she'd be running around in her brassiere and I don't know what all, and fiftyseven varieties of consternation would break loose, whispered conversations and whatever, and he'd sit stiff as overstarched laundry in the front room for half an hour, and the girl's mother and father would have to entertain him and feed him coffee and maybe cookies or who knows what, orange rinds maybe. And he's the only person I've ever known whose head never moves when he speaks. Have you ever noticed that? What I mean is . . . his *lips* move . . . or at least they *twitch* and give *some* sign of life . . . but it's as though his *head* has been *strapped* to a . . . oh, I don't know . . . a cement collar. And here Victoria's father grinned more widely. Snorting, he said: Can't you imagine poor Frank sitting in all those front rooms? And Victoria's mother said: I feel sorry for the people who had to sit with him. And the Rev Mr Tabor said: That is a fact. And here Victoria spoke up, saying: "Is Uncle Frank a bad person?" And her father glanced at her and quickly said: No. I don't mean to imply that at all. It's just that he's a little impatient. And Victoria said: "Why do people have to be impatient?" And her father hesitated a moment before saying: It's the world we live in. And Victoria's mother said: Victoria, so much is rush, rush, rush. There are a lot of, um, pressures. Everything has to occur *right at this instant.* There's no such thing as *anticipation.* It all has to be *now.* Instant soups. Microwave ovens. Frozen lasagna. Do you think you understand? And Victoria said: "Yes." She frowned a little. Why did her mother and her father so often ask her did she understand?

She scrunched herself so that she was looking away from her mother and her father. She blinked at the fat bearded man who had the HEINEKEN flight bag, and he smiled. Victoria quickly looked down, and Bear whispered to her that it probably would be a very long day, what with one thing and another. Victoria nodded. She looked around. She hugged Bear. She saw a fat woman who wore green slacks, a blue sweater, and a brown coat. The fat woman was holding a baby, and the baby was asleep, and it was sucking a thumb. It was wrapped in a pink blanket. The woman and the baby were with a skinny man who had a wobbly jaw, and the skinny man was holding the hand of a little girl who was perhaps Victoria's age. The little girl was fat, and she was wearing a red snowsuit, and her hair was knotted, and she jumped up and down, and she said: Knuckleheads! Knuckleheads! You're all knuckleheads! She blinked straight at the fat bearded man who had the HEINE-KEN bag. They promised me a Mars bar! she said. And the fat bearded man cleared his throat and said: Well, um, I'm sure everything will be just fine. And the girl said: What do *you* know about it? You're *ugly!* What do you want, knucklehead? A knuckle sandwich? And she tried to move toward the fat bearded man, but she was held back by the skinny man with the wobbly jaw, who said to her: Now, Sophie, he nice. Sophie turned to the skinny man with the wobbly jaw, and she tried to jerk her hand free of his, and she said: I want my Mars bar! What kind of a daddy is it who doesn't keep his promises? And the fat woman said: He only told you *maybe*. And Sophie said: That's not true! That's a *lie!* He said he *would!* Now everyone was looking at Sophie and the fat woman and the baby and the man with the wobbly jaw. Victoria supposed the fat woman and the man with the wobbly jaw were Sophie's parents. A voice came over a loudspeaker, and it said something about the delay of a Flight Something or Other arriving from Madison. The little towheaded boy pushed his locomotive toward Sophie. A thin blond woman motioned to him not to move too close to Sophie, but he did not notice. Victoria held Bear up to one of her ears, and he whispered: I don't like the looks of any of this. Stay clear of it. And Victoria whispered: "Why?" And Bear whispered: Just *trust* me. Stay *clear* of it. I *mean* that. Then the baby began to bawl. *Now* see what you've done, said the fat woman to Sophie. A tall woman in a fur coat seated herself next to the man with the wobbly jaw, and Sophie tried to kick the tall woman. Mind your own beeswax! said Sophie to the tall woman. I beg your pardon? said the tall woman, smiling a little, smoothing her coat. Give me my Mars bar! said Sophie to the tall woman. I'm real sorry, said the fat woman to the tall woman. The fat woman bounced the baby and clucked at it, but it continued to bawl. It drooled, and the fat woman wiped at its little leaking mouth with a corner of the blanket. There, there, Ernestine, said the fat woman to the baby, who poked at the fat woman with its thumbs. You are a ratfink! said Sophie to the tall woman. The man with the wobbly jaw smacked Sophie across the face. Sophie drew an enormous shuddering breath.

Now everyone was looking at Sophie. The fat bearded HEINEKEN man was looking at Sophie. The tall woman was looking at Sophie. The little boy was looking up from his locomotive at Sophie. Victoria's parents were looking at Sophie. Victoria was looking at Sophie. Bear was looking at Sophie. A woman in a United Air Lines flight attendant's outfit was looking at Sophie. Two young nuns were looking at Sophie. Two young black men were looking at Sophie. One of them was carrying a small satchel that said ADIDAS, and the other had a goatee and a waxed moustache. Sophie began to squirm. She rubbed her face where the man with the wobbly jaw had smacked it. You can't hurt me! she said to the man with the wobbly jaw. Then she again kicked out at the tall woman, and she was successful. Ow, said the tall woman, and she looked around. The fat woman looked up from the bawling baby and said to the tall woman: I'm real sorry. And the tall woman tried to smile, but at the same time she was wincing. She bent over and rubbed the place on her leg Sophie had kicked. Communist! said Sophie, and abruptly she wrenched her hand free of the hand of the man with the wobbly jaw. The young black man with the ADIDAS satchel shook his head and said to the other young black man: Sheesh. Sophie glared at them and said: Dinges! And the goateed young black man said: Hold on, now, you. And the fat woman blinked up at the two young black men and said: I'm real sorry. Sophie ran to the little towheaded boy and stepped on his locomotive, crushing it. Dummy! said Sophie to the little boy, and she kicked out at him, but he rolled away. The man with the wobbly jaw ran toward Sophie, but she ducked past him. The little boy was weeping. The thin blond woman came to him and hugged him, and then they tried to gather up what was left of the crushed locomotive. The man with the wobbly jaw chased Sophie, and Sophie was whooping. Perhaps there is something the matter with her glands, said one of the nuns to the woman in the United Air Lines flight attendant's outfit. A chemical imbalance, said the other nun. Oh, yes, I wouldn't be surprised, said the woman in the United Air Lines flight attendant's outfit, and she smiled. Her forehead appeared to be a little damp and shiny. The man with the wobbly jaw chased Sophie down a corridor, and there was a sort of silence. But it wasn't much of a silence, since the baby still was bawling and the little boy still was weeping. The fat bearded man removed a book from his HEINEKEN bag. The title of the book was *Something Happened*. He opened the book, crossed his legs, squinted at the page. The fat woman and the baby were sitting smack next to him, and he hunkered down with the book, literally hiding his face in it. Sophie came clattering back up the corridor, and the man with the wobbly jaw still was pursuing her. She ran past Victoria, and she whacked Bear on the head. Sissy! she said. Sissy with a teddybear! Then Sophie stopped run-

ning. She turned and faced the man with the wobbly
jaw. All right, turkey! she said, and her teeth were
gleaming. Come and get me! And she placed her
hands on her hips and braced herself. And the wobblejawed man advanced on her. Briskly she kicked him
in a shin. Ow, he said, and he hopped on one leg.
Laughing, Sophie scurried past him before he could
recover. She went past the fat bearded man and
seized the copy of *Something Happened*. She threw
the book at Victoria's father. The book bounced off
Victoria's father's chest onto his lap. He glanced down
at the book, and it fell open. Thoughtfully he rubbed
his chest. *TAKE THAT, YOU BUZZARD!* said
Sophie to Victoria's father. Then she ran back down
the corridor, and she was whooping, and she nearly
knocked down an elderly woman who had a moustache and was walking with the aid of a crutch. The
wobblejawed man still pursued Sophie, and he also
nearly knocked down that elderly woman. Woopsy!
said the elderly woman, flailing for a moment with
her crutch. The fat woman smiled at Victoria's father
and said: I'm real sorry. Victoria's father cleared his
throat. The fat bearded man went to Victoria's father
and reclaimed the book. The fat bearded man
shrugged, rolled his eyes. Animal spirits, I guess, he
said. He returned to his seat. The fat woman hushed
and murmured over the baby. She's not really to be
blamed, said one of the nuns. Oh, no, not when it's
a chemical imbalance, said the other nun. The fat
woman tickled the baby's chin, and the baby began
to gurgle. Good baby, said the fat woman. Victoria
whispered with Bear, but she kept an eye out for the
return of Sophie. For surely Sophie would return.
"Like a bad penny," she whispered to Bear. Indeed,
whispered Bear. "Mean as thumbtacks," whispered
Victoria. Without a doubt, whispered Bear. Then,
howling, Sophie came careening back up the corridor,
and she said: *I HATE ERNESTINE! ERNESTINE*

SUCKS! And she went to the baby and pounded it on the head with a fist. The fat woman gasped. The baby screeched. The nuns embraced one another. The fat bearded man turned a page of *Something Happened*. See here now, said Victoria's father, and he got to his feet and started toward Sophie. The nuns retreated a step. The young black men shook their heads. This ain't, you know, all that cool, said the one with the goatee. The thin blond woman was holding the little boy on her lap, and she was telling him she would see to it that Mister Choochoo was fixed up good as new. Neither she nor the little boy appeared to be paying a bit of attention to Sophie. Victoria hugged Bear, and Victoria's mother touched one of Victoria's shoulders and told her to stay right where she was. The wobblejawed man came up on Sophie, but she ducked out of his reach. The fat woman kissed the baby's skull, and then she said to everyone: I'm real sorry. (The baby had turned a moist pink). Sophie headed straight for Victoria's advancing father. She brought a foot down smartly on his instep. He made a whinnying noise, and she ran past him. Victoria kissed Bear's head where Sophie had whacked it. Victoria hadn't even bothered yet to ask Bear if he felt any pain. Shame on Victoria. Sophie ran past Victoria's father. He had bent over to rub his shin, and so she kicked him in the buttocks. Victoria's mother gasped, got up, ran to her wounded husband. He was staggering from the force of Sophie's kick. The nuns and the black men were closing in on Sophie. The wobblejawed man and the woman in the United Air Lines flight attendant's outfit were closing in on Sophie. But Sophie ducked through the encircling cordon. Laughing, she began another dash toward the corridor. But she had to pass where Victoria was sitting, and so Victoria was able to stick out both legs. Sophie tripped over them at full speed. She flew horizontally,

and she landed on her belly, and she slid forward,
and she gave a mighty scream, and the bearded man
looked up and smiled at Victoria. He inserted a thumb
in the book and closed it. The fat woman looked at
Victoria and said: I'm real sorry. The wobblejawed
man went to Sophie and knelt next to her. She needs
her lithium, he said to no one in particular. And one
of the nuns said: See? And the other nun said: Oh,
yes, Catherine, that I do. And Bear whispered: Nice
going, my friend. I do believe my head has been
avenged. And Victoria whispered: "Well, enough was
enough." The thin blond woman smiled at Victoria.
The tall furcoated woman smiled at Victoria. Even
the two black men smiled at Victoria. Even the
woman in the United Air Lines flight attendant's outfit. Even the nuns. Even the little boy whose Mister
Choochoo had been crushed. And Victoria's parents
came to her, and her mother said something about
violence not always being the way to deal with
violence, but the words were flat and perfunctory,
and they were about as passionate as a list of Fire
Drill Regulations. And Victoria's mother kept smiling,
and so did Victoria's father, which meant the words
vanished as soon as they were spoken. The fat bearded
HEINEKEN man bought Victoria a bag of peanuts,
and then everyone rode to Chicago in a big bus, and
Victoria and her mother sat across the aisle from
Sophie and the wobblejawed man, and Sophie slept
all the way in the wobblejawed man's arms.

There was snow and snow and snow, and Victoria
was reminded of a paperweight in her parents' bedroom. The paperweight had a snowman inside. You
turned the paperweight upside down and snow fell
on the snowman. Victoria had a name for the snowman. She called him Frosty, and she hoped someday
to inherit him. Sophie slept. The baby slept. The
fat woman and the wobblejawed man sat erectly.
Victoria was sitting next to the window, but she was

able to hear distinctly when the wobblejawed man leaned into the aisle and said to her mother: I'm real glad your little girl done what she done. It put a stop to the thing. When Sophie gets like that, and we're out of the lithium, don't seem like there's nothing we can do. I mean, we ain't nothing much, no matter how you look at it, and we just don't know how to handle her when she's like that. And Victoria's mother said: I can sympathize with you. I only wish there were some words of real comfort I could speak. I do want you to understand, though, that my daughter meant your little girl no harm. And the wobblejawed man nodded. Sophie was pressed against his chest, and her body was in a tight ball, and he stroked her hair and the back of her neck. Victoria saw this, and so she stroked the back of Bear's neck, and she whispered: "Are you all right? Your head, I mean." And Bear whispered: I'm very comfortable, thank you. Hush now. Let's look at the scenery and maybe catch a little nap. Nodding, Victoria turned Bear so that he faced the window. Everything was gray and awhirl with snow, and so there wasn't all that much scenery. The ride in the bus took four hours, and Uncle Frank was just about eating his lips when Victoria and her parents (and Bear) finally arrived in Chicago. Uncle Frank's wife, Aunt Marian, and Uncle Frank's three children—Bobby, Frank Junior, and Barbara—also were on hand. And everyone spoke at once. And Uncle Frank said something to the effect that my God, why were the airlines so reluctant to give any information when there was an emergency? Uncle Frank was bald, and he had pink palms, and he wore a heavy overcoat that was making him sweat, and the odor of the overcoat caught high in Victoria's nostrils after everyone crowded inside his Buick. Victoria sat on her mother's lap, and she closed her eyes and tried to listen to Uncle Frank, but the remembered bleating harshness

of Sophie's voice kept intruding. Snow crunched
under the Buick's tires, and other cars skidded past,
and Uncle Frank continued talking, talking, and his
voice was splintered, forever grabbing at air and
gulping it, and his voice was Sophie's voice, and it
all put Victoria in mind of instant soups, microwave
ovens, frozen lasagna. (She glanced back at her mother
and started to whisper something. But then she
changed her mind. Bear was curled on her lap. She
looked down at him and whispered: "I guess we're
lucky." And Bear whispered: That is a fact.)

In 1977, when she was eight, Victoria stole a large
box of Brach's chocolates from a cupboard in the
diningroom. It was Christmastime, and she wrapped
each piece of chocolate in a scrap of Christmas paper.
Then she went into her father's study and stole a
small box of gummed labels. She wrote the names
of her dolls and animals on the gummed labels, and
the total was twentysix gummed labels. She licked
the labels, made numerous faces, attached the labels
to the tiny packages. She hid the empty chocolate
box under her mattress. She was the first to awaken
on Christmas morning. She took the tiny packages
downstairs with her and scattered them under the
Christmas tree with the other packages. Then she
brought down all her dolls and animals and arranged
them around the tree. Even the retired nightlights
were included. The dolls and animals sat and sprawled
and crouched, and they admired the tree, and *then*—
after Victoria had switched on the lights—they all
murmurously exclaimed. The lights were the sort
that flickered, and they threw quick aimless shadows
on the walls and the ceiling, and everyone applauded.
A little later, when Victoria's parents awakened and
came downstairs and saw the tiny packages, they
told her ah *hah*, now they had solved the mystery
of the missing box of chocolates. They tried to scold
her, but it was Christmas morning, and finally they

simply smiled and shrugged and told her they hoped her friends had a merry Christmas. Victoria had counted on this sort of reaction, and she looked at Bear, and she winked, then set about the glorious business of opening her own presents. And she heard Bear make amused conspiratorial noises somewhere maybe in his belly.

In 1978, when she was nine, Victoria accused her teacher's grandmother of sucking canal water through a leaky straw.

25 ⁓ Stripes

So IT WAS indeed perhaps once a year that Victoria was a genuinely bad girl . . . and even then, such as in the incidents of the streaking Marybeth and the demented Sophie, she wasn't all that bad, and perhaps she wasn't bad at all. She really did believe in respect, love, warmth, quiet, blankets, baths. And there were certain questions that sorely vexed her, questions that had nothing to do with deportment or morality. Take stripes as an example. One day, while she was pulling Cat around the kitchen, she hesitated, frowned at him for a moment, then abruptly flopped down next to him and said: "I need to talk to you about your . . . about your, um, stripes."

Pardon? said Cat.

"Um, you have orange stripes, and you have black stripes. What I want to know is—which are the stripes and which aren't?"

Pardon? said Cat.

"Are you all orange with black stripes? Or are you all black with orange stripes? You have to be one or the other, correct?"

Oh, said Cat. Well, I don't know . . .

Victoria rubbed her chin. "Unless of course someone did a real careful job and painted *both* stripes," she said. "But why would anyone do *that*, when it is so much easier to paint black on orange, or orange on black?"

You have a point, said Cat.

Victoria squinted at Cat. "I really can't tell by *looking*," she said.

And myself, said Cat, I can't remember. It was all so long ago. I was only a little kitten.

"You were wood before you were painted," said Victoria.

I still am wood, said Cat.

"But I mean you were wood *color*," said Victoria.

Oh, said Cat.

"But it wouldn't be fair to expect you to remember."

True, said Cat.

"Especially since you have to be led by the nose," said Victoria. "Which, um, which doesn't exactly make you altogether so smart, you know?"

No, I *don't* know, said Cat. Just because I'm led by the nose, that doesn't mean I'm *stupid*. It only means I have no choice. I was *created* so that the only way I could get around was to be led by the nose. You think I'd *choose* to be led by the nose? Now, that *would* be stupid.

Victoria giggled.

What's so funny? said Cat.

"I don't know," said Victoria, giggling.

Big deal, said Cat. You and your stripes. You and *my* stripes, I mean.

Victoria squealed. She scrambled to her feet. She pulled Cat by the string that was attached to his nose, and they clattered through the downstairs rooms, even Victoria's father's study. Cat's red wheels clapped and bounced. Victoria giggled again, but she also kept squealing. She thought of stripes and silly questions. Big deal indeed. Crazy Victoria. Ah, but this sort of thinking at least most of the time occupied her attention, which meant she seldom had room in her days for mischief. So she picked at Cat's stripes with a fingernail, and one day she figured they were black on orange, and the next day she figured they were orange on black, but she never really made up her mind. All right, perhaps this wasn't a very important question to be occupying her attention, but it didn't hurt anyone, and it surely fulfilled the function of seizing her brain, of taking up some of the mornings and afternoons of persons such as herself, persons who were alone a great deal, persons who rode in beds that clicked and rocked along on flanged wheels, persons who trafficked in dialogue with dolls, stuffed animals, a wooden cat, retired nightlights, a soap fish. So the soft miraculous palaver persisted, the happy secret debates.

26 ❧ Grandpa

THE FLESH on Grandpa Bird's face was wattled and slabbed. It put Victoria vaguely in mind of the cellophaned ground meat she saw in the butcher's case at Heinen's when she accompanied her mother grocery shopping. I'm something from out back of the privy for sure, said Grandpa Bird, and I got more wrinkles than a dog has fleas, and maybe I ought to be condemned by the sheriff, or the Board of Health, or the Catholic Church. I expect I don't really know.

Victoria and her parents visited Grandpa Bird out near Chagrin Falls about once every two weeks—usually Sunday afternoons, after the Rev Mr Tabor had completed his duties at Wrexford Methodist. Grandpa Bird had four rooms in the retirement village, and his little place and all the other little places there adjoined one another in a chain of little places that was maybe like a chain of cages (with wooden American eagles over the front doors, all of them painted gold; with patches of pansies and petunias clustered in the narrow dooryards; with numbers spelled out over the front doors, *Twenty Three* and *Six* and *Thirty Seven*, the letters very Early American, wriggly, arcane, snootier than a camel with a sinus condition), and the people who owned this retirement village called the little places condominiums, and Grandpa Bird and all the other old folks who lived in those condominiums surely did get a chuckle out of *that*, no two ways about it. Not that the walls were thin, understand, but there was a couple named Salisbury who occupied a condominium adjoining Grandpa Bird's place, and Grandpa Bird was there to testify he could hear the Salisburys every time they groaned in their sleep, or passed gas, or exchanged whispered reminiscences of sweet times past. Mr Salisbury had led a dance band for four decades, and his wife had been its vocalist, and there were times when all they talked about was tuxedos and colored balls. Not balls held by colored people, but rather the sort of balls that used to hang from gymnasium and ballroom ceilings and slowly turn, casting dotted shadows on great crowds of clutched and swaying foxtrotters.

I like the Salisburys just fine, said Grandpa Bird one day, but I don't really want to hear their most intimate conversations. Especially since all they seem to talk about is *dancing*. I mean, what do I care about Bunny Berigan and Woody Herman at *this* late date? And especially since it's been a long time since I've exactly been a promtrotter. A very long time.

Grandpa Bird and Victoria and Victoria's parents were sitting in his tiny front room. Victoria's mother glanced at Grandpa Bird's legs, then abruptly looked away.

That's all right, Sandra, said Grandpa Bird. He had fixed tea for himself and Victoria's parents, and he had given Victoria a glass of milk. Now he sipped at his tea. He shook his head. He spoke softly to Victoria's mother: It's been more than fifty years.

I'm sorry, said Victoria's mother. I didn't mean to stare like that.

Nothing to be sorry *about*, said Grandpa Bird. It's been more than *half* a *century* since Herb Sheppard piled up the Packard. And so I lost my left foot. Herb and the girls lost a good deal more, didn't they? And anyway, I don't really want to look back.

Victoria's mother nodded.

Grandpa Bird leaned down and tapped his wooden left foot. This is the fourth one, he said. I've actually worn out three, can you imagine? Worn them to nubs, so to speak. What do you think of that, huh? No one spoke.

Grandpa Bird blinked at his daughter. He blinked at his daughter's husband. He blinked at Victoria. He sipped at his tea. He sat next to Victoria on a loveseat that was decorated with a brilliant design of peacocks. It was mostly purples and blues, and there were times when it hurt Victoria's eyes. The room was clean, redded up, with magazines and both the Cleveland newspapers stacked neatly on a coffee table, and Grandpa Bird liked to boast of the fact that he vacuumed the four rooms of his condominium every other day, come rain, come shine, come hemorrhoids, come croup. There was a breakfront in a far corner, and it abounded with china owls. Grandpa Bird always dusted those owls after doing the vacuuming. His wife had collected them. His *late* wife. His wife who had been dead since the summer of 1952, which was as remote to Victoria as eternity and the moon. The woman had been Grandma Bird, and Victoria had seen photographs of her, and the photographs had shown a thin woman with lips that were pressed too tightly together. Victoria wasn't altogether certain she would have liked Grandma Bird very much. She had heard it said that Grandma Bird had been quite close with a dollar and always had bought bread that was a day old. What sort of person was it who always bought bread that was a day old? A poor person or a cheap person, and Grandma Bird never really had been poor, at least as far as Victoria knew. Which meant Grandma Bird more likely than not had been a cheap person. Victoria did not know why Grandma Bird had been a cheap person, but she supposed the reason wasn't really important anymore. Perhaps it still affected Grandpa Bird; perhaps

it still had a sting to it, a sting that created a remembered anger or sadness. And perhaps it even still
affected Victoria's mother. But as for Victoria, well,
her late grandmother's reputed cheapness didn't really
occupy too much of her thinking time, and she'd
never even bothered to discuss it with her friends—
not even Bear, who knew so much. But something
else having to do with Grandma Bird did occupy quite
a bit of Victoria's thinking time. It was the breakfront—or, more specifically, the owls that were inside
the breakfront. They stood blank and mute; they were
white; they were brown; they were mottled. Some of
them were large, and others weren't. Some of them
were chipped, and others weren't. Some of them
glistened; others were too old to glisten. There was a
regular multitude of them inside Grandpa Bird's
breakfront, and it was a job of work to dust all of
them, he said. He had a little key on his keyring, and
that little key opened the doors of the breakfront,
and sometimes he would unlock the doors and allow
Victoria to hold an owl or two. The biggest of them
was perhaps five or six inches high, and it had a
toothily quizzical expression on its plump face, and
it had a moustache and wore a pince nez with ribbon,
and the legend LOUISIANA PURCHASE EXPOSI-
TION ST LOUIS MO 1904 had been carefully inked
on its chest. This was probably her favorite of the
owls. There were fiftyfour of them, all told (Grandpa
Bird had counted them), but this big fellow was the
only one that gave any sign of having a sense of
humor. The others were altogether too solemn, and
Victoria wished she could do something to cheer
them up. She supposed they were solemn because
they were confined in the breakfront. Occasionally,
when she had a few moments alone with them, she
would press her mouth to the glass doors and try
to whisper to them, asking them what she could do
to help. And she was able to hear a hollow and rueful

mixture of voices drift to her from the poor imprisoned owls, but it was too faint, and she coud not
make out the words. Only the big owl ever spoke with
Victoria, and then just briefly, while she was holding
him after Grandpa Bird had unlocked the breakfront
doors for her a few Sundays after the conversation
having to do with the Salisburys and his wooden
foot. He and Victoria's parents sat chatting in the
kitchen, which was in an alcove just off the front
room. Grandpa Bird had told Victoria to take care
not to drop the big guy, and he went on to say
that this particular owl had been Grandma Bird's special favorite. Victoria nodded. She held the big owl
with both her hands, and she sat scrunched far back
on the peacocked loveseat. That way, if she dropped
the owl, it simply would bounce off her lap onto the
cushions, and it would not break. Holding her breath
a little, she leaned over the owl and whispered: "My
name is Victoria. What's yours?" And the owl whispered: I am Teddy. And Victoria whispered: "Pleased
to meet you, I'm sure." And the owl whispered:
Bully. And Victoria whispered: "Why do you wear
those funny glasses?" And the owl whispered: They
are not *funny glasses*. It just so happens I am afflicted
with day blindness, and it is no joking matter. I shall
be very angry if you see me as a figure of ridicule.
Ask those Spaniards at San Juan Hill if *they* saw me
as a figure of ridicule. Bloody damned greasers. We
gave them Gatling guns right in their bellies, and we
were brave men, all of us. San Juan Hill, and I fired
a pistol that had been salvaged from the wreck of
the *Maine*. Oh, we were splendid, I tell you. We
were not ridiculous, and I am not ridiculous. Just
because I have a touch of day blindness, that is no
reason for you to joke. And Victoria whispered: "I
didn't mean to hurt your feelings." And the owl
whispered: All right—you can make it up by helping
us escape from this damnable breakfront. I have been

elected President of the Owls—by acclaim. Which
means I have the vested authority to ask you to assist
us. And Victoria whispered: "But how can I do that?"
And the owl whispered: We leave that to you to
figure out. And Victoria whispered: "But I don't
have a key. What am I supposed to do? Come here
and break the glass doors and carry you all away in
a . . . in a *truck?*" And the owl whispered: A bully
idea.

Victoria was about to reply, to tell the owl he was
crazier than a bedbug in a pan of Crisco, but just
then Grandpa Bird and her parents came wandering
back in from the kitchen, and Grandpa Bird took the
owl from Victoria and returned it to the breakfront.
He closed the breakfront doors and locked them.
Then he hobbled to a straightbacked chair and seated
himself. He shifted his weight. He sighed. He leaned
forward and rested his hands on his knees. He got
to talking about the family. He smiled vaguely at
Victoria's mother. Snuffling a little, he said: I don't
suppose it's escaped your attention that I've had I
believe three beers today.

No, said Victoria's mother. It has not.

I was thinking about my son. Your brother.

Oh, said Victoria's mother.

Morris the Three. Morris Bird the Eye Eye Eye.
Perhaps it is just as well he died.

Pardon? said Victoria's mother.

My father was the original Morris Bird. I am Morris Bird the Eye Eye. Your brother was Morris Bird
the Eye Eye Eye. If he had survived, and if he had
sired a son, that young man undoubtedly would have
been Morris Bird the Eye Vee. The Eye Vee, don't
you get it? Morris Bird the Intravenous.

Oh, Daddy, for heaven's sake . . .

I see what you mean about the beers, said Victoria's
father to Grandpa Bird.

Well, I expect I'm entitled, said Grandpa Bird.

Entitled to what? said Victoria's father.

To *whatever* I *want*, said Grandpa Bird. He hesitated. His vague smile focused shakily on Victoria. Roman numerals, he said to her. I have a Roman numeral after my name, and your late Uncle Morris had a Roman numeral after *his* name. But now there will be no more Roman numerals. Nor will the name exist. Since I leave no male heir, the name will be rendered extinct.

But not the *line*, said Victoria's mother.

No indeed, said Grandpa Bird. A great deal of the vagueness went out of his smile. His eyes tightened, and more lines dug themselves into his slabbed cheeks, and he said to Victoria: *You* are the *line*. It all comes down to *you*. What do you think of *that*, eh?

Victoria glanced toward the breakfront. She did not know what to say.

Whatever was before is now distilled into one very nice little person, said Grandpa Bird to Victoria.

She looked at him. "Me?" she said.

I'm not talking about Mickey Rooney or King Zog of Albania, said Grandpa Bird.

"Pardon?" said Victoria.

He means you are the last survivor of his family, said Victoria's father.

And that's important, said Grandpa Bird. A responsibility. I mean, no man likes to think of his blood, um, petering out.

"Oh," said Victoria.

You'll understand that when you're older, said Grandpa Bird to Victoria. You see, I . . . I haven't been all that, ah, exemplary a person, and now, seeing as how I'm a whisper and a spit from seventy, I'm full of regrets. Oh, not that I haven't been full of regrets for a long time. Back in 1952, when your Grandma Bird died, she called me a pig, and she was absolutely—

Please, Daddy, said Victoria's mother. Please. *Please.*

Grandpa Bird hesitated, but only for a blink, maybe two blinks. Then, continuing, he said: Victoria, listen to me. Never mind the interruption. Your Grandma Bird was on her deathbed, and she called me a pig, and she was absolutely right. I never was anything more than a *voice*, first in radio and then in television, and I never made an awful lot of money, which was the one thing on this earth your Grandma Bird understood and appreciated. She married me so long ago I forget right now what the year was, but I do remember what the *reason* was, and it had to do with what she *expected* of me. I mean, I'd already lost the foot, but she didn't care about the foot. All she cared about was the fact that she saw me as having a capacity to provide her with a lot of money, since my folks in those days were in pretty good financial shape and then some, especially in the context of Paradise Falls, Ohio, where crickets chirp, you know? where the river makes an ardent hushing sound, you know? where everyone prays so earnestly that the heavens just about curdle, you know? where old women sit on porches and fan themselves and talk about funerals and kittens and homemade soup, you know? But then, well, along came a thing called the Depression, and someday you'll learn about the Depression in school, and it probably won't mean a sack of stones to you, and that's too bad. On account of, you see, right now you are listening to someone who is close to you, and that someone who is close to you was torn down by the Depression, which maybe means the Depression was an important thing even for you, but you'll never understand that, will you? Or why I came to Cleveland because a friend of mine fixed me up with a job bonging chimes for a radio station. Because it was the only job I could find. And your Grandma Bird, oh, how she was after me all the time, blah blah blah, nya nya nya, Morris, you aren't worth the powder to blow you up, and that is an absolute fact, you poor sorry windbag you. And oh, yes, I regret to say that is the way she spoke to me, and all the chirping crickets were silent, and I heard no ardent hushing river, and I no longer was a young man, and I wore out a wooden foot, and I wore out another wooden foot, and then I just plain wore out, *period*. And there were what we adults call other women, and I—

I'm sorry, but I don't think you should go on like this, said Victoria's father to Grandpa Bird. She doesn't really know what you're talking about, and we don't really want to confuse her, do we?

Be quiet, said Grandpa Bird to Victoria's father.

Daddy! said Victoria's mother to Grandpa Bird. She had lighted a cigarette, and now she snubbed it out in an ashtray that was in the shape of a frog. She snubbed out the cigarette in the frog's throat (and Victoria winced a little). Enough of this, she said. *Please.*

Not quite yet, said Grandpa Bird to Victoria's mother. But I don't want either you or Carl to worry. I'm not about to say anything dirty, and I'm not about to corrupt her. Why, my God, you know better than that. You know how I love her. You know how I am when you bring her out here. I mean, I give her milk, and I let her touch Alice's precious china owls, and I keep trying to make her understand that I believe the world still has a future, if the young people would only stop to think about it. But the thing is—*I want her to know where she's come from*. That way, maybe she can—

"And I want to know," said Victoria.

Everyone looked at her.

Victoria concentrated on Grandpa Bird. "I want to understand all I can," she said. "I don't know for sure what you mean when you talk about crickets and the river and old women and a lot of the other stuff you've brought up, but maybe in time it'll all come together, you think?"

I hope so, said Grandpa Bird.

Victoria shifted her attention to her parents for a moment. "Forget how old I'm not," she said.

Come again? said her father.

"If you forget how old I'm not," said Victoria, "then maybe you'll think I am old, and so it won't matter what Grandpa says, on account of I'll be old enough to handle it."

Victoria's father frowned.

Grandpa Bird grinned. I couldn't have expressed it better myself, he said to Victoria. He cleared his throat, then resumed: Well, to put an end to this story, your grandmother had every justification in the world to say what she said at the end. I mean, look around this place. Does it put anyone in mind of palatial luxury? Four rooms, and you have to move sideways so you fit in them.

But *that* doesn't mean Mama was *right*, said Victoria's mother, lighting another cigarette.

Lack of, um, worldly goods certainly doesn't mean a person is *evil*, said Victoria's father, clearing his throat. And it gives no one the right to use such a word as *pig*.

Grandpa Bird chuckled. You don't understand, he said. You never have understood. Either one of you.

Understood *what?* said Victoria's mother.

Please try to explain it, said Victoria's father.

All right, said Grandpa Bird. I'll try. Back in '52, just before he died, Morris asked me to explain it, and I said to him, I said: Morris, a *nothing* who thinks he is *something* is a *pig*. I've never been—

Victoria's mother interrupted. Daddy, at this late date it doesn't matter, she said, inhaling.

I thought you wanted to understand, said Grandpa Bird.

Well, I've changed my mind, said Victoria's mother.

Victoria's father nodded toward Victoria and said: Please, Mr Bird, please try to remember who's here.

"It's all right," said Victoria.

They all looked at her.

"Just *go ahead* and *talk*," said Victoria. "And try to *forget* how old I'm *not*. I *want* to hear. I *want* to know." She smiled at Grandpa Bird. "I love you. I, um, I love everybody in this room. Please, everybody, please just say whatever it is you want to say."

Grandpa Bird shook his head.

"What's wrong?" said Victoria.

Nothing, said Grandpa Bird, only . . . well, sometimes you talk like you're forty years of age and you've been through three world wars and nine earthquakes and sixtysix flu epidemics.

"Is that good?" said Victoria.

Maybe, said Grandpa Bird.

"Then okay," said Victoria.

Okay what? said Grandpa Bird.

"Okay," said Victoria, "then please just say whatever it is you want to say." She smiled at Grandpa Bird and her parents. She pressed down her skirt. Her knees were touching, and her legs and feet were precisely aligned. She was wearing a blue dress that had a white sash at the waist. "I'm not going to bawl or anything like that," she said. "I don't like to bawl. I only think it's right to bawl when I hurt. Like last week when I bit my tongue." Now the smile was directed at her grandfather only. "It was breakfast," she said, "and I was eating Granola, and I bit down on something hard, and I don't know, somehow my teeth slipped, and the something was knocked down into my throat, and I got to coughing, and then I bit my tongue. The *side* of it, you know?" She made a face. "When you bite the *side* of your tongue, that's the worst way. So I, um, I bawled."

That she did, said Victoria's mother to Grandpa Bird.

She moves from being a child to being a woman to being a child, and just like that, said Victoria's father to Grandpa Bird. She is really very remarkable.

So is Mount Rushmore, said Grandpa Bird.

What? said Victoria's father.

Um, maybe we shouldn't talk about her as though she's not here, said Grandpa Bird to his soninlaw. Maybe we shouldn't talk about her as though she's an abstraction. If she is *remarkable* or whatever, maybe we shouldn't stuff her and put her under glass. I mean, *look* at her. She's a *little girl*.

Victoria wanted to kiss Grandpa Bird, but she did not move. She simply continued to smile at him, and she hoped the smile was telling him what she really wanted to do. She thought very hard: Kiss kiss kiss. I kiss your eyes, Grandpa Bird. I kiss your ears and your nose and the funny flesh on your cheeks.

Never mind about the world wars and the earthquakes, said Grandpa Bird to Victoria's father. I was just making a joke. A little joke. A very little joke.

Victoria's father shrugged and looked away.

Victoria's mother snubbed out her cigarette in the frog's mouth (and again Victoria winced a little).

Grandpa Bird folded his arms over his belly. A life is breath and days and smiles and loss, he said to Victoria. It can't be analyzed the way chemicals can be analyzed, and it can't be summed up on an IBM machine. You think you stay the same, but you never do. You think the whole rest of the world changes, gets older, but you stay the same, and you know what? You're a fibber. Oh, now just a second, Victoria. I'm talking about all us older people; I'm not talking about you as *you*. I'm talking about all the rest of us you see staggering around, or tiptoeing, and always holding our breath, sucking broken glass, whatever.

Daddy, *please*, said Victoria's mother, quickly lighting another cigarette.

Grandpa Bird paid the interruption no mind. He hugged his belly. He said to Victoria: But we don't too many of us think about the breath and the days and the smiles and the loss. Instead we try to find one *moment*, a couple of hours, a night perhaps, that marks an I don't know what, a *center point*, which your average adult can look back on and tell himself: Ah *ha*, if I'd done *Thus* and *So* instead of *This* and *That*, then maybe I would have amounted to something. Are you, um, doing all right with all this?

"I think so," said Victoria.

Good, said Grandpa Bird. Now he was hugging his belly so tightly he was leaning forward a little, and his large mushy voice was pinched around the edges. He said: For me, it was so long ago . . . the center point, if it means anything, which maybe it doesn't . . . all right, I just told you it doesn't mean anything, and I *know* I just told you that . . . but I still can't help, um, summoning it. Is that all right with you?

"Yes," said Victoria. Now most of Grandpa Bird's words had moved beyond her, and so she knotted her face, and she pressed a fist against her chin. She did not *want* them to move beyond her, and perhaps she would be able to pull them back.

Daddy, none of this is any good, said Victoria's mother, puffing, inhaling.

She's right, said Victoria's father.

I guess it's you and I—me?—against the world, said Grandpa Bird to Victoria. He smiled, then: It's important you know your, um, origins. Especially since you are the last of the Birds.

"That's scary," said Victoria.

Maybe so, said Grandpa Bird, but it's something we have to face, isn't it?

"Yes," said Victoria.

You're frightening her, said Victoria's mother to Grandpa Bird.

"I'm all right," said Victoria to her mother.
Her parents stared at her.
"I'm *all right,*" said Victoria to her parents. She
frowned at Grandpa Bird. She kept the fist pressed
against her chin. "I want to hear it," she said to him.
"Whatever it is. I don't care. I want to *hear* it. Please,
Grandpa . . ."
You betcha, said Grandpa Bird. And anyway, it's
not all that terrible, which I've been trying to say
all along, right?
Victoria nodded.
I'm not going to hurt her, said Grandpa Bird to
Victoria's parents.
Victoria's father shrugged.
Victoria's mother inhaled.
Victoria kept the fist pressed against her chin. Her
panties were caught up a little, and so she wriggled,
freeing them, giving more room to her crotch.
All right, then, said Grandpa Bird, I want to tell
you a little something about my center point, which
may or may not be important, which I leave for you
to decide, Victoria, and I'm sure you'll do a good
job of it. It goes back to 1927, and there was a girl
named Rhoda Masonbrink, and she was the most
beautiful girl I've ever seen. This takes nothing away
from your mother, and it takes nothing away from
you, on account of you both *know* you're pretty
and you don't need an old goat like me to tell you.
You have to remember that I was only eighteen years
of age at the time, which is an impressionable age,
believe me, and this Rhoda Masonbrink, um, was
every day like a hair in my throat and, um, stones
in my belly. Maybe that sounds uncomfortable to
you. Well, it *was.* I mean, it was *uncomfortable.* But
there wasn't anything I could do about it, and there
wasn't anything I wanted to do about it. There was
only one catch. Down in Paradise County, the Masonbrinks aren't worth much, and they never have been.

They've been poor dirt farmers, and they've been bootleggers, and I seem to recall that a whole long time ago there were two Masonbrink brothers who earned their living by cleaning the streets of Paradise Falls of, um, horse mess, and—

"Horse mess?" said Victoria.

Horse *bad*, said her mother, speaking quickly.

"Oh?" said Victoria.

The streets were full of it in the olden days, said Victoria's father.

Now everything's full of it, said Grandpa Bird, grinning.

"Oh," said Victoria.

Victoria's father made a dry sound with his tongue and his palate.

But anyway, people who shoveled horse mess for a living weren't exactly your pillars of the community, said Grandpa Bird to Victoria. I'm only bringing up the matter, you understand, in order that you get a clear idea of the sort of people the Masonbrinks were. It's necessary that you—

Baloney, said Victoria's mother to Grandpa Bird.

He looked at her. His arms unwrapped themselves from his belly, and he leaned back. What do you mean? he said.

It's all baloney, said Victoria's mother. You've built it up, Daddy. You've built it up and built it up and *built it up*. What do you call it—a center point? Well, *I* call it baloney.

I expect you're right, said Grandpa Bird. It's what I said when I started out on all this.

Then why do you *bother* with it? said Victoria's mother.

I don't want to. I don't even like to talk about it.

Then why *are* you talking about it?

Because it doesn't matter whether the thing is an illusion. Not as long as my mind and my memory see it as being real. And after all, it really did mark the first time I betrayed your mother, didn't it?

Victoria's mother did not reply. She exhaled, shifted her weight, snubbed out her cigarette, jammed the butt down the poor frog's throat.

Grandpa Bird turned to Victoria again. He said: Rhoda Masonbrink was tall, perhaps as tall as five feet seven inches, which was extremely tall in those days. Her eyes were blue the way certain summer sunsets are blue, sunsets that reflect light just so, with a sort of misty effect. She had a long neck, and she kept her hair short, and there was a mole on the back of her neck. As closely as I can recollect, that mole was two or three inches, maybe four inches, from her left ear. I remember it as clearly as I have you locked in my vision right now, maybe more clearly. You see, Victoria, for a lot of people, when you get to be the age of your grandfather here, the past takes on a reality that Here and Now can't hope to duplicate. It was the time, you see, when we were *alive*, when we, um, when we didn't realize that we did change. All right? Does that make sense?

"Yes," said Victoria. She was fibbing, but she figured it was in a good cause.

Good, said Grandpa Bird. Anyway, Rhoda Masonbrink. Her neck. That mole. There are times when young men, boys really, get peculiar notions into their heads. For me, in those days, the peculiar notion was a very strong wish to kiss that mole.

"Uck," said Victoria. "Ish."

No, said Grandpa Bird. There's no reason to say uck or ish. I'm not talking about anything dirty. There's nothing wrong with wanting to kiss a mole that happens to reside on the back of a pretty girl's neck. After all, I'm not talking about the sort of mole that burrows in the earth. Nobody in his right mind would want to kiss *that* sort of mole.

Victoria giggled. She covered her mouth. (A mole

was like a rat or a mouse, wasn't it? Victoria could just see it clinging to the back of this Rhoda's neck. And she could just see Grandpa Bird kissing it. And she could just hear it wriggling and squeaking.)

Grandpa Bird smiled. Yes, it is a stupid thought, isn't it? he said.

Victoria nodded.

Victoria's mother fumbled in her purse for another cigarette.

Victoria's father linked his fingers and stared at them. Then he stretched his arms as far forward as they would reach. He turned his linked fingers inside out, cracking all his knuckles.

Victoria's mother jumped a little. *Carl,* she said, lighting a cigarette.

Still smiling, Grandpa Bird said to Victoria: Pay no attention to them. I'll finish this story if it takes all year.

Hallelujah, said Victoria's mother.

Grandpa Bird chuckled. Then, to Victoria: Even though Rhoda kept her hair short, it had a richness, a body. Oh, now there he goes, folks, the announcer, Morris Bird the Eye Eye, doing a commercial: *For hair with richness and body, look at Rhoda Masonbrink.* Well, I'm sorry, but I don't know any other way to put it. Rhoda was, you see, a girl of much richness. And body. I don't mean richness of purse. I mean, um, *generosity.* And I mean *lushness.* In those days, most girls kept themselves sort of bound and cinched, but not Rhoda. She believed that her blessings should be shared with the world at large, and so she did just that. Her mouth was immense, and she had good teeth. And her, well, her chest . . . her chest was—

Daddy, said Victoria's mother, shaking her cigarette in Grandpa Bird's direction.

Grandpa Bird nodded. Sorry, he said to Victoria's mother. Then, to Victoria: Well, take my word for it, Rhoda Masonbrink was some cookies. And all the boys at Paradise Falls High School were tormented by her, but in a sweet way, of course, a way that you'll come to understand in time. Her family was poor, and her dresses were always out of style, and sometimes they were a trifle too tight on her, a fact to which none of us made objection, believe me. She carried herself well at all times, and there was nothing in her voice or her manner to make you believe she was anything less than the daughter of landed nobility. Oh, not that she was *snooty*. The people with real class never are. It was just that she carried a serenity that said to all of us: It doesn't matter that I am a Masonbrink, does it? You love me anyway, and come to think of it, I love you. Oh, I know. The years perhaps have made her larger in my mind than she really was, and I suppose there's no perhaps about it; I suppose she is a legend, a dream, whatever. All right. I am willing to grant that, but there *are* certain *facts* about Rhoda that can't be ignored. The fact of her smile, for example. The fact of that mole, the fact of what was revealed when she wore dresses that were too tight on her. And she was secretary of the Class of '27. A *Masonbrink*, and she had been *freely elected*. It probably was the greatest thing that had happened to a Masonbrink since about the time of the invention of the wheel or maybe the discovery of fire. And it was not only *that* distinction she had. She was the president of the Odyssey Literary Society, and she could throw a baseball farther than any girl in the school, and she was the best dancer, and her grade average was right near ninety. Why, it was possible to be so taken with her that you actually forgot she was a Masonbrink, and her father, old Joe Masonbrink, was a bootlegger. Or at least *I* forgot it. The only thing is—my parents didn't. Rhoda and I started running around together when we were both juniors. I was what they called hot stuff in those days.

I was center on the basketball team, and I had a good baritone singing voice, and my people had money, and my father, who was the original Morris Bird, the Morris Bird the Eye, so to speak, edited a newspaper, and we even had a Packard. We—

"What's a Packard?" said Victoria.

Pardon? said Grandpa Bird.

"A Packard," said Victoria. "What's a Packard?"

It *was* an automobile, said Grandpa Bird.

"Oh," said Victoria.

A very fancy automobile, said Grandpa Bird. Only people who were *important* owned Packards. They were built as though they were intended to, um, supply protection from the end of the world. And they were expensive. You drove a Packard, you were the cat's whiskers and the cat's meow and maybe even the bee's knees.

"The bee's knees?" said Victoria.

That was an expression we used in those days, said Grandpa Bird.

Victoria smiled. "The bee's knees. I like it. I mean, I've never even thought much about a bee having knees. What would they be like?"

I don't know, said Grandpa Bird. Little spiky things, I imagine. Probably yellow and black.

I don't believe any of this, said Victoria's mother.

Grandpa Bird looked at Victoria's mother.

Victoria's mother twisted out her cigarette in the scorched and tortured frog's poor blistered throat.

Victoria's father rubbed the knuckles of his right hand with the palm of his left hand. He breathed with his mouth open, and his tongue rubbed his lower lip. He spoke to Victoria's mother. He said: Sandra, if we let it run its course, if we don't interrupt, then it'll be *over*. And if it does your father good, perhaps we can be generous enough to tolerate it.

Thank you very much, I'm sure, said Grandpa Bird to his soninlaw.

Sir? said Victoria's father.

Who the hell do you think you are?

Sir?

Tolerating me. My God, what is it that I'm doing? Pouring vinegar down my granddaughter's throat? Showing her a dirty movie?

I didn't mean—

I'm trying to explain to Victoria what I am. I'm trying to cite a little history. And I get sarcasm from my daughter and condescension from my soninlaw. What is it that's so terrible? I mean, is an ancient grief so terrible? All I want to do is get straight in Victoria's mind this matter of the *center point* in my life. If it's an illusion, it's an illusion. Myself, I keep switching from one side to the other, from saying center points are too easy and convenient to saying yes, yes, all right, until a certain night in June of 1927 I was one sort of person, and then I became another sort of person, and you see that person to this day. I want Victoria to choose her own side, to draw her own conclusions—that's all. You keep saying to me that she isolates herself, and you're worried about it. Well, I'm not so sure she does isolate herself. How can you isolate yourself in *this* world? I mean, everyplace you go, the walls are too thin, and you hear old folks pass gas and talk about old dance bands and Russ Columbo and Tex Beneke and I don't know who all. I'll grant you Victoria is very dainty and feminine and fond of gentle things, sentimental, whatever, but does that mean she has pushed herself away from reality?

"No," said Victoria.

Everyone looked at her.

Victoria's panties again were giving her discomfort. She wriggled. "I'm not . . . I'm not *crazy*," she said.

Oh, said her mother.

Hey, now, said her father.

Victoria's mouth made an *o*, but no sound emerged.

I wasn't saying you're crazy, said Grandpa Bird to Victoria. I think you're a little *different*, but you're certainly not *crazy*.

Victoria nodded. Her mouth continued to move, but it was unable to form any words.

Grandpa Bird smiled a little. From all this fuss, he said to Victoria, you'd think I was about to confess to a murder. Well, no such melodramatic luck.

Victoria moistened her lips and tried to form at least one or two words.

It's *all right*, said Grandpa Bird.

Victoria coughed.

It's only a story, said Grandpa Bird to Victoria. A story from the Long Ago and the Far Away. Don't let it upset you. It's not supposed to upset you; it's only supposed to be a part of your education, and you can accept it or throw it out the window, whichever you choose. Please . . . don't be frightened, all right?

Victoria tried to nod.

You're not crazy, said Grandpa Bird, and we don't want you to be afraid, either.

Victoria managed to nod.

That's better, said Grandpa Bird.

Again Victoria nodded.

That's very good, said Grandpa Bird.

Victoria's mouth moved. "I'm . . . I'm okay," she said.

Fine, said Grandpa Bird. Now let's get back to my story, my *center point* story, all right?

"All . . . right," said Victoria.

Rhoda Masonbrink, said Grandpa Bird to Victoria. Rhoda Masonbrink and Yours Truly. My sweetheart of golden antiquity, all right? The bee's knees, all right? Well, in my own way, I was the bee's knees, too. Which made us quite a couple—at least in our own eyes. But one of these days you'll learn a word, and the word is *caste*, and it exists wherever people

exist, and it has to do with your rich people versus
your poor people, your fancy people versus your
plain people, your people of position versus your
people of no position. And it's a very important word
to a lot of grownups. It was certainly a very important
word to my parents, and one evening they sort of
trotted me into the front room, and they sat me down
on the sofa, and my father—who was a man of the
world, at least in his own estimation—poured me a
glass of Harvey's Bristol Cream sherry (the real stuff,
smuggled in from Canada), and I drank that Harvey's
Bristol Cream sherry, and I remember that it tasted
a little like warm prune juice, and my father said
to me: Look, Son, I don't blame you a bit. That
Masonbrink girl is prettier than sunshine on a mountain lake, and a young fellow such as yourself
would have to be out of his mind not to be attracted to her. And my mother said: Oh, Morris,
we are not so old that we don't know what hot
blood is. And my father said: Don't think we're trying to stand in your way. And then it was *my* turn
to speak up, and so I rolled some of the sherry around
on my tongue, and then I swallowed the sherry,
and I said: If you're not trying to stand in my way,
then why are you talking to me? How come you've
brought me into the front room? How come I'm
drinking this Harvey's Bristol Cream? And my father
said: Because we don't want too much seriousness to
enter into all this. And I said: Seriousness? And my
father said: Sunshine on a mountain lake is pretty.
Maybe it's even beautiful. But it goes away. The light
changes. It's not *permanent*. And I said: What's *that*
supposed to mean? And my father said: Your Rhoda
Masonbrink. Do whatever you like with her. Be
happy, laugh, dance, sing songs, kiss, ride merrygo-
rounds, pull taffy. Only always remember that it's
not *permanent*. And I said: But why couldn't it be?
And my father said: Because that's not the way of

the world. Because certain *standards* are maintained, certain *levels*, whatever you want to call them, and the son of Morris Bird the newspaper publisher and editor cannot seriously plan to spend the rest of his life with the daughter of Joe Masonbrink the bootlegger. I'm not being cruel, Son. Believe me, I'm not. I'm only acknowledging the way the world functions. The *world*, Son. *People.*

"What world?" said Victoria.

The world they knew, said Grandpa Bird. The world most people still know. I expect even you'll come to know it. In time.

"I don't know if I want to," said Victoria.

Clearing her throat, Victoria's mother snubbed out her cigarette in the frog's throat. She'd probably burned out its tonsils by now. Its tonsils and its voicebox, its croaker, its *ribbit* apparatus.

Victoria's father sucked at his lips.

Grandpa Bird spoke to Victoria. He said: But what did I know in those days? Maybe I *was* the bee's knees. Maybe I *did* play a mean game of basketball and sing a mean baritone and pass through my schooldays with half the girls in love with me. But none of that meant I *knew* anything. And so I, well, not to make too fine a point of it, I accepted what my father and my mother had to say. And my attitude toward Rhoda underwent a change. Oh, it was gradual, but it *was* a *change*. You see, up to that point my notions were more or less gentle, reserved. But then they . . . changed. An adjustment took place.

Careful now, said Victoria's father to Grandpa Bird.

Remember her age, said Victoria's father to Grandpa Bird.

Victoria looked at her parents.

I am being *very* careful, said Grandpa Bird to Victoria's parents. Then, to Victoria: I can't say too much, but I can say that I, well, I became more demanding than I had been. And Rhoda didn't take too kindly to the, um, adjustment.

"Adjustment?" said Victoria. "Like when the TV's out of focus?" She glanced at her father. "Isn't that the word you use?"

Victoria's father nodded.

Grandpa Bird also nodded. Yes, he said to Victoria, it was like I wanted the focus to be changed. But Rhoda didn't want the focus to be changed. And she finally wanted to know what sort of girl did I think she was. We had been down street one evening, which was a way the people in Paradise Falls had of saying we had gone into the center of town, along Main Street, past the Ritz Theater and Steinfelder's and Pop Korn's Popcorn Palace, and I'd bought her an ice cream cone, and we'd crossed the river, on account of it was a warm night, you see, and we'd sat on a bench that was in a grove of I think they were tulip trees, and no one could see us in there, and one thing led to another, you see, and we were washed by the quick sound of tree frogs and the white sound of the river, and I remembered what my mother had said about my blood being hot; I was full of *juices* and *arrogance* and I can't really recollect *what* all, and my palms were all sticky, maybe from ice cream, maybe from nervousness, maybe from that forever new thing boys must endure before they feel. themselves to be men, but at any rate I—

Careful, said Victoria's mother to Grandpa Bird.

All right, said Grandpa Bird to his daughter. Fine, Sandra. *Fine.*

Victoria's mother looked away.

I, um, I lost out, said Grandpa Bird to Victoria.

"Lost out at what?" said Victoria.

Something important, said Grandpa Bird. Something you'll learn about soon enough.

"But *what?*" said Victoria. "You mean *kissing* and like *that?*"

Kissing is part of it, said Grandpa Bird.

"Like on TV?" said Victoria.

Like on TV, only better, said Grandpa Bird.

Careful, said Victoria's mother to Grandpa Bird.

Grandpa Bird nodded. Don't *worry,* he said to Victoria's mother. Then, again to Victoria: There was something I wanted to *do* with Rhoda, but she wouldn't let me, and so I lost out. She told me I was trying to take advantage of her. She said to me: Morris, just because I'm a Masonbrink, that doesn't mean I'm something that can be picked off a back shelf at Woolworth's for three cents. I'm a Masonbrink like none of the other Masonbrinks, and you *know* it. Or if you don't, you should. And then she sort of, um, gathered herself together, and she got up from that bench, and she marched out of the park, and I followed along like a little puppydog, and I tried to *plead,* you know? I just wrung my hands, you know? And a lot of good any of it did. When Rhoda was angry, she walked as though the heels of her shoes were biting the sidewalk or the earth or whatever, biting or maybe gouging or maybe both, and she would not look at me, and her lips were pressed so tightly together that her upper lip actually curled over her lower lip, and she didn't say a word to me, all the way from the Elysian Park to the little house where she lived with her dad, old Joe, and her mother and her three sisters and her four brothers. Yours Truly felt as though he wanted to go somewhere and boil his head and put himself out of his misery. But he did not do that. Instead he said to himself: Well, she'll get over it, and then she'll do what I want. But she didn't get over it, not at first, and she never did do what Yours Truly wanted her to do, even though the two of them were at the end reunited. And I do mean at the end. But that's getting ahead of my story. Suffice it to say that Rhoda Masonbrink, that beautiful heiress to the Masonbrink millions and the

glorious Masonbrink name, decided she no longer
wanted to be seen with Yours Truly. We were to
have attended the senior dance, or prom, together,
but she told me she would sooner have attended the
senior prom in the company of a baboon, and not a
particularly bright baboon, at that. She further told
me she *would* attend the prom with the most ridiculous person she could find. That way, she said, I
would be publicly humiliated. And, well, *I* told *her*
fine, *two* could play at *that* game, and *I* also would
find a ridiculous person. We both were successful.
Her escort the night of the prom was a pasty little
fellow named Charley Light, who later became an
undertaker and came to a bad end back in the summer of 1950. But that's another story. She knew that a
prom date with that poor foolish Charley Light would
affect me like, um, hot railroad spikes in my throat.
Which it did. If she'd tossed me aside for *John Gilbert*, fine, since John Gilbert was a famous movie
star of the time and much admired by the feminine
segment of the population. I could understand *that*.
But that slippery little *Charley Light* . . . oh, I was
sorely irritated, and I won't lie to you and say I was
anything else. So I retaliated the only way I could
retaliate. I found a girl whom I saw as being the
female equivalent of Charley Light. She was a skinny
and nervous girl who sort of *shook* and *clicked,* and
she had had a crush on *me* every bit as long a
time as Charley Light had mooned over Rhoda.
She was the sort to send a Valentine, sign it *Guess
Who?*, and write a return address on the envelope.
She was a silent little thing, and a lot of people
actually went so far as to say she was *cranky*, and
they had a point—as I was to learn in the fullness of
time. This girl, of course, was your Grandma Bird,
Alice Anna Jones, as she was known then. I called
her silent, didn't I? Well, she wasn't all *that* silent,
come to think of it, and especially when she was

aggravated, or when people did not live up to what she saw as decent behavior. Oh, to be with her was about as enjoyable as cutting your tongue on a loose fingernail, which meant, of course, she was a perfect girl for me to ask to the senior prom. She was a year older than I (she'd had pneumonia in 1916, and it had kept her out of school for a year), which made her the oldest member of the Class of '27, but this was a piece of statistical information one did not bring up in her presence. I know, speaking for myself, I always was careful what I said in her dear sweet *presence*. Such a presence. Sometimes listening to her was like having my thumbs pounded by a ballpeen hammer. Well, anyway, she was a perfect candidate to be my prom date, and she wasted no time with coyness when I decided to invite her. This dramatic scene took place in a hallway at Paradise Falls High School, and she seized me by a wrist and said: This is no joke? And I said: Of course it's no joke. And she said: You'll be proud of me. I don't care whether you're mad at Rhoda Masonbrink or *what* you are. I promise you you'll be proud of me. And then she squeezed the wrist, and I just about jumped out of my bones. A great big *athlete* such as myself, and I wanted to yelp like a dog with its tail caught in a bicycle wheel. But I managed to restrain myself, and she must have admired my tolerance of pain, since she then decided not to crush my wrist in her steely grip. Instead she released my wrist, and then she almost *caressed* it, laying a dry opened palm on it, and she said to me: Morris, whatever I can ever do for you, whatever favor or *what*ever, I want to be allowed to do it. And *then*, while I was mulling over all those whatevers, she turned and ran away from me. I think I was a little touched by what she said. At any rate, I stood there, shifting my weight from one foot to the other, feeling a trifle ratty, if the truth be known, and the thought crossed my mind that maybe I hadn't done the right thing, that it was not proper to *use* someone the way I was planning to use your Grandma Bird. But the die had been cast, so to speak, and an adolescent melodrama was under way. So the big night arrived. I remember the day and the date. It was Saturday, June 4, 1927. This is not a particularly remarkable thing, remembering the day and the date. Adults have a way of remembering exact days and dates when something important happens to them. Especially if it represents a center point in their lives. Lindbergh was still over in France after making his historic flight, one that I'm sure you'll read about in school one of these days. He'd gone to London to visit the King and Queen of England, and I remember all the whoop and commotion there was in the papers. Anyhow, it was an exciting year to be alive, and I think the nation had dreams. I know *I* had dreams . . . to be perhaps a great athlete or perhaps a great baritone, it didn't really matter. The future was all sunshine and daffodils, and I just about thought I was followed around by photographers, and the world was enormous, and I would defeat it. But first it was important that I defeat Rhoda Masonbrink, show her that what was good for the goose was also good for the gander. It was a glorious night, and I brought a corsage of orchids to my skinny little friend, Alice Anna Jones. I was hoping to show Rhoda Masonbrink I didn't care about either her or the silly prom, and Alice obviously was hoping to bewitch Yours Truly with her charm and her beauty. Oh, the poor, poor thing. I mean, all right, so perhaps I sound condescending, but Alice's good points did *not* include a talent for bewitching. She was presentable enough that night, and she even perhaps exhibited a certain skinny pallid prettiness, and her mother had put together a fine summer formal dress with lace and the rest of it, making Alice almost seem to be moving in a great rustling cloud of who knows what, and then—after I carefully and somewhat apprehensively had pinned the corsage to Alice's bodice —Alice's coloring (what there was of it) was brought out by the brilliance of the corsage. But in no way would she have been mistaken for a great beauty, and —in my view—compared with Rhoda Masonbrink she had all the charm of, um, a boy of twelve. Still, I had gone too far in my game to turn away, and so I told Alice she looked very pretty indeed, and I believe I even said something to the effect that if she didn't watch herself, people would go around comparing her with the bee's knees. She smiled, but she said nothing. She appeared to be holding her breath. You know the look people sometimes display on their faces when they are just about biting their tongues because they want something important and valuable to happen to them? Quiz show contestants, lottery finalists, beauty pageant candidates, people of that type? Well, that's how Alice Jones looked that night. It was as though she were holding a slippery and exceedingly precious balloon made of delicate glass that barely was visible to the naked eye. It was as though she were telling herself: Any abrupt movement, Alice old girl, and you'll drop the silly thing and probably ruin your life forever. Well, I suppose it was funny, and believe me, I did want to laugh, but I don't know, something, perhaps an intensity . . . *something* kept my face straight, and I solemnly escorted her to the car, which was of course the Packard. I opened the car door for her and helped her inside, then carefully closed the door, making sure it did not catch her skirt. Then I went around the car and climbed in beside her. I mention this only as a matter of historical interest. Still, surely your generation, and the generations yet unborn, will find it at least moderately quaint that there once lived a race of men and women who observed what were known as *amenities*. Among these amenities was the practice known as The Young Man Helping The Young Woman Into The Car And Even Making Sure Her Skirt Is Not Caught. These customs, these amenities, have gone the way of the dodo, the auk, the condor, the passenger pigeon and the nickel candy bar, but I nonetheless do feel they should not be forgotten by history. And oh, by the way, isn't it strange that we not only have buried amenities, but we ridicule them? If we are so liberated, why are we so afraid of the past? That's one of the things I like about you, Victoria. I think you have a feeling for amenities. It can only come to you from books, but it's very real to you, isn't it? Oh, this is not to denigrate your parents, and I'm sure your mother has taught you a great deal, and your father has given you more than adequate spiritual guidance, but in the final judgment *you* are the one who has the feeling; *you* are the one who has chosen to be a little lady of standards and grace. I salute you. I really do. You are indeed a love. But I do digress. Please forgive me, but I am an old man. And, hah, perhaps *you'll* be an old *woman* by the time I finish, eh? Well, I hope not. I suppose I have had too much of a past, and every time I summon it, I seem to find more threads, scraps, pieces of broken crockery, fragments of metal, patches of yarn. Stories breed stories, and I tend to forget which is the original story, and I cannot make up my mind which story is important. But then perhaps none is important. Or perhaps all are important. But then what becomes of my theory of the center point? You see, that's why I keep going back to defining a life in terms of breath and days and smiles and loss. And it's why I have my doubts about analyzing. But analysis interests me. Rummaging interests me. Scuffling through odd moments as though they were old rags, costume jewelry. So my story continues. If I stray, if I hallucinate, if my memory wanders all around Robin Hood's fabled barn, well,

so be it. No one is perfect. And anyway, longwinded-
ness is not such a terrible thing. So be it. Now, then,
as for the night of Saturday, June 4, 1927, when the
world was spelled Lindbergh and dreams still were
a commodity available on the open market for all
those of good will, I drove Alice to the dance, which
was held in the Paradise Falls High School gymnasium. And I remember, as I escorted her in, and as
we looked at the ribbons and the banners, and as a
sort of gentle racketing bleat and puff of music
curled around us, with all the boys stiff and splendid
in their dinner jackets, with all the girls more perky
and provocative and downright *beautiful* than they
had a right to be, it occurred to me that my troubles
with Rhoda Masonbrink probably didn't amount to
very much; it occurred to me that this night would be
irreplaceable, that it was enormous, that I and every
other member of the Paradise Falls High School Class
of 1927 were taking part in a gentle rite of passage
that we would never forget. In the face of all *that*,
what did it really matter that Rhoda and I were
feuding? what did it really matter that we were using
other people? what did it really matter that we were
being cruel? Well, of course it *did* really matter, and
I suppose I knew that, but I didn't *want* to know it.
Not *then*. If there was some sort of bill to be paid,
I was willing to settle it later, but not *then*. I mean,
I am not a religious man the way your father is a
religious man, Victoria, but I do know that the Lord
maintains a great and, um, infallible Ledger, and He
frowns on those who do not keep their individual
Ledgers in balance. I know that now, and I knew it
then, but I figured oh what the heck, one night of
fun wasn't too much to ask before I began paying the
piper. But I was wrong, and later that night I had it
eloquently demonstrated to me just how wrong I
was. And I am reminded of that demonstration every
day. All I have to do is look down and study the

place where my left foot should be. Or all I have to
do is remember Rhoda Masonbrink . . . her laughter
. . . that mole on her neck . . . and oh, yes, I know
we *deserved* to be punished, and I know it was not
right, what we did to Alice Jones and that Charley
Light, but did the punishment have to be that severe?
Is it possible the Lord made a mistake? Oh, well,
there's no sense speculating on all that. I'll know soon
enough, I expect. What I'm really trying to describe
here is a particular moment. It took place at perhaps
nine o'clock in the evening of the aforementioned
Saturday, June 4, 1927, when Alice Anna Jones and
her escort, the dashing Morris Bird the Eye Eye, came
walking into that gym, that place of streamers and
music and laughter and beauty and the discreet sipping
of punch. Talk about your bee's knees. That night we
all were the bee's knees. Even Alice, and perhaps
even Charley Light. At any rate, Alice was given a
dance program, and I dutifully signed up for about
half a dozen dances, including, of course, the last
one, and I remember she told me she hoped she
would not embarrass me. And I told her aw, shucks,
little lady, I'm just a smalltown boy and all I gots is
two left feet. (*Very* funny, right? Especially since
I came out of the evening with no left foot at all,
let alone *two*.) And then we danced, Alice and I;
we actually for the first time in our lives *touched*.
That first dance with her wasn't really very much.
It was an easy foxtrot, and all she really had to do
was follow me and the beat of the music and, um,
close her eyes and *relax* . . . but Alice never understood how to relax, and so our first dance had a
hesitant and, ah, *tiptoeing* quality that was enough to
make a person think we were moving around the floor
with our pockets full of hand grenades, all of them
with loose pins. And I said to her: We're not going
to break. And Alice said: Don't be too sure of that.
And I grinned. And I was aware that just about

everyone was staring at us. But Rhoda was nowhere to be seen. I supposed she would make a grand entrance with her ratty beau of a Charley Light, and I was correct. Alice and I were into our sceond dance (another easy foxtrot) when Rhoda and Charley, as they say these days, *made* the *scene*. She was in red, and my God, *such* a red. Think of cardinals. Think of the devil. Then maybe you have an idea of the sort of red it was. She was wearing a corsage of white flowers. I don't know what they were, but apparently she'd consulted beforehand with Charley Light, since those white flowers set off that incredible red in a way that I can only describe as, um, *incredible*. And she *blossomed* in that dress. I can think of no other word. Dear me, I am too old to be remembering this so vividly. But I *do*, and it's all just about enough to give me palpitations and sweats. But you're not interested in my present physical condition, are you? You want to know what happened the night of June 4, 1927, don't you? And you want this story to end before you drop dead of hardening of the arteries and aggravated senility, correct? So I shall press on, and please forgive me for all my ridiculous digressions. Your grandfather is a flawed human being, Victoria, and that is the absolute truth. Well, ah, to make a long story long, both Alice and I sort of *stumbled* when Rhoda and Charley came into the gym, and the first thing I said to myself was: What's the matter with me? Why did I let myself become so influenced by my parents—and by what? animal stupidity?—that I antagonized the most beautiful girl on this planet? And I think I exhaled rather loudly. At any rate, I must have done *something*, since Alice abruptly pulled me closer to her, or *tugged* me closer to her, and she pressed her lips tightly shut and breathed through her nose, if you know what I mean. But it was too late, and Alice knew that as well as I did. There was no way in the world she could shield me from a *manifestation*. She could have *chained* me to her, and it wouldn't have made a pin's worth of difference. All that mattered to me was that somehow I take Rhoda aside and explain and apologize and do whatever else was necessary to reclaim her. And it didn't matter about Alice; it didn't matter about Charley Light; it wouldn't have mattered about a soul, even President Coolidge, even Lucky Lindy Lindbergh. I don't really know how I did escape Alice, and I have no idea how Rhoda got away from Charley Light, but somehow Rhoda and I were dancing, and I held her carefully, and I tried not to touch her flesh, and various words and fragments of words rolled on my tongue, and finally I was able to tell her she looked finer than fine in her red dress; I was able to tell her she was in fact the bee's knees for fair and for certain. And she smiled a little and said: You're just telling me all that because you *want* something. And I said: All I want is to tell you I'm sorry about what's happened. And Rhoda said: I suppose I'm expected to believe that. And I said: That surely would be nice. And she said: Is there any proof you can give me? And I said: No. And my voice was flat. And I said: I'd like to give you a guarantee, like maybe on the parts to a bicycle or an electric fan, but I can't do that. Nobody can. (By this time, Rhoda and I were standing at the punchbowl, and Alice was standing a few feet away, and if looks could kill . . .) And I said to Rhoda: I've missed you. That's the whole truth. Honest. And Rhoda said: Now I suppose *you* want the whole truth from *me*. And I said: I wouldn't mind. And Rhoda said: Well, if it gives you any pleasure, Mister Bird, I expect I've missed *you* too. I don't know what it is about you. It surely isn't your *manners* or your sweet way of *talking*, but it does sit inside me like a hatching hen, and I can't seem to find a place to hide from it. And so then I said to Rhoda: Does that, um, does that mean we can maybe get together again? And Rhoda said: Maybe. And I said: Starting now? And Rhoda said: That wouldn't be fair to my Charley, and it wouldn't be fair to your Alice. And I said: Don't call her *my* Alice. She's not *my* Alice. She's not *anybody's* Alice. She's too busy grinding her teeth. And Rhoda said: *Grinding* her *teeth?* And I said: Something like that. Every time I dance with her, she's so tense it's a wonder she doesn't bite her jaw in half. And Rhoda said: Well, you picked her. And I said: And you know why I picked her. For the same reason you picked Charley over there. I mean, *we* picked *them* because we wanted to get *at* each other. Which means we're dumb, doesn't it? And Rhoda said: You won't get an argument from *me* on *that*. And Rhoda took one of my hands. She squeezed it. I wish we could get away from here, she said, and I wouldn't even care if you got fresh. But we can't. We got to be decent. We got to think of *them*. And I said: Oh? And Rhoda said: *Yes*. And then she let go my hand and turned away from me. She started across the floor toward Charley, who was standing with his hands in his pockets. He looked like an undertaker waiting to arrange flowers and folding chairs. This was very appropriate, since he in fact eventually turned out to *be* an undertaker. I helped myself to some of the punch, and I drifted back to my tense and coiled Alice Anna Jones, taking her a cup of the stuff—which was pink, as I recall, with little soggy slices of what I believe were mandarin oranges. The slices floated. She drank the awful stuff in about three gulps, and she actually told me it tasted good. Then she asked me whether I'd had a nice dance with my old flame. And she said: Rhoda certainly is dressed for the part, isn't she? Flaming red for an old flame. And I said: It was only one dance. We're trying to be, um, civilized. And Alice said: What do you know about being civilized? You're eighteen years old. And I said: And you're nineteen, which gives you a whole lot of wisdom, right? On account of you had to stay out of school for a year because you had the pip or the croup or whatever, right? And Alice said: It was *pneumonia*, and I almost *died*. And I said: *Almost* only counts in horseshoes and field mortars. And Alice said: You're trying to get my goat so I'll walk away and then you can go running to Little Miss Red Dress with her *chest*. And I said: You're my date. And Alice said: And you asked me because you wanted to annoy her. If you take poor plain Alice Jones to the prom, poor plain Alice Jones who is so washed out she looks like a pile of bleached underwear in the hot sun, then you really show Rhoda what you think of her, correct? And I said: That's not true. And Alice said: *Stop lying*. And I said: *Don't call me a liar*. And Alice said: *Then tell the truth*. And I said: *We can go around forever with this sort of talk*. And Alice said: *I don't care*. And at that point I'm afraid I turned away from Alice. My face was warm. It was altogether *too* warm. She knew more about me than I wanted her to know. It was one thing that she had a crush on me. Despite the ravaged appearance of what you see before you here today, at one time this poor old bag of wrinkles was attractive to girls, and quite a few had crushes on him. I was used to them, and I believed I knew how to handle them. But how could I handle a crush that also obviously included the most ferociously close *study* of me? And so my footsteps were loose, and I just about shambled. It all sort of put me in mind of the germ theory of disease. In order to prove the germ theory, scientists have to examine the most sickening little things under microscopes. Well, fine and dandy, but what right did *Alice* have to examine *me* that way? Could that by some insane perversion of logic be called *love*? If I wanted Alice Anna Jones to disassemble me and pick apart my motives, by

God I would *ask* her. In the meantime, I would prefer that she minded her own beeswax, as they used to say. Now then, you might think I was reacting too strenuously. Well, I'm sorry, but guilt does have that sort of effect. So this time I deliberately sought out Rhoda . . . Rhoda and her eyes that tore away whatever they wanted to tear away, Rhoda and her red dress, Rhoda and her *chest* . . . I said to her: I don't think it matters about them. And Rhoda, who been dancing with a fellow named Herb Sheppard, said to me: You mean Alice and Charley? And I said: Rhoda, I love you. You are the most beautiful girl in the world. And Rhoda said: Shovel me another ton, Mister Man, and I'll have the best garden in the county. And I said: *Don't make fun*. And Rhoda said: And don't *you* make a big *fib*. All that's talking now is your . . . your *human desire*. And I said: May God strike me dead if I am making a big fib. May a bolt of lightning tear away the roof of this place. And I held her tightly, and she told me she was having trouble breathing, and I told her I didn't really care; it was more important that she know I was speaking the truth. And she said: But what good will that information be if I'm dead? And then Rhoda laughed: Don't you see they'd be angry with us forever if we . . . if we had a *grand reunion* right here in the middle of the dance floor? And I relaxed my grip on her, and I said: These things happen. And Rhoda said: But they don't *have* to. We can wait until *tomorrow*. I have *my* date, and you have *yours*. And we have how many more years to live? a million? And I said: But we could die by tomorrow. And Rhoda said: Don't be *morbid*. I don't *like* boys who are morbid. They go around looking like they want to wash their hands in formaldehyde. Take Charley Light. Do you know what he said to me tonight? He told me it was his humble opinion too many people were too afraid of death. He said death was as much a part of life as birth. Now, I ask you—what sort of way to talk is *that?* And I said: Well then, if he's so crazy, why should you worry about sneaking out of here with me? And Rhoda said: *Because* it's sneaking. Because it isn't right. And then I said: All right. Let's not sneak. Let's just walk out, big as life and twice as sassy. And I took both of Rhoda's hands in both of mine, and we broke away from the music, and I pulled her toward a side door, and I said to her: Smile. If anybody gives us a dirty look, just smile and smile. It doesn't matter if your lips fall off, just keep *smiling.* And then I released her hands, and I took one of her arms and squeezed it, and we could have been a bride and groom marching back down the aisle from the altar, with the organ playing, and our mothers weeping, and all the rest of it. We nodded at I don't know how many of our classmates, and I have no recollection of where Alice was, and I have no recollection of where Charley Light was, but they could have been cardboard dummies for all *I* cared. Because, you see, *they did not exist.* They were not even as real as your dolls and your animals, Victoria. So Rhoda and I smiled our way out of that place. I knew she was reluctant, but she did not try to pull away from me; she matched me step for step, and she nodded, and she kept her teeth exposed. So Rhoda and I were reunited, and never mind the embarrassing fact of my *human desire.* We walked along a gravel path that led away from the gymnasium, and no doubt we had left behind us consternation, broken hearts and who knows what all else, but we *smiled;* we *embraced;* we murmured fragments of words, and then I managed to say to her: In the long run, it won't matter. It isn't as though you'd promised to *marry* him. He's only your *prom date.* And Rhoda said: I don't want to talk about him. And I don't want to talk about Alice, either. We've gone and done it, and I don't see what good a lot of talk would

be. I mean, I don't want to think of whatever they're
doing back there, or however they're feeling. And I
said: Yes. All right. I can understand that. And Rhoda
said: I love you, Morris. And I hesitated. I looked at
Rhoda. We never had used the word before. Either
of us. She began to speak quickly, and she stood right
there on that gravel path, and her arm was curved inside mine, and she was sort of hunched forward, and
the words came in such a rapid flow that I had to
listen carefully in order to make out what they all
were, and she said: It doesn't *matter* what you think
of me, and if I'm something that comes off the back
shelf at Woolworth's, if that's the way it is, then
that's the way it *is*, but I *love* you, Morris, me, a
Masonbrink, and I've surely got my nerve, right?
Loving *you*, I mean. I'm Joe Masonbrink's daughter,
and Joe Masonbrink is a *bootlegger*, which means he's
a *criminal*, and it's like something out of a movie,
isn't it? The poor girl of bad family loving the rich
boy of good family, right? And so you take me for
a walk, and we go to the Elysian Park, and one thing
leads to another, doesn't it? The *human desire* thing
rears its ugly head, right? And oh, am I the proud
one . . . I tell you to unhand me, you villain, just
what sort of girl do you think I am? And maybe, if
it were a movie, I'd roll my eyes. But I . . . I don't
care about any of that anymore. It's all . . . it's all
bushwah, isn't it? Do you know what I do at night
before I go to sleep? I curl myself into a ball. I hug
my knees. And then I squeeze my eyes as tightly
shut as they'll go, and I see you, and you're smiling
at me, and we're in the Elysian Park, and I'm saying
to you . . . the biggest word is, um, *yes*. And there's
a rush of leaves, a feeling of sweet breath, warm hands,
all of it, um, *candified* and, um, *beautiful*. Let's *do*
whatever it is you want to *do*. Let's *go* wherever it
is you want to *go*. I give up, Morris. I love you,
Morris. And here my glorious Rhoda embraced me,

and we kissed, and then we began to run, and we laughed, and she bobbed along beside me, and various portions of her anatomy moved in various directions, and no tightness remained in her, and we stumbled off that gravel path and across a field to the place where the Packard was parked, and we piled into the Packard, and we were wheezing and giggling, and we sprawled across the front seat, and we kissed, and then we were aware of voices, and we sat up straight, and Rhoda made a sort of squealing noise, and it turned out Herb Sheppard was in the back seat, and his girl was with him. Herb and I had been basketball teammates. His girl's name was Lois Newman, and she said to us: The upholstery is so *comfortable*. And Herb said: Thank God you never lock this thing. Both Lois and Herb were sitting up in the back seat, but they were, um, *brushing* at themselves, and it was apparent, Victoria, that they had been . . . ah, let's just say that they had been exercising their capacity for *human desire*. And Lois said to me: Morris, my goodness, unless my eyes deceive me, isn't that the famous Rhoda Masonbrink with you? And, laughing, Rhoda said: No, my name is Norma Talmadge, and I'm *slumming*. And Herb said: With *him*, you'd *have* to be. And then it was my turn to speak, and I said: As the driver of this here Packard, which as we all know is the finest automobile an ambitious young fellow's father can buy in order that certain fancies and pursuits be indulged, I must protest the rude way you people are addressing myself and my ladylove here. And, cooing, Lois said to Rhoda: Well, dear me, *Alice*, haven't we changed? And Rhoda said to Lois: The day my name is Alice will be the day your name is Dead. Or Mud. And Lois said: Oh, my goodness dear me suz, it *is* Rhoda Masonbrink, isn't it? And then we all got to laughing, and I reached back and smote Herb across a knee, and Rhoda allowed as how she and I were being just *terrible* as far as Alice and

Charley were concerned, but we just couldn't wait another *minute* to be with each other, and if that was selfishness, well then, all we could do was plead guilty. And Herb said something to the effect that oh, what the heck, everybody had known Rhoda and I would get back together sooner or later. And Lois said she figured Alice and Charley would get over it. People usually did. You waited long enough, and damage was forgotten, or you laughed about it, or the damaged thing fell down in a heap. Herb and Lois and Rhoda and I giggled and joked for a few more minutes, and then someone—I believe it was Lois—suggested it might be a good idea if we went for a little ride. And Rhoda said: Maybe it ought to be a *long* ride—so we won't have to come back. And I said: Don't you *want* to come back? And Rhoda said: Not really. I don't think I'd be able to look at Alice or Charley. I mean, could *you?* And quickly I said: No, I guess not. And Lois said: Well, *I* want to come back. A little ride would be real nice, but I've got some really spiffy fellows signed up in my program, and I don't want to miss out on them. And Herb laughed, saying: Spiffy fellows? Since when did spiffy fellows have such poor eyesight? And then Lois began whacking Herb about the head and shoulders with her dance program, and there was a great deal of scrambling and gasping and snickering. But order finally was restored, at which time Herb asked me if he could drive, and I told him I would be delighted. If Herb drove, it meant Rhoda and I would take possession of that pleasant domain known as the back seat, and we could, um, well, attend to matters having to do with hugging and kissing and sweet words and *human desire.* So Rhoda and I surrendered the front seat to Lois and Herb. We climbed into the back, and we settled into a sort of snuggled position, and I seem to recall that her face was pressed against my shoulder. Herb had never driven this car, but he assured me oh, well, after all, a car was only a car, and they all more or less were alike, correct? And anyway, he would be driving for only half an hour or so, since Lois was so bound and determined to return to the prom and her regiment of spiffy fellows. I grinned and handed the keys forward to him . . . and here began for me a brief time—less than an hour, actually—that was clearly the center point of the center point. Herb was a trifle unsure with the gears, and he hit the brakes too hard several times, but by and large he did well with the Packard, considering it was his first time at the wheel. We headed northwest out of Paradise Falls on the road to Lancaster, and I murmured placid endearments into Rhoda's ear, and gradually she settled back until her face again was resting against my shoulder. It was a splendorous night. An immense hand had scattered stars and clouds across the horizon, and the Paradise County hills rubbed and nudged the stars and the clouds. The Packard's tires hushed and thudded over the road's uneven brick pavement, and I lightly kissed Rhoda's hair, and Herb and Lois were whispering and giggling up in the front seat, and I'll tell you something, Victoria: For that fraction of an hour or however long it was, I had a grasp of a reality I never had known before and never would know again. Farmhouses, barns, cornfields, orchards, pastures . . . all of them *comfortable* and *stolid* and *orderly* . . . prim, sequential, logical, straight, swept, blanketed, applebuttered, Scriptured, haymowed, chickencooped, stabled, corncribbed. Oh, how they spread themselves *so* easily outside the windows of that fine brave hurtling Packard, and I had warm thoughts of a structured life with my magnificent Rhoda, of taking over the paper from my father, of rearing fine strapping children who would have good minds and the wisdom to savor quiet pleasures. Oh, there are *times*, Victoria. Or at least for your old granddad here there was *one* time. Less than an hour, actually. The placid endearments rolled from my lips like, um, apple butter, and Rhoda wriggled herself closer to me, and she said she wanted to creep inside my skin with me, which is a wish common to most lovers, I expect. But then neither of us was seeking originality that evening; neither of us was seeking to make any points in rhetoric. All we sought was to taste the evening, to renew our love, and on my part, to erase the flavor of Harvey's Bristol Cream and the words my parents had spoken. So then please, Victoria, please, please try to understand that neither Rhoda nor I was vicious, or vile, or anything other than young, and impetuous, and a bit fast and loose with the feelings of others. Please see us only as careless, not cruel. I bet you think this story will never end, don't you? I bet you see me as being some sort of mechanical talking contraption that somehow hasn't yet had the good taste and sense to wear itself out. Well, I'm sorry if you feel that way, but I am spreading the essence of a life in front of you, a shabby life, to be sure, but nonetheless a *life*, and it happens to be *my* life, and if *I* don't have a right to dwell on it at some length, then just who does? So bear with me. The story is nearly completed. It was on a curve near a village called Egypt that Herb somehow lost control of the Packard. The pavement was perfectly dry, and the car had an excellent steering mechanism (for its time), but somehow we went straight ahead when the road curved to the right. Our speed was estimated at perhaps fortyfive miles an hour. We went hurtling down a shallow embankment, and I remember that we all hollered. Somehow Rhoda bounced into the front seat with Herb and Lois, and then somehow Herb and Lois bounced into the back seat. I bounced into the front seat, and I recall looking though my legs at the sky and the stars and the dark nudging hills, and I bleated, and Rhoda was slammed into

me, and Herb came flying atop me from the back
seat, and Lois screamed, and then the sky and the
stars and the dark nudging hills were directly *below*
me. And then the car seemed to explode itself against
an old blighted chestnut tree. It somehow burst from
within, like a plum. I remember the sounds our voices
made, a sort of great final falsetto *sigh,* coming in the
exact same crazy unison one hears from all the whooping people desperately hanging on aboard a really
good rollercoaster, but the sound of the *car* was
simply a great *pop!* It was quite a sound. Oh, there
was a sound of the tree being splintered and actually
uprooted, and there was a sound of metal and glass,
but it was the *pop!* that I remember the most vividly.
Rhoda and Herb and Lois were killed immediately.
I'll not go into the details. I don't want to make you
sick, and I know your mother and father wouldn't approve, and I can't say as I blame them. As for myself,
let's just say my foot went through the windshield,
and the doctors couldn't save it. My foot, I mean. Not
the, ah, windshield. And that is the exact story of
the center point of your grandfather's life—as he re-
calls it. Oh, not that I altogether subscribe to the
theory of the center point. As a matter of fact, I
probably don't subscribe to it at all, but you will have
to admit—if Herb hadn't lost control of the car, well,
my life would have been diffcrent. All our lives would
have been diffcrent. You wouldn't have been you,
Victoria. You'd have been someone else. And your
mother would have been someone else. It's all enor-
mously complicated, isn't it? Right now I probably
would be surrounded by inlaws named Masonbrink,
and perhaps one of them would be pouring me a
little of that old Paradise County white lightning.
Oh, yes, there still are Masonbrinks in the bootlegging
business. There still are Masonbrinks in the *still* business, if you'll pardon the little play on words there.
And their blood would be flowing in your veins to-

day, Victoria, if Herb Sheppard's foot hadn't slipped on the accelerator of that legendary old Packard. Oh, you should have seen the *Journal* and the *Democrat* the following Monday afternoon. Rhoda and Herb and Lois and I pushed Lucky Lindy Lindbergh clear off the front pages of both papers, and all sorts of photographs were published. Photographs of the wreckage, graduation photographs of the four of us, photographs of our parents (including even old Joe Masonbrink, who was described as an unemployed roofer, which probably made every drunk in town just about expire from laughter). I was taken to a hospital in Lancaster, and I understand it was touch and go for a few hours as to whether I would bleed to death. I don't remember anything from the time of the *pop!* until late the following afternoon, when my eyes opened, and Alice and my parents were sitting next to the bed, and Alice said to me: There's nothing you need to worry about. She spoke before my parents had a chance to utter a single syllable, and her words penetrated the weeping noises my mother was making, and they penetrated the wheezing noises my father was making. And Alice said: Morris, everything will be just fine. And I looked at her. There were facts I needed to know, but I was unable to form the necessary words. As for my foot, well, I wasn't even aware it was missing. I simply looked at Alice. One of my arms was resting outside the sheets. I tried to lift the arm and reach toward Alice, but there was no strength in the arm, and so all it did was flop a little. Alice saw the movement, though, and she touched the arm, and she stroked it, and then she squeezed my hand. I believe it was from that moment that I began to give way to her, and so— in a sense—perhaps I experienced a second center point. I had the feeling that somehow she had pushed away my parents, and I also had the feeling that perhaps they welcomed being pushed away. It was Alice who told me Rhoda and Herb and Lois were dead, and it was Alice who told me I had lost the foot. And it was Alice who visited me seven days a week at that Lancaster hospital, riding back and forth from Paradise Falls on the interuban line, and it was Alice who visited me seven days a week after I was brought home (and my father and mother sort of hovered at the door, if you know what I mean, and my mother gnawed on her lips and picked at cuticles), and it was Alice who said to me: If you want to weep for yourself, that is your right. But it seems to me you're lucky. It seems to me you ought to be grateful. The others are *dead*. You're *not*. Your family has money, and you still have your looks and your intelligence, and an artificial foot will fix you up good as new, so fine, go ahead and weep, but don't expect a whole lot of sympathy from *me*. And Alice spat her words at me. She sat rigidly, and she lost weight, but her words came like moist little pellets, and it was as though I were a reclamation project, some sort of great historic *landmark* seriously in need of restoration. And it was as though she were the only person on the planet capable of doing the job. And yes, I'll admit it. I did weep. I suppose you might even say I wept a great deal. And my parents often wept right along with me, which meant they weren't much of a help at all. But Alice never wept. She was too busy being rigid. She was too busy giving me pep talks. And do you want to know something? Never once— *never once* did she bring up the matter of the prom and the way I had treated her that night. But then, of course, she didn't have to. Her presence and her pep talks were all the reminding I needed, and she was intelligent enough to understand that. So she eventually married me, Victoria. She and I attended Ohio State together, and I could neither escape her nor resist her. But I don't want you to think she forgave me. She never did, not really. And perhaps she never thought in terms of forgiveness. Not that she ever bothered to say much of anything about it . . . except later, after we were married, and after the Depression had taken all my parents' money. You see, she had counted on me to be such a *big cheese*. Well, I was a *big cheese* all right, but it turned out to be Limburger. I was nothing more or less than a bankrupt cripple. And my socalled show business career was nothing more or less than a joke. A bonger of chimes was Morris Bird the Eye Eye, a reader of commercials having to do with used cars and nose drops. And now I sit in this wonderful place and drink beer and talk too much and probably bore my little granddaughter half out of her mind. Maybe twothirds out of her mind. Who knows? Who is to tell? But I have made at least a start. A start. At laying open her roots. When my wife died, it was 1952, and she tried to sit up in bed, and she called me a pig. She spoke clearly, Victoria, and there were witnesses, and your mother was one of the witnesses, and Alice said: *You pig.* She said that, you see, because for many years I still had believed I would amount to something. But your grandmother had believed no such thing—not since the Depression. You see, it was like this: Alice remained steadfast because she thought she would be rewarded. The patient Alice Jones who visited me every day eventually became Alice Bird, and she figured she was on her way to all sorts of wealth. And there was nothing she valued *more* than wealth. I mean, coming from a family that had, um, too many mouths and not enough worldly goods, she valued money more than anything. Oh, I suppose she loved her children, and perhaps at the beginning she even had loved *me* a little, but it always was money This with her, and money That, and the Extra, and she would walk fifteen blocks in order to purchase a loaf of dayold bread and thus save herself perhaps seven cents. You can understand

what a disappointment I must have been to her, can't
you? When she died, she was in much pain, and it
could not have been easy, but still she managed to
say: *You pig.* I was there, Victoria, and your mother
was there, and your late Uncle Morris was there,
and we all heard her very distinctly. So what does
it all come down to, eh? I had been a whole *something*, and then I had been a crippled *something*,
but Alice had not complained. Why? Because the
money still had existed. But then along came Old
Man Depression and the money vanished. Poof. Good-
bye, Bird family fortune. And the *something*—namely
and to wit, myself—became a *nothing.* But I still
nourished dreams for so many years. Morris Bird the
Eye Eye and his golden throat. But Alice saw through
me. She saw my lack of talent. And so the days
mingled, and so many of them. Breaths were expelled.
Alice collected her china owls, and they were the only
trivial things I ever recall that she paid for with cash,
and I have no idea why *owls.* Perhaps because a
great many of them had been handed down from the
estate of my father's mother, who once had been a
singer of grand opera and had started the collection
I don't know how many years ago. The renowned
diva, the town used to call her—Hortense M. Bird,
my grandmother, which makes her your greatgreat-
grandmother, Victoria, which is going back a bit,
isn't it? But anyhow, she began the collection of the
owls, and for some reason my Alice became interested
in perpetuating it and enlarging it. Don't ask me
why. I don't know . . . it just never occurred to me
to ask the question. Perhaps this is one of the reasons
she called me a pig on her deathbed. Apparently I
was a selfish person. But I believe the real reason
goes deeper than that . . . to my pretensions, to my
insistence, carried for so many years, that I still was
a *something* when I really was a *nothing.* At least
that's the way I see it. Oh, there were other consider-

ations . . . women and, ah, *entanglements* . . . but in
the interest of delicacy I won't go into them. Enough
is enough. What you see before you, Victoria, is
a man who is, heh, far from perfect. But he represents
your beginnings, and you'd better pay attention to
what he says. Why? Because there will come a day—
or more likely a night—when it will not be enough to
be alone with your dolls and your little animals, when
you will need to know (out of loneliness, sadness,
fear, curiosity) where you came from. Not that it
will explain why you are what you are. That's all
probably a matter of chemicals, accidents, who knows
what. No. The reason you'll need to know where you
came from is because you are *human*, because no one
who is human can avoid the consequences of the past,
no matter how painful they might be. Look, I know
a lot of what I'm saying is downright gibberish (at
least to you), and I know I've been talking far too
long, and I know your father and your mother would
like to strangle me, but I hope and pray some of the
words have penetrated, and I hope and pray there'll
come a time when you'll say to yourself: He may
have been silly, and he may have been boring, but
he meant well. And maybe you'll *also* say to yourself:
Whatever he did that was bad, we should forgive
him. He certainly didn't mean to—

Victoria's mother interrupted. Daddy, she said, for
heaven's *sake*. You've been talking for more than an
hour.

More like an hour and a half, said Grandpa Bird.

Victoria's father's eyes were heavy. He poked at
them with his fingers.

Nobody's fallen asleep yet, said Grandpa Bird.

Is that the *purpose* of all this? said Victoria's
mother. To *lull* us to *sleep?*

No, said Grandpa Bird. Actually, there's only one
more point I want to make, and then I'll let you all
go, and if you want to let all I've said drain out of

your ears or your skulls or whatever, that is your right. *But there is one more point I want to make, and I insist on making it.*

Victoria's mother blinked at Grandpa Bird. She had smoked so many cigarettes the frog's mouth was overflowing with butts, and they put Victoria in mind of fangs.

Grandpa Bird smiled at Victoria. The point is an important one, he said, and I think it represents a question you'll sooner or later have to face. It is a point that has to do with what I called the *center point*. Remember the center point theory that I outlined awhile back? Well, my center point was that business with Rhoda and the accident involving the Packard. And as I said, if she'd lived, you wouldn't have been you. You'd have been someone else, because I would have married her. All right. That is one theory of existence. The other theory that I've outlined to you is the one having to do with breath and days and smiles and loss, what we adults call *attrition*. Or, if we are less harsh, we call it *maturing*. It rejects the notion that there is a specific day or moment that determines what we are. As I also have said, I think I lean toward this second theory. Oh, the story of Rhoda Masonbrink is reasonably romantic, I suppose, but would I have been much different if she'd lived and I'd married her? Would the self-important bonger of chimes have vanished? Most of the time, I don't think so. Now and then, I do think so—when I yield to sentiment and romantic imaginings. The night of June 4, 1927, has had an impact on me, and it certainly changed me to the extent of costing me a foot, but was the change anything more than a small physical change? I doubt it. Or at least I do when I view the situation with any degree of rational detachment. But we can't *always* view situations with rational detachment, can we? So all I ask is that you recognize the *possibility* of a center point, but I don't ask you to embrace that possibility, and as a matter of fact, I hope you don't. And why do I bother to talk at such length about all this? Well, perhaps because I am old. Perhaps because I want to get it all *out* before I expire. I thank you for bearing with me. I don't know how much you've understood, but I appreciate the fact that you've been so patient. Thank you.

Victoria moistened her lips, made an *o*. One of her ears was giving off a faint ringing noise. She cupped it with a hand.

Ah, you look like an oldtime radio announcer, said Grandpa Bird, grinning.

"Grandpa?" said Victoria. Her throat was dry. She coughed, covering her mouth.

Oh, would you like a glass of water? said Grandpa Bird. A little Pepsi maybe?

"No thank you," said Victoria.

Did I talk too long? said Grandpa Bird.

"I don't know," said Victoria.

Victoria's father smiled and said: A diplomatic answer, if I ever heard one.

Victoria's mother snorted.

"Grandpa?" said Victoria. "Grandpa?"

Yes? said Grandpa Bird.

"You said I would have been somebody else if you had married that Rhoda."

That is correct, said Grandpa Bird.

"I wouldn't have been somebody else," said Victoria.

Pardon? said Grandpa Bird.

"*Somebody else* would have been somebody else," said Victoria. "I mean, um, I wouldn't have been anybody at all. And what about Mommy? She wouldn't have been anybody at all, either."

Oh, said Grandpa Bird.

"But that's okay," said Victoria to Grandpa Bird. "I *am* here, so I'm not, um, upset or anything."

Grandpa Bird nodded.

Nor am I, said Victoria's mother to Grandpa Bird. And I do thank you for leaving out some of the more gory details.

You're very welcome, said Grandpa Bird to Victoria's mother.

I don't really believe sarcasm is called for here, said Victoria's father to both of them.

Grandpa Bird shrugged.

Victoria made another *o*.

Everyone looked at her.

Victoria smiled at Grandpa Bird.

Yes? he said.

Victoria poked at the *o* with her tongue. Then she said: "Grandpa, can I go to the bathroom?"

27 ⬙ Analysis

LATER THAT DAY, in the car on the way home, the Rev Mr Tabor said to his wife and daughter: I'm not quite sure I know what he was driving at.

He wasn't *driving* at anything, said Sandra Tabor. He was *crawling*. Good grief, he wasn't telling us a story; he was reciting the Yellow Pages. He wasn't talking; he was filibustering.

When did we get there? said the Rev Mr Tabor. Two o'clock? Well, do you realize it's past seven now, and it's dark? When was the last time we visited him and didn't get home until after dark?

I don't know what I'll be able to fix for supper, said Sandra Tabor. Maybe we ought to stop somewhere for chicken. Or hamburgers. Or how about that delicatessen, Corky and Lenny's? Wouldn't a nice corned beef sandwich hit the spot along about now?

It was a compulsion, said the Rev Mr Tabor.

I've heard it all before, said Sandra Tabor. And I don't know how many times. And you've heard it all before, too.

But never in such detail, said the Rev Mr Tabor.

"Mommy?" said Victoria.

Yes? said Sandra Tabor.

"I didn't mind," said Victoria.

Mind what? said Sandra Tabor.

"All his talk. If it made him feel better, it was okay."

You really mean that, don't you?
"Yes," said Victoria to her mother.
Did you understand much of it?
"Um, some of it," said Victoria.
Victoria's mother nodded. She said: What do you think he was trying to say to you?
"Um . . ." said Victoria, and she let her voice trail away. She was in the back seat, and her mother had scrunched around up in the front seat, and her father was bent forward a little over the wheel.
Her mother nodded, smiled. Go on, said Sandra Tabor. Let the words come out.
"But I'm, um, I'm not sure," said Victoria.
Well, try, said Sandra Tabor.
Victoria nodded. "Grandpa . . . ah, Grandpa was maybe trying to say to me that there could come a day when . . ."
When what? said Sandra Tabor.
"When I'll maybe have to make a choice . . ."
Between what and what? said Sandra Tabor.
"I don't know," said Victoria. "Only that it'll be a *center point* day. And it'll change me."
From what to what? said Sandra Tabor.
"I don't *know*," said Victoria. "And, um, the thing is . . ."
Yes? said Sandra Tabor.
"Well, from what he said, it might never come. And, um, which would mean that only *time* would come. *Days*, I think he said."
Isn't that all sort of complicated?
"Yes," said Victoria.
Do you think it's worth all the trouble, trying to think it all through?
"Maybe," said Victoria. "I mean, it depends."
On what?
"On how much I love him."
Love him?
"Yes. I mean, I'm *young*, and I've got *time* to think

things through, haven't I? So all right, maybe he talks
too much, but it's not like I'm going to *die* and I've
got a whole lot of real, more important, um, *problems*
buzzing around inside me."

You're saying, then, you found his words valuable?
"Maybe," said Victoria.

Well, said Sandra Tabor. Goodness.

Victoria shrugged a little, made another *o* with her
lips.

Victoria's mother turned until she was facing forward again. She shook her head, then said to Victoria's
father: It would seem that our daughter has a lot of
stuff moving around in her skull. I don't know
whether it's good or bad.

Perhaps only time will tell, said Victoria's father.

I wish I'd said that, said Victoria's mother.

Oh, I'm sure sooner or later you will, said Victoria's
father.

Then there was a sort of dry laughter, and Victoria leaned back in her seat and looked at the lights
of Chagrin Boulevard. They stopped at Corky and
Lenny's, and they were served corned beef sand-
wiches and chocolate phosphates by a waitress who
wore spectacles that had pink rims. The waitress was
perhaps fifty, and she had Midriff Bulge, and she
called everyone Dear. There were free pickle slices,
and Victoria ate three of them. Victoria's corned beef
sandwich was juicy, and the flavor of the phosphate
tickled the base of her throat. She enjoyed her bath
that night, and her mother's hands felt especially
gentle. She became all puckery and pink, and she
giggled. She took Marybeth to bed with her that
night, and they discussed lingerie and nailpolish. Then,
much later, after Marybeth had fallen asleep, Victoria, who did not approve of tears, who tried to
make it a point to defeat tears, who never really
bawled (except when she bit her tongue or did other
things that brought an abrupt pain that she was

unprepared to resist), got to thinking of how old she wasn't, and of how old Grandpa Bird *was*, and then, her ears and memory all awash with Grandpa Bird's words and his pain and his slabbed and polysyllabic bafflement, she covered her eyes with one of her arms. And she embraced Marybeth with the other arm. And she was sorry she wasn't as old as she should have been. And she mourned Grandpa Bird's vanished foot. She mourned it more than she had mourned that poor old comb. What was done with a foot after it was removed? Victoria Anne Tabor, she of a tight warm arm across her eyes, shuddered. It had been a long day. She was *young*, and she had *time*, but it had been too long a day, and that was the truth. She moaned a little, but she did not moan too loudly. She did not want to awaken Marybeth. That would have been unfair.

28 🐿 Owls

VICTORIA GATHERED them all together, the dolls, the animals, the retired nightlights. She arranged them neatly on her bed, aligning them just so. Then, after waiting to make sure she had their undivided attention, she placed a finger to her lips and whispered: "There are these owls I know, a whole lot of them, and the biggest one is named Teddy and he wears funny glasses, and I think maybe they would like to come live with us." Victoria hesitated. This was the night of the day following the long speech that had been delivered by Grandpa Bird. It was a Monday night, and Victoria was warmly and fragrantly clean, all nicely puckered, and she said: "They're trapped in a big thing that's like a glass case, and Teddy says they're not happy. He says it is not *bully* to be as unhappy as they are, and I guess maybe I ought to do something about their situation. Maybe I can talk to Grandpa Bird. Maybe, if he knows how they feel, he'll let them go. He's a nice man. I want to go to him and tell him how they feel."

Are you that brave? whispered Bear.

"I think so," whispered Victoria.

Are they good conversationalists? whispered Bear.

"Well, *Teddy* is," whispered Victoria. "The others haven't said a word yet."

It would be nice to have even one good conversationalist, whispered Bear.

Aren't *we* good enough for you? whispered Rabbit.
Are you addressing *me?* whispered Bear.
Yes, whispered Rabbit. You and no one else.
Ah, you're all *wonderful* conversationalists, whispered Bear. Just absolutely *terrific*. But variety is the spice of life, to coin a phrase, and I would appreciate the opportunity to exchange ideas with someone new. Still, don't misunderstand. I meant no offense.
"Please don't fuss," whispered Victoria to Bear and Rabbit. She swiveled their heads so that they were looking directly at her. "And anyway, I don't know whether Grandpa Bird will give them up. After all, he's had them I don't know how long. Most of his life, I guess."
Try to be very nice to him, whispered Bear.
"Oh, I *will*," whispered Victoria.
You say the big owl wears funny glasses? whispered Bear.
Victoria nodded.
Are they attached to a string? whispered Bear.
"Yes," whispered Victoria.
And he uses the word *bully?* whispered Bear.
"That's right," whispered Victoria.
Imagine that, whispered Bear.
"Pardon?" whispered Victoria.
He'll be an interesting conversationalist, all right, whispered Bear, just as long as he doesn't bore us with a lot of talk about the Panama Canal. When I was president of Harvard, I took tea with him several times in the White House, and I remember once we had brandy with our tea, and he seemed a bit tired, and he shook his head and asked me whether I would care to exchange presidencies with him, sight unseen. I smiled and told him I declined. He asked me whether I might change my mind if I were plied with brandy. I told him I truly was sorry, but there wasn't enough brandy in the world.
"That's very interesting, I'm sure," whispered Vic-

toria. She didn't have the remotest idea what Bear was talking about.

It's strange, at that, whispered Bear.

"Pardon?" whispered Victoria.

That *Teddy* should wind up as an *owl*, and *I* should wind up as a *bear*. You see, I am what is known as a teddybear, and the first teddybear in the entire world was patterned after *him*. Really. I wouldn't pull your leg. And I am, if I am anything at all, owlish. So why is he an owl and why am I a bear?

"I, um, I guess I don't know."

Very peculiar.

"If you say so."

Yes. I do say so.

"All right," whispered Victoria.

Please make me smile, whispered Bear.

Victoria nodded. She seized Bear by the head and pulled at the corners of his mouth with her thumbs.

Ha ha ha, whispered Bear.

29 ~ Chicken

BUT TAKING THE OWLS from Grandpa Bird wouldn't be that easy. The more Victoria thought about it, the more she had to ask herself: But how much does he have? She looked around Grandpa Bird's condominium each time she visited the place with her parents (and she saw Teddy and the rest of the owls staring through the breakfront's glass doors), and she asked herself: What's so great about a peacocked loveseat? If I ask him for the owls and he says yes, what will be left?

She decided she couldn't do that.

She tried to avoid looking at Teddy and the rest of the owls.

She decided she was either softhearted or chicken. Maybe both. Probably both.

30 ᥫ Comfort

IT WAS TRUE. She had come to believe that she never
would know why she was the way she was. Oh, it
was true enough. There had been no *center point* early
in her life that had caused her to keep to herself.
All she knew was that she needed to be by herself—
provided, of course, warm baths were available, and
a cupped palm now and again. There was no real
pain in any of this. It always was possible to place
her bed on flanged wheels and take all her dolls and
animals and nightlights and even Henry the soap
fish on a journey to realms that abounded with hot
juicy chicken breasts, with easy smiles, with lipsticks
and rubber balls and copies of *Five Little Peppers
and How They Grew*, to her particular Peaceable
Kingdoms, where there was no coldness and dirt,
where no one hollered, where all graspings were
gentle, unhurried, where beauty was understood and
applauded (by quietly appreciative crowds that
gathered in misted and golden streets). Oh, yes, it
was true, it was true. She had come to believe that
she never would know why she was the way she was,
but she was not unhappy. She was pretty enough,
or at least just about everyone said so. She was small
for her age, but she was slender, which made her
appear taller. Her pigtailed hair was dark and heavy,
and her eyes were gray verging on blue. She had fair
skin, and she tried not to scratch or bruise herself.

She liked her dresses too much, and she did not want any tacky old *scratches* or *bruises* to divert attention. She did not want her life to be disturbed. (Cupped palms and soft miraculous palaver are too precious.)

31 🐿 Disturbance

BUT THEN CAME that particular Saturday morning in early June of 1978, and Victoria had managed to force herself back to sleep, and she was not burdened with dreams—not even the mostly benevolent nightmares having to do with repentant trolls and the like. She slept with her face pressed against the pillow, and her hands were in warm pink fists. She slept with her mouth open, and her mouth was twisted a little because her face was pressed a trifle too tightly against the pillow. She slept thickly, and her breath came moistly, and it wasn't until nearly eight o'clock that she came awake for the second time, that she again heard the new leaves and the fragile bell of a Rapid Transit car. Nearly eight o'clock? Oh, wow! She couldn't recall having slept this late in her whole entire life! She scrambled out of bed. She hugged herself, and she patted several of the canaries on her nightgown. She wriggled into her bathrobe (it was pink, and it had what was known as a fun fur collar) and hurried into the bathroom. She kind of urgently had to Go. A little later, after the Going, she brushed her teeth, then washed her hands and her face, using a washcloth and towel that were white with brown ducks sitting plumply on the initials VT—sort of entwined inside them, actually. She heard someone moving around downstairs in the kitchen, and she supposed it was her mother. She had not told her parents of yesterday's dispute that had involved Miss Platt's grandmother and the canal water and the leaky straw.

180

Maybe she should have told them, but she had used up her supply of courage for one day. The scene in the schoolyard, the visit to Mrs Bee's office, the words that had been exchanged . . . well, the truth was, it all had *drained* Victoria, and she'd said nothing about any of it last night. Ah, but now was the weekend, which was just fine. Since there was no school, Victoria wouldn't have to worry about the famous canal water incident, not for two days. She might be in for some trouble on Monday, but Monday was a universe away, and she would let Monday take care of itself. So she had at least a temporary reprieve, and it made her grin into the bathroom mirror as she washed her face. A reprieve from what? Her parents, of course. She did not care if they ever found out about the incident, and that was a fact. And this wasn't only because they would be angry with her. It also had to do with a sort of knotted feeling that somehow they would be disappointed in her for being so rude and not showing the proper respect for *fellowship*, which meant *cooperation*, which meant *not being alone*, which meant diverting too much time away from silence and the soft miraculous palaver of things stuffed, things made of plastic, things made of wood and metal, things made of glass and china and even soap. Victoria shook her head and sighed. She wiped her face and hands. She adjusted her braids. She hung her towels neatly on a rack, and her initials and the entwined ducks were precisely aligned.

She heard her father moving around in her parents' bedroom. She heard him clear his throat, and she heard the thudding of his bare feet. He had been out late last night on a pastoral call, visiting a Mrs Schroeder, who had a suite in the Shaker Towers and was very rich and was dying of pancreas trouble. The woman had told Victoria's father the Wrexford Methodist Church would receive generous attention in her will, and so Victoria's father visited Mrs

Schroeder whenever Mrs Schroeder wanted him to
visit her. With the economy and the church's books
being what they are, he had told his wife and daughter, I would visit the old girl every ten minutes if
it came to that. And then he had smiled. And Victoria's mother had smiled. But Victoria had not smiled.
She had been unable to understand why that remark
was funny. She believed in God (she almost had to,
didn't she?), and she was not quite able to grasp why
her father would be amused simply because he was
protecting the Almighty's interests. The poor old
thing has tasseled wallpaper, Victoria's father had reported to his family, and it's that sort of off pink, if
you know what I mean. Salmon pink, I believe it's
called. And the place has bowls of feathers, white
feathers, purple feathers, even green feathers, and
about twelve zillion little china figurines, fancy ladies
in long skirts, and all of them look like Norma Shearer
in *Marie Antoinette*. And all the chairs are spindly
and a bit precarious, and there are glass candlesticks
and even an enormous wooden bulldog that serves as
a doorstop. Oh, I expect you would like the place well
enough, Victoria, but to me it's like a museum, all full
of fuss and clash, very remorselessly Early Nouveau
Riche Jewish, which is sort of an inside way adults
talk among themselves to one another now and then,
and I'm afraid not a very charitable way to talk, but
sometimes very appropriate. The bulldog is brown
with blue sequined eyes, if you can believe such a
thing. But would I lie to you? Do you really think I
am gifted with such an imagination? Ah, listen to me.
Listen to the way I'm talking. I'm beginning to sound
Jewish. Oy. And here Victoria's father had begun to
laugh, and the laughter had cut off his recitation.
And Victoria's mother had also laughed. But Victoria
had not laughed. If an old woman was dying, wasn't
she entitled to bowls with feathers in them? Wasn't
she entitled to just about anything she wanted, as

long as no one else was hurt by whatever it was? The way Victoria's father had spoken of Mrs Schroeder, was it any less insulting than what Victoria had said to Miss Platt about Miss Platt's grandmother? Was it any less hurtful? Victoria shook her head. She decided she was tramping too heavily in stuff that was too sticky for her. She scurried out of the bathroom. She did not want to encounter her father just now. She closed her bedroom door behind her just as her father was crossing the hall to the bathroom. He shouted a good morning to her, and he told her he hoped she hadn't steamed up the mirror. Victoria said nothing. Carefully she took off her robe and her nightgown. She hung them in her closet, and then she dressed herself in panties, a reddish orange plaid skirt, a white blouse, reddish orange knee socks, and a pair of brown shoes. Her mother had on more than one occasion complimented her on her sense of color. Victoria glanced at her Hobbit calendar, and today's date was Saturday, June 3, 1978. She decided she would take Bear downstairs to breakfast with her. She went to the bed and smoothed down the sheets and the blanket and the spread. Bear was lying on his back, and so she tickled his armpits. He came awake giggling, and she said to him: "Would you like a special treat today?"

You mean . . . breakfast downstairs? said Bear, suppressing his giggles.

"Yes," said Victoria.

I would be delighted, and I thank you very much, said Bear.

"You're very welcome," said Victoria. She scooped up Bear. His loose eye wobbled. Today she would ask her parents to do something about it. There apparently was some sort of spring or hook that had become disengaged. She hugged Bear to her chest. She looked around the bedroom, and she said to the rest of her dolls and animals: "You be good now."

They were silent. They stared at her.

"Now don't be angry," said Victoria.

That's easy for you to say, said Rabbit.

I've never gone downstairs with you *once*, said Kermit the Retired Nightlight. I mean, not even for so much as a lettuce leaf.

"Don't be rude," said Victoria.

Rude, my foot, said Kermit. I'm only a little bored, that's all. I'm told there's life outside this bedroom, and I'd like to see it someday before the end of the century. Or the end of the world. Whichever comes first.

"You will," said Victoria.

I'll believe that when it happens, said Kermit.

"Do you think I would go back on a promise?" said Victoria.

Ah . . . well, no, I suppose not, said Kermit.

"That's better," said Victoria.

Some of the others made indistinct murmurous sounds, but nothing more was said so Victoria could hear it. She took Bear downstairs to the kitchen with her, and on the way he whispered: You really do have us all under firm control. I admire you.

"Thank you," whispered Victoria.

You are to us like the Mind of God, whispered Bear.

"Pardon?" whispered Victoria.

Never mind, whispered Bear. It was just a lot of pretentious nonsense.

"Okay," whispered Victoria, shrugging.

Bear made a small sound that might have been a chuckle.

Victoria's mother's hair was in curlers, and she was wearing a flannel bathrobe. She glanced at Victoria, the skirt, blouse, knee socks, shoes, and she said: Well, I'll say this for you, Little Miss Slugabed, you look awfully well turned out for so early in the morning.

Early? Ah, not so early, I guess. Not for you. What happened?

Victoria seated herself at her place at the table. A glass of orange juice had already been poured for her, and she sipped at it. She set Bear squarely on her lap. "I overslept," she said to her mother. "I woke up real early, and I—"

Very early, said Victoria's mother.

Victoria nodded. "And I got to thinking, and I couldn't get back to sleep. For awhile."

Victoria's mother was frying eggs and bacon. She pushed at the eggs with a spatula. Thinking about what? she said.

"Nothing," said Victoria.

You had to be thinking about *something*. A person doesn't think about *nothing*. If a person thinks about nothing, he's not thinking about anything. Or, in this case, she.

"Pardon?" said Victoria.

If a person is thinking about nothing, he is not thinking at all. Or, in this case, she.

"Mommy?"

Yes?

"Are you putting me on?"

Victoria's mother smiled. She scooped eggs and bacon onto a platter. She brought the platter to the table. She set down the platter and said to Victoria: Don't mind me. There are times when I can be a fussbudget.

"That's true," said Victoria, nodding.

Her mother sniggered and said: Mind your manners.

Victoria then did some smiling of her own. The kitchen faced east, and there already was a good deal of sunlight. It streaked the kitchen. It splattered the kitchen. It shadowed the kitchen. Victoria squinted into it. Perhaps this morning she would take some of her dolls and animals out onto the back patio. Saturday mornings her mother usually went grocery shopping at Heinen's, and her father usually did some lastminute sermon work in his study. Victoria often went to Heinen's with her mother. She enjoyed breathing the place's various supermarketed odors, and she even *kind of* enjoyed all the commotion, a special commotion that made Saturday mornings in Heinen's such a hassle of breath, bodies, voices, the thuck and ring of cash registers, the pooosh and smackkk of large paper bags being filled, folded, squeezed. Victoria always stayed near her mother during these visits to Heinen's, and she wouldn't have let her mother out of sight for the world and all the planets, and she had to admit there were times when all the noise made her want to turn her ears insideout and tuck them behind her forehead, but still there was something about Heinen's on a Saturday that brought a sweet excitement to her, that gently laid a hint in her mind that there perhaps existed noise and confusions that would not necessarily harm her. In other words, maybe she didn't *always* have to be alone. At least the possibility existed, and it pleased her. And certainly later, when she would be out on her own in the big wide world (or whatever it was), occasional visits to Heinen's would be helpful in preventing her from starving to death. So she was glad she was able to cope with Heinen's. She hadn't always been able to. As a very little girl, at three and four and even five, she often had wept when her mother had taken her to Heinen's. And she often had covered her face when her mother had wheeled her up and down the aisles in a shopping cart. Her mother sometimes had bought her Animal Crackers in an attempt to calm her, but the Animal Crackers had been a disastrous failure, since how could Victoria be expected to eat bunnies and elephants and pussycats that were so small they fit in the palm of her tight pink frightened little hand? And so, quietly, reluctantly, Victoria had wept. She hated herself when she wept, but there were times when she could not help it. Those early times in Heinen's stood out in her mind as being perhaps the worst. She would chew on a thumb. She would jam shut her eyes, and she would twist her face tight as a raisin, and she would hold her breath, and she would bite her tongue. She would do everything she knew to keep from weeping, but still she would weep. Victoria the sissy. Victoria who was showing too much.

Well, now she no longer wept. Or at least she no longer wept when she was taken to Heinen's. She was *older*. She had outgrown those particular tears. She had responsibilities now, to her dolls, her animals, her retired nightlights, her soap fish. When a person had responsibilities, tears were weakness, and Victoria Anne Tabor did not have the time for weakness. She supposed this was the main reason she had come to terms with all the roar and hassle at Heinen's. And she had to admit there were things about the place she really did *kind of* enjoy. She was a little proud of herself because of all this. She knew how much it had taken out of her. And she knew she now was at the point where she didn't have to go to Heinen's with her mother *every* Saturday morning. Now if she didn't want to go, it was because she simply didn't want to go—and *not* because she was afraid. This morning, for instance, she knew it would be nicer to stay home, to go out on the patio and play with her chosen dolls and animals and enjoy the sunlight, and she knew she would do just that—and *not* because she was afraid. Or ashamed. This all made her feel good. It made her feel that she wouldn't be a whimperer and a whiner all her life, that she actually was growing up. And hooray for growing up, as long as she was allowed to do it her way.

Her mother sat down across the table and spooned some eggs and bacon onto Victoria's plate. She glanced briefly toward the ceiling and said: There's no sense waiting for your father to finish his mucking about in the bathroom. We might as well eat before the food gets cold or we die of terminal impatience.

Still smiling, Victoria nodded. She held her glass of orange juice in front of Bear's mouth. "Now, drink your orange juice," she said to him. She inclined his head forward and down until his mouth rested against the rim of the glass.

He likes his orange juice, doesn't he? said Sandra Tabor, spooning herself eggs and bacon.

"It's good for him," said Victoria. "He says it really wakes him up in the morning."

He is a nice Teddy, isn't he?

"His name is Bear."

But he is a *teddy*bear.

"Okay. But Teddy is named Teddy. Bear is named Bear."

I'm sorry.

Victoria glanced down at Bear. "Had enough?" she said to him. She moved his head up and down. "Good," she said. She lifted the glass and drank from it. The juice was so cold and puckery it made her shudder a little. Then she spoke to her mother. "I know somebody *else* who is named Teddy," she said.

Oh, said Sandra Tabor, chewing. I think I get what you mean. Now then, eat. There's nothing worse than cold gummy eggs and bacon.

Victoria nodded. She began to eat. She buttered herself a slice of toast and spread it with grape jelly. She offered food to Bear, but he declined. He always seemed to be having a weight problem, did Bear. Victoria nodded. "Suit yourself," she said, "but it's good."

I beg your pardon? said Victoria's mother.

"I was talking to Bear," said Victoria.

Ah, yes, said Sandra Tabor. I should have known.

Victoria's father came into the kitchen just as her

mother was lighting a cigarette. He seated himself at the table. He was wearing light white trousers, and he was wearing a T-shirt that said OH, GOD! It showed a picture of George Burns, the comedian. It had been given to him last Christmas by Victoria's mother. He said something to the effect that he probably was rushing summer a little, what with his white britches, but he just couldn't help feeling a sort of euphoria on such a fine sunny day. Victoria's mother went to the stove and began fixing him eggs and bacon. She snubbed out her cigarette in an ashtray. He smiled at Victoria, poured himself a cup of coffee. Well, he said, and what are Victoria's plans for today? Will she take advantage of the sunshine while her poor father is upstairs laboring over his sermon?

Carl, I wish you wouldn't talk to her as though she weren't here, said Victoria's mother, cracking an egg.

Oh, said the Rev Mr Tabor. Well, I, ah, I meant no offense.

Do you talk that way to Mrs Schroeder?

No. Of course not.

Then don't talk that way to your daughter.

What's Mrs Schroeder got to do with this?

Victoria's mother shrugged. She was peeling bacon, dropping it into the skillet. There's something about you that can be awfully condescending, she said. That's all. I mean, the way you talk about Mrs Schroeder's wallpaper and her bowls of feathers, I sometimes think you . . . oh, I don't know. I'm not being fair. Forget what I said.

Victoria's father sipped at his coffee. He held his cup up with both hands. No, he said. Please go on.

Not in front of Victoria.

No. Whatever it is you might have to say, I think Victoria is mature enough to hear it.

Victoria's mother turned from the stove and faced the Rev Mr Tabor. She said: I like the way you just blithely judge what I'm going to say before I say it.

Ah, I'm sorry, but it can't be all that terrible.

Don't be too sure of that, Carl.

Really, I—

Carl, do you like people?

What?

I am asking you a very simple and basic question—*do you like people?*

You're right, Sandra. We definitely should not be talking this way in front of Victoria.

Well, it's too late now. So please answer my question.

I love you. I love Victoria. You know that.

Carl, answer my question—*do you like people?*

That's enough, Sandra. I mean it.

Victoria's mother turned back to the stove. She pushed at the eggs and the bacon with the spatula. All right, she said.

Victoria's father sipped more of his coffee. Then he looked at Victoria and said: We . . . um, there are times when, what with one thing and another, we all of us get up on the wrong side of the bed. Do you understand?

Victoria nodded.

Victoria's mother brought the skillet to the Rev Mr Tabor and scraped eggs and bacon onto his plate. She took the skillet to the sink and soaked it with cold water. It hissed. She brought the ashtray to the table, seated herself, poured herself a cup of coffee. Her cigarette was down to a butt, so she stubbed it out and lit another. She used one of those Bic throwaway lighters. She inhaled so deeply that for a moment it seemed that the smoke would come from her ears. But it did not come from her ears. Instead, it came from her nostrils in what was close to a snort.

Victoria looked away from her mother.

The Rev Mr Tabor chewed on his eggs and his bacon. He drank more coffee. He drank orange juice. He spread himself a slice of toast. He was sitting next to Victoria's mother. Speaking quietly (the words were a bit indistinct, what with the eggs and bacon and toast that were in his mouth), he said: Sandra, I'm sorry if I upset you.

Victoria looked at her mother.

It doesn't matter, said Sandra Tabor to her husband.

Are you sure?

Yes, said Sandra Tabor to her husband. Yes. *Yes.*

Are you *really* sure?

Yes.

I suppose I *can* be condescending.

That is correct, said Sandra Tabor to her husband.

The Rev Mr Tabor touched one of his wife's hands . . . the one that was not holding her cigarette.

Victoria wriggled a little. Her panties were caught up. She held Bear steady on her lap. She glanced down at Bear and whispered that she truly was sorry for having disturbed him.

The Rev Mr Tabor looked at Victoria. Pardon? he said.

"I was talking to Bear," said Victoria.

Oh. Sorry.

"That's okay," said Victoria to her father.

Her father smiled. Even her mother smiled. Her father patted her mother's hand, and her mother shrugged, puffed, inhaled. Victoria hoped they had enjoyed their little argument. They seemed to have so many of these little arguments that surely they had fun. Otherwise, why would they have bothered? Victoria patted Bear's head, and she pressed at his loose eye with a thumb. Her mother asked her whether she would like to go along to Heinen's this morning. Victoria said no, thank you, she believed she would rather play out back in the sunshine. Her mother smiled and nodded and said yes, it appeared to be a nice day for that sort of thing. Victoria also smiled. And then she said: "This is a *good* way to talk, isn't it?"

A good way? said her mother.

Her father looked up from his food.

"I mean, no fussing," said Victoria.

Her mother hesitated for a moment, then nodded.

Victoria smiled.

Her father quickly forked up a mouthful of eggs.

"Can we talk about something else?" said Victoria.

Are you talking to me? said her mother.

"I'm, um, I'm talking to both of you," said Victoria.

Again her father looked up from his food. Go on, he said, swallowing.

Victoria held up Bear. She moved his head from side to side, and his eye slipped forward. "Bear has a loose eye," she said, "and I was wondering if maybe it could be fixed."

Victoria's father glanced at her mother, than again at Victoria.

"It's *serious*," said Victoria.

Her father quickly smiled. Of course it is, he said, nodding at her. He looked at her squarely, openly, and he idly ran a hand across his shirtfront, rubbing the OH, GOD! and George Burns's forehead and cheeks. Now his face had the sort of expression he often wore when he was delivering his sermon. It was full of teeth, with perhaps a drop of saliva at a corner of his mouth.

Victoria held out Bear and said to her father: "Can you look at him, please?"

Of course, said the Rev Mr Tabor. He took Bear and began fussing with the loose eye, prodding and twisting it.

"Oh," said Victoria.

Be careful, said Victoria's mother.

The Rev Mr Tabor grunted. He frowned. He fussed.

"*Please* be careful," said Victoria.

Of course, said the Rev Mr Tabor.

Victoria's mother reached across the table and

patted one of Victoria's hands. She smiled at Victoria and said: He'll be very careful, I'm sure.

Yes indeed, said the Rev Mr Tabor, biting his tongue. I think if I just . . . ah, twist it, it'll pop into place very easily. It seems to be held by . . . by a sort of . . . ah, little clip of some sort . . . or perhaps *spring* would be a better word.

Don't twist too hard, said Victoria's mother.

The Rev Mr Tabor nodded. He grunted. Bear's eye popped out, bounced off the Rev Mr Tabor's lap and rolled across the floor, coming to a stop in front of the refrigerator.

"Oh," said Victoria.

Oh, *dear*, said her mother.

Victoria howled. She snatched Bear from her father. There was a raveled hole where the eye should have been. She hugged Bear to her chest, and she told him it was all right if he wanted to bawl. She scooted across the kitchen and retrieved the eye. She pressed it against the raveled hole, but nothing was there to hold it in place. (She listened closely, and she was able to hear Bear gasp and whimper.) She ran out of the kitchen before her parents could say or do anything. Cradling Bear, she hurried upstairs and went into the bathroom, slamming and locking the door behind her. She was sniffling. She was breathing with her mouth open. But she no longer was howling. In point of fact, she had howled only the one time. There was too much to do, and she did not have the time for howling. And anyway, howling was for *babies*. Bear was howling, though, and she couldn't say as how she blamed him. She hugged him. She said: "Yes. Yes. All right."

I, oh, I *hurt*, said Bear.

Victoria nodded. "Of course you do," she said. She tried not to look at the raveled hole. Carefully she set Bear on the closed commode. "But I think there's something I can do for you," she said.

Then please *do* it, said Bear.

Victoria nodded. She opened the medicine cabinet that was over the sink. She removed a swab, a bottle of tincture of merthiolate, and a package of Curad bandages. "They're ouchless," she said.

Wha . . . what? said Bear.

"Curad bandages are ouchless," said Victoria. "You've seen the Curad TV commercials, haven't you?"

No, said Bear.

"Well, take my word for it," said Victoria.

I am very . . . pleased, said Bear.

Victoria nodded. "But first, though, a little mathiolate," she said, opening the bottle.

That's pronounced *mer*thiolate, said Bear.

"Oh," said Victoria. "Thank you very much." Carefully she poured some of the tincture of merthiolate onto the swab.

And tincture of merthiolate is *not* ouchless, said Bear.

"I know," said Victoria, and quickly she dabbed at the raveled hole with the swab.

Ouch, said Bear.

"I kind of thought you'd say that," said Victoria. She set aside the swab and opened two of the little Curad strips. Carefully she placed them over the raveled hole. There was a rattling at the door. She paid no attention to it. She pressed down on the strips, and they felt firm. There was more rattling at the door. She paid no attention to it.

Victoria's mother's voice came from the hall: I want you to unlock this door, please.

"You know, if I got some shoepolish and painted your bandages black, you'd look like a regular Long John Silver," said Victoria to Bear.

Oh, said Bear, snuffling. Wonderful. That's been my lifelong ambition.

Victoria, *please*, said her mother from the hall.

"I'm working," said Victoria.

Pardon? said her mother from the hall.

"I'm *fine*," said Victoria.

Her mother again set to rattling at the door.

"How do you feel now?" said Victoria to Bear.

Please unlock this door, said her mother from the hall.

I believe I'd . . . I believe I'd like to lie down, said Bear.

Now you do as I say, said Victoria's mother from the hall.

"The bandage too tight?" said Victoria to Bear.

I am losing my patience, young lady, said Victoria's mother from the hall.

It is a fine patch, said Bear. Yo ho ho and a bottle of rum.

Would you like for me to call for your father? said Victoria's mother from the hall.

Avast, me hearties, said Bear.

Grinning, Victoria gently picked up Bear. She unlocked the door and opened it. She brushed past her mother. She stroked Bear and murmured to him. She carried him into the bedroom. Her mother followed. She stretched Bear out on the bed, then brought Rabbit and Cat and Kermit and Marybeth to him. She placed them in a semicircle around the place where he lay. Her mother stood by a window and watched all this. Finally, after kissing Bear's nose and one of his ears, Victoria turned to her mother and said: "Excuse me. I was busy."

Sandra Tabor sighed, grunted, shook her head. You are the limit, she said. The absolute most farout wacko incredible daughter any woman could want. He's really hurting, isn't he?

"Yes," said Victoria.

Poor Teddy, said Victoria's mother.

"His name is *Bear*," said Victoria.

Oh, said Victoria's mother. That's right. Sorry.
"Am I really those things?"
What things?
"Farout. Wacko. Incredible."
I think you are. But I don't want you to worry
about them. They're nice things to be.
"Does Daddy think so?"
Um, sometimes.
Victoria had dropped Bear's eye in a pocket on the
front of her skirt. She retrieved the eye from the
pocket. She walked to where her mother was standing.
She held out the eye and said: "Will he be able to,
um, do something about this?"
I can ask him.
Victoria glanced down at the eye. Then she stared
directly at her mother and said: "I'd appreciate that.
So would Bear. It *hurts* him."
Yes, said Victoria's mother.
"Here," said Victoria, holding out the eye.
All right, said Victoria's mother. She took the eye
and rolled it for a moment between the thumb and
forefinger of her right hand. She inhaled. Her breath
whistled a little. It really *does* hurt him, doesn't it?
she said.
"If you don't believe *me*, ask *him*," said Victoria.
Victoria's mother quickly shook her head. She
closed her hand over the eye. I believe you, she said.
"Thank you," said Victoria.
Victoria's mother glanced out the window for a
moment. She made a fist with the hand that had
closed over the eye. She touched her mouth with the
fist. She nodded. She coughed softly. Fine, she said.
She blinked at Victoria, then went out of the room.
She did not look back. Gently she closed the door
behind her.
Victoria looked around the room. She looked at
all her friends. Then, smiling, she said: "Wacko?"

32 ❧ Concern

VICTORIA DECIDED to gather *all* her friends around
Bear, and so she carried them to the bed. For the
most part, they admired Bear's eyepatch, and Marybeth swore up and down it gave him an absolutely
dashing look. Victoria picked up Marybeth and
pressed Marybeth's mouth against one of Bear's
cheeks, and he grunted a little—and at the same time
he said maybe his missing eye was worth the pain;
maybe he was a very lucky fellow indeed. Then
Bonnie, who was wearing the Dolly Parton outfit
Victoria's mother had made for her, spoke up. She
told Bear she was jealous. She told Bear anything
Marybeth could do, she could do better. In West
Virginia, said Bonnie, we may not know a whole lot,
but we do know how to kiss. Bonnie's sequins glit-
tered, and her dyed blonde hair was unmussed, and
she smiled in Bear's direction. So Victoria picked her
up and pressed *her* mouth against the same cheek
that had been kissed by Marybeth. Bear made a smug
noise that perhaps came from the area of his belly-
button. Victoria asked him whether he would like to
go outdoors. Smiling at the others, she wondered
aloud whether they all should go out on the patio
and catch some sunshine and fresh air. She put the
question directly to Bear, asking him how he was
doing in the strength department. There was then a
general commotion, and all the dolls and animals
began talking, assuring Victoria that sunshine and

198

fresh air would be just the ticket for dear old Bear, just the ticket to take his mind off his pain. Victoria gently tugged at the corners of Bear's mouth, and so he smiled, and he allowed as how yes, sunshine and fresh air had never hurt a soul. Victoria fetched a white wicker doll bed from the bedroom closet. It had a blanket and a pillow, and it smelled faintly of lavender. She tucked Bear into the doll bed, and he said something to the effect that he hoped he wouldn't gag on the lavender. Victoria smiled, then gently punched him in the belly and just as gently tickled his armpits. He giggled, and so did Victoria, and he said: All right. All right. I *give*. Victoria made several trips to the patio. She brought down every single doll and animal, every single retired nightlight and even Henry the soap fish. Six patio chairs were folded just outside the back door. Victoria unfolded the chairs. She set out the dolls and the animals and the nightlights and Henry the soap fish on the chairs. Part of the patio was shaded by a forsythia bush, and she placed the doll bed in that shadow. She did not want Bear to be bothered by any sort of glare. Everyone talked quietly so as not to disturb Bear. Bonnie said it was a shame there was not even a single Dolly Parton LP in the family's record library. Victoria told Bonnie that perhaps the *Star Wars* music would be fun to hear some evening. "I got the album for Christmas from my mommy and my daddy," said Victoria to Bonnie. "I've played it over and over again on my little recordplayer, but *some of these people here*—or *whatever they are*—got to complaining because I played it too much. Bear was one of the biggest complainers. Bear and Cat. Bear and Cat and Rabbit. Kermit, too. But I held out for a long time. I liked that movie a whole lot. I especially liked the little Droids, you know? They were my favorites. Ah, anyway, I played the music and *played* it, and finally Bear and Cat and some of the rest of them told me they were absolutely going deaf. And they said to me would I like that on my conscience. I decided I wouldn't, and so I put the record away. But it's been a few months now, and if you'd like me to, I could get it out, and I could play it, and I could talk to you about the Droids." And Bonnie said: I thank you kindly, but I don't know nothing about no Droids. I just would like to have a listen to old Dolly Parton, on account of I look so much like her, you know? And Bear broke in, saying: Good for you, Bonnie. And Cat said: Victoria, with Bear on his deathbed, would you subject him to *Star Wars* again? And Bear said: *Deathbed?* And Cat said: Sorry. I was just trying to make a point. And Victoria shook her head. She clucked her tongue against the roof of her mouth. She shook a finger at everyone and made a rather severe announcement that she did not want a lot of bickering. After all, the day was too nice. There was a general murmur of what she hoped was agreement. She listened to traffic and leaves. She held Bonnie up to the sunlight so that it caught at Bonnie's excellent hair. She smoothed Marybeth's skirts, and she checked Cat's wheels to find out whether they squeaked. Last week she had talked her father into oiling Cat's wheels, and the oil had stopped the squeaks. But that had been then. Now was now, and Cat was squeaking again. Victoria pulled him across the patio, and his wheels squeaked so loudly it was as though they had never been oiled at all. He told Victoria he didn't know what the matter was; perhaps he was suffering from acute old age. Victoria told him she didn't see anything cute about old age. Cat told Victoria he didn't see anything cute about that pun, either. Victoria giggled. So did Marybeth and Bonnie. Cat told them not to encourage Victoria, and so of course they giggled some more. Kermit told Victoria this surely was a nice outing. Victoria smiled. She went to Bear and asked him how he was feeling.

He told her the pain had begun to die down. Now it was only a dull ache, and he told Victoria he thanked the Lord for small favors. She nodded. She patted his head, scratched him under his chin. The dolls and animals chatted among themselves. Typing sounds came from upstairs, which meant Victoria's father was working on his sermon. Victoria's mother, dressed now in a flowered blouse, white bellbottomed slacks and white sandals, with her hair pulled back and sunglasses perched above her forehead, came out onto the patio and told Victoria last chance for Heinen's. And Victoria told her mother no, thank you, this was too fine a morning, too *warm* a morning, and it was necessary that Bear be comforted, what with the catastrophe at the breakfast table. Victoria's mother glanced at Bear and the little white wicker bed. Victoria patted Bear's frayed ear. Her mother nodded, walked briskly to the garage, backed the family's station wagon out of the driveway and went off to Heinen's. Victoria smiled. She spoke to her dolls and her animals. "Well," she said, "I do believe we just about have the morning to ourselves." She decided to drag the patio chairs closer to Bear's little bed. That way, everyone would be able to *talk* to him, and no one would have to *shout*. Bear told her he appreciated her considerateness. There was now and again the sound of a bell of a Rapid Transit car. Chocolate was discussed, and birds clambered carefully in the fresh moist trees. Victoria hunkered on a bench, and she crossed her legs like The Brave Little Tailor, but she made sure she did not muss her skirt or dirty her skirt or show anything she shouldn't. Now and then she wriggled her panties, but otherwise she was motionless, and all she really did was listen. An ant crept up her arm. Carefully she flicked the ant away, and she hoped she hadn't injured it. She watched it crawl into a crack in the patio's brick floor, and it did not appear to be in particular distress.

Cat spoke of milk, and Bear spoke of honey, and
Bonnie spoke of the Nashville sound. Victoria breathed
odors of earth. They were heavy and brown. They
caught at her nostrils, and they nearly made her
sneeze. She plumped Bear's pillow for him, and he
thanked her. Both Rabbit and Cat agreed that Bear's
eyepatch was a work of art. And Pluto said: Art
who? And Rabbit said: That's about as funny as a
wart in a bowl of peas. And Victoria said: "All right,
everyone. Let's not fuss." And then Victoria breathed
with her mouth open, and she listened to the quick
uneven sound of her father's typewriter. She heard
the telephone ring. The sound of the typewriter
stopped. She supposed the call had something to do
with church business. People were forever telephoning
her father about church business. She asked Bear
whether he was receiving enough comfort. He assured her he had never received so much comfort
in his life. He told her it had been a very long time
since his pillow had been plumped for him. Nothing
sets me up better than having my pillow plumped for
me, he said. A fellow who has a plumped pillow
can't hardly ask for much more. Victoria nodded.
She told him it was nice he was properly appreciative.
She unfolded herself from the bench, went to Bear,
squatted over him and tucked his blanket a little
more firmly around his shoulders and his arms. Her
father came out onto the patio. He was frowning,
and his chest was moving in and out, and the OH,
GOD! on his T-shirt became OH, GO, and then
O OD, then G D! He went to Victoria and stood
over her and said: It has come to my attention that
yesterday you told your teacher her grandmother
sucked canal water through a sieve.

33   Wishes

VICTORIA WISHED she was a lima bean. She wished she was a black person. She wished she was a forsythia bush. She wished she was in the land of cotton. She wished she was a frog. She wished she was a trumpet. She wished she was invisible. She wished she was a garage, a television aerial, a doily, a cheese sandwich, a brassiere, a cup of coffee. She wished she was Rapunzel, Bambi, Cinderella, Snow White, Heidi, Minnie Mouse. She wished she was old and bald and withered and dying and sad. But she was none of those things. She was Victoria Anne Tabor, which was too bad, since this was not really the time to be Victoria Anne Tabor.

34 ₰ Interrogation

VICTORIA PATTED Bear's blanket, then straightened and faced her father. Her left knee popped. She rubbed it.

Well? said her father.

"I said straw."

What?

"I, um, I said *leaky* straw."

Oh, is that so?

Victoria nodded. "It's bad enough to suck canal water through a leaky straw," she said. "Wouldn't it be even worse to suck it through a sieve?"

I just had a telephone call from your principal, Mrs Bee. She and your teacher are on their way over here. She says your teacher is very upset.

"Oh?"

She says your teacher can't understand why you said what you said.

"I was, um, angry."

Angry with your teacher?

Victoria nodded.

Her father placed his hands on his hips. Mrs Bee spoke of a class project, he said. She told me you refused to participate.

Victoria nodded.

Just who do you think you are to refuse to participate? said Victoria's father.

Victoria shrugged.

And have your mother and I taught you to insult your teacher?

"No," said Victoria.

Do you think it's *smart* to insult your teacher?

"No," said Victoria.

Mrs Bee said your teacher was up all night. She said your teacher even *cried*. She said the class project had been very important to your teacher.

"Cried? Miss Platt cried?"

Platt? Is that her name? Well, she cried.

"She shouldn't have cried. She's too old to cry. A person should cry only when something hurts . . . a bitten tongue, something like *that*."

I don't know what I'm going to do with you.

"Pardon?" said Victoria.

I don't care what the provocation was. You had no right upsetting that woman. There is such a thing as respect. There is such a thing as good manners. It doesn't matter how wrong she was.

"It doesn't?" said Victoria.

You have to get out of your dream world. You have to understand how *other* people feel. You can't spend your whole life talking to dolls and that Teddy.

"His name is *Bear*," said Victoria.

Well, I don't care if it's Algernon Charles Swinburne. You're going to have to learn that you can't isolate yourself from reality the way you do.

Victoria was silent.

Do you understand me? said her father.

Victoria blinked down at her shoes.

You're not *hiding* from me by not *looking* at me, said her father. They're coming over here, both of them, and you're going to have to look up when they arrive. And you're going to have to apologize. It doesn't matter what your justification was, or what you *thought* it was. You upset those women very much. Or at least you upset one of them very much . . . your Miss Pratt.

"*Platt*," said Victoria, murmuring. "Her name is Winifred *Platt*."

I met her at Parents' Night, didn't I?
Victoria looked up, nodded.
A skinny woman, correct?
Victoria nodded.
As I recall, she wore a short skirt.
"Probably," said Victoria. "She usually wears short skirts."
But it doesn't matter what she wears, said Victoria's father.
Victoria exhaled.
The apology must be rendered, said Victoria's father, and that's all there is to it.
Victoria glanced toward Bear, and he was motionless in his little bed.
No sense looking at that thing, said Victoria's father. It won't help you. It won't utter so much as a peep.
Covering her mouth, Victoria coughed.
But it interests me that you looked at the thing, said her father. It backs up what I've been trying to say to you.
"Pardon?" said Victoria.
No one really lives alone. Not even you.
"Pardon?" said Victoria.
And who would *want* to live alone? said her father.
"I try so I don't bother anybody," said Victoria.
Her father paid no attention to her words. He said: You and your *friends*. Your conversations with them. Your concern for them. That bear there, the way you carried on when his eye came out. Oh, ah, hey now, he's . . . is that an *eyepatch* I see on him?
"Yes," said Victoria.
He looks very comfortable.
"He says he *is* very comfortable."
Is he angry with me because of the eye?
"He hasn't said."
But he *is* talking? taking nourishment?
"Yes," said Victoria.

Well, that just goes to show you.

"Pardon?" said Victoria.

It just goes to bear out what I've been saying, said Victoria's father.

Victoria again seated herself on the bench. She scrunched up her legs, and at the same time she tugged down her skirt. She crossed her legs, and again she was The Brave Little Tailor.

Her father tried to smile. His voice was pallid, lame: I made a little pun. *Bear* out. Not much of a pun, I'll grant you.

Victoria said nothing. She figured there wasn't anything she really *had* to say.

Her father cleared his throat. He rubbed his hands across his shirtfront, pressing his palms against George Burns' cheeks and nose and mouth. He said: Well, never mind *that*. I . . . ah, Victoria, listen to me. I don't mean to sound cruel about any of this, but you're just going to have to learn to *cooperate*. That is a hard and I suppose a distressing truth. But you see, none of us is an island.

Victoria nodded.

Do you agree? said her father.

Victoria shrugged.

If you agree, said her father, why were you rude to your teacher?

Victoria looked away from her father. She was aware of all her dolls and animals staring at her. She especially was aware of Bear staring at her—with his one good eye. Perhaps he could call to her and suggest what she should do. And just think how flabbergasted her father would be if Bear spoke up! Or if any of them spoke up! But Bear was silent. They all were silent. Victoria almost always loved silence, but this was one time she did not love it. She listened for a moment to leaves. Somewhere someone slammed a door. She swallowed, and she listened to her throat.

Never before had she listened to her *throat*. Never before in her *life*.

Please answer me, said her father. And please *look* at me.

Victoria looked at her father. She formed an *o*.

When you nodded, said her father, it indicated to me that you agreed with me. But then you shrugged. Perhaps you were trying to shrug it all away. Perhaps you do not agree with me after all. Which means perhaps you do not believe you were rude. Which means perhaps you think it's all right to say terrible things to your teacher.

Victoria made dry sounds against the roof of her mouth, but no words were formed. She curled back her tongue and rubbed the roof of her mouth, but still no words were formed.

When we get to a certain age, said her father, we have to make compromises. Right now you think the world's at your feet, don't you? Well, it's not. It never has been, and it never will be. It doesn't matter whether a person is Caesar or Napoleon or Queen Elizabeth or Winston Churchill or Jimmy Carter or, ah, Farrah Fawcettwhatshername, the planet cannot really be conquered. This means the aim of the truly intelligent person must be to *abide*, to *understand*, to *accept* the *knowledge* that everything cannot be retained . . . all the elements of freedom, I mean.

Victoria frowned.

I don't care how *beautiful* or *brilliant* or, ah, *charismatic* you are, said her father. You must from time to time make concessions.

Victoria rubbed at her eyes with her thumbs. Then, and she hadn't felt it coming, she yawned.

All right, said her father. That does it.

Victoria blinked, and her eyes were hot.

Her father looked around. He made an abrupt movement with an arm. I want you to clear your, your *friends* . . . all this *junk* . . . off the patio, he said.

I want you to take it all up to your room, and I want you to *stay* in your room until I give you permission to come out. You have been rude to your teacher, and now you have been rude to me.

Victoria managed to speak: "Daddy, I didn't mean to—"

I don't *care* what you meant. It doesn't *matter* what you meant. It's what you *did*.

"But all I did was yawn. It snuck up on me."

Sneaked.

"Pardon?"

It *sneaked* up on you. If you insist on being rude, that's one thing. But there's no need for you to assassinate the English language as well.

"Oh," said Victoria.

Bad little girl, said her father.

Victoria moistened her lips. She swiped at her mouth. She almost wanted to spit. (*Bad little girl,* her father had said. *Bad little girl.* His voice had been the voice of a man addressing a naughty pet—a dog probably, a dog that had made bad on an expensive rug.)

Get cracking, said Victoria's father. He strode back toward the house. He paused, glared at Victoria over a shoulder. *Now,* he said.

Victoria nodded. She came off the bench and went to work gathering up her friends.

When her father entered the house, he took care to slam the kitchen door behind himself.

Victoria winced.

35 ᝈ Exile

TENDERLY VICTORIA gathered up Marybeth and Bonnie and Bear (the little doll bed and all), and she
carried them back upstairs to her room. They told
her to pay no attention to what her father had said.
A man can be real mean sometimes of a morning, said
Bonnie. It has to do with the side of the bed he gets
up out of, said Marybeth. Or perhaps he's having
trouble formulating a coherent sermon, said Bear.
Victoria nodded. She told her friends she appreciated
their concern. She placed Bear's little doll bed at the
head of her own bed. She placed his little doll bed
right up on her pillows. Ah *hah*, he said, I feel like a
regular King of the Mountain. Victoria smiled. She
placed Marybeth and Bonnie next to Bear's bed, and
she whispered to them to chat with him, tell him
jokes and in general do anything they could to distract him from the pain he no doubt still was experiencing. She returned to the patio several times to
fetch the rest of her dolls and animals. Then she
replaced the patio chairs where she had found them.
She was in enough trouble, and she really didn't want
to add to it because of carelessness with patio chairs,
for goodness' sake. Back upstairs in her room, she sat
on the bed and arranged all her dolls and animals
and whatnot in a tight semicircle around herself.
She sat with her back against the headboard. She
had removed her shoes. She did not want to dirty the

bedspread. The sound of her father's typing had resumed.

She did not know where Mrs Bee and Miss Platt lived, and so she had no idea how long it would be before they arrived. Don't be afraid, said Cat to Victoria. You're in the right, said Rabbit to Victoria. The issue is clear, said Bear to Victoria. And Victoria nodded. And she assured everyone she would be just fine. But her chest felt as though something damp and lumpish had come up from her belly. The semicircle of her friends was a comfort, though. She felt good about all of them. She even felt good about poor undemonstrative Henry the soap fish. She patted him and said to him: "You didn't want to, um, *dissolve*, did you?" He did not reply, but this didn't really bother Victoria, since she seldom heard a syllable out of him from one week to the next. She tried to smile, and perhaps she was successful, but she did not know. All she *did* know was that the moist and lumpish thing gave no sign of breaking apart. It was about as much fun as a graveyard on a rainy afternoon. Blisters on the tongue. Sour cottage cheese, watery and gray. Quickly Victoria shook her head. She looked at her friends and said: "If I'm very brave, then I'll be fine." She bent over Bear and moved his head up and down. She took care not to touch his eyepatch or his frayed ear. But make sure you don't let it all inflate itself out of proportion, he said. It's a matter of principle, and none of us wants you to retreat. On the other hand, though, we don't want you to be damaged. So please remember that. You are the best friend we've ever had, and you are the best friend we ever hope to have, and we can't afford to lose you. And Victoria said: "Lose me?" And Bear said: The possibility always exists that you will be too, um, *steadfast*—in which case your father might forcibly remove us from you. Better, ah, bedfast than too steadfast, I always say. And Victoria

said: "Pardon?" And Bear said: Pay no attention to
me. I do believe I am hallucinating. And Victoria
said: "Well, I *guess*." Bear chuckled, and Victoria
helped him shake his head in a more or less exasperated manner. Gentle laughter came from many
of the dolls and animals. Victoria nodded, and she
knew she never would betray any of them. If this
required being steadfast until the clocks all melted,
then she would be steadfast until the clocks all melted,
and that was all there was *to* it. She folded her arms
across her chest. She tucked her feet under her buttocks. She made a tight face. That was all there was
to it, amen and period. Her hands tightened into
fists, and the fists pressed against her ribs. Then she
was aware that the sound of her father's typewriter
had given way to silence. Either he had finished his
sermon or he was stuck. *Or* he was so upset with
Victoria that he could not concentrate. She certainly
hoped it wasn't that. She didn't believe he had ever
been *that* upset with her. Oh, boy, if he was, she
surely was in for it. Grimacing, she rubbed her
knuckles against the sides of her ribs. Her dolls and
animals made murmurous comforting sounds, but she
was unable to concentrate on them. Words probably
were involved, but she could not make them out. She
felt herself begin to shake and gasp a little. She shook
her head and she told herself: *No. Stop this.* She
heard the station wagon pull into the driveway, and
then she heard her father walk into the kitchen. And
then she heard her father's voice. And then she heard
her mother's voice. And then she heard her mother
say: *Whaaat?* And then she heard a sound of what
might have been laughter. It was quite loud, and it
came from her mother. Maybe her mother wasn't
taking any of this very seriously. Maybe her mother
would intercept Mrs Bee and Miss Platt at the front
door and tell them to go away. Victoria looked at
Bear, and he must have been reading her mind, for

he said: I don't believe that's likely. When push comes to shove, your mother almost always goes along with your father, and you know it. And Victoria nodded. She did know it.

She pressed her teeth together, and she was able to do away with the shaking and the gasping. She closed her eyes, and she tried to think of palm trees and snow angels and pink mints. She tried to think of ribbons and jewels and Droids. She tried to think of laughter, of bravery. She tried to think of clouds, summer clouds, high and majestic clouds, clouds that were softer and puffier than her father's Gillette Foamy. She swallowed something that perhaps was sand. She had meant no *harm*. She had done nothing except take advantage of an option. But then a promise had been broken, and she had been hassled over that broken promise (as though it had been *her* promise and *she* had done the breaking), and finally her outrage had been too much for her, and she had made a public announcement of Miss Platt's grandmother's awful secret. There really was nothing more to it than that, and so why was the world coming to an end?

Victoria unfolded her arms. Her fists flew up and pressed themselves against her eyes, and she saw detonations of red, purple, green, blue. Her dolls and animals persisted with their murmurous comforting sounds. Now the voices of her mother and father were coming from the front room, and her father's voice was wintry and abrupt. Victoria rubbed her eyes, and she swallowed more of the sand or whatever it was. Then she distinctly heard the front doorbell ring. She groaned aloud. Steady now, said Bear. She looked at Bear. He said: Hang in there. Do whatever it is you have to do—only don't forget us. Victoria nodded. Now more voices drifted up from the front room, and she was able to recognize Mrs Bee's and

Miss Platt's. Then came the inevitable footsteps on the stairs. Her father opened her bedroom door without knocking. All right, he said. It's time for you to come downstairs.

36 ⟨🕭⟩ Surrender

MRS BEE AND MISS PLATT sat next to each other on
the sofa. Victoria's father led her into the room and
told her to sit in a hardbacked chair across the room
from the sofa. Victoria's mother was making hurried
noises in the kitchen, which meant she probably was
fixing something for the visitors. Mrs Bee wore dark
slacks and what appeared to be an Indian sweater.
It was white with zagging blue stripes. She patted her
streaked hair, and she tried to smile at Victoria. Miss
Platt, though, did not even look at Victoria. Victoria's
mother came into the room. She was carrying a tray,
and it held a pot of coffee, four cups, four spoons, a
cream pitcher and a sugar bowl. She poured coffee
for Mrs Bee and Miss Platt and her husband and
herself, and it turned out everyone opted for black
coffee. She smiled, ran her tongue over her lips, said
something to the effect that this surely was a hardy
crew. Victoria briefly thought of the Hardy Boys
television show, and at the same time she wondered
how long it would take everyone to get down to
the business at hand. She glanced at her father, and
he was staring at Miss Platt's legs. Miss Platt was, of
course, wearing one of her pleated miniskirts, and it
had worked itself up so high that she almost appeared
to be wearing no skirt at all. But she evidently was
not aware of Victoria's father's stare. She sipped at
her coffee, and she wriggled a little. Her eyes were
moist. She rubbed a pointed elbow. Mrs Bee patted

Miss Platt's lap, but Miss Platt appeared not to notice. Victoria's father stood in front of the mantel and frowned at Mrs Bee and Miss Platt, then folded his arms across his OH, GOD! chest. His arms were large, and so both the words and George Burns vanished from view. Victoria's mother brought him a cup of coffee, and then she stood with him there in front of the mantel. Victoria scrootched forward and hugged her knees. Her father shifted his weight forward and sipped at his coffee. Then, grimacing a little, he looked directly at Miss Platt (her face, not her legs) and said: For myself, Miss Pratt, I apologize. I leave it to Victoria to do her own apologizing.

Platt, said Miss Platt.

I beg your pardon? said Victoria's father.

My name is Winifred *Platt*, said Miss Platt. All my life I have been called Pratt. I believe some people even think it's funny. By that I mean, I often get the distinct impression it's an accidental on purpose sort of mistake.

Victoria's father placed his cup of coffee on the mantel. He again folded his arms across his chest. He said: I apologize, Miss Platt. But I assure you I was not trying to be funny.

He has trouble knowing how, said Victoria's mother.

What? said Victoria's father, frowning.

Oh, said Victoria's mother. Sorry.

Which means I now have apologized twice to you, said Victoria's father to Miss Platt. Nothing like getting off to the right sort of start, I always say.

Victoria squirmed, rubbed her lower lips with her tongue. She tugged at her skirt, and then she pressed a knee with a palm.

Mrs Bee again patted Miss Platt's lap. Winifred and I were up all night, she said to Victoria's father, and so we're both more than a little tired. I really regret that we had to come barging over here on a Saturday, but a resolution is needed. Yesterday I thought I had found one, but I was wrong.

Oh? said Victoria's father.

Mrs Bee glanced at Miss Platt.

You explain it, said Miss Platt to Mrs Bee.

Ah, all right, said Mrs Bee, nodding. Then, to Victoria's father: You see, Mr Tabor, there is a certain degree of ambiguity here. Myself, as principal *and* as Winifred's friend, I have had serious reservations about her race.

Her race? said Victoria's father.

She doesn't mean my race, said Miss Platt to Victoria's father, in the sense of flesh pigmentation. She means my race in the sense of having the children run back and forth across the schoolyard.

Oh, said Victoria's father.

That was more or less explained to you over the telephone, wasn't it? said Miss Platt.

Yes, said Victoria's father.

Competitiveness is the nature of mankind, said Miss Platt.

Humankind, said Victoria's father, swallowing wetly. All right. Yes. Humankind. Hostility. Aggressions.

Yes, said Miss Platt. Exactly.

You believe conflict makes the world go around, said Victoria's father.

Yes, said Miss Platt. Don't you?

I suppose, said Victoria's father, shrugging a little.

Victoria's mother looked at him and said: Carl, don't you think we ought to get *on* with it? There's a lot here I, for one, need to understand. It wasn't fifteen minutes ago that I came home with my arms full of groceries, and you told me these ladies were upset with Victoria, so upset that they had to come over on a Saturday morning.

It is Winifred who is upset, said Mrs Bee. Myself,

I am hardly upset at all, even though there *is* a rather significant moral issue involved.

Which is? said Victoria's mother.

Miss Platt broke in. It's respect, she said. It's decency.

Oh, said Victoria's mother.

You, as a *minister*, should be able to understand that, said Miss Platt to Victoria's father.

But I'll have to have more of an explanation, said Victoria's father.

Miss Platt started to speak, but Mrs Bee interrupted, saying: Winifred, let me tell it. The thing needs a reasonably disinterested description. Otherwise, it becomes unutterably absurd.

Ab . . . absurd? said Miss Platt.

Yes, said Mrs Bee. And you know I wouldn't lie to you. I am your closest friend in the entire world.

I know, said Miss Platt to Mrs Bee.

Victoria looked around the room. She rubbed at her mouth with a fist.

Mrs Bee leaned forward and resumed speaking to Victoria's father. Every year, said Mrs Bee to Victoria's father, Winifred has her little thirdgraders run races that to her have enormous symbolic importance. For some reason, she sees nine as being a very important year for them, a year when certain *truths* must be opened to them. Don't ask me why she picks nine as being such a magic age. Perhaps it is because she teaches the third grade. Perhaps it is *that* simple. I don't know.

It's just that they're old enough, said Miss Platt to Mrs Bee.

And you're the judge, said Mrs Bee to Miss Platt.

Well, *someone* has to take the initiative, said Miss Platt.

Good for you, said Mrs Bee.

Whose side are you on? said Miss Platt. Are you

on this little girl's side, even after what she said to me?

I'm not on anybody's side, Winifred, said Mrs Bee. I'm only trying to get this *thing* resolved.

Victoria made a squealing noise. She formed an *o*. Everyone looked at her.

Is there something you want to add to the conversation? said her mother.

Victoria looked away from all of them.

Silence.

Victoria rolled her tongue against the *o*, but she said nothing.

Mrs Bee was the one who finally spoke. Mr Tabor, she said, I think we'd better get back to the main thrust of all this.

Victoria glanced at the ceiling. She glanced at the floor, her feet, her knees. The moist and lumpish thing had begun to harden in her chest, and she felt a little sick to her stomach.

Mrs Bee continued: Winifred calls what she tries to do with the races a pursuit of excellence. She hearkens back to John F. Kennedy. He meant a great deal to her. She remembers Camelot as though it were yesterday. It is all *very* serious to her, and I respect that, don't you? I mean, there would appear to be so little genuine *belief* in the world these cynical days that it's refreshing to encounter a person such as Winifred. She *cares*, and I do believe that amounts to something. From time to time she becomes, I suppose, a little *overly enthusiastic*—

Miss Platt spoke up. Nadine, she said, how can a person be *overly* enthusiastic when she is right?

Mrs Bee looked at Miss Platt and said: Before we left home, didn't we agree on something?

Yes, said Miss Platt.

And what was it? said Mrs Bee.

That you would do the talking, said Miss Platt.

You gave me your word, didn't you?

Yes.

It means something, doesn't it?

Yes.

All *right* then, said Mrs Bee to Miss Platt. Then please let me continue.

Miss Platt nodded.

Thank you, said Mrs Bee to Miss Platt. Then Mrs Bee again turned her attention to Victoria's father. She said: Yesterday, after Victoria made that remark about the . . . the canal water, and Winifred here brought her to my office, I tried to work out a compromise—or at least a standoff. After all, in large measure that is why school principals have been put on this earth, to work out compromises and standoffs so that some sort of order may be retained and that thing we call the *educational process* may be, um, protected. My idea was that Winifred here would admit she had been unreasonable, while at the same time your Victoria here would apologize. After all, Winifred *had* made the races optional, and so Victoria *was* within her rights in refusing to participate.

Victoria's mother interrupted. So what's the big problem? she wanted to know. She crossed to an ottoman and seated herself. She sipped at her coffee, and she blinked up at Mrs Bee.

Sandra, *please*, said Victoria's father. I want to hear the rest of what Mrs Bee here has to say.

There's really not all that much, said Mrs Bee to Victoria's father. In my opinion, Winifred was wrong in scolding Victoria for not participating in a thing that was optional. On the other hand, though, I think Victoria's remark was uncalled for, to say the least.

Rude? said Victoria's father. I mean, rude as well?

Yes, said Mrs Bee.

Now let me get this straight, said Victoria's mother to Mrs Bee. Is this such a profound question that you have to resolve it on a Saturday morning by coming over here and behaving as though it's the worst emergency since the Cuban missile crisis?

I'm afraid so, said Mrs Bee.

But why? said Victoria's mother.

I want to answer that, said Miss Platt to Mrs Bee.

All right, said Mrs Bee.

I know we agreed that you would do all the talking, but this is one thing *I* want to explain.

All right, Winifred. The floor is yours. But please try not to become too emotional.

Miss Platt nodded. A moustache of perspiration had formed a thin arc above her mouth. She wiped at it with a finger, and then for a moment she absently licked the finger. She tried to smile at Victoria's father. She said: Mr Tabor, I shall try with all my might and main not to be emotional. When Nadine telephoned you this morning and gave you an outline of what happened yesterday at school, it is my understanding that you told her you would see to it that your Victoria apologized. All right then, that is what I want. I want to hear her apology. I want her to stand in front of me and admit she was disrespectful and tell me she is sorry. I am fortyfour years of age, Mr Tabor, and oh, yes, I know, most women are reluctant to admit their age, but *I* am not *most women*. I am *Winifred Kathleen Platt*, and I hate to seem immodest, but I am a fine and dedicated teacher. The talent I have is very real, demonstrably so. I come from a family of teachers. I have three sisters who are teachers, and my mother retired only four years ago after some forty years of teaching in the school system of Waverly, Ohio, which is down on the Scioto River a little north of Portsmouth. It would be fair, then, to say that I was reared in an academic atmosphere, wouldn't you admit? Mama rushing home, fixing supper, then laboring at the diningroom table over papers that had to be graded, over lesson plans and activity programs. Our father died of a

coronary thrombosis when Mabel, the youngest of my sisters, was only three, and Mother was both mother and father to us from then on. She was strict, yes (remember strictness? remember when there were standards of behavior that we all obeyed without *debating* over them or insisting that others *persuade* us?), but there was never anything less than a profound love and sense of community in our home. And so it was only natural and logical that my sisters and I became teachers. I am the oldest and the only one who never married, and Mother and my sisters insist I am the most dedicated, but I don't see where there's any sort of yardstick that can measure the comparative dedication of the four Platt girls and their mother. My sisters have fourteen children among them (and believe me, Christmas shopping just about *demolishes* my poor little schoolteacher bank account), but they all are still teaching, come children, come war, come pestilence (so to speak), and so who is to say that I am the most dedicated? *I* never would claim such a thing for myself, and anyway, what does it matter, as long as we all are doing the best we can? I was graduated with honors from Waverly High School. I received my BS in education from Ohio University, and I received my master's from what used to be known as Western Reserve, and I have been teaching in the Shaker Heights system since the fall of 1957. In that time I have never missed a day of class. And I have never failed to prepare a lesson plan. In other words, Mr Tabor, I have never faked it. I have never given the children anything less than my best efforts and my undivided attention. When I was younger, I had many opportunities to go out dancing and drinking and partying, but would the dancing and the drinking and the partying have been fair to the children? I would say to myself: Winifred, where does your primary responsibility lie? And the answer was clear, which meant the dancing and the drinking and the partying were placed on the back burner, so to speak. And I *am* human, Mr. Tabor. My rejection of most social activity has not been without a certain degree of discomfort, as I am sure you must understand. *But that's all right. I'm not complaining.* Winifred Platt is not a complainer, or at least most of the time she is not a complainer. At the same time, though, I do believe I am entitled to at least a minimum of respect. So therefore, when I am *publicly humiliated* by a *child*, I am *hurt*. Nadine here actually tried to work out *two* compromises yesterday. First she wanted both myself and your daughter to apologize. Which didn't work. For one thing, your daughter was stubborn. For another, I saw no reason why I should apologize for doing my job. Then Nadine came up with the notion that oh, well, since both your daughter and I (in *Nadine's* opinion) had been wrong, then our mutual wrongness sort of cancelled itself out. Well, I didn't buy *that*, either. I am a teacher, and respect must be forthcoming or the entire structure will topple, wouldn't you say? So an impasse was reached, but it is an impasse that must be resolved. And the resolution is obvious, isn't it, Mr Tabor? When you talked with Nadine on the telephone, you *understood* it was necessary that Victoria apologize. And you've said so right in this room. But then just a little while ago you said you needed more explanation. *More explanation?* Of what, Mr Tabor? I am a trained, qualified teacher, and I am respected by my peers, and I have spent nearly half my life attempting to provide knowledge, and perhaps even a bit of wisdom, to little ones whom I honestly love. And I have attempted to introduce them to the real world, using various means, including the running of the races. And in all those years they have at least respected me to the extent of going along with me. Until yesterday. Until your Victoria stood off to one side and refused to participate and *then* became rude and vulgar, and in so doing embarrassed me. So I ask you—isn't it understandable why I am upset? Can you imagine the hours I have put in? the days? the *years?* Do you think I have no knowledge of the world? Do you think I am *incorrect* when I say the world is a race that is won by those who must at all times be zealous and unflagging in their pursuit of excellence? All I sought was a demonstration, and would it have *killed* your Victoria to have participated? What am I? some cardboard caricature? some ridiculous *travesty* embodying all that is pompous and absurd in the educational process? Well, *I* say I am not. I may not be brilliant, but I am *serviceable,* and I am a *human being,* and I . . . and I deserve a minimum of . . . oh, you know . . . a minimum of *consideration* . . .

Now, *now,* said Mrs Bee to Miss Platt.

Miss Platt's words had faded away, and she was pressing her cheeks with her palms. She moaned.

Victoria's father looked at Victoria and said: Do you feel proud of yourself? Isn't it good to know the rewards that can be brought by a little straightforward lack of manners and respect?

Mrs Bee embraced Miss Platt, and Miss Platt wept.

"No," said Victoria. It wasn't clear to whom she was speaking, and not even she really knew.

Mrs Bee and Miss Platt came apart, and they looked at her. Her father looked at her. Her mother looked at her. Miss Platt snuffled, swallowed.

"No," said Victoria.

What's . . . what's that supposed to mean? said her father.

Victoria began to shake, and the sickness in her stomach began to roll and boil. And now the thing in her chest was like a boulder.

Victoria? said her mother. What's wrong?

"*No,*" said Victoria, and she embraced herself.

You're still saying no—is that it? said her father.

"*No,*" said Victoria, and she belched.

I think perhaps she is a little ill, said Mrs Bee to no one in particular.

She can join the club, said Miss Platt.

Now, Winifred, said Mrs Bee.

Well, how do you think *I* feel? said Miss Platt. Up all night. Wondering, wondering. Feeling the pain that comes from doubt. I mean, suppose she sets an example, and suppose from now on—

"*No*," said Victoria, and tears squirted from her eyes, and she blinked at Miss Platt, and she said: "I'm . . . I'm sorry . . . I was wrong . . . I don't hate you . . . you're a good teacher . . . you're a *real* good teacher."

Victoria's mother went to her, knelt next to her chair and hugged her.

Weeping, Victoria pressed shut her eyes. Her stomach was full of canal water and worms and dead mice.

You'll be a good girl in school from now on? said her father.

Victoria pressed her face against her mother's belly and nodded.

Do you understand that you can't exist just for yourself? said Victoria's father.

Victoria nodded.

People are more more important than *dolls* and *stuffed animals*, aren't they? said Victoria's father.

Victoria nodded. She heard juices gurgle in her mother's belly.

So do you promise from now on to confront the real world and not escape it by conducting a lot of nonsensical conversations with things that don't exist? said her father.

Victoria nodded.

Good, said her father.

Well, Winifred, are you satisfied? said Mrs Bee.

Yes, said Miss Platt. All I want is respect. If I was

wrong about my races, that is *one* thing. But lack of respect is *another*, and I—

Wailing, Victoria began vomiting against her mother's belly. Her mother sprang back, and so Victoria vomited on the rug, spraying her legs and shoes in the bargain.

37 ～ Grief

SHE SAW MEN with axes, and they laughed at her.
She saw men who carried great blunt hammers, and
they told her she was stupid. Scrawny old women
plucked at all her dresses, tearing them. Undertakers
arrived, and they happily chatted over tubes and
bottles. She lay in her bed, and she felt as though
her throat had been shredded with a hot knife. The
covers were up to her neck, and her dolls and her
animals all had been knocked to the floor. Her father
spoke to her. Victoria, look, he said, I don't mean
to be cruel. Please believe that. On the other hand,
though, maybe today you've learned something about
the limits of privacy. Your mother and I aren't about
to live forever, and *then*, after we are Gone, will be
time enough for you to be alone. Victoria turned her
head away from her father. She closed her eyes. The
men with axes began breaking furniture. Her mother
asked her whether she would like a sip or two of
bouillon. She shook her head no. She opened her eyes.
She supposed beginning Monday she would have to
seek out *friends*. Martha Bemis, who had a voice that
sounded like scissors and waxed paper. Barbara Israel,
who read poems and liked to tear off her thumbnails.
Nancy Reeves, who giggled a lot and was able to hit
a softball farther than most of the boys could. Mary
Schoen, who had pierced ears and whose father was
vice president of a bank. Melissa Williams, whose
family owned three German shepherds and who there-

fore always gave off an emanation of Fur and Doggy
Poop. Now Victoria would have to choose among
them and the other girls in Miss Platt's room for
friends . . . girls with whom she could giggle and
run. She supposed today she had reached a center
point of the sort Grandpa Bird had described. An
accident had changed his life, and now an angry remark about canal water had changed hers. Otherwise,
why had she thrown up? Why were those men
swinging their axes? And why were the other men
swinging their great blunt hammers? Why were the
old women tearing all her dresses, and why were the
undertakers having such a good time? The next time
she saw Grandpa Bird, she would have to tell him
yes, life *was* governed by center points, melodramatic
events that forever changed a person, shaping his or
her life. All that other talk . . . about *breath* and *days*
and whatever . . . was incorrect. Huh. What a life.
She supposed it now would be necessary for her to
begin wearing jeans and T-shirts from time to time.
She shuddered. Her throat was as sour as it was hot.
Mrs Bee and Miss Platt had left no more than five
minutes after the vomiting. Mrs Bee had said something to Victoria about not taking it so hard, but
Victoria had not been able to reply. Which probably
was just as well. After all, what would Victoria have
been able to say? That it didn't matter? Well, it *did*
matter. Nothing in her life had ever mattered more.
A person just could not escape *fellowship* and *cooperation* and *going along*, and it apparently didn't
matter that a promise had been pushed aside like a
pile of old gum wrappers. The way of the world was
the way of the world, and those who didn't *go along*
barfed all over their shoes and their legs and the rug,
not to mention their mother's stomachs. And so a
Miss Platt would weep, and the weeping of a Miss
Platt would bring the most terrible sorrow (since
weeping was not right, since weeping created a sound

that curled the belly), and the terrible sorrow would cause a Victoria Anne Tabor to weep, to fall apart, to hug her mother, to apologize, to barf. And so now the tension was gone. Only exhaustion remained— and the sounds of the happy wreckers and tearers and undertakers. All that remained was for Victoria Anne Tabor to do those final things that would enable her forever to change her ways. They would involve destruction. No, they would involve death. Burial. Farewell. Grimacing, Victoria sat up a little. She was able to see the floor at the foot of the bed. Her dolls and animals were scattered on the rug. She covered her mouth. She rubbed her eyes. Bear had toppled from his little bed. Marybeth lay on her back with her legs in the air, and her crotch was exposed. Cat lay across Rabbit, and one of Cat's wheels rested against Rabbit's throat. Henry the soap fish had lost his tail, and there was a hole in one of Kermit's flippers. Victoria's father had thrown back the covers with a sort of exasperated grunt after carrying her to bed, and all the dolls and animals had gone flying. The men with the axes embraced the men with the hammers. The old women whooped and hollered with the undertakers. Victoria's father and mother were both out of the room, and she could have whispered to her friends, but they no longer could be her friends. She had given her word, and she would see to it that her word would be better than Miss Platt's had been. She made an *o*. She lay back. She tried not to listen to the happy sounds of the people who were smashing and pulling apart all her rooms and dreams and loving memories, but she could not do that. She would have had to have been deaf. Perhaps she would have had to have been more than deaf. Perhaps she would have had to have been dead.

38 ❦ Farewell

VICTORIA LAY IN BED all day long, and finally she did accept a cup of bouillon from her mother, who told her she genuinely regretted the way things had turned out. I think I know how you're feeling, said Sandra Tabor, and I know it can't be easy. Victoria sipped at her bouillon but said nothing. So her mother knew how she was feeling. Victoria had wept, and she had thrown up, and her friends were scattered all across the floor, and her mother knew how she was feeling. Well, goody goody gumdrops, how observant her mother was. The bouillon had a chicken base, and it was too hot, and it rubbed harshly against Victoria's throat. But she did not complain. She held the little cup with both hands, and she sipped, and at least the warmth of the cup was pleasant against her palms. The wreckers had finished their work, and all her secret rooms were gone. She finished the bouillon, handed the cup to her mother, then dug at her eyes with her forefingers. She twisted her forefingers, and she held her breath for a moment, and after a time she said: "I'll be a different person now forever, won't I?" She stopped fussing with her forefingers. She blinked, and her vision exploded for a moment, all bright and sort of sequined, and then her mother's face came into focus.

Different? said Sandra Tabor, frowning.

Victoria nodded. "And forever," she said.

Ah, well, perhaps so.

"And that'll make you and Daddy happy?"

Yes.

"I don't want to fight with anybody," said Victoria.

We know that, said Sandra Tabor. She was sitting next to the bed, and she would not look directly at Victoria. Instead she looked into the empty bouillon cup.

"I don't want to make anybody *cry*," said Victoria.

We know that, said her mother.

"I won't talk to them anymore," said Victoria. "I mean, I got carried away too much, didn't I?"

By *them*, do you mean your dolls and your little animals?

"Yes," said Victoria.

Well, perhaps yes, perhaps you did get carried away too much, as you put it. Myself, I believe I know how you feel, but I have been, um, overruled.

"I'll be good from now on," said Victoria.

Fine . . .

"Mommy, please don't cry."

Who's . . . who's crying? said Sandra Tabor. She began digging at her own eyes with her own fore fingers, and then she said something about needing a cigarette. She gave Victoria a shaky smile, then stood up and went out of the room without saying anything more.

Victoria pressed her face against a pillow. The boulder was gone from her chest. Her belly was empty. She closed her eyes, and her interior vision was empty. She was as empty as empty could be, and it was a wonder to her that she did not go spinning up to the ceiling, like a balloon or a dry leaf. Her father had not bothered to pick up her dolls and animals. Neither had her mother. Victoria did not really want to think about her dolls and animals. She tried to keep her interior vision empty, but gradually it began to

abound with images of Bear and his eyepatch, Cat
and his stripes, Bonnie and her Dolly Parton hair.
Victoria shook her head. She would have to bid farewell to all of them. It now was necessary that they
be gone from her forever. They were not real
enough. They did not pass muster. Victoria shuddered. Oh, what a big, big center point *this* was. She
thought of Grandpa Bird. She thought of the death
of that Rhoda Masonbrink. If Rhoda Masonbrink had
not died, then Victoria Anne Tabor never would have
lived. The date had been June 4, 1927, and—hey!
Tomorrow would be June 4, *1978!* Victoria opened
her eyes. She frowned. Twentyseven from seventy-
eight was, um, fiftyone. It would be the fiftyfirst,
um, *birthday* of Rhoda Masonbrink's *death*, and it
would be the first day of Victoria's new existence as
a person who *cooperated*, who *went along*, who understood the value of *fellowship*. Surely this was some
sort of sign. Victoria began to breathe in spasms. She
wanted to weep, but all she did was breathe in the
spasms. She tried to imagine that historic senior prom.
She tried to imagine what Rhoda Masonbrink must
have looked like. She tried to imagine what Grandpa
Bird must have looked like . . . young, tall, handsome,
the possessor of two feet. Oh, if Rhoda Masonbrink
had not died, there would have been no Victoria
Anne Tabor here today weeping and apologizing and
barfing, and wouldn't that have been better? And
then no one would have been hurt or bothered, and
Victoria Anne Tabor, who was *selfish*, who thought
only of *herself*, who *refused to run a silly race*, who
hurt her teacher's feelings, who stubbornly formed
o's with her lips and *refused to speak*, who in effect
was telling the world to stay away from her and
not bother her in order that she *dream* and *mope* and
give herself to *false imaginings*, never would have
caused a speck of trouble—on account of she never
would have breathed a drop of air, on account of she

never would have occupied an inch of space, on account of she never would have *existed*. Victoria shook her head in a loose and mournful rhythm. She wanted baths. She wanted cupped palms. She wanted to ride away on flanged wheels. But no, the baths and the cupped palms and the flanged wheels were out. They were just as ridiculous and harmful as the dolls and the animals. Oh, of course she would continue to take baths, but no longer would they help her relax so that her imaginings could remove her from the house and Wrexford Road and Shaker Heights and Ohio and the USA and the world. Baths from now on would be *baths*, and their existence would be confined to the real world everyone seemed to think was so important, a world where people broke their word, a world that punished you when you resisted and showed your displeasure, a world that gave you immense pain when your enemies wept. Victoria wiped some spittle from a corner of her mouth, folded her arms across her chest and decided ah, there was no getting around it; she would have to dispose of her friends as quickly and painlessly as she knew how. Which probably meant burying them. Yes, burying them. Suppressing their voices with earth, sand, rocks, stones, whatever. She would wait until dark. She would wait until beyond dark. She would wait until her parents were asleep, and Shaker Heights was asleep, and the streets had been given over to the chirr and whick of insects, the sounds of new damp leaves moving in the wind. She sat up and scrunched to the foot of the bed and looked down at her friends. No, they were no longer her friends. How could they be her friends when they no longer existed? From now on, her friends would be the likes of Martha Bemis and Barbara Israel and Nancy Reeves. Victoria blinked at Bear and his silly eyepatch. No, no, *no*, he was not *Bear*, he was *a teddybear* . . . and Cat was not *Cat*, he was *a pulltoy* . . . and Marybeth was not

Marybeth, she was *a doll in a fancy dress.* Victoria cleared her throat. She made an *o.* She rocked from side to side. Speaking aloud to herself, she said: "Shame on you, you turkey." She made another *o.* She licked it, but there really was nothing else she needed to say, and so she remained silent. She looked around for Henry's tail, but she could not see it. No, no, *no . . .* he was not *Henry,* he was *a piece of soap.* Victoria grunted. It apparently would take her awhile to adjust her thinking, and she would have to be patient with herself. She sighed. She scrunched back. She knew she would not be able to sleep, but she closed her eyes anyway. She had been asleep perhaps an hour, and she had had vague and misted dreams of remorseful trolls and a certain weeping teacher who *hint hint* almost always wore pleated miniskirts and who may have been related to certain of the trolls, when her mother came into the room and awakened her and sat down next to the bed and said: You'll get over it.

Victoria rubbed her eyes. Had her mother awakened her just to tell her *that?*

I understand how large the change will be, said Victoria's mother.

Victoria said nothing. Her right shoulder had fallen asleep. She busily rubbed away the tingling feeling.

We know you thought you were doing the right thing. And in a sense, of course, you were.

"A sense?" said Victoria.

Well, your teacher *did* go back on her word. But that's not the issue here. Do you understand?

"I . . . I guess so," said Victoria, nodding.

The issue is order. The issue is the acceptance of truth.

Victoria rubbed. She said nothing. She pressed her lips tightly together, and all the color went out of them.

Your father thinks you are angry with him, said Sandra Tabor.

Victoria shrugged.

Suddenly Sandra Tabor smiled. But I know my Victoria, she said, and my Victoria never holds a grudge very long. Inside she's a real softie. I often think she should have been named Victoria Marsh-mallow, the way she is so sweet and sentimental about things.

Still rubbing, Victoria frowned in the direction of the foot of the bed and her fr—*things* that were scattered on the floor.

He wants to talk to you, said Sandra Tabor.

Victoria looked directly at her mother and said: "Well, why doesn't he come in and talk? What does he think I'm going to do? kick him in the rear end?"

Victoria!

Victoria exhaled. She said nothing. She shook her head.

Now you're talking like the canal water girl, said Sandra Tabor.

"Well," said Victoria, "he's talked to me and *talked* to me. I was asleep before you came in here. If I'm talking like the canal water girl, maybe it's because I *am* the canal water girl. I mean, wouldn't that make sense?"

Please. Try to remember I've been on your side all through this.

"Oh," said Victoria. The tingling feeling was gone from her shoulder. "Oh. I didn't know that. I'm sorry."

Sarcasm doesn't fit you too well.

"What?"

It's not your nature.

"What's sarcasm?" said Victoria.

It's . . . it's *being nasty* . . .

"Oh," said Victoria.

Sandra Tabor pressed her hands against the knees

of her slacks. Wouldn't you like to come downstairs for a little while? she said.

"No," said Victoria.

We could have a little talk, just the three of us, and then maybe—

"*No*," said Victoria.

You're being rude again, do you know that? You're being holierthanthou, do you know *that?* You're behaving as though *you* were right and *we* were wrong.

Victoria began to cry.

What? said her mother.

"I'm . . . I'm sorry," said Victoria, "and if you . . . if you want me to change my ways, okay. I'm doing that. But I just don't, um, I just don't want to *talk* about it anymore, with you or Daddy or *anybody*." Victoria pressed her palms against her eyes. Enough had long ago become enough, and why wouldn't her mother and father leave her *be?* She wept dryly, and she made sounds that were like gravel and paper. Her mother tried to embrace her, but she pushed her mother away. Grunting, she managed to say: "Um, tell Daddy I'm, um, I'm not mad at him, but it's just that I . . . it's just that I don't want to talk to him . . . or to you, either, or to *anybody*. I'll be a good girl, I promise you, so please just . . . please just *leave me be*."

You . . . you pushed me away, said Victoria's mother.

Victoria nodded, swallowed, nodded again.

My *word*, said Victoria's mother.

Victoria blinked at her mother and said: "I'm not mad at you."

You *pushed* me *away*.

"I didn't mean . . . I didn't mean anything *bad*."

I've never been pushed away by you before.

"Well, um, before was different. Now is new, and I got to get used to it."

Oh.

"I don't hate you."

Oh.

"I just want you and Daddy to, um, *leave me be.*"

Victoria's mother slowly nodded. She stood up. She shrugged.

"You'll see," said Victoria.

Pardon? said Sandra Tabor.

"I'll make it so everything'll be real nice. I'll wear *jeans*, and I'll make *friends*, and I'll *run* and *skip* and *hop* and *holler*, and you'll be as proud of me as proud can be, and Daddy'll stand up in church some Sunday morning, and he'll tell the world how I've, um, come to know *fellowship*, and—"

That's enough, said Sandra Tabor. *That's just enough.*

Victoria looked away from her mother.

Sandra Tabor went out of the room, and the door slammed shut behind her. Probably right about now she needed a cigarette in the worst possible way, whatever that was.

Nodding, Victoria said aloud: "The canal water girl strikes again." She snuffled. She squirmed out from under the covers and slid from the bed. She felt a little dizzy for a moment, and she had to lean back against the mattress. She closed her eyes, shook her head, wiped away the last traces of her tears. Then, when she opened her eyes, she no longer felt even a little dizzy. She swallowed. She was *Victoria Anne Tabor*, and she was *in control*. She moved to the foot of the bed and scrunched herself down on the floor with all her scattered dolls and animals. She set upright all those that had been overturned, but she said not a word to any of them. And she tried not to look directly at any of them. She looked at the walls. She looked at a curtain, at the closet doorknob, at the dresser. She slid across to the place where Bugs, the operating nightlight, was plugged into the baseboard. She unplugged Bugs. She curled

her fingers around him, and that way she would not
have to look at him. She stood up, walked to the place
where her dolls and animals lay, then hunkered down
and carefully placed Bugs with them. She nodded.
She straightened. She tried to smile, and perhaps she
succeeded. She had not spoken to them. This no doubt
meant a beginning had been made. (And they, of
course, had not spoken to her. She supposed this was
because she had made it so they no longer existed.
From now on it would be Martha Bemis who truly
would exist. And Barbara Israel and Nancy Reeves
and Mary Schoen and Melissa Williams and Darth
Vader and President Carter and trees and trolleycars
and the Wrexford Methodist Church.) Victoria returned to bed. All that remained now was to wait,
and then she would get all these *things*, all this *stuff*,
forever out of her life. She slid herself back under
the covers. She was able to hear her parents' voices
coming up from the front room, but she had no desire
to eavesdrop. She supposed they were *concerned* and
wondering and whatnot. Well, beginning tomorrow,
they would see a different Victoria Anne Tabor. A
Victoria Anne Tabor who would be so cooperative
it would frost their minds. Victoria nodded, sucked
at her lips. She closed her eyes. She would rest them
for awhile. She swallowed, and she was aware that
most of the sour heat was gone from her throat. She
lay flat on her back, and she stretched her legs, and
she felt her bones crack. She grimaced. She was aware
of something gray, soft, puffy, sad. Warm things
closed in on her cracked bones. She hadn't had a bath
tonight, and she missed feeling puckery, and she supposed she didn't smell very good. But then her mother
probably was too upset to preside over a bath tonight.
Victoria wanted to move her arms and push away the
thing that was so gray and soft and puffy and sad,
but there was no strength in her arms. Perhaps their
bones   had   been   cracked   too   severely.   Victoria

breathed so that her cheeks became as puffy as the gray thing. It was almost as though someone were trying to push a pillow over her face. Trolls came to her, and they stared regretfully at her through their squishy eyes, and one of them said to her: *Where will we be able to say we're sorry?* Victoria did not understand what the troll was trying to say, and so she asked it please to clarify its words. And the troll said: *Your dreams received us with benevolent hospitality. There's no one else in the world who has such pleasant dreams. Where else will we find the proper setting so that we can become Bornagain Trolls and occupy our share of The Peaceable Kingdom?* And Victoria made an *o*, and trapped noises moved up and down from her belly to her throat and back again. She wanted to tell the poor trolls that from now on she would be a different person, a *real* person, but how could she explain such a thing to *trolls?* The trolls simply would have to find someone else to grant them forgiveness. Victoria looked around. She saw lions, lambs, chickens, foxes, sheep, kittycats, frogs and squirrels and bears and oxen. She saw a misted river, and she saw a tall gaunt farmer whose overalls were navyblue and whose eyes were brown and gently remote and who had a great stringy beard. And he smiled as regretfully as the trolls had stared. And he said: *We hate to see you go.* And the lions, the lambs, the chickens, the foxes, the sheep, the kittycats, the frogs and the squirrels and the bears and the oxen all gathered closely around Victoria and the old farmer. And they made reproachful sounds that came to her in a quiet blur. And she wanted to slouch away, but the old farmer somehow sensed this (he apparently was a miraculous old farmer), since right then he held up a hand and said to Victoria: *There aren't that many remaining of you. We wish you would reconsider. You are our Victoria, and we love you, and you have always taken the time to listen to us.* And

the lions, the lambs, the chickens, the foxes, the sheep, the kittycats, the frogs and the squirrels and the bears and the oxen all shuffled and murmured, and Victoria was aware of fur, straw, warm placid breath. And now oh *dear* how she wanted to slouch away, to curl, to turn her head insideout and tuck it down her gullet. But she could not move. The animals all shook their heads, and there was noplace she could look where she was able to escape their eyes. And she supposed she would be trapped forever. But she was not. The old farmer released her. Sighing, dabbing at his eyes that were brown and gently remote, he said to the animals: *We don't exist. If BEAR and CAT and RABBIT and MARYBETH and the rest of THEM don't exist, then how can WE exist, eh?* And the old farmer began to back away from Victoria. And he said to her: *I surely do wish more of you would be able to reject being made to FACE UP and GO ALONG. You were such a good friend, and we enjoyed your dreams very much. We'll be a long time forgetting you, and probably the trolls never will. I mean, hardly a soul sees them the way you did. Ah, the poor things.* Then the old farmer motioned to the animals, and they also backed away from Victoria. He herded them across a meadow and through a grove of sweet reedy trees and into a low misted place beyond the misted river. Then they were gone, and silence crouched all around Victoria, and she hated it. She had never hated silence *before*. Why did she hate it *now?* Ah, but *now* she was a different person, and she *had* to hate silence. She was a person who valued the *fellowship* of those who occupied the *real world*, correct? And such a person could have no use for silence, correct? Victoria nodded. She looked around. Here now was a city, and people, and money, and loud voices, and soot, and television sets, and slogans. And arms were joined. And banners were waved, and the banners proclaimed: FEL

LOWSHIP FOREVER! And more banners were waved, and they proclaimed: OH, GOD! Roofs were falling in, and Victoria's happy wreckers were ripping up the streets, and a black man came up to Victoria and said: REALITY. PASS IT ON. And Victoria nodded. She turned to an old woman, and the old woman had no teeth, and Victoria said: REALITY. PASS IT ON. And the old woman smiled, and the smile was all gums and dry lacerations, and the old woman turned to a little blond boy and said: REAL-TY. PASH IT ON. And the old woman nudged Victoria and began to laugh, but Victoria could not laugh. Victoria's bones were all cracked and bent, and too much pain was involved. She decided the best thing she could do was spin away, even though spinning away meant NOT FACING REALITY and therefore probably was contemptible and cowardly, but she went whirring up, up, up anyway, over the ruins and the slogans and the voices and the urgent banners, and she found herself back inside the thing that was so gray and soft and puffy and sad, and it whispered and swirled, and she lay back, and it curled around her, and she supposed that from now on everything would be taken care of for her, that from now on she would not have to weary herself with dreams and laughter and silly games, and maybe now *this* sleep (for surely she was sleeping) was the best sort of sleep, since its only dreams obviously came from good old cold remorseless bonebreaking drymouthed REALITY. PASS IT ON. So then her dreams were closed off, and she simply slept.

She pressed her face against a pillow, and her right hand crept up, and a thumb slipped into her mouth, and she sucked that thumb, and her cheeks moved, making unrhythmic hollows. Now she slept as though her face had been dipped in ink and fur. She slept beyond sleeping. She slept as though she did not exist. Surely all this had to be a center point. In a sense, she was as dead as Rhoda Masonbrink. Certainly she was as dead as her erstwhile friends on the floor at the foot of her bed. Bear was *a teddybear;* Cat was *a pulltoy.* And et cetera and et cetera and et cetera. They had no existence in reality, which meant they had no existence at all, correct? Victoria groaned in her sleep. Her head hurt. She sucked. Hours fell away like clipped toenails, absurd, useless, without comfort. Vaguely she was aware of her mother looking in on her, but she refused to wake up, and she refused to remove her thumb from her mouth. She hadn't sucked her thumb since she didn't know when, and okay, let her mother see it; let her mother see everything that had to do with the change, with the entrance of Victoria Anne Tabor into the glorious kingdoms of FELLOWSHIP and REALITY. (Where wreckers wrecked, and old women mouthed what they were told to mouth.) So Victoria Anne Tabor sucked, but everything other than her mouth was immobile.

It was 2:47 by her little bedside clock when she awakened. She blinked at the clock's luminous dial and hands, and then she was aware of the thumb in her mouth. Slowly the thumb came out of her mouth. The thumb was cold from her saliva, so she blew on it, then wiped it with the edge of the sheet. She heard a remote snapping noise, and she believed it came from somewhere in the backyard. The breaking of a twig, perhaps. A cat, perhaps. She made fists and rubbed her eyes. She knew what she had to do, and now was as good a time as any to do it. The sooner she did it, the sooner it all would be finished, and she would have passed through a center point as profound as the death of Rhoda Masonbrink. And she would not cry. She had done enough crying. From now on, crying *definitely* would be restricted to times when she bit her tongue, or when other physical pain was involved. Never again would crying come *out* of Victoria Anne Tabor. Never again, even if she lived past the moment when all the clocks melted. She cleared her throat. She closed her eyes for a moment. She clearly saw her old sandbox that was in the back yard. Her father had built it back in the days when she had been a little itty baby cooing over sticks and mud. It had been deep and comfortable, and she had been grateful to her father. She no longer played in it (after all, she *was* nine!), but it was in reasonably good condition, and she didn't believe the sand would be too difficult to dig up. There were several shovels in the garage, and an hour's work probably would get the job done. Victoria Anne Tabor was no weakling, and afterward she would pat down the sand and put away the shovel and give herself a bath, and no one would know the difference. And her mother and her father could question her all they liked; she would never tell. She simply would say: Look, I now believe in your REALITY, and so what I did was logical, and so why don't we let it go at that? Victoria opened her eyes. She sat up. She rubbed her mouth. She told herself her parents ultimately would understand. They had to, didn't they? It was their idea, wasn't it? Surely it made sense for them to understand their own idea. Ha. Ha. Ha. Victoria snorted. She told herself she was a nerd and a dumbbell. She told herself to stop behaving like a *child*. She sat up in bed and told herself everything would be just as fine as fine could be. She told herself she would cry no longer. Now it was time to do what was necessary.

She slid out of bed and tiptoed to her closet. Carefully she opened the door. She felt a trifle woozy, and so she leaned against the door for a moment. She swallowed. Briefly she embraced herself. But she was okay, and she knew she was okay. She had been sick *then*, but this was *now*, correct? So she blinked, shook her head, cleared her throat. She was fine, and she knew it. She was *just fine*. She groped inside the closet. Stay on the ball, she told herself. She came up with a pink bathrobe, and she came up with the MY TOTE BAG tote bag. She closed the closet door just as carefully as she had opened it. She gnawed her tongue—but gently, since *pain* was the *last* thing she needed. She hesitated in front of the closet door. She leaned forward a little and listened, but she heard nothing. Not. A. Sound. Nothing from outdoors. Nothing from her parents' bedroom. Nothing from anyplace else in the house. She nodded. There was work to be done, and she was wasting too much time. When a person lived in the real world, time was valuable beyond measure, correct? Granted, Victoria wasn't that familiar with the real world (after all, she *was* very new to it), but she did accept the value it placed on time. She supposed, come to think of it, she accepted *all* its values. As a newcomer to them, this was the least she could do. But then . . . oh, phooey, it didn't matter. She made a tiny impatient clucking sound, then hurried to the foot of the bed and knelt on the floor. She pulled open the MY TOTE BAG tote bag. She began scooping up dolls and animals and stuffing them into it. Frowning, she felt around for Henry's missing tail. She found it under the bed. She dropped it into the bag along with the rest of him. She was able to identify Cat and Bear from the way they felt, but she did not speak. It would have been foolish to have spoken, since what sort of person was it who spoke to things that did not exist in the real world? She did squeeze Bear a little, though, and she did spin Cat's rear wheels. Again she was being a nerd and a dumbbell, but she could not help it. She made a flat and tentative sound, and it confined itself to the base of her throat, and she didn't suppose anyone in the world could have heard it.

She filled the tote bag. Her eyes had become accustomed to the darkness, and she counted the dolls and animals and retired nightlights that still were on the floor, and she figured she probably would need at least three trips downstairs altogether. So she'd better concentrate and get down *to* it. Still, she paused for a moment and asked herself whether she needed slippers. Urgency or no urgency, she didn't want to catch cold from sneaking outside in her bare feet. After all, wasn't there already enough to occupy her attention? So she reached under the bed for her slippers, and she stuck her feet into them. She wiggled her toes, and for a moment she was put in mind of warmth, but it was the wrong sort of warmth (an abandoned and anachronistic warmth having to do mostly with murmurs and polite laughter, a scholarly fellow named Bear, a place called The Peaceable Kingdom—plus all sorts of other things, dreams and ideas that now were without value), and so Victoria Anne Tabor made a face and pushed away that old useless warmth, and she picked up the tote bag, and she hugged it to her chest. She was able to feel the back of Bear's head, and she was able to feel one of Cat's axles.

She opened the bedroom door and crept out into the hall. She felt her way along the hall toward the stairs. She passed her parents' bedroom, but she heard nothing. She surely hoped they felt good about the way this canal water thing had been resolved. She did love them. It now was clear to her that she had been wrong. Anything that disturbed her parents *that* much *had* to be a bad thing, correct? This whatever it was . . . this *realization* . . . had been working at her all day and night, twisting and ripping, penetrating her tears and her despair. And when it came to a choice between *people* and *things*, there was only one choice that could be made, correct? To do away with the *things*, correct? Victoria sighed. She inched toward the stairs, feeling her way with the tips of her slippers. She started down the stairs on tiptoe, and then somehow Cat fell from the tote bag. Victoria had no idea how. Cat bounced, first against the spokes of the banister, then on the stairs, then against a wall. At the same time Victoria lost her balance. Perhaps she had tripped on the stairs' thick runner, but at any rate, she went sprawling forward, and the MY TOTE BAG tote bag spilled its contents in front of her, and so she went bouncing over several of the dolls and animals, and finally she smacked her head against the banister. She yelped, but she cut short the yelp as soon as she realized this was neither the time nor the place for such a thing as a yelp. She arranged herself so that she was leaning against the banister and sitting with her legs straight in front of her. She had banged one of her knees against something or other, and so she rubbed the knee. Then she rubbed her head, the place where it had smacked against the banister. In addition to all this, her *ears* hurt, and she was just about ready to believe she could hear an *echo* of her little yelp, as though she really had given off an enormous howl, like some large hairy thing trapped in a cave. Oh, phooey and phooey and *phooey*.

She supposed her mother and father would now come storming out of their room. And they would see what she was trying to do. And they would say to her: *You don't have to go this far.* And: *We KNOW you love us.* And: *Your promise was good enough for us. And besides, we still want you to be a little girl. We never intended for you to turn your back on ALL of it.* And embraces would be exchanged, and Victoria's mother probably would brew some nice cocoa. And right now it all sounded awful to Victoria Anne Tabor, but there was nothing she could do. For she was suddenly so very tired. She was not quite sure why. She was just nine years of age, and was it fair for her to be so tired? Wasn't she supposed to have great happy balls of energy at her age? She exhaled. Her hands slowly came away from her face. She was able to see the dolls and animals lying all scattered and indistinct at the foot of the stairs. She rubbed her sore knee. She rubbed her sore head. She waited for her mother and father to come storming out of their room. She frowned. She rubbed the back of her neck, then twisted around and looked up the stairs. She waited. She pressed her tongue against her lower lip. All her parents had to do was come down these stairs, and she would not run or hide from them. She was altogether too tired. So she waited. And nothing happened. She rubbed her ears. It was coming to her that nothing *would* happen. It was coming to her that her parents had slept through all the commotion. They had *slept*. Victoria just about envied her parents, and that was the truth. Oh, sure, she was glad they had slept through all the commotion, but at the same time she almost wished they had awakened, caught her, told her to calm herself, given her the cocoa, then tucked her back in bed. Good old sleep. It did not matter that she had slept most of the day and much of the night away. Right now she very much wanted to lie down and close her eyes—and here on these stairs, for all *she* gave a whoop. And it didn't matter that her parents would find her tomorrow morning, just as long as she was able to—*no!* What was she thinking? She was *Victoria Anne Tabor*, and she had set out to do a thing, and she would *do* it. *Then* would be time enough for good old sleep. What was she *really* doing right now anyway? *Waiting* for her parents like a little baby waiting for Christmas? Hoping they would *stop* her? Oh, talk about your pits. A grunt came from Victoria. Shaking her head, she seized the banister and pulled herself to her feet. She clung to the banister railing for a moment, then silently scooted down the stairs and set to work refilling the MY

TOTE BAG tote bag. She supposed maybe her
parents had gone deaf. Or maybe they had drunk
some sort of magical sleeping draught. It certainly
was a miracle that they hadn't been awakened by
the racket, and Victoria said to herself: Hey, maybe
it's a sign that what I'm doing is right. Nodding, she
dropped the last of the dolls and animals into the
tote bag. She even had been able to find Henry's
severed tail. She tiptoed along a downstairs hallway
to the kitchen. She felt her way to the back door,
and she bumped into nothing. She went out the back
door, and she crossed the patio, and again she was
hugging the tote bag, and now she was cold. She came
to the sandbox, squatted next to it and emptied the
dolls and animals onto the hard congealed sand.

She made two more trips into the house for the rest
of the dolls and animals—and retired nightlights. She
had no more trouble on the stairs, and her parents
did not awaken. It was almost as though they had
been clubbed by a troll, but of course this was a lot
of baloney. Victoria Anne Tabor was a new Victoria
Anne Tabor, and she no longer believed in trolls.
Instead, she believed in good old REALITY, and she
supposed she forever would be obliged to PASS IT
ON. She grimaced. She told herself to attend to the
business at hand and never mind all her dippy *thinking.* She tossed the MY TOTE BAG tote bag aside
and went into the garage, entering through a side
door. She made her way past the family car and the
family station wagon to a far wall, where a number of
shovels and hoes and rakes were hanging. She chose
a small shovel. She nodded. She cleared her throat,
and she tried to flush everything from her mind.
She knew that from now on her mind would have
to be as dull and silent as what? something without
memory? something without love or sentiment?
something *dead?* She squeezed the shovel, and quickly
she went out of the garage and recrossed the yard

to the sandbox. She tossed the dolls and animals aside and began digging up the sand. She grunted, but she tried to be quiet about it. Clammy sand squished at her slippers, but she paid it no mind. Later she would take a bath, a good warm bath, perhaps even a puckery bath, and it would wash away all the icky feelings she was having right now. Or would it? Ah, probably not, but maybe it would wash away *something*. Victoria sighed, tried to concentrate. She did concentrate. She dug, and she concentrated. She dug what she figured probably would be a pretty fair little mass grave, perhaps a foot deep and five feet square. Then, when she had finished digging, she hugged herself. She suddenly was so cold she was sure her teeth would fall out. She told herself it was *June*, for crying out loud, and she was being *stupid*. She hunkered down and began arranging the dolls and animals and nightlights flat on their backs in straight lines in the grave. These were the dolls, and these were the animals, and these were the retired nightlights, that lay on their backs, all sad and forlorn, on the sand, all clammy and worn, in the pretty fair little mass grave Victoria had dug. She heard someone moan, and she flinched, and then she realized the someone was herself. She tried not to look too closely at the dolls and the animals and the retired nightlights, and she was grateful for the darkness. She rubbed the knee she had hurt on the stairs. She winced. She wondered whether she deserved the pain, and she supposed she did. She worked faster, and she snuffled, and she broke a fingernail. She sucked at the finger, and she was able to taste wet sand. She spat. It was just then that Bear spoke. He said: No.

"I'm afraid so," said Victoria, and the words came without thinking.

This is nonsensical, said Bear, and you know it is.

"*What?*" said Victoria. "How can you be *speaking?* You're a . . . you're a *teddybear*."

Not so loud, said Bear, and now his voice was a whisper.

We don't want to wake up your parents, whispered Cat.

"*Hush*," said Victoria.

Shh, whispered Bear.

We don't want nobody coming down here and yelling at you, whispered Bonnie.

A joke is a joke, but this is enough, whispered Rabbit.

My dress is dirty, whispered Marybeth.

Shame on you, Victoria, for making her dress dirty, whispered Kermit.

I've got my work to do, whispered Bugs. Please take me back upstairs and plug me in and stop being so silly.

"*Hush*," said Victoria.

That's easy for *you* to say, whispered Mickey. *You're* not about to be buried in a lot of wet old sand.

"I don't believe this," said Victoria.

Oh? whispered Bear.

"You don't exist," said Victoria. "It's all very clear to me, and *you don't exist*. And you never *did* exist. I just sat in my room and *made you up*, and I was a *bad girl*, and I made a whole lot of *trouble*."

Then how can we be talking now? whispered Bear.

"What?" said Victoria.

We are talking now, whispered Bear. *You are hearing us*. What does that tell you? Doesn't it tell you that we can't be pushed away? Doesn't it tell you that your mind and your heart are too large to be bullied by your world? All that talk about *fellowship* and *cooperation* is a lot of rat poop, and you know it. And as for giving respect to that woman, why should you give her respect after she went back on her word? How has she earned that respect? Remember this morning when we told you to be careful? Well, maybe you were too careful. Maybe we were wrong.

Victoria rubbed her forehead. "I don't understand," she said.

Yes you do, whispered Bear.

"*No*," said Victoria. "I don't want to *bother* at it anymore." Snorting, she shoveled a spray of sand in the direction of Bear's voice.

Mumpf, whispered Bear, coughing.

Victoria shoveled more sand in the direction of Bear's voice.

You're getting sand under my eyepatch, whispered Bear.

"Be quiet," said Victoria. "Be quiet. Please be quiet. Please."

Now all the dolls and animals and retired night-lights (and Bugs, who simply wanted to get back to his job) set to murmuring and clearing their throats.

"Patooey," said Victoria. Somehow her mouth was full of the taste of wet sand.

Serves you right, whispered Cat.

Victoria shoveled sand in the direction of Cat's voice.

Thanks a lot, whispered Cat.

Victoria shoveled more sand into the little mass grave.

This is very wrong, whispered Bear.

You don't know what you're doing, honey, whispered Bonnie.

Victoria shoveled. She wanted to cover her ears, but there was no way she could cover her ears while shoveling. She sprayed sand across all her former friends.

This is really outrageous, whispered Bear.

My poor dress, whispered Marybeth. It's ruined.

And sand doesn't do an awful lot for sequins, either, whispered Bonnie.

I believe my patience is being tried, whispered Kermit.

Wahpf, whispered Rabbit. Bluh. Yuk.

She really means it, doesn't she? whispered Pluto.

I'm afraid so, whispered Bear.

I can't see, whispered Mickey.

I can't *breathe*, whispered Cat.

Rabbit began to cry.

"I'm . . . I'm sorry," said Victoria, wheezing.

Big . . . deal, whispered Rabbit.

Victoria told herself she would not weep. She shoveled all the sand back into the grave. She heard murmurs and cries. She *told* herself she *would* not *weep*. She paused for a moment and looked at the sky. She blinked at the sky. She inhaled. The sky had no particular color beyond a sort of blurred grayness from the light of the moon and perhaps some reflected light from Shaker Heights or who knew where. She *told* herself she *would* not *weep*. She heard more than the murmurs and the cries. She heard her own breath. She heard coughings, the clearing of throats. She *told* herself she *would* not *weep*. Groaning, she looked down at the sandbox. She raised the shovel.

No, whispered Bear.

"Yes," said Victoria, closing her eyes.

Please? whispered Bear.

Victoria brought down the shovel and began tamping the sand.

Bear groaned.

Victoria tamped sand over all her former friends. She opened her eyes, and her vision had no definition, and so she was able to tamp and tamp. And tamp and tamp and *tamp*. And she kept *telling* herself she *would* not *weep*. The murmurs and the cries diminished. She did more than tamp. She pounded. She brought the shovel over her head, and the shovel came down, and the impact against the sand jarred her hands and her arms and her shoulders and the

back of her neck. Now the murmurs and the cries,
the few that remained, were broken, muffled, clogged
with wet tamped sand. The shovel thudded, and Victoria was aware of a cold and almost syrupy perspiration on her chest and her back and her face and her
neck. She almost never perspired, but then it wasn't
often she buried former friends. She tamped and
pounded, pounded and tamped and perspired. She bit
her tongue, and she kept tamping and pounding until
all the sand was flat and she could hear no more
murmurs and cries. Then all she heard was her breath
and the thudding of the shovel. Finally she stopped.
She gasped, dropped the shovel, embraced her chest.
She looked down and saw the empty MY TOTE
BAG tote bag. She made an involuntary gagging
sound, but then she held her breath and managed to
suppress the sound. Her tongue was sore where she
had bit it. She stuck out her tongue and rubbed it
with the back of a wet sandy hand. Grimacing, she
spat. She shuddered. She *told* herself she *would* not
weep. She picked up the empty MY TOTE BAG
tote bag. She dropped the shovel and began tugging
and twisting the bag. It occurred to her that back
awhile ago, while all her former friends had whispered, she had spoken in a normal voice. What had
that meant? Had she wanted her mother and father
to emerge from the spell of their magical sleeping
draught and come storming out into the backyard and
rescue her former friends from all the tamping and
pounding? Victoria shook her head and tried to clear
her mind of such a stupid thought. She concentrated
on the tote bag, and finally a seam gave way, and
she was able to rip it lengthwise and then across,
then lengthwise again. Then she began plucking at
the remnants, shredding them. Finally she tossed up
the scraps of cloth. They whirled for a moment, but
there wasn't much of a wind, and so they quickly
and dispiritedly fell, scattering themselves across the

tamped sand. Victoria shrugged and picked up the shovel. She wandered back to the garage. She said to herself: Center point. One of her pigtails had come unbraided. She seized it and tugged it. She winced, and she said to herself: Serves you right. She returned the shovel to the place where it had been hanging in the garage. (They did not exist, so how could they have spoken? She supposed she was crazy. Center point indeed. You'd better believe it.)

39 ✒ Dirt

VICTORIA CREPT BACK to the house, and she took care not to look in the direction of the sandbox. Her mouth tasted gummy, sandy, and she knew she *had* to be absolutely *filthy*. Well, dirt probably was one of the prices a person had to pay for a center point. Grandpa Bird had paid with a foot, though, and so Victoria supposed she was lucky. A little dirt beat the loss of a foot any old day, correct? Victoria entered the house through the kitchen. She groped her way upstairs. Still no sounds came from her parents' room. Suddenly she yawned. The tiredness had returned, quick as light and loss and despair. Her eyes watered, and again she yawned. She hurried into her room and took off her bathrobe and slippers. She went to the dresser and silently pulled open a drawer. She found a clean pair of pajamas. She held them up to the window. They were pink, with a design of sailboats. She went to her closet and found a pair of slippers that weren't all wet and yucky from sand and grass. She yawned. She let herself out of her bedroom and crossed the hall to the bathroom. She turned on the HOT tap of the tub. She took off her dirty pajamas and dropped them in a hamper. She stood naked and embraced herself. The tub was beginning to fill, and steam rose and swirled. She breathed it. She exhaled. She breathed it again. She exhaled. She tempered the bathwater with a stream from the COLD tap. She tested the bathwater with an elbow. The water was too hot, and she grimaced. She ran more water from the COLD tap. She *told* herself she *would* not *weep*. She yawned. She again embraced herself, and this time she squeezed herself. She listened to the running water, and suddenly she felt she had to Go. She went to the commode and sat down and performed Number One. Now the steam had fogged the mirror over the sink. Victoria flushed the toilet and returned to the tub. Again she tested the water with an elbow, and now the temperature of the water was fine. She turned off the taps, climbed over the side of the tub, and lowered herself into the water. She sighed. Maybe she would fall asleep and drown, and maybe that wouldn't be so bad. She soaped a washrag and listlessly dabbed at her chest and neck. She inhaled. Bubbles came off the soap, and she made an *o* and blew at them. Sand was underneath her fingernails, and she soaped it away. Briefly she sucked on the finger that had the torn nail. Her face felt sandy, and so she scrubbed it. Then she reached up and unbraided her hair. She would have to wash it as well. She used the bath soap as a shampoo. It would be good enough. This was not a beauty bath. It was a bath that had as its aim the cleansing of Victoria Anne Tabor. The *cleansing*. The ridding her of the last of her notions having to do with voices where no voices existed, of grief that focused itself on *things*, of love that did not include fellowship and all the rest of that stuff. From now on, reality would govern all her days, and she would seek out fellowship like a squirrel rooting and scrabbling for acorns. And she would respect people, teachers, whomever, whether they deserved it or not. She supposed that was the beauty of a center point— it put a person's days in order and gave them direction. She shook her head, and some of her hair trailed down over her face, and she began to push the soap back and forth on her head, pulling her hair, soaking it and soaping it, with some of the soap leaking down into her eyes and making them smart. She had no awareness whatever of any sort of cupped palm. She was just rinsing her hair (by lying back and immersing her head) when the door opened and her mother came into the bathroom. Well, goodness gracious *me*, said Sandra Tabor, blinking, pushing at the steam.

Victoria's head came out of the water, and she rubbed her eyes.

Her mother was wearing a blue cotton bathrobe. I *thought* I heard something in here, she said.

Victoria said nothing. She swiped at her wrists and hands with the washrag. Water streamed down from her hair.

Her mother leaned against the door and said: You must be feeling better.

Victoria shrugged.

A bath always makes a person feel better, said Sandra Tabor. Even if it comes at whatever time it is —four o'clock in the morning or whatever. It's very comforting, isn't it?

Victoria reached forward with soap and rag and began washing her toes.

Your stomach all right? said her mother.

"It's fine," said Victoria.

Good, said her mother.

Sand was underneath Victoria's toenails, and she scraped it away. Then she scrubbed her toenails, and her feet made quiet plashing sounds.

Victoria's mother seated herself on the edge of the tub and said: Would you like some help?

"No," said Victoria, scrubbing.

Please don't take it out on *me*, said her mother.

Victoria was finished with her toes. She washed her feet, and then she began soaping her legs and thighs.

I've tried to be on your side, said her mother.

"Fine," said Victoria, scrubbing.

And you know that, said Victoria's mother.

Victoria shrugged. She rinsed her legs and thighs. She was warm and wet enough, but she didn't feel hardly puckery at all.

You're acting like you hate me, said her mother.

Victoria looked at her mother and said: "I don't *hate* you. I did what you and Daddy wanted me to do because I *love* you. And so now I want everything to be fine. I'm not mad at you or Daddy or anybody in the world. I won't be any bother. Whatever you want me to do, I'll do it. I mean, you feed me, don't you? And you care about me, don't you? And you more or less some of the time leave me alone, don't you?"

You were wrong.

Victoria shrugged and said: "Okay. Whatever you say."

It's not right to go around hurting people and saying nasty things about their grandmothers.

"Okay," said Victoria, soaping her chest.

There are certain simple compromises everyone has to make.

"Fine," said Victoria, splashing water on her chest.

I held out for you as long as I could.

Victoria blinked at her mother and said: "Did you?" There was a residue of soap in her eyes, and she rubbed at it with her wrists.

I *did*, said her mother.

"That's real nice," said Victoria.

40   Hurt

V<small>ICTORIA'S</small> <small>MOTHER</small> went shrugging back to bed a few minutes later, but not before she told Victoria there really wasn't anything to be gained by being *snippy*. Victoria nodded but said nothing. She couldn't really understand. What further proof did her mother need of her love? She had apologized. She had barfed. She had promised to change her ways and *cooperate* and accept the same *reality* the world accepted. Every day she would make a point of saying: REALITY. PASS IT ON. What more was necessary? Grunting, Victoria stepped out of the tub almost as soon as her mother was gone from the bathroom. She wrapped herself in an enormous white bathtowel, and then she drained the tub, and she scrubbed away the ring, and she saw to it that all residual grains of sand were sent swirling down the drain with the last of the gray and vaguely scummy bathwater. She dried herself, and oh, yes, she was warm, but she did not feel a bit puckery. She put on her clean pajamas and slippers, switched off the bathroom light and darted across the hall to her bedroom. Something that may have been a sound of suppressed voices came from her parents' room, but she paid it no mind. She hurried to her bed, and she looked neither to the right nor to the left. That way, she would not have to confront those places where her former friends had been. And never would be again. *Never.* Never never *ever.* She squeezed her eyes tightly shut and burrowed

263

under the covers. Her tongue pressed the roof of her mouth, and a trace of sandy flavor was still there. Perhaps she would always live with a trace of that sandy flavor. Perhaps her father's God intended it to be a reminder of all her stupid and inconsiderate behavior. Briefly she wondered what this room would be like in the daytime, and the thought made her groan. She held her breath. She listened for the suppressed voices, but she heard nothing. Whatever her parents' conversation had been, it clearly hadn't been very important, since they probably were asleep again, and big deal, Victoria really had caused them a sleepless night, hadn't she? Sighing, she rolled herself into a ball. She did not believe she would be able to fall asleep, and she fell asleep in perhaps ten minutes. Her head still hurt, and her knee still hurt, and there wasn't a single cupped palm within a thousand miles. Maybe there wasn't a single cupped palm in the entire world. Victoria's right hand made its way to her mouth, and she set to work sucking her thumb. Her mouth popped, and her throat gurgled. She sighed in her sleep. Occasionally she made angry little squeaking sounds. They came out all frayed and dry. Her arms and back were a trifle stiff from the tamping and pounding. But she *had* not *wept*.

41 🐿 Sunday

THERE WERE NO CLOUDS accompanying the sun that
morning, which meant nothing lay between Victoria
and the universe, nothing shadowed her vision as she
blinked, yawned and looked around her bedroom
that now was empty. Or at least it was empty as far
as she was concerned. (Her thumb was wet, and she
wiped it across the front of her nightgown.) Oh, the
walls were still there, and the floor, and the window
and the dresser and her Hobbit calendar and her
recordplayer and her albums and her books, but it
wasn't the same room, and it wouldn't ever be the
same room. There were no ears to dust. There were
no dresses to arrange. There was no dyed blonde hair
to comb, and there were no squeaky wheels or ret-
icent fish. (Her nose was clogged, and she snuffled.)
It was Sunday, June 4, 1978, the fiftyfirst *birthday*
of a *death* that had placed Victoria Anne Tabor on
this earth, and she made a face and licked the roof
of her mouth. (She patted her hair, and it was soft
from the washing she had given it, but it also was
tangled.) She breathed deeply, shakily, and it was as
though she were sitting in some sort of cart or wagon
that was passing over the most awful rocks and sticks
and potholes, and she told herself she *would* not *weep.*
Maybe someone had taken away her bed's flanged
wheels, and it was bumping along on its axles. Probably so, considering what had happened yesterday and
early this morning. *No,* Bear had said, but Victoria

had ignored him. She'd known what she had to do, and she'd *done* it. And now everyone would live happily ever after, and she *would* not *weep*. Her mother would come into this room sometime today, and she probably would wonder what had happened to all the dolls and animals and nightlights (including Bugs, who still had been functional), but Victoria wouldn't tell her. Victoria simply would say: They are gone, and that is all you need to know. And Victoria most definitely absolutely without question *would* not *weep*. (Her throat felt as though it had been scraped with a fork. She coughed.)

Sunday was, of course, the busiest morning of the week in the Tabor household. Victoria's father always had a light breakfast (coffee, orange juice, one poached egg, one slice of toast) by no later than seven o'clock, and then he would retire to his study to rehearse his sermon one last time and perhaps make a few revisions. Victoria and her mother always were as quiet as mice with tiny pillows tied to their feet, and they had a habit of talking behind their hands, like kids whispering in a classroom. Victoria wore a blue blouse and a pink skirt that particular morning, and she had braided her hair tightly. (She was proud of the fact that she was able to braid her hair without her mother's assistance. She was not *stupid*, for heaven's sake. Just because she had been fond of puckery baths and cupped palms, that didn't mean she was unable to take care of herself. When a little girl lived in a home that had no other children, she learned to do a great many things for herself. As her father once had said to her: Victoria, there'll be times and times, I think, when you'll need to make do, to be resourceful—by which I mean, times when you'll have to figure out how to handle a situation with no help. It, well, it is the sort of thing that often falls to children who are alone so much. I think you can handle it, though. Victoria is our very *competent* little girl, isn't she? And then her father had grinned, and perhaps he had kissed her. She could not quite remember.)

Victoria dressed herself quickly that particular morning, but not quickly enough. The absence of her former friends lay flat and blank in her sunny bedroom, and she could not avoid feeling it. Sleepers were in her eyes, and she swiped at them, but they were too soft and moist to be real sleepers, and quickly she told herself she *would* not *weep*. The blue blouse and the pink skirt were the first things she found in her closet, and then she fled her bedroom, crossing to the bathroom and washing her face and hands and braiding her hair. She squinted at herself in the mirror, and she hoped she would be presentable enough for church this morning. She supposed she looked okay. She brushed her teeth. Usually she dressed herself after washing her face and hands and brushing her teeth, but this morning she had been in too much of a hurry. All she had wanted to do was get dressed and flee the bedroom with its sunny emptiness and all. She went downstairs, and her father was eating his breakfast, and her mother was drinking coffee and smoking a cigarette, and her father asked Victoria whether she was feeling better. And Victoria assured her father she felt a hundred percent better, maybe more than that. And her father smiled and said: Good. Time wounds all heels, to coin a phrase. And Victoria's mother said: Carl, that's not very funny. And Victoria's father said: Well, life does go on. That was the only point I was trying to make. (Victoria looked away from both of them. There was a small cluster of potted violets on the windowsill above the sink, and several of the violets had opened. Victoria stared at the violets. Her father and mother continued to speak, but she did not hear their words. She wanted to press the violets against her face. But they were so *small*, and she was being silly even thinking such a thing.)

Later, after Victoria's father had gone upstairs for his rehearsal or whatever, she dried the breakfast dishes for her mother, who did them in the sink while smoking a cigarette and complaining in her Sunday-morning mousevoice about the family's lack of an electric dishwasher. I don't really believe I'm all that strung out on gadgets and worksavers and what have you, said Sandra Tabor, but I really *would* like a dishwasher. I mean, if there is any human activity that is utterly without a socially redeeming value, it is the washing of dishes by hand. I wish I had a dollar for every dish I've washed. Oh, I wish I had a penny for every dish I've washed. You and your father and I would be lolling on Majorca, and we'd never have to lift a finger for the rest of our lives. I've always wanted to loll on Majorca. I don't know what one does when one lolls on Majorca, but whatever it is, I'm all for it. I've washed dishes and dried dishes for your Grandma Bird, for your Grandpa Bird, for your Uncle Morris, for your father, for *you*, for *myself*, for my various roommates when I was single and working at County Welfare and living in apartments and marching in civil rights demonstrations and doing all sorts of things the nature of which I don't really need to describe just now. But, anyway, I am *weary* unto the *death* of the washing of dishes. Of the washing of dishes, is there to be no end? Gadzooks.

Victoria figured she had to say something, and so she said: "I'm real sorry."

Her mother rinsed the skillet and handed it to her. Nobody knows the trouble I've seen, said Sandra Tabor.

Victoria wiped the skillet. She formed an *o*, but she had run out of conversation, and so she said nothing. She had a quick image of Bear, his eyepatch,

his frayed ear. She shook her head. She finished with
the skillet and placed it in the dish rack.

Something wrong? said her mother.

"Wrong?" said Victoria.

The way you just now shook your head. Are you
bored with my words, or are you still thinking about
what happened yesterday, or are you just being
snippy, or *what?*

Victoria said nothing.

We love you, said her mother.

Victoria nodded. "That's . . . that's what you keep
saying."

It'll pass faster than you can imagine, and you'll
actually even feel *better.*

"That's . . . nice."

There are cruel lessons we have to learn early.

"Curl lessons?"

I said *cruel* lessons. Not curl lessons. This has nothing to do with hair, you ninny.

"Oh," said Victoria the ninny.

Lessons having to do with the fact that we can't
always have our way all the time, if you'll pardon the
redundancy. Myself, if I had *my* way, I'd never wash
another dish, pot, pan, knife, fork, spoon, skillet,
spatula or double boiler as long as I lived. But I'm
not having my way, and I never will. And so, to make
a little poem of it, the Ivory Snow will continue to
flow, and Procter and Gamble will continue to rejoice
in my aggravation.

"Oh," said Victoria.

Your first sermon of the day.

"Yes."

Try to bear up.

"All right."

We love you.

"*Fine,*" said Victoria.

Are you tired of hearing me say it?

Victoria made an *o*. She said nothing. She dried a handful of knives and forks.

You can play, you know, said Victoria's mother. It's not as though your life has been destroyed. We want you to run and laugh and have a good time. The only new thing we want from you, or different thing, is an acknowledgment of the rules.

Victoria cleared her throat. "Like, um, like when a person makes a promise to me and breaks the promise, it's okay, and, um, *I'm* the one who's to blame. On account of, um, I get mad and say something."

You're not being nice.

"Nice?" said Victoria.

You're *not* being *nice*, said her mother. Now the last of the dishes and pots and pans and knives and forks and whatnot had been washed, and so Sandra Tabor opened the drain, and the dishwater made soft soapy gurgling sounds. It swirled, and Sandra Tabor frowned at it. We feel bad about this, she said. We discussed it last night before we went to bed, and then we discussed it after you and I had our little encounter in the bathroom, and believe me, we get no pleasure out of any of it.

Victoria nodded. She folded the dishtowel and hung it on a rack.

But that's no excuse for you to be nasty, said Victoria's mother.

"Yes," said Victoria. "I know. And you *love* me. I *know*."

Oh, my God, said Victoria's mother. Something's vanished, hasn't it?

Victoria made an *o*.

Her mother was wearing an apron that had pink horizontal stripes. Sighing, Sandra Tabor took off the apron and hung it on a hook that was attached to the door that opened into the diningroom. I have to get ready for church, she said. I'll have to do some vanishing of my own. Then Sandra Tabor tried to smile, but nothing much emerged, a flutter at a corner of her mouth, a vague crinkling at the corners of her eyes.

Victoria licked at the *o*.

Victoria's mother went out of the kitchen, and the door closed heavily behind her.

Victoria flinched. She spoke to the door. She said: "I did it for, um, you. Ah, you and Daddy, I mean." Nodding, Victoria picked at an elbow. Then she said: "They're dead and buried, and everything's okay. *Okay?*"

The door said nothing. The door was a *door*, and who ever heard of doors that spoke? If doors spoke, then teddybears also spoke. And pulltoys. And dolls with silly dyed Dolly Parton hair. And if you believed *that*, you were in trouble—and the world might even deny you its precious REALITY. PASS IT ON.

Victoria went out onto the patio and sat in one of the chairs. She was just settling back when she realized the chair was facing squarely in the direction of the sandbox. She turned the chair so that it faced the house. Of course, she *could* flee upstairs to her room, but that would be just as bad. It would be just as much a reminder of her former friends—who, of course, no longer existed, if indeed they ever really had existed at all. Victoria glanced down at her hands and picked at her torn fingernail. She wished she knew how it all really had started. Flanged wheels and cupped palms and *Veritas*. Good grief, Charlie Brown, the world sometimes surely had peculiar ways of sorting itself out. Victoria felt a chill. She rubbed her arms. She glanced toward the sky, the merciless sky that this morning was providing her with no clouds to protect her from sunlight and reality and all the rest of that great neat stuff the world held so dear. She looked for a moment in the direction of the Wrexford Methodist Church, which was just up the street. Its architecture was colonial, and it was painted white every spring. The painters had finished their annual job only about three weeks ago, and the place still had a trace of an odor of Spred Latex. It was a low building with a narrow spire, and people called it *graceful*. Victoria liked the church. It had plenty of windows, which meant plenty of sunshine, which meant plenty of good eyewatering brightness, which helped her concentrate on her father's sermons, his words having to do with fellowship and love and all the rest of *that* great neat stuff the world *also* held so dear. But none of his words had given her even a clue as to why she was the way she was. Oh, people talked of *only children*, saying how an *only child* was different, and sometimes Victoria actually wondered whether those people thought *only children* had grapes growing from their toes and elves dancing in their armpits. It surely was almost funny. The only thing was, nothing had come clear. It all was noise and blurs, unformed words. Victoria was just as baffled now as she had been when the question had first occurred to her.

She supposed she probably never would understand why she was the way she was. She supposed there was a chance most people were accidents. After all, wasn't Victoria Anne Tabor herself an accident? If that Rhoda Masonbrink hadn't died in an *automobile* accident fiftyone years ago *this very day*, then Grandpa Bird never would have married Grandma Bird, and Victoria's mother never would have been born, which meant Victoria never would have been born, which meant the world sometimes had peculiar ways of sorting itself out, correct? Victoria sighed. She said to herself: You think too much. She said to herself: You are silly, and f.r years you've heard voices when there haven't been any voices, and it's about time you got yourself organized. Grimacing, Victoria wriggled off the patio chair and went into the kitchen and

poured herself her second glass of milk of the morning. For some reason, her mouth felt dusty. Perhaps
this was because of all her silly thinking. She drank
the milk eagerly. Some of it leaked from a corner of
her mouth, and she rubbed the spill away before it
had a chance to drip and perhaps spot her blouse.
(Was Miss Platt weeping *today?* Or was Miss Platt
rejoicing? Was she on her knees and offering thanks
to Almighty God that a certain snippy little girl had
apologized for her inexcusable rudeness? It wasn't
likely Miss Platt was weeping today. Not *today*. And
Victoria would have bet any amount of money anyone would have cared to name.) Victoria went to the
sink and rinsed out her glass. Her mother called down
from the bathroom and told her everyone would be
leaving for church in just a few minutes. "Okay!"
hollered Victoria. She went upstairs to her room and
fetched a little black patentleather purse she always
took with her to church. The purse was in a drawer
of her dresser. She tried not to look around the room.
She dropped a comb and half a roll of orange Life
Savers into the purse. She hurried out of the room.
She encountered her father in the hall just as he was
coming out of his study. He told her she looked very
pretty. She said nothing. She pushed past him and
went downstairs. She seated herself on the sofa in the
front room and waited for her parents to come down
and escort her to church.

Sunday mornings were times her father insisted it
was important that the three of them be a *family* and
show braves faces to the world. Victoria couldn't
quite understand this. Were Sunday mornings somehow more important than, say, Tuesday afternoons?
Friday nights? a Wednesday twilight? a sunrise from
some anonymous forgotten Monday? Huh. It all certainly was strange, and Victoria was grateful she was
so young. It probably meant she would have a lot of
time to try to figure out such questions. (Was Miss

Platt hugging Mrs Bee, and were they dancing around
a room somewhere?) Victoria reached up and touched
her braids, and they felt properly tight. She told herself she probably was a dumbbell for bringing along
a comb, but then she clearly was far from perfect,
and so she just had to accept being a dumbbell now
and then. Her mother and father came downstairs.
Sandra Tabor was wearing a gray dress with a white
kerchief at the neck, and she had framed her face
and her blonde hair with a large floppy white hat. The
Rev Mr Tabor was wearing a brown suit with brown
shoes, a brown tie, and a white shirt. He put Victoria
a little in mind of a door, or a stone, or faded wallpaper. She supposed, though, that was the way he
had to be. She'd never seen him wear any other sort
of clothes on a Sunday morning. When one con-
fronted the Lord, one apparently dressed as though
He had weak eyes and would be offended by color.
Victoria had often wondered about this, but she'd
never found a real opportunity to discuss it with her
father. And she knew that now would not at all be
the time. So she rose from the sofa and went to her
parents, and her mother took her by a hand and
squeezed it. Victoria nodded and even smiled a little.
She always held hands with her mother Sunday
mornings when the *family* showed its brave faces to
the world. Sometimes she also held hands with her
father. Of course, all this handholding only lasted for
the short time it took the *family* to walk the few
dozen yards to the Wrexford Methodist Church, and
Victoria never really had minded all that much. At
least the old Victoria hadn't, the Victoria who had
spoken with things that did not exist in REALITY.
PASS IT ON. This new Victoria, though, felt a sort
of sourness at the base of her tongue. Her mother led
her out the front door and and down the front walk.
There was an odor of grass newly mown. Victoria's
father followed along. Then, once the *family* was

walking along the sidewalk, he took Victoria by the other hand. A manila folder was tucked under one of his arms, and he inclined his head toward the folder and said: Victoria, I'm pleased you always seem to listen so closely to my sermons.

"That's nice," said Victoria.

I did some revising yesterday.

Victoria looked at the Rev Mr Tabor.

You will listen especially closely this morning, won't you? said the Rev Mr Tabor to Victoria. There are things I'll say that have to do with yesterday's, ah, *situation*.

Victoria's mother spoke to her husband over Victoria's head, saying: Carl, don't you think she's heard enough?

Not as long as she still holds out.

Holds out?

Yes, said the Rev Mr Tabor. There's a part of her that resents all this, which means she is still holding out. Look, I love her as much as you do, but she is barely speaking to either of us . . . and when she does, well, she's not exactly *friendly*, is she?

I do wish you wouldn't talk about her as though she weren't here.

Sandra, that's a small point.

Maybe to you—but not to her, and not to me.

Now you listen to me. Just a few minutes ago, upstairs in the hallway, I bumped into her and I told her how pretty she looked. And do you know what she said to me? She said nothing—*that's* what she said. She uttered not a syllable, not even a grunt. So there's still work to be done, wouldn't you say?

Work to be done? What is she? a highway project?

Well, I expect her to reply when I speak to her. I am her father, and I love her, and it . . . well, hasn't it ever occurred to her that she can't go around ignoring people without perhaps angering them and perhaps even hurting their feelings?

Carl, this has all gotten very much out of hand.

I suppose it has.

We'll have to talk about it after church.

"Talk about it," said Victoria.

Both her parents looked down at her. The *family* now was walking toward a side entrance of the Wrexford Methodist Church. Is there . . . is there something you want to say? said Victoria's father.

Victoria stopped walking. The abruptness caused her hands to come free of her parents' hands. She said: "I am what you want me to be. Maybe there'll be more times when I won't say anything, and maybe there'll even be more times when I'm, um, *snippy*. But, ah, I promise I'll be good. I mean, by and large good, okay?"

Her parents stood and said nothing. Her mother's hands were on her hips, and her father now had both arms wrapped around the manila folder. His face was shadowed by leaves.

"I said I'd protect them until all the clocks melted," said Victoria.

Pardon? said Victoria's mother.

"Stand up for them," said Victoria.

You mean your toys and whatnot? said Victoria's father.

"Yes," said Victoria. "But I didn't. Miss Platt bawled, and so I caved in, and *okay, I give,* all right? I love you, Daddy, and I love Mommy, but what more am I supposed to do? Run around and laugh and holler and sing?" Victoria shook her head. She ran toward the church, and her parents called after her, asking her what she meant, but she didn't listen to their words. She told herself she *would* not *weep*. She pushed into the church and went clattering down into the basement. She supposed she knew this church nearly as well as she knew her own home. She went

into the Sunday School classroom, and it was being
swept and tidied by a Mrs Rhodes, who was dark
and tall and curved and pretty, who had enormous
gray eyes, who was from England, who had nice
little chats with Victoria nearly every Sunday morning, early, before the place became too busy. Mrs
Rhodes liked to speak to Victoria of a place called
Devon, of fields and hedges and a city called Plymouth
and a body of water called the English Channel.
Sometimes, to hear Mrs Rhodes speak of Devon,
Victoria just about was put in mind of The Peaceable
Kingdom. Mrs Rhodes's voice had a fluted and tentative quality, and it almost was as though she were
forever afraid she would be interrupted and perhaps
told to go sit down and be silent. And yet Victoria
sensed a strength in Mrs Rhodes, an ability to with-
stand pain and, furthermore, remain quiet about it.
There was no Mr Rhodes (no one had much of an
idea what had happened to him), and Mrs Rhodes
had no children, either. She was perhaps thirtyfive,
and she worked in a travel bureau somewhere in
downtown Cleveland. She lived in a small apartment
off Shaker Square, and the Tabor family had once
been her guests for dinner. Something called beef
olives had been served, together with the most de-
licious rice pudding Victoria ever had eaten (warm,
fluffy, drenched in heavy cream and abounding with
plump raisins), and the Tabors had agreed that Mrs
Rhodes unquestionably could have been a gourmet
cook in any restaurant in the world. Mrs Rhodes had
been flattered, and she even had blushed a little, and
she had made nervously disorganized little movements
with her hands. She wore her dark hair in a great
curving upsweep, emphasizing her high cheekbones
and long neck. There was nothing at all stylish about
the way her hair was done, but at the same time it
was admirable and probably gallant. And Victoria's
mother had said: Her hair is *her* hair. It is *no one*

else's hair. And on her it looks good. I believe that's
the secret of women who have true class. They don't
give a whoop for *fashion*, which means they have
the courage to *be* what they *are*. And Victoria's father
had agreed, adding: Whoever Mr Rhodes was, I feel
sorry for him that he's no longer among the present.
I mean, um, and please excuse me if I seem overly
enthusiastic, she is some gorgeous woman. I mean, she
is a fooler, so quiet and wellbred and all, and yet look
at her eyes. And the way she smiles. And that *corpus*
of hers. It is an experience simply to watch her
breathe. And, smiling, Victoria's mother had said:
Easy, boy. And Victoria's father had said: Well, there
ought to be a law against a woman such as Nancy
Rhodes. On the one hand, she has such a shy manner.
On the other, she has a face and, um, *apparatus* that
won't stop. And, laughing by then, Victoria's mother
had said: Why, Carl Tabor, you old lecher! And
Victoria's father had said: Guilty as charged, your
Honor. I throw myself on the mercy of the court.
And Victoria's mother had said: It is too late for
mercy. But then she and Victoria's father had embraced, and so apparently their argument hadn't been
very serious. Victoria was glad, since she liked Mrs
Rhodes very much. After all, Mrs Rhodes also believed in being quiet, in speaking softly. And Mrs
Rhodes appeared to have just as many secrets as Victoria had, and perhaps more. No one knew why Mrs
Rhodes was living in Cleveland. No one knew what
had happened to Mr Rhodes. No one knew why such
an attractive woman apparently spent most of her
time alone, except once a week, when she taught Sunday School to the little ones at the Wrexford Methodist Church. Maybe it was crazy of Mrs Rhodes to
be alone so much, but Victoria could understand that,
and perhaps she even loved Mrs Rhodes a little because of it. And on this particular Sunday morning,
after having disposed of her former friends, after

having tamped them and pounded them, after the umptyumpth conversation with her parents about how *sorry* she was and how much she *loved* them and how henceforth and forevermore, world without end, she would *go along* and believe in *fellowship* and stare sternly into the wrinkles and warts that covered the face of *reality*, Victoria needed to be with Mrs Rhodes, however briefly. And so Victoria hurried into Mrs Rhodes' classroom and went to its little blackboard and gathered up the blackboard's three erasers and took them to an open window, where she began beating them on the sill. Chalkdust came up, and the wind sucked it away. Mrs Rhodes, who was just finishing sweeping, smiled at Victoria. She tucked the broom inside a tiny closet, and then she said: I thank you very much indeed, Victoria.

Victoria nodded. "You're welcome," she said. She still was pounding the erasers.

There's no need to beat them to death, you know, said Mrs Rhodes, crossing to her desk, where she sat down. She wore a black skirt and a red sweater, and she appeared to move in many directions. She folded her arms across her bosom and she said: Are you angry about something?

"No," said Victoria.

I beg your pardon. It is none of my business.

"That's okay," said Victoria. Now the erasers were dusted to her satisfaction. She returned them to the blackboard, where she neatly arranged them in a little tray. "Is there anything else you want me to do?" she said.

No, thank you, said Mrs Rhodes. I believe I am pretty well caught up.

Victoria stood for a moment in front of the blackboard. She looked around. "Can I sit down?" she said.

Yes, of course you may, said Mrs Rhodes.

"Thank you," said Victoria. She went to one of the little classroom chairs and seated herself. She had attended Sunday School in this room from the time she was five until the time she was seven. Since then, she had attended the services upstairs, and she had listened to all her father's sermons. Mrs Rhodes had been her Sunday School teacher, and it had been at Mrs Rhodes' suggestion that Victoria had made the change. You're so very far along, Mrs Rhodes had said. You understand so much. Victoria never really had understood what Mrs Rhodes had meant. Maybe now was a good time to ask. She looked around. Crayon drawings of Jesus were displayed on a bulletin board. He was white and He was black, and in one of the drawings He wore what just about appeared to be a pair of jeans. Victoria formed an *o* with her mouth.

Mrs Rhodes smiled. You look very pretty today, she said.

"Thank . . . thank you," said Victoria. "So do you."

I thank *you*, said Mrs Rhodes.

"Everybody thinks so," said Victoria. "The whole world thinks so."

Oh? Have you taken a survey? You mean to say that there's not even a single Hottentot off in some obscure corner of the globe who disagrees with that view?

"Not a one," said Victoria.

Thank you very much indeed. I do believe you have made my day. Perhaps my year.

"Why did you say I was special?"

I beg your pardon?

"Two years ago, a whole long time ago, when I was, um, *seven*, you said to me I should, um, worship with the people upstairs. You said something about how I was, ah, so very far along."

I did?

"Yes."

Well, I simply meant you did not need to sit down

here and work with crayons and listen to stories
having to do with loaves and fishes. I didn't think it
was necessary that you be bored. I saw a great deal
of myself in you. I still do.

"Yourself?"

Yes, said Mrs Rhodes. She folded her hands on her
desk. I've never exactly been a mixer, she said. My
maiden name was Piper, Nancy Piper, and in school
the other girls called me a snob. They believed I was
a bit too standoffish, I think. You see, all my life I've
attached great importance to the value of privacy,
which we pronounce *privvissy* and you pronounce
pryvassy. Anyway, my *privvissy* gives me time to
dream, and even now, at my advanced age. And I
believe you hold your *pryvassy* in the same high re-
gard . . . because, you see, you also can appear to be
standoffish. The Victoria Tabor I see before me has
certain definite similarities to the Nancy Piper of times
gone by. I had a cat names Giles and a budgie named
Winston and a little white dog named Arabella, and
they were the closest friends of my childhood. *Budgie*,
by the way, is short for *budgerigar*, which is a sort
of parakeet. At any rate, my father was a chemist,
druggist to you, and we lived in a village to the
northeast of Plymouth, and every afternoon I took
tea with Giles and Winston and Arabella. *Took tea*
with them, if you can imagine such a thing—and I
believe you can. And I would relate the events of
the day to them, and after a time I assigned *words*
and *thoughts* and *personalities* to them, which of
course meant that my *privvissy* became even more
important to me, since my imagination had taken
such possession of me. But whom did I hurt, eh? And
whom do *you* hurt, eh? You're a—

"I hurt *people*," said Victoria, blurting.

I'm sorry. What did you say?

Victoria told the story as quickly as she could.
The races. The scolding. The remark. The scene in

Mrs Bee's office. The words yesterday in the front room. The tears. The apology. The barfing. Even the burial of all the dolls and animals and nightlights. And then she said: "Mrs Rhodes, how long will it be before I'm back together again?"

Mrs Rhodes looked away.

"Mrs Rhodes?" said Victoria.

Mrs Rhodes said nothing.

"I don't want to hurt people," said Victoria, "and I don't care whether it's Miss Platt or my mommy or my daddy or who it is, and *all right*, I don't care who goes back on whose word. *It doesn't matter.* I'm sorry about the canal water. I'm sorry about all of it."

They used to call me Nancy Piper the Human Viper, said Mrs Rhodes.

"What?" said Victoria.

Mrs. Rhodes looked directly at Victoria. She smiled. There was a gardenia in her hair. She patted the gardenia. She stood up. She came around her desk and stood over the place where Victoria sat. She still was smiling. She said: It was only a bad rhyme. It *meant* nothing. It was only a phrase some schoolgirls dreamed up because one of their number had the nerve or the foolishness to prefer the company of a cat and a budgie and a dog. I never was a viper, human or otherwise. I may have been stupid, Victoria, but I never was malicious. And neither are you. And you didn't hurt anyone. Not really.

"Then how come . . . how come Miss Platt bawled?"

She had a pet notion, and you interfered with it. But you didn't *hurt* her. And anyway, even if you *had* hurt her, she was in the wrong.

"But she *bawled*."

It's not the *fact* that she bawled. It's *why* she bawled.

"I'm sorry?" said Victoria.

Mrs Rhodes leaned against the back of Victoria's chair. Now, please listen to me, she said. Please listen to me very carefully. Your canal water remark was perhaps a bit rude, and I shan't deny that, but we must also consider its source. Why did you say what you did? You said what you did because a promise had been broken, and the breaker of the promise had had the nerve to scold *you*. The scolding should have been the other way around. Surely you must understand all that. You do, don't you?

"Yes," said Victoria.

Then you shouldn't allow yourself to be black-mailed. On the contrary. You should stand firm.

"I'm sorry?"

If I were you, I'd hurry home and dig up your dolls and animals. Maybe they're . . . maybe they're, ah, still breathing. One never can tell. Stranger things have happened.

"I can't do that," said Victoria, speaking quickly.

And why not? said Mrs Rhodes.

"Because I'm *different* now, and they wouldn't *mean* anything, and they're better off gone forever."

That's nonsense, said Mrs Rhodes.

Victoria blinked up at Mrs Rhodes.

Mrs. Rhodes patted one of Victoria's shoulders. Mrs Rhodes smelled good, and maybe the gardenia had something to do with it. She said: You are exactly the person you were yesterday. Otherwise, you wouldn't be concerning yourself so deeply about all this. You see, I really do detect a great deal of myself in you . . . dear old Nancy Piper the Human Viper. And I know how I would have felt if something similar had happened to me. I would have been just as desolate as you apparently are. *But I would not have changed, and neither will you, not really. You may think you will, but you will not.* Listen to me. My words are to be taken seriously, young lady.

Victoria nodded.

Thank you, said Mrs Rhodes. Now then, after church you are to go home and dig up your dolls and animals. I order it.

"I *can't*," said Victoria, almost whispering.

Can't or won't? said Mrs Rhodes.

Brightness flooded the little classroom. It came in a burst, and it brought motes, and Victoria blinked.

Mrs. Rhodes glanced toward the windows and said: Ah. The sun. Such a sudden manifestation. Perhaps it is a sign. Ah, but then there has been sun all morning, hasn't there? Still, perhaps there was a haze we hadn't noticed. Otherwise, why all this quick brightness?

"I can't dig them up," said Victoria. "Never mind the sun. *I can't dig them up.* I made a promise."

A promise? To do what? Bury your dolls and animals?

"No," said Victoria, choking.

A promise to go along?

Victoria nodded.

Mrs Rhodes sighed. She knelt next to Victoria's chair. She said: I live alone. I had a husband, and he was a perfectly fine fellow, and I loved him dearly, but he never understood about *privvissy*. And so, much as I loved him and perhaps still do love him, I no longer am married to him. I live alone, and I suppose I am experiencing the ultimate *privvissy*, and there are times when it is painful indeed, but isn't that particular pain my right if I choose it to be? I came to this country because my husband had a job here, and I have stayed on because I find my own job rewarding, and I don't really want to return to England and live with relatives and encounter former inlaws and have myself passed from relative to relative as though I were a *burden*. And this choice is mine and only mine to make. Oh, there are times when I yearn for home, when I look around myself in this country of yours and become terribly frightened, when I require the company of others. (After all, why do I teach Sunday School?) Nancy Piper the Human Viper is *human*, after all. The word is even included in her terrible nickname. But it also is human to seek to conduct one's own affairs in one's own way, and if this causes a certain loneliness, then that is the risk one undertakes, and it is a risk one is *entitled* to undertake. I bathe three times a day, once in the morning, once in the late afternoon as soon as I arrive home after work, and then just before I retire for the night. To some, all this bathing may seem excessive. All right then, let them think whatever they like. All I ask is that they leave me alone. For example, I would rather gather mushrooms than drink whiskey. I know quite a lot about mushrooms, actually. I drive into the country, and I trudge about, and my hair is held back in a kerchief, and I gather mushrooms in a little wicker basket, and I am able to separate the good from the bad. When I was a girl, I often took along my cat and my dog when I went on mushroom expeditions. I even occasionally took along my budgie, dear old Winston, keeping him in his cage, of course. And they have been my only companions on my mushroom expeditions. *Ever*. Giles and Arabella. Occasionally little Winston. Of course they all are Gone now, and not a single living creature has accompanied me since my girlhood. Not even my husband—when he was my husband—went along. He played golf instead. Or sat at home and read books about highway construction. He was an engineer, you see, and he was quite ambitious, and he took his work very seriously indeed. He still does. He has married again, and he and his new wife have two little girls, and they live out near Aurora, and the three of us occasionally meet for cocktails, which is all very *civilzed* and *decent* and *reasonable*, wouldn't you say? Well, *you* might say so, but *I* wouldn't. Ah, but pardon me, this has nothing to do with your dilemma.

Goodness, listen to me ramble on. Forgive me. I, ah, I have no more advice for you. I think you should go home and dig up your dolls and your animals and try to explain to them that you had a brief loss of reason. I know you say you can't, but perhaps you really can, if you think seriously enough about the situation.

"*No*," said Victoria. She dug at her eyes with her fists, and she told herself she *would* not *weep*. Her fists came away from her eyes. She opened her eyes.

Mrs Rhodes straightened up. Wincing, she rubbed one of her knees. I'm afraid I'm not as young as I once was, she said.

Victoria blinked up at Mrs Rhodes and said: "You're beautiful."

Oh, now . . .

"Everybody says you're beautiful, and everybody's . . . correct."

Really, Victoria, you don't have to—

"But I can't . . . dig them up."

I don't believe that. If you try to follow what I've been saying, then you—

"You're the most beautiful person I know, and I *want* to dig them up, but I just *can't*. Please, Mrs Rhodes, please don't keep after me about it."

Did your parents *order* you to bury your dolls and your animals?

"No. They don't even know about it."

Then rescue them before it's too late. The dolls and animals, that is. Not your parents.

"Too late?"

Yes.

Victoria swallowed. Her head moved from side to side. She said: "I shouldn't have told you about any of this."

And why not? said Mrs Rhodes.

"Because . . . because I don't *tell* people things. I

never have. I, oh, you know, the more people who
know things, the more, um, confused I get."
I understand that.
Victoria nodded. She tried to smile at her beautiful
friend.
Mrs Rhodes patted the gardenia in her hair. She
tugged down her sweater. She returned to her desk
and seated herself and said: Just try not to think of
the situation as closed. Please do that for me.
Again Victoria nodded . . . a little.
Privvissy forever, said Mrs Rhodes, smiling.
Victoria squinted toward the windows and the sun-
light.
I really mean that, said Mrs Rhodes.
"Okay," said Victoria, shrugging.
If we don't know who we are, how can we survive?
said Mrs Rhodes. Unless, of course, we, ah, *go along.*
Victoria nodded.
But there's a better way, said Mrs Rhodes.
"No," said Victoria.
Yes, said Mrs Rhodes, smiling.
Victoria glared at the sunlight. "Fellowship," she
said.
I beg your pardon? said Mrs Rhodes.
Victoria abruptly stood up. The sunshine was a
sign, all right, but it was the wrong sort of sign. It
said: *Open up, Victoria. Open up and let the real
world come pouring in on you. Never mind that silly
Mrs Rhodes. If her life is so wonderful, how come she
has nothing to show for it except maybe now and
then some yucky MUSHROOMS?* Victoria moaned.
She went stumbling out of the room. Mrs Rhodes
called after her, but she did not look back. She held
her little black patentleather purse with both her
hands, and she just about wanted to hug it. Now the
building was beginning to fill with people, and most
of them recognized her as the minister's daughter.
They smiled at her, and it was necessary that she

smile at them. And this was especially necessary now
that she had pledged allegiance to REALITY. PASS
IT ON. So she smiled at them. Mrs Vanauken, who
had a moustache and sang alto in the choir. The Tid-
blad twins, Barton and Martin, who were sixteen and
very fat and still attended Sunday School, perhaps
because of Mrs Rhodes. Mr and Mrs Trowbridge,
who once had been missionaries. Mrs Johnson, an
elderly widow who had a lacerated elbow that always
scabbed but never fully healed. Dr and Mrs Higley,
both of whom were dentists. Orville Sigafoos, an
ancient and gaunt fellow who reportedly had been
married to four women named Alice. F. DeWitt
Hoover, bald, dentured, fifty, who played the organ
and conducted the Wrexford Methodist Church choir
and taught music at Green Road Junior High School.
The Rev Mr Purcell, who was thin and optimistic,
with a high fractured laugh, who had been Victoria's
father's assistant for the past two years. Mrs Purcell,
who was as heavy and dour as her husband was thin
and optimistic, who was not yet thirty but already was
a mother of five, which perhaps explained why she
was unable to share her husband's thinness and op-
timism. Miss Patricia Forbes, tall, black, sharply cheek-
boned, with a baritone voice, numerous fur coats, and
a reputation as one of Cleveland's three or four most
successful fashion models. The Derwent sisters, Molly
and Gertrude, fortyish, giggly and flirtatious and
rather trim, who both were licensed embalmers and
operated a successful funeral home they had inherited
from their late father and a bachelor uncle. Calvin R.
Bing, a prosperous trial lawyer. Mrs Alice Slagle, a
widow who allegedly had once been married to Orville Sigafoos. Victoria smiled at all those people, and
she smiled at dozens more, and she nodded when some
of them told her how pretty she looked, and now and
then she even allowed herself a murmured exclamation
of modest denial. She joined her mother and father

in her father's office, and they all sat quietly. Her
parents did not ask her about her toys. Her father
leaned back and blinked toward a window. He also
glanced from time to time at his typewritten sermon,
and after awhile he looked at his wife and said:
Sandra, you know, I've been saving these things for
as long as I've been delivering them. Why do I save
them? Do I expect them to be published? Do I believe a groaning and anxious humanity is falling all
over itself waiting for a massive tome entitled: *The
Collected Lifetime Sermons of a Humble Shaker
Heights Methodist Sky Pilot?* Or perhaps: *Days of
Piety and Platitudes—The Wit and Wisdom of Carl
J. Tabor, Pastor to the Multitudes and Servant of
God?* And Victoria's mother smiled and said: Darling,
you want to know something? As long as you can say
things like that, there just may be hope for you, after
all. And Victoria's father looked at Victoria and said:
Do you agree? And Victoria said: "I agree." And
Victoria's father said: Will you come here and hug
me and say that? And Victoria nodded. She went to
her father and hugged him and said: "I agree." And
her father kissed her on a cheek. Even if I *am* too
dense, he said to her, I do love you very much. And
Victoria swallowed air, pulled back from him and
said: "Yes." And Victoria's mother said: Wellnow,
you two, how nice. And Victoria returned to her
chair and sat down and picked at her damaged fingernail. Her mother and father had *forgotten* about her
toys. And whatnot. Which meant they didn't care.
So big deal. They spoke, but she tuned out their
words. If they were talking to her, or if they wanted
to know about her toys (and whatnot), they could
shake her or otherwise seize her attention. In the
meantime, she would try to keep her mind vacant.
She knew there was nothing more she could face.
Not right now. Perhaps tomorrow, or perhaps even
an hour from now, but *not right now.* Enough was

enough. The words of the beautiful Mrs Rhodes had pushed away the last of Victoria's strength. Oh, sure. She never should have confided in Mrs Rhodes in the first place, but things have a way of sort of boiling out, don't they? And a person such as Mrs Rhodes is a good listener, isn't she? She is quiet, and she is beautiful, and she does not become angry or impatient. She speaks of a cat and a budgie and a dog and mushrooms, and her words reveal a calm and understanding that finally become altogether too much, don't they? And there you are, dear Victoria —*thinking* again. Grunting, Victoria stood up and went out of her father's office without saying anything. She entered the sanctuary, and more people smiled at her, and she tried to smile at all of them. The church was crowded, and she was grateful for her father's sake. Yes, he *was* dense, but yes, she *did* love him. She was able to smell perfumes and breath, facepowders, mints, papery things. The sunshine slammed at her. She walked up the center aisle to the pew where she always sat with her mother. Up in the organ loft, F. DeWitt Hoover began to play something appropriately thoughtful and anticipatory. It was mostly in the bass, with occasional little treble cries. Victoria sat down, and she was joined by her mother a few moments later. Her father entered the sanctuary through a side door, and he seemed to be in good voice. He led the prayers firmly, and he stood erectly, and he was precise in his enunciation of such words as JESUS and SALVATION and GOD and BLESSED and JERUSALEM and GALILEE and SAVIOUR and THESSALONIANS and MALACHI and MOUNT OF OLIVES and even good old FELLOWSHIP. She spoke the prayers, and she followed along, and from time to time she felt her lap being patted by her mother. And she smiled at her mother, who really was very pretty, perhaps not as pretty as Mrs Rhodes, but *almost*. There were hymns, and the choir sounded fresh and enthusiastic, almost as though it were welcoming summer and picnics and sweet kisses, and F. DeWitt Hoover's head and torso moved in urgent spasms as he played the organ, and the music came all bright and hopeful, and many of the choristers were smiling. And then came the sermon, and Victoria's father stood grinning in the pulpit (his forehead was a little moist, and now and then he rubbed his tongue across his lower lip), and he said: *Surely this is a time of year for renewal, and it is almost as though we have traded in our bones, isn't it? This week, while working on the text of the words I am now speaking to you, I often felt my attention being deflected . . . by the song of a bird . . . by leaves . . . by a gentle rain . . . odors of earth . . . the sound of a laughing child. And I said to myself: This is such a glory, to be surrounded by such simple richness. Why is it, then, that we permit our lives to become so complicated, especially when the complications so often lead to weariness and pain? And I thought: DEAR LORD, HELP US RETAIN SIMPLICITY. HELP US LOVE ONE ANOTHER OPENLY AND WITHOUT ARTIFICE. HELP US RENEW OURSELVES. HELP US, IF YOU WILL, TRADE IN OUR BONES. And oh, yes, I know . . . this planet has progressed beyond our poor powers of understanding, and matters of politics and finance and resources are more than any single human being can comprehend . . . and there are perhaps too many of us . . . and we are becoming too standardized per- haps . . . too bland, too intimidated by our environ- ment . . . but does all this mean that God's blessings are forever denied us? I say no, in thunder, if you will. I say that the RENEWAL, the POSSIBILITIES, are still open to us. It is never too late for us to change . . . to SEIZE THE BEAUTY and CHERISH IT . . . to find the tiny flame within us that is never without hope . . . to lay aside SELFISHNESS and*

SILENCE and turn to COMMUNICATING and SHARING . . . to say to our friends and neighbors: Ah, such a gift is this planet, and we must JOIN TOGETHER TO PRESERVE IT. For it will be THEN, you see, that we truly shall be able to treasure the private moment, since it will have been earned through our consideration of others. Here Victoria's father hesitated. He smiled in the direction of his wife and daughter. *I cannot conceive of a life without sharing,* he said, *any more than I can conceive of a life that does not have its rich moments of personal contemplation. But I must not let the personal contemplation interfere with my responsibilities. We are indeed our brothers' keepers. And we are indeed the keepers of all those we love, and all those who love us. So yes, this morning I do indeed rejoice in the fine weather, the sweet sounds and odors, the feeling of renewal, the thought that perhaps I have traded in my bones. But I do so in the context of my membership in the community of the human race, not as an isolated man brooding in an empty room. I cannot imagine anyone wanting the situation to be any different.* Here Victoria's father again hesitated. *My bones,* he said. *I am trading in my bones. Glory be to God in the highest.* And he smiled at the people who had crowded into the Wrexford Methodist Church that morning in early June of 1978, and there was a politely suppressed suggestion of laughter, and he said: *Oh, yes, perhaps I am strange, but I do try to say what I mean. God's most splendid Name be praised.* And now he was smiling directly at *Victoria,* and it was necessary that she look away. Then came more hymns and prayers, and the choir sang something having to do with abiding and patient angels. F. DeWitt Hoover moved his head and torso gently in time with the music. A fly crawled across Victoria's nose. She tried not to brush it away. She wondered how much willpower she had. She made fists, and then the fly flew

off, and she hadn't had to brush it away, which meant
maybe she had at least a little willpower, correct?
Or maybe more than a little. After all, she hadn't wept
even once since burying her dolls and her animals and
her nightlights. (Her toys and whatnot, as her forget-
ful father had called them.) The change was coming
along just fine, and Mrs Rhodes's words hadn't really
penetrated. Mrs Rhodes and her silly mushrooms. Poor
dumb beautiful Mrs Rhodes, so alone and all. And
there was nothing worse than being alone.

The service was concluded just before noon, and
Victoria and her mother stood at the main entrance
with her father, and a whole lot of handshaking took
place. And a whole lot of teeth were displayed. This
was a tradition and the congregation seemed to enjoy
it. A feeling of *family* was created, and Victoria always took care to display as many of her own teeth
as she could. She stood squinting and grimacing into
the sunlight, and there was a midday breeze that
caught at her skirt. Mrs Rhodes came out of the
church, and Victoria smiled at Mrs Rhodes. So did
Victoria's father, who told Mrs Rhodes she appeared
to be in blooming good health. The thin and optimistic Rev Mr Purcell was standing with Victoria's
father, and he grinned and briskly moved his head
up and down. The dour Mrs Purcell, who was standing nearby and holding two babies, glared at Mrs
Rhodes, and Mrs Rhodes looked away. But only for a
moment. Quickly, before Victoria could move, Mrs
Rhodes squatted in front of her and whispered: *Dig
them up.* Then Mrs Rhodes straightened. She hurried
down the church's front steps and did not look back.
Her body flowed, and the Rev Mr Purcell cleared his
throat. Calvin R. Bing shook Victoria's father's hand
and told him the analogy of the bones was a felicitous
one indeed, very amusing, just the thing for such a
warm and promising morning. Victoria's father
thanked Calvin R. Bing and said: Coming from such

a person as yourself . . . and believe me, your eloquence as a trial lawyer, Mr Bing, is acknowledged
by everyone . . . those words are much appreciated.
And Calvin R. Bing, portly, vested, shaggy, smiled at
Victoria's father and said: You should have taken up
politics. And Victoria's father said: I believe I already
have, the politics of salvation, I mean. And Calvin R.
Bing said: Sounds mighty portentous to me. And,
grinning, Victoria's father said: You can always trust
me to sound portentous. Snorting, Calvin R. Bing
moved on down the steps, and Victoria's mother
frowned at her husband and made a clucking sound.
You are the *limit*, she said, nudging him, shaking her
head. (Victoria looked down Shaker Boulevard and
watched Mrs Rhodes climb inside a little red car.
Dig them up, Mrs Rhodes had whispered. *Dig them
up. Dig them up.* Well, Mrs Rhodes would have to
be disappointed. The little red car started with a sort
of grunt, and Mrs Rhodes drove away. Victoria
wished she could do what Mrs Rhodes wanted her
to do. But Victoria couldn't. She knew Mrs Rhodes
had tried very hard to get her to dig up the dolls and
the animals . . . even going so far as to speak of the
vanished Mr Rhodes, thus providing Victoria with
more information about that gentleman than anyone
else at Wrexford Methodist probably possessed. And
that sort of talk no doubt had damaged Mrs Rhodes,
which meant it really was too bad Victoria would
have to ignore her. But Mrs Rhodes just could not, or
would not, respect the proper value of REALITY.
PASS IT ON. So Victoria would not dig up her dolls
and her animals and her nightlights. And she *would*
not *weep*.)

It was perhaps half an hour later that Victoria and
her parents walked home. They would be visiting
Grandpa Bird this afternoon in his condominium out
in Chagrin Falls. He had been ill all week with a
spring cold, and Victoria's mother had fixed a pot of

homemade vegetable soup for him. He's always been fond of my cooking, she said, and I know he's been fonder of it than I am.

Now, don't put yourself down, said the Rev Mr Tabor. You are a very good cook.

You're prejudiced, said Sandra Tabor.

I should hope so, said the Rev Mr Tabor.

It was nearly two o'clock in the afternoon now. Victoria and her parents were sitting at the dining-room table. Her mother had fixed a midday Sunday dinner of pork roast, lima beans, lyonnaise potatoes and applesauce, and there would be lemon sherbet for dessert. Neither of Victoria's parents as yet had gone into her bedroom, and so they still did not know that her dolls and animals no longer existed. Her *toys* and *whatnot*. The subjects of the questions they had forgotten to pursue. Huh. Victoria pushed her food around her plate, but she did not eat much of it. She did not have the space in her stomach. It was too knotted. There were too many things she had to concentrate on pushing away. Her father's sermon today, for instance. All that stuff about *sharing*. It surely was what he had meant this morning when he had announced he had revised the sermon more or less at the last minute . . . no doubt with the thought in mind to lay another good old zinger on good old Victoria.

I liked your sermon, Carl, said Victoria's mother.

Thank you, said Victoria's father.

Oh, I got the message, all right, and I'm sure so did Victoria, but at least it was delivered with some humor.

Which is unusual, coming from me?

Well . . .

The Rev Mr Tabor stabbed at a slice of pork roast. He popped the slice into his mouth, chewed, swallowed, then looked at Victoria and said: Your mother has a wonderful habit of praising me with faint damns.

Victoria frowned at him.

Now, *Carl*, watch it, said Victoria's mother.

The Rev Mr Tabor did not acknowledge his wife's words. Still looking at Victoria, he said: Did you understand the sermon?

Victoria nodded.

Did you understand how it applied to you? said the Rev Mr Tabor.

Another nod.

Good, said the Rev Mr Tabor. Then he turned to Victoria's mother and said: It was necessary.

Victoria's mother nodded. Of course it was necessary, she said. If sermons were not necessary, what would clergymen do to keep themselves off street corners and out of pool halls? Let's hear it for sermons, folks. Let's hear it for the eloquence of Sunday mornings.

The Rev Mr Tabor chuckled.

Victoria looked at her parents. Her eyes were dry. She supposed it was nice her parents were enjoying themselves so much. (Nothing maybe ever would be said about toys and whatnot.)

They all set out for Grandpa Bird's condominium shortly before three o'clock. Victoria's mother had piled the dishes in the kitchen sink, and she had said something to the Rev Mr Tabor about a dishwasher, but he hadn't replied. And so Sandra's mother said: I've never known *anyone* who's been such a . . . such a *virtuoso* at hearing only what he wants to hear. It is a rare gift. And again the Rev Mr Tabor chuckled. He had a good voice for chuckling. It put Victoria in mind of cement blocks bouncing in a gymnasium. He was driving the station wagon today. There was something wrong with the car's transmission, and he planned to take it to the Qua Buick people tomorrow. He drove the station wagon out

Shaker Boulevard and then Chagrin Boulevard toward the retirement village in Chagrin Falls. There was a great deal of slow Sunday traffic. Victoria curled up her legs, pressed her elbows against her knees, cupped her chin in her hands, and stared at the traffic. She was sitting, curling, rather, in the back of the station wagon. She wished it was fifty years from now. If it was fifty years from now, all this would be forgotten. She wished it was a hundred years from now. If it was a hundred years from now, everyone would be dead. The windows were open, and Victoria breathed shallowly so as not to inhale too many of the fumes from all the traffic. Sunlight reflected off hoods and headlights. Tires hissed. Tires slapped over chuckholes. Car radios were playing, and Victoria recognized the voices of Elton John and the late Elvis. She read signs that said CAR WASH FREE HOT WAX and GAS and DAIRY QUEEN and NURSERY and HEALTH SPA and ETON SQUARE and JAMES TAVERN. A car passed, and a little boy leaned out a window and made a face at Victoria, pulling at the corners of his lips with his little fingers while at the same time cackling shrilly and poking his tongue in and out, in the manner of a demented serpent. *Up yours, honeybunch!* he hollered, and then the car sped ahead. Victoria blinked. This was all she needed. Her mother frowned back at her and said: Did that little boy shout something at you?

Victoria shook her head no.

Are you sure? said Victoria's mother.

Victoria shrugged. "I don't know," she said. "If he did shout at me, I didn't catch the words."

All right, said Victoria's mother. She turned to her husband and said: How come our little girl is so good and all the rest of the children in the world are so bad?

We're lucky, I guess, said the Rev Mr Tabor.

I was thinking . . .

Good for you.

Now, don't *be* that way. I was thinking, Carl, she has given us her word, and she's never really gone back on it, and I was thinking, well, perhaps, um, no more sermons will be necessary. I think we have made our point about fellowship or whatever. Don't you?

Yes, said the Rev Mr Tabor.

Victoria's mother looked back at her and said: Excuse me. I'm talking as though you're not here.

"That's okay," said Victoria.

I just may have the habit as badly as your father does.

"That's okay . . . really."

Thank you, said Sandra Tabor. Again she turned to her husband. She said: Well, what about it?

What about what? said the Rev Mr Tabor.

Discontinuing the sermons.

Oh.

Well?

I suppose . . .

Look, she knows she was wrong. She has apologized.

But what about this morning when she wouldn't speak to me?

She's upset. It'll take awhile. This . . . this *business* . . . this canal water thing . . . because of it, a large change has been forced on her. Oh, I suppose it's a necessary change, but we do have to give her time to make the adjustment. In the meantime, she has promised us she'll be good and relate more to other people. How much more can we ask of her? I mean, can't we give her a little bit of the benefit of the doubt?

I . . . yes, I suppose so . . .

She's given us *her* word. Now can we have *your* word that you'll get off her back and stop hassling her and directing sermons at her?

We?

Yes, Carl. *We.* I admit the change is necessary, but you don't have to indulge in . . . overkill.

Overkill?

I'm afraid so.

The Rev Mr Tabor called to the back seat: Victoria?

"Yes?" said Victoria.

Do you feel overkilled?

"Pardon?" said Victoria.

Your mother seems to think I am leaning on you too heavily. Do you agree?

Victoria formed an *o*, but she said nothing. Now the station wagon was tooling along in what almost was open country, and she was able to breathe deeply. She scrunched around and faced away from her father and squinted into the sunlight. Cars whisked past in the opposite direction. She thought of her toys and whatnot. She thought of forgetfulness.

Do you agree? said her father.

Victoria shrugged.

Answer me, said her father.

Victoria turned and spoke directly toward the back of her father's neck. "I love you," she said. She wriggled forward and kissed him behind an ear. "I love you. I love you." She flopped back. She supposed forgetfulness didn't really matter all that much.

It doesn't matter, said the Rev Mr Tabor to his wife.

What doesn't matter? said Sandra Tabor.

Whatever she did, it's over and done with. And if I've overkilled, I'm sorry. I shall cease and desist. I cannot continue being the villain in the face of this love.

Thank you, said Sandra Tabor to her husband. Then, to Victoria: Did you hear that?

Victoria's little black patentleather purse had been lying on the seat next to her. She opened the purse and extracted an orange Life Saver. Her mouth was very dry, and she really needed the orange Life Saver. She opened her mouth and placed it on her tongue. She closed her mouth and began sucking. Moisture came, and then she was able to say to her mother: "I heard it."

Sandra Tabor reached back and patted one of Victoria's knees. Then: Everything will be fine.

Slowly Victoria nodded. She sucked on the orange Life Saver. She continued to breathe deeply. She blinked at cars. She blinked at a sign that said CHAGRIN VALLEY LITTLE THEATER ONE MILE. She saw a girl on a horse. The horse was brown, and it stood motionless in a field. The girl was perhaps twelve, and she was leaning forward and patting the horse's head. The field was speckled with some sort of small white flowers. Victoria briefly had a vision of The Peaceable Kingdom, but this was no time to be thinking of The Peaceable Kingdom, and so she made a face, and the vision went away. So her father no longer would overkill. Well, good enough. It surely would make it easier for her to keep loving him—and never mind his forgetfulness. And she needed to keep loving him. And she needed to keep loving her mother. She needed to keep loving as many *real* persons and things and ideas as she could find. Now that she had passed through her personal center point, she would always have to keep in mind the importance of REALITY. PASS IT ON. Oh, not that her new life was perfect. Ha. Just now, for instance, when she told her father she loved him, he perhaps could have done more than make some sort of flat remark having to do with villainy and something called overkill. He might have stopped this station wagon. He might have told Victoria to step outside into the sunlight so he could hug her. But perhaps the real world did not permit such behavior. There was a great deal Victoria would have to learn.

Or relearn. Or rethink. The last of her orange Life
Saver had liquefied, and she swallowed the juice. Now
her mouth was just as moist as moist could be. She
wondered what that horse girl had been thinking
while patting the horse's head. She said to herself:
Maybe when I'm older I'll be a horse girl, and I'll
be able to talk to the horse without anyone hollering
at me. A horse is real, isn't it? Suddenly Victoria was
bonebreaking tired again. And her head began to
hurt.

Now the station wagon was in Chagin Falls. Victoria's mother called Chagrin Falls *atmosphery*. There
was a gazebo in the middle of town, and the business
district architecture was mostly Victorian. Today the
business district was crowded with Sunday promenaders and observers—young couples holding hands;
children (and adults) licking at ice cream cones; girls
giggling and scuffling along in T-shirts and cutoffs;
boys, slack and unfocused, nudging one another and
pointing at the girls; elderly people, hatted and
wheezing, leaning on the rail of the bridge that passed
over the Chagrin River and afforded a view of the
falls. There was a languor to the afternoon, and most
of the promenaders and observers seemed almost in
nocent to Victoria, as though they were still loosely
seeking their own center points. But only loosely.
Slowly, what with the warmth of the sun. The station
wagon turned off the main drag and climbed a long
hill. Now the business district gave way to a neighborhood of homes, and most of the homes were old
and small and painted white. Most of them had been
built more than a hundred years before, and their
style (also *atmosphery*, according to Victoria's
mother) was known as Western Reserve. Victoria
had no real idea what Western Reserve meant, and
perhaps it wasn't all that important. After all, in a
world that was *real*, who cared about the style of a
lot of old houses?

I hope Daddy likes my soup, said Sandra Tabor.

He'll love it, said the Rev Mr Tabor. He always does.

At his age, a summer cold can be dangerous.

Well, I'm sure it'll be slayed by your soup.

As long as *Daddy* isn't slayed by my soup, said Sandra Tabor.

Again the Rev Mr Tabor chuckled. The station wagon entered the retirement village, passing between immense wooden white gates and under an arch that had the words CHAGRIN HILLS written in metal scrollwork. The station wagon moved slowly along a narrow street, and Victoria saw a number of old people sitting in folding chairs on the tiny lawns in front of their condominiums. Others were squatting over flowerbeds, and a few were simply standing in their doorways, as though perhaps they were awaiting visitors whose arrival time was uncertain. Her father parked the station wagon in front of Grandpa Bird's place, and everyone piled out. Grandpa Bird greeted them at the front door of his condominium. He wore only a purple striped bathrobe, a wrinkled pair of cloth trousers, and slippers—no doubt to hide the artificial foot. His slabbed flesh appeared to be blotched, and his hands were shaking. He smiled, though, when he saw that Victoria's mother had brought him soup. She asked him how he felt, and he shrugged and told her his throat was scratchy and he was having sweats. He looked past his daughter at Victoria, and he asked Victoria how everything was going. She shrugged, and then her father chuckled and told Grandpa Bird the past couple of days had been eventful. Grandpa Bird frowned, but Victoria's father explained no further. Instead he said: Mr Bird, I really think you need to lie down.

Everyone was standing in Grandpa Bird's tiny front room. He looked from the Rev Mr Tabor to Victoria, then back to the Rev Mr Tabor. He placed his hands

on his hips. What's *that* supposed to mean? he said.
You don't look well, said Victoria's father.
I don't mean my health, said Grandpa Bird. I know
I'm sick. But what I *don't* know is what you mean
when you say the last couple of days have been
eventful for Victoria. Stop running me up the flag-
pole, Carl. I may be an awful piece of old meat for
fair, but I'm not quite yet all senile, so tell me what
happened.

Victoria's mother broke in: Daddy, we're not going
to tell you a thing until we get you into bed.

Grandpa Bird blinked at Victoria. He gathered the
bathrobe more closely around him. His hands began
shaking again—now that they no longer were pressed
against his hips.

"I'm okay," said Victoria.

Really? said Grandpa Bird.

"Really," said Victoria.

You want your grandfather to go lie down, don't
you? said the Rev Mr Tabor to Victoria.

Victoria nodded.

And then Carl and I will tell you all about it, said
Victoria's mother to Grandpa Bird. She glanced at
Victoria and said: And you won't mind staying out
here, will you? I mean, you've heard it all and then
some, haven't you?

"Yes," said Victoria.

Grandpa Bird embraced himself.

Victoria's mother touched Grandpa Bird's forehead. Oh, *my*, she said, it's really *warm*, isn't it?

Grandpa Bird shrugged.

Victoria's mother went to her and gave her the
pot of soup and said: Please put this in the refrigerator. Then Victoria's mother returned to Grandpa
Bird, and she and Victoria's father began steering
Grandpa Bird toward the door that opened into his
bedroom. We won't leave out a thing, she said. Not
a single solitary smidge.

Victoria held the pot and watched them.

Her mother turned at the door and said to her: You can wait in here, or you can go outside and catch some of the sunshine, all right?

"All right," said Victoria.

Good, said her mother.

Victoria's father opened the door, and he and her mother were helping Grandpa Bird into the bedroom when Victoria said: "Grandpa?"

They hesitated. Grandpa Bird looked back over a shoulder at Victoria.

"It's been fiftyone years today," said Victoria.

Pardon? said Grandpa Bird.

"Rhoda Masonbrink," said Victoria. "The center point."

Grandpa Bird frowned, and his slabbed flesh moved heavily. Is this the fourth of June? he said.

"All day," said Victoria.

Now both Victoria's mother and father also were looking back at Victoria.

The fourth of June, said Grandpa Bird. My God.

Victoria nodded.

Never mind, said Victoria's mother to Grandpa Bird.

We can talk about it when we get you into bed, said Victoria's father to Grandpa Bird.

Just a second, said Grandpa Bird to both of them. He hesitated, then smiled at Victoria and said to her: I thank you very much.

"You're very welcome," said Victoria.

Victoria's mother sighed and made a clucking sound, but she said nothing. She and Victoria's father helped Grandpa Bird the rest of the way into the bedroom. Victoria's mother looked back at Victoria and said: Don't forget to put the pot in the refrigerator. And if you need us for anything, feel free to come on in. It's not that we're trying to hide from you or anything. Then Victoria's mother closed the

door, and Victoria was alone. She took the pot to
the kitchen and put it in the refrigerator. She glanced
out the kitchen window at the sunlight and decided
she didn't really want sunlight just now. She didn't
really want to be with those elderly people and their
folding chairs and their flowerbeds. One elderly person at a time was enough, at least for today. Later,
when she was rested, when she was more accustomed
to the new and very *real* way she was living, she no
doubt would have the time and the energy for the
entire world, plus the moon and who knew what all
else. But right now all she really wanted to do was
rest. So she went back into Grandpa Bird's tiny front
room, and she seated herself in his peacocked loveseat. Mutters and hissings came from Grandpa Bird's
bedroom, and she supposed her parents were giving
him an earful and then some, but she didn't really
care. She was altogether too pooped. Her eyes felt
gummy, and so she rubbed them. Now the mutters
and hissings seemed to come from all around her, and
she supposed she was so tired she had gone a little off
her good old rocker. She snuffled, and her eyes were
hot, but she *would* not *weep*. She looked around the
room, at rugs, chairs, the television set, endtables,
even the breakfront. She sniffed, and she was able to
smell Endust. Well, Grandpa Bird had always taken
pride in how well he kept the place dusted. *The
breakfront.* Some of the furniture was scratched, and
the rugs were worn thin and stringy, and the television set probably dated from about the time the
Romans were throwing the Christians to the lions,
but Grandpa Bird had everything in alignment, and
the newspapers and magazines were just so, and it was
nice that he took such pride. Victoria's mother and
father had agreed on this, and she had gone along
with them. *The breakfront with its collection of
china owls.* Oh, all right, maybe Grandpa Bird did
talk too much on occasion, and maybe there even

were other occasions when he drank too much beer, but it wasn't as though he was some sort of fiend planning to blow up the world. He was just an old man whose walls were too thin, who still mourned the lost and legendary Rhoda Masonbrink from fifty-one years ago, who dated his life from the night of her death, which didn't make much sense, but then how many things really did? *The breakfront with its collection of china owls, and its doors were open.* Victoria blinked at the breakfront. A rag and an opened spray can of Endust were on a table next to the breakfront. *The breakfront with its collection of china owls, and the doors were open, which meant Victoria could set them all free.* She grimaced. She saw Teddy, the big fellow, and now she knew why the mutters and the hissings were seeming to come from all around her. The owls had joined in, augmenting the sounds her parents and Grandpa Bird were making in the bedroom. But of course this was impossible, and Victoria supposed she was *more* than a little off her good old rocker. *China owls* did not *speak.* They no more spoke than a stuffed bear spoke. Or a cat that was a pulltoy. And china owls did not even mutter and hiss. This was the real world, and its china owls were forever silent, and all this was right and proper and logical. (That's what you think, my dear young lady, said Teddy.) Victoria smacked her ears with her palms. (There is no hiding, said Teddy.) Victoria's head moved from side to side. (If your friends become free, so do you, said Teddy, and the situation will be utterly bully all round. You must hurry home to your sandbox, and you must dig up your friends, and you must tell them you're sorry, and then—mark my words—you'll dine on milk and honey until all the clocks melt. And maybe you should invite your sweet and beautiful friend, Mrs Rhodes.) Apparently Grandpa Bird had been dusting the owls and the breakfront when Victoria and her parents had arrived. Sick as he had been, he had still wanted the place to be just so. Victoria was proud of him. (Don't try to force your mind elsewhere, said Teddy. We're just as proud of your grandfather as you are, but he's not the principal issue here.) Victoria rubbed her forehead. She was not hearing what she was hearing. She could not be hearing what she was hearing. If she really was hearing what she was hearing, then what really was really real? She stood up. She walked to the breakfront. Teddy looked at her through his funny glasses. She picked up Teddy, and she used both her hands. She read the legend *LOUISIANA PURCHASE EXPOSITION ST LOUIS MO 1904* that had been carefully inked on his chest. He was *such* a big fellow, and she liked the toothily quizzical expression on his plump face, and he no doubt would have enjoyed meeting Bear, and she . . . this Victoria Anne Tabor . . . abruptly threw him to the floor. And he bounced, but he did not break. He lay on his back, and he hadn't even flinched, and she knew this. She squatted next to him, and she stroked him, and she told him she was sorry, and he said: Bully for you. It takes a large person to admit such a serious mistake.

42 ᔍ Teddy

"MISTAKE?" said Victoria.

Of course, said Teddy. And now you must dig them up.

"No."

And why not?

"I gave my word."

So did your delightful Miss Platt.

"Well, my word ought to be better than hers."

Not when you promised to do something that you cannot and should not do.

"Pardon?"

Your father doesn't understand at all, and your mother understands only a little. Of all the human beings you know, only Mrs Rhodes sees the situation with any accuracy. Now, then, you *are* hearing me, aren't you?

"Yes."

Which means that either I exist or you are insane, correct?

"Correct."

Which do you think it is?

"I don't know."

Could it perhaps be a little of both?

"I guess so."

Bully. Now I do believe we are getting someplace. It all has to do with dreams, doesn't it?

"Yes."

If it weren't for a particular dream of mine, there would be no Panama Canal. I was denounced as being a lunatic, do you know that? And an imperialist. And I don't know what all. But the canal was built, and it still exists, and it has helped the world. Oh, there are *some* dreams that are not so fine. Simply because a thing is a dream, it is not necessarily good. Napoleon and Hitler had dreams, too. But still, we cannot condemn all dreams because some of them are corrupt. You understand this, don't you?

"Yes."

And my voice is coming clearly to you, isn't it?

"Yes."

Which means that I in fact do exist, correct?

"Yes."

Which means you cannot hide from your dreams, can you?

"Ah . . . I don't know."

Just now, when you threw me to the floor, you apologized. As soon as you did that, you acknowledged my existence. Which means you have readmitted all your . . . *notions*.

"No."

Oh, *yes*, young lady. As President of the Owls, I will not tolerate being contradicted. You've done nothing to warrant having your . . . notions . . . torn down.

"But what about the canal water thing?"

What about it?

"I met a little girl once. Her name was Sophie, and she was very rude, and she hollered a lot, and she called people names. And today, just a little while ago, a boy in a car called to me, and he said: *Up yours, honeybunch*. And . . . and, um, the thing is . . ."

The thing is what? Kindly get on with it.

"The thing is, um, when I told Miss Platt her, um,

her grandmother sucked, um, canal water through a leaky straw, how was I, um, any different from that little girl or the boy in the car?"

You really don't know the answer?

"If I did, I wouldn't ask the question."

But the answer is simple. If what you tell me about that little girl and the boy is true (and I'm sure it is, since you do not strike me as the type to wallow around in falsehoods), they acted the way they did for no reason. You, on the other hand, had reason. Ample reason. You had been betrayed. A promise had been broken.

"Pardon?"

Look, what had you ever done to that little girl? What had you ever done to that boy? Nothing, correct? Your teacher, though, did a terrible thing to you. So you had a right to say what you said, and I applaud you. I have always been a believer in strenuous measures against adversity and one's enemies.

"All right . . . but what about now?"

You must go home and dig up your friends.

"No. I made a promise, and I would be breaking my promise . . . which would, ah, make me just like Miss Platt."

That is not the same—

"And anyway, they're my, ah, *former* friends."

Victoria, there is something I must tell you.

"Yes?"

You are not to interrupt me. I will not tolerate that. I deserve respect.

"I'm . . . I'm sorry."

All right. Just don't let it happen again. *Now.* There are several more points that must be made. First, you made no *promise* to *anyone* to bury your friends . . . your *former* friends, as you incorrectly call them. Second, the promise you *did* make, the one having to do with your acceptance of this planet's socalled *reality*, was made under false and, yes, *unreal* pretenses. Third, since that was the case, you are under no obligation to honor it. Fourth, since the promise was invalid, then you would not be behaving badly—like Miss Platt, that is—if you walked away from it.

"But it all comes back to what I said before."

What?

"That, um, my word ought to be better than Miss Platt's."

You are impossible, young lady. *Impossible.*

"Why?"

Put as simply as I know how, it is just as, ah, immoral to keep an immoral promise as to break a moral one.

"Immoral?"

The promise you made to your parents was an immoral promise.

"No."

You have set your thinking adrift, Victoria. Kindly reel it back. *You* did nothing *wrong*, and I don't care what your father said or what he thinks. And the devil take his, ah, *stature.* He may be a widely revered clergyman and all that, but he is absolutely incorrect on this issue. And as for the burying of your dolls and your animals and your, ah, nightlights, that was a totally voluntary action on your part. No such demand was made on you, but you decided to take that drastic step out of what? love for your parents? a desire that no reminders of your former sweet existence be permitted to survive? Well, Victoria, to put it in the vernacular of your times, you have by and large behaved like a nerd.

"No."

Yes.

"No."

Do you want to cry? Is that it?
"No."
Oh, yes. Yes. I see. All right. Good. Now we're
getting somewhere. Good girl. Bully for you.

43 🦉 Tears

Victoria Anne Tabor, who *would* not *weep*, wept. She cradled Teddy against her chest, and she rocked easily and joyfully from side to side, and she mumbled choked little words having to do with how sorry she was that she had thrown him to the floor. He told her it was all right. He told her he was made of stern stuff. He told her it was bully she finally was able to weep. His voice was muffled and heavily cheerful against her chest. She wept quietly, and she was able to hear every word he said. She closed her eyes and felt the tears squirt, sting, flood her interior vision. She smiled, though, and the smile was a smile, not a grimace. She saw the misted river, and the creatures were making their way back across it, and she heard muted lowings and purrings and quick hopeful chipping sounds. She opened her eyes, and she held Teddy at arm's length, and she sniffled, and she told him she remembered their former conversation, and she told him yes, all right, she would see to it that he and the other owls would be freed from the breakfront. She told him she would take them all home with her, and they could watch while she dug up her dolls and animals and nightlights from the sandbox. But Teddy told her he was sorry; he and the other owls had made an adjustment in their thinking. Wiping at her eyes, Victoria asked Teddy what he meant. He told her he and the other owls had decided to stay here with Grandpa Bird. Your grandfather is a fine

315

gentleman, said Teddy, and we cannot leave him. We thought we could, but we cannot. Later, after he is Gone, will be time enough. For now, however, we choose to remain here and do whatever we can to distract him from his loneliness. Do you understand that? And Victoria told Teddy yes, yes, *yes,* of *course* she understood that, and she just bet Teddy and his friends were the best, the most decent and generous china owls in the whole entire world. And she kissed Teddy on the top of his head, and she wept some more. She lurched across the room, and she sprawled on the peacocked loveseat, and her knees hurt from squatting on the floor with Teddy, but who cared about *knees?* She hugged Teddy, and she stroked his belly, and she rubbed his smooth face across her warm eyes. Bully, said Teddy. Splendid. Good girl. You are fine and brave, and you will flourish. Victoria nodded, and more animals came back across the misted river, and the old farmer came back across the misted river, and the old farmer said to her: The secrets will return. The magical tablets. The private joy. And the poor trolls once again will have their compassionate champion. And the old farmer looked squarely at her with his brown and vaguely remote eyes, and he locked his thumbs in the straps of his navyblue overalls, and he said: You must hurry home. I do believe a happy ending just might await. Sand or no sand, they might all still be breathing. As long as the magical tablets exist, as long as the private joy exists, then they might all be restored, wouldn't you say? Magical tablets. Have you thought of magical tablets in connection with all this? Have you heard the sweet ceremonious words . . . and they are *harmonious* words as well, words that surely do have their place in any Peaceable Kingdom . . . that are written on the magical tablets, words that have no shape and dimension, yet lie so warmly at the heart of all this doughty and private benevolence? Of course you have heard those words, and of course you have seen the tablets. We return to you then. We gather within you. Only you could have exiled us, and only you could have caused us to return. Your glory is that you again understand that secret tableted language for which the words have not been devised. And oh, yes, your glory also is tears. They renew the misted fields and the misted river. Bless your tears. Bless their benevolence. For where is it decreed that we cannot embrace puckered fragrant warmth? What is the crime of possessing dreams that have a loving essence? that create loving identities? that enable us gently to survive? You and Bear and Teddy and Marybeth and Cat and Mrs Rhodes and your grandfather—and all the rest of your friends, whether they be of the earth, earthy, or of the heart, loving and humorous—carry the banners and the sandwich signs and the billboards and the trumpets and the neon lights and the tambourines and the electric guitars and the bullhorns of the Lord, and no day is trivial to you; no pain goes unfelt; no grief goes unrecorded, and you forever are occupied with the business of miracles, kisses, chocolate cake, home runs, cupped palms. So then bless your tears. May they come green and warm and lovely as the first day of a perfect universe. And then the old farmer slowly winked one of his brown and remote eyes, and he told Victoria (who still was weeping, or at least dabbing at her eyes) it was time she went into Grandpa Bird's bedroom and told her parents—and Grandpa Bird, of course—she needed to go home so this matter could be brought to its proper resolution. And so, nodding, Victoria rose from that peacocked loveseat, uncoiling herself and rubbing her knees, and she carried Teddy to the breakfront, where she carefully returned him to his shelf (and he thanked her, and he told her he just knew she would be brave and splendid in Grandpa Bird's bedroom with her parents, and he told her he wished her good health and all good things forever, or at least until her famous clocks melted), and then (nodding back at Teddy, thanking him for his kind words) she moved loosely and on flat splayed feet toward Grandpa Bird's bedroom door. And she opened that door, and she entered the room, and her mother was fussing with the sheets that covered Grandpa Bird in his bed, and her father was standing by a window, and Victoria said: "I don't want anybody please to interrupt." She closed the door and leaned against it. She swallowed, dabbed at her eyes. Then she tried to focus them on Grandpa Bird's slabbed flesh, but they were still too wet. And so she blinked, and she coughed a little, and no one moved, and she said: "It's all . . . no good. I can't . . . your world. I'm sorry, but I can't go inside . . . um, I can't go inside something that makes me *hurt*. I, um, *please don't anybody say anything right now . . . please?* I can't keep my promise. I can't go inside the things you say I got to go inside. It's none of it . . . good . . . for me." And here Victoria curved a hand over the doorknob, and she clutched the doorknob; she squeezed the doorknob, and she said: "I know I . . . all right, I know I hurt Miss Platt's feelings, and it's not right to hurt people's feelings . . . but how come I have to . . . how come I have to tear down everything? Well, I won't. I just *won't*. I mean, you, um, you don't know about my dolls and my animals, do you? *Do you, huh?* You don't know I buried them all in the back yard in the sandbox, do you? I buried them because I thought they were, um, *silly* and, um, *stupid*, and because *I love you*, and because I wanted to show you that okay, I understand what you were talking about . . . okay? *okay?* do you follow that? But it isn't right." Victoria's hand was moist from squeezing the doorknob. She released the doorknob. She flexed the hand. Her parents and Grandpa

Bird stared at her. They were motionless. Victoria blinked at them, and then she raised a hand, and she pointed a finger at them, and she shook the finger, and she said: "*I will not put up with this.*" The finger pointed directly toward Grandpa Bird. She said: "Remember when you talked about Rhoda Masonbrink? Remember when you told us all that happened that night was something you called the *center point* of your life? But you, um, you *also* said maybe you didn't *believe* in center points, remember? You said something about a life being . . . um, *breath*, right? um, *days*, right? um, *smiles*, right? Well, you were right." The finger moved up and down. "You were *right*," said Victoria. "It *is* breath and days and smiles . . . at least as far as *I'm*, ah, concerned." The finger moved from side to side. "For me, what happened Friday and yesterday—and they've told you all about it, haven't they, Grandpa?—was *no* center point. *Why should I change what I am because some silly woman broke her word to me and I told her what I thought of her and all of a sudden it was VICTORIA who was wrong; it was VICTORIA who didn't know the . . . um, the shape of the world; it was VICTORIA who had to show she was sorry?* Well, I . . ." Victoria hesitated. She looked at the finger. She grunted. She embraced herself. She said: "I, um, I want to go home now. I need to . . . um, dig them up. I love you, but I love them, too. They are as much of the earth, earthy, as you are. See, I can read the tablets, and I understand the ceremonious harmonious words, and I am the only person in this room who is loved by trolls, and do you understand? Daddy? Mommy? Grandpa? Have you ever heard me talk so much? Do you know how big this is for me? Do you think I . . . do you think I would talk like this if it wasn't like knives and forks and shovels and rakes and hoes, um, like all of them together *scooping* at me, huh? *Huh?* Listen, I am only nine years old, and I . . . and I . . . *I love you, but I love THEM, too.* I can do both, I know I can, and if I'm alone a lot, then I'm alone a lot, but that doesn't mean . . . that doesn't mean love gets blown away. Listen to me. *Listen to me. I LOVE YOU, BUT THERE'S MORE.* A whole lot. The things that were torn down, um, well, I'm building them back . . . on account of I can't change . . . on account of this is no center point . . . on account of that wouldn't be fair. I made a bad promise. I'm sorry, but I can't keep it. I mean, I want to hear those certain voices. I'm sorry . . . only I'm not sorry, you know? I can't be . . . I . . . oh, *please please please take me home right now.*" And Victoria felt her knees give way. And slowly she slid down leaning against the door, until she was sitting with her back propped against the door, and she continued to weep, and it was then that her father and mother went to her, and they knelt in front of her, and her father said: Yes. All right. Fine. And her mother said: I do believe we understand. And, calling from the bed, Grandpa Bird said: *Good for you!*

44 ⤳ Speed

VICTORIA WAS EMBRACED by her father, and she was embraced by her mother, and then she stumbled to the bed, where she was embraced by Grandpa Bird, and it didn't matter a bit about his breath. Victoria now was damp, ceremonious, harmonious, splendid and brave, and she smiled at everyone, and Grandpa Bird told her she would live as long as dreams lived, which perhaps meant forever. And then Grandpa Bird told her she had work to do back home, and she'd better get going. Your friends will be more than a little miffed with you as it *is*, he said. Victoria's mother hovered over Grandpa Bird for a moment, but he told her oh, Sandra, in the name of the Lord Almighty, will you and Carl kindly take your daughter home so she can do this thing that makes an old man's cold about as important as sawdust in a high wind? And Victoria's mother nodded. And she told Grandpa Bird she would telephone him as soon as Victoria's, ah, *business* was completed. She tucked up Grandpa Bird's covers, and now Victoria was standing first on one foot and then on the other, so Victoria ran into Grandpa Bird's bathroom and had herself a hurried Number One. Then her mother and father were ready to leave. They met Victoria in the front room, and Victoria's mother called to Grandpa Bird not to forget the soup, and Victoria nodded briefly in the direction of the breakfront and its now voluntarily imprisoned owls led by Teddy, their intrepid and outspoken President, who was so large and quizzical, who wore such peculiar spectacles, who carried the legend *LOUISIANA PURCHASE EXPOSITION ST LOUIS MO 1904* so proudly on his smooth white chest. He was a good old fellow, this Teddy, and from now on it would be great fun chatting with him when she was taken on these visits to Grandpa Bird's condominium. Right now, though, what with her tears, what with that *sermon* of her *own* she had delivered in Grandpa Bird's bedroom, all she wanted was to get home so the happy ending could take place. So she went to her mother and seized her mother by a hand and began pulling her mother toward the front door. And her mother made a small wry sound but allowed herself to be pulled. (The small wry sound came from behind a mouth that was happily crooked, like the mouth of someone savoring something sweet beyond reason and comprehension.) And Victoria's father followed right along, and good-byes were shouted back to Grandpa Bird, and his great mushy voice called to them to hurry, and it bade them good luck, and everyone now was smiling —even Victoria's father, that hortatory advocate of REALITY. PASS IT ON.

They piled into the station wagon, and this time Victoria sat in the front seat between her mother and her father. She was snuggled against her mother, but she was tall enough so that she could see above the dashboard . . . so that she could see the hatted elderly people, so that she could see the folding chairs and the flowerbeds, the arch that proclaimed CHAGRIN HILLS, the Western Reserve houses, the promenaders, the observers, the gazebo, the lickers of ice cream cones, the moist and awkward gigglers, the slack and unfocused nudgers . . . so that she could see the slow disintegrating afternoon begin to crouch, make plans to slink away from this pretty and *atmosphery* place . . . so that she could see and feel

how fast the station wagon was moving as it descended
a long hill and passed the field where the horse girl
had been patting the horse's head. And Victoria's
father said: All right. Now we know. And Victoria's
mother said: You *buried* them. Dear me. You *buried*
them because you *love* us. Oh, my goodness me. Oh.
And Victoria's mother curved an arm around Victoria's shoulders and squeezed Victoria, and again
Victoria wept. But this time she wept only a little,
and her tears were not unpleasant. The station wagon
zipped in and out of the heavy dawdling Sunday-
afternoon traffic, and Victoria's father said: See? We
are doing very nicely, aren't we? We are picking
them up and laying them down, aren't we? That's
an old phrase from my boyhood. When people said
an athlete, for instance, could pick them up and lay
them down, they meant that athlete had speed. The
ability to pick up his feet and lay them down. There
once was an outfielder for the New York Yankees
named George Twinkletoes Selkirk, and this George
Twinkletoes Selkirk was the first man I ever heard
described as having an ability to pick them up and
lay them down. Oh, since then there have been men
who have made George Twinkletoes Selkirk seem
almost *stationary*. Men such as Jackie Robinson,
Maury Wills, Lou Brock. But it's always George
Twinkletoes Selkirk who comes to mind when I
remember that old phrase having to do with picking
them up and laying them down. Say, do you want
to know something, Victoria? Perhaps you and I
aren't so different, after all. If I am able to project
myself backward in time a good forty years and
mull over an athlete the world has forgotten, anoint-
ing him with a legendary grace and speed that probably nowhere existed as vividly as it exists in my
memory, then perhaps I am not altogether an un-
imaginative, ah, turkey. Which means, ah, please try
to have patience with me. Please. And then Victoria's

father brought his foot down heavily on the accelerator, and the station wagon swerved around three cars, a pickup and a camper. And Victoria's mother said: Hang on, Victoria! He's in earnest! And Victoria's father grunted and said: That is a fact. And the station wagon careened in a wide arc off Chagrin Boulevard north on Richmond Road. It passed two cars by crossing a double yellow line on Richmond, and it had just turned left onto Shaker Boulevard when a siren sounded, and Victoria's father glanced into the rearview mirror and said: Oh, God.

45 ∽ Safety

THE POLICEMAN was small, and he had long side-
burns, and a little American flag had been sewn on
an arm of his shirt, and he wore a badge that said
MIGCHELBRINK. Victoria's father had pulled off
to the side of Shaker Boulevard, and MIGCHEL-
BRINK's cruiser was parked just behind the station
wagon. Lights flashed on the roof of the cruiser. They
spun around and around, and Victoria thought they
were pretty.

Victoria's father and MIGCHELBRINK were outside, and Victoria's father was showing his driver's
license to MIGCHELBRINK, and MIGCHELBRINK
said: You shouldn't endanger your family this way,
Mr Tabor.

I know that, but we were . . . in a hurry.

I wouldn't be surprised, said MIGCHELBRINK.

I don't normally drive that way.

That's very encouraging, said MIGCHELBRINK.

We have a sort of family emergency. My daughter
here

MIGCHELBRINK was writing in a pad. She is
very pretty, he said, interrupting Victoria's father,
and I can appreciate the fact that people do have
emergencies, but I think maybe you ought to put
your priorities in order, Mr Tabor.

Priorities? said Victoria's father.

Yes, said MIGCHELBRINK. You say it is an
emergency. Suppose you had lost control of your

car and it had hit a tree and your daughter and the
lady there had been seriously injured, wouldn't that
have been more of an emergency?

Yes.

MIGCHELBRINK nodded. He said: The lady is
your wife, isn't she? She is very pretty. I had a pretty
wife once. But she died in an automobile accident
because her brother was drunk and was joyriding at
about a hundred and ten out on Interstate 90 near
Mentor. So, as you maybe can understand, I have a
thing about reckless operation.

Yes, said Victoria's father.

MIGCHELBRINK was still writing in the pad.
He said: You look like a nice man, Mr Tabor, and so
I'll only give you a speeding ticket. Fortyeight in a
thirtyfive zone, okay? But try to remember what I
just said about my wife and her brother, okay?

Yes.

Whatever it is you're rushing to do, it can wait for
an extra five minutes. It isn't worth killing yourself.
It isn't worth killing other people. Am I making
sense?

Yes, said Victoria's father, nodding.

She was very pretty, and she was a graduate student
in English at Cleveland State, and she wanted to teach.

Oh, said Victoria's father.

MIGCHELBRINK finished writing. He tore off a
piece of paper and handed it to Victoria's father. Try
to stay alive, he said. Perhaps you can make a contribution.

A contribution, said Victoria's father, folding the
ticket and slipping it into a pocket of his trousers.
Yes. Fine. Thank you.

Now. This emergency. Is there anything I can do?
Would you like an escort?

A contribution. You mean a contribution to the
world?

Yes.

Oh.

What other sort of contribution did you think I meant?

Oh . . . none, said Victoria's father.

Did you think I meant some sort of bribe?

No.

Good, said MIGCHELBRINK. He smiled. I was only trying to be kind, he said. I may be the only policeman in the world who believes in kindness, but I spend a lot of time alone now that Joanne is dead, and kindness enters my thoughts more often than you might think. So would you like an escort?

Victoria's father nodded. Ah, well, you know, it might not be a bad idea, he said. The emergency has to do with my daughter.

Is she ill?

Not exactly, but she does need to get home as quickly as possible. We live on Wrexford in Shaker—the address on my license. She needs to do something that is very important to her. And, ah, it's very important to my wife and myself as well.

Fine, said MIGCHELBRINK. Then hop in your wagon. And let me lead the way. *How will I escort thee? Let me lead the way.* The only thing is—drive carefully. All right?

Yes, said Victoria's father.

Good, said MIGCHELBRINK. He hurried to the crusier, and he drove it in front of the station wagon. He turned on the siren, and it was one of those new sirens, and it went woop, woop, woop.

I think he may be crazy, said Victoria's father, starting the station wagon's engine.

Good for him, said Victoria's mother.

Amen, said Victoria's father.

Victoria smiled.

46 ～ Escort

MIGCHELBRINK waved the station wagon forward, and his cruiser went wheeling ahead, and the woop, woop, woop scattered traffic. Victoria continued to smile. Her tears all had leaked away. She concentrated on the pretty blue lights atop MIGCHELBRINK's cruiser. She decided that if MIGCHELBRINK was crazy, maybe there was hope for this world. She embraced her mother, and the woopings laid back her ears, and she displayed her teeth. Then she again concentrated on the pretty blue lights. Maybe the best center point was the day a person discovered there would be no center point. Victoria snorted, and her mother was saying something to the effect that none of this really was to be believed, and there was a whir of warm air and new leaves outside the station wagon's open windows, and the woopings curled around and through the air and the leaves; the woopings laid themselves braying and rude among the fat trees and the stolid lawns of Shaker Heights, and perhaps she should have been afraid, but the happy ending was too imminent, and she did not have the time to be afraid. MIGCHELBRINK's cruiser crossed the Rapid Transit tracks onto Wrexford, and a Rapid Transit trolley was approaching, but the woopings brought it to a stop, and the station wagon bounced over the tracks, and Victoria saw MIGCHELBRINK grin back at her from his cruiser. The trolley made a clean little dinging sound, and it was a sweet and familiar sound, and Victoria began to nudge her tongue a little with her teeth. MIGCHELBRINK's crusier and the station wagon passed the Wrexford Methodist Church, and the woopings persisted, and then the cruiser came to a stop in front of Victoria's home as the station wagon pulled into the driveway. Victoria and her mother and father got out of the station wagon as MIGCHELBRINK came running up to them. Victoria hurried toward the garage, and her parents and MIGCHELBRINK followed her. The woopings were beginning to subside. Her father was telling MIGCHELBRINK about the dolls and the animals and the nightlights, and she heard MIGCHEL-BRINK say something to the effect that yes, yes, okay, you're right, Mr Tabor; it *is* an emergency. At the same time it occurred to Victoria that the name MIGCHELBRINK almost sounded like Masonbrink. She ran into the garage and pulled down the shovel she had used to bury and tamp and pound her dolls and animals and nightlights. Briefly she wondered how many of them she had broken. She drew a sharp breath. She rushed out of the garage and ran toward the sandbox. She was moaning a little, and perhaps there wouldn't be a happy ending, after all. She heard her father go into the garage and fetch another shovel, but then she heard MIGCHELBRINK say: Hold it, Mr Tabor. Don't you think she ought to do it all herself? And then, speaking slowly, her father said: Ah . . . well, yes, you do have a point. And MIGCHELBRINK said: Good.

47 ❧ Exhumation

VICTORIA TOSSED ASIDE her little black patentleather
purse. She was standing by the sandbox now. Carefully she laid down the shovel. She spat on her hands,
then rubbed them together. She picked up the shovel.
The woopings had subsided entirely, but not before
several neighbors had come into the Tabor backyard.
They included old Mrs Portman, from across the
street. She was wearing a flowered dress. The Grassos
from next door also had been attracted by the woopings. They included Mr and Mrs Grasso, their twin
sons, Danny and Donny, who were fifteen, and their
daughter, Rosalie, who was twelve. Danny and Donny
were wearing identical T-shirts that said Cleveland
Cavaliers. Mr and Mrs Hinchcliffe also showed up.
Mr Hinchcliffe was a lawyer, and he had a purple
birthmark on his neck. Mrs Hinchcliffe belonged to
the National Organization for Women, and her nickname for her husband was Piggy. Mrs Hinchcliffe
had extremely heavy arms and thighs, and they often
flapped. All these people, together with Victoria's
mother and father and of course MIGCHELBRINK,
stood in a semicircle and watched Victoria as she
went to work with her shovel. She was aware of
whispered questions, but she did not bother to try
to follow the words. She dug carefully. She tried to
focus her ears on the sandbox. She motioned for
silence, and all the persons in the semicircle stopped
their whispering. She dug. The shovel scraped some-

thing or other, and so she dug even more carefully. Sand began to pile up outside the sandbox. She listened, but she heard nothing other than the shovel, the sand, a hissing of trees, her own breath. Her tongue rubbed a corner of her mouth, and her head began to hurt. She tried to think of misted fields, a misted river, beasts, an old farmer, sorrowful trolls. She tried to think of the beautiful Mrs Rhodes, of *privvissy* and mushrooms. Now the shovel was beginning to scrape all sort of things . . . cloth, metal, glass, plastic . . . things furry and yielding . . . things hard . . . things that rattled. And then, speaking hollowly and with some weariness and exasperation, Bear said: Well, it's about *time*.

48 ⚘ Resurrection

VICTORIA TOSSED the shovel aside. She dropped to her knees, and it didn't matter that she was dirty; it didn't matter that her skirt and her blouse and her stockings and her shoes were dirty. She worked with her hands, scooping, and she pulled Bear from the sand, and his eyepatch was intact, and sand drained from his ears, and he said: Patooey. Yuck. Victoria hugged him, and he said: I really was beginning to become a little vexed. And Victoria nodded. And gently she set Bear aside. And she dug up Cat. And she dug up Bonnie (whose poor Dolly Parton hair was absolutely *filthy*). And she dug up Rabbit, Pluto, Mickey, Marybeth, Kermit, Bugs, even Henry (and even Henry's missing tail). And the semicircle of witnesses murmured baffled little words. And the semicircle of witnesses murmured loving little words. And MIGCHELBRINK made a satisfied sound that came from high in his nose. And Victoria's mother and father came to her and crouched next to her. And they kissed her. And she nodded. And people began to move away. She heard one of the Grasso twins say wow, it sure did take all kinds. And she heard MIGCHELBRINK say wow, thank the Lord it took all kinds. And she heard herself weep, but she smiled at her parents, and they continued to kiss her, and her hands brought from the sand all her former friends who were her friends again, and the sand was warm (she remembered it as having been so

terribly wet), and MIGCHELBRINK squatted next to her and told her she was out of sight, and he kissed the top of her head, and then he straightened and walked away, and now Victoria was alone with her parents and her friends, and twilight rushed across the sky, staggering, happy, loud, free.

Victoria began gathering her friends in her arms. And she took them inside the house and upstairs to her room. This required several trips, and she asked her parents not to help her, and they smiled, and her father told her yes, all right, they understood. And how the animals did joyfully low and purr in The Peaceable Kingdom. And how the old farmer did clap and grin. And the trolls said: Thank you. And all the tablets were displayed to Victoria, and they were as clear as ice and laughter and perfect final glory.

49 ☙ Comments

THAT NIGHT Victoria sat on the floor of her bedroom. Newspapers were spread all around her, and she cleaned her friends, and just about all of them had comments to offer.

Said Bear: I kept seeing my life passing in review. About the third time, I began to worry. I figured if I wouldn't expire of suffocation, I would bore myself to death.

Said Cat: A squeaky wheel is supposed to get grease, not sand.

Said Bonnie: I think I lost maybe a dozen sequins back there in that old sandbox. And my *hair*, Lordy, Lordy.

Said Bugs: It's good to be back on the job.

Said Rabbit: Be careful with my nose. I do believe it's chafed from all the sand.

Said Marybeth: I'm not *cracked* anywhere, am I? My *face* is all right, isn't it?

Said Bear: I hope someday I'll be able to meet your friend Teddy. He must have been a great help to you. And I would like to remind him of the meetings we had in the White House. He always was a bit too belligerent for my taste, but he had a good heart, and his courage was not altogether reckless.

Said Pluto: I felt as though I were taking part in a short story by Edgar Allan Poe, which wasn't much fun, believe me.

Said Mickey: Myself, I kept wondering whether a

335

cat would come and . . . ah, what with the sand, I mean . . . ah, come and *use* us.

Said Marybeth: Ugh.

Said Pluto: You can say that again.

Said Marybeth: Ugh.

Said Bear: The change is no change, and it does not matter what you said about Miss Platt's grandmother and the canal water. You are what you are, and no one has a right to step in from the outside and hurt you and betray you because you choose not to change, or adjust, or *go along*, or indulge in the practice of *fellowship*. I love you, Victoria. We all love you. We are glad you have returned to being what you always have been.

Said Kermit: There may be a hole in my flipper, but my heart will always belong to you.

Said Bear: Happy endings are the best.

Said Henry: Thank you.

50 ❧ So

So PASSED, then, the matter of Victoria's rudeness and the premature burial of her friends. So passed, then, the matter of a center point that did not exist. Victoria's mother gave her an excellent, fragrant puckery bath that night, and the house abounded with cupped palms. Victoria got to wondering whether such a person as MIGCHELBRINK would have any interest in mushrooms. Victoria's mother and father both tucked her in bed that night, and she was joined by all her friends. Victoria's mother had telephoned Grandpa Bird and told him everything appeared to be all right. She had conveyed Grandpa Bird's congratulations to Victoria. And Victoria had smiled. And she continued to smile as she slipped off to sleep. She wondered if there ever would be a way she could explain the situation to Miss Platt. She did not suppose there ever would be. She should have been sad about this, but all she could feel was a vague regret. All persons did not understand all things, and this was a new truth Victoria Anne Tabor would have to remember. She slept, and she did not suck her thumb. Her dreams were serenaded by choirs of happy trolls, and Bear's head lay against one of her shoulders. She saw mushrooms, and she heard a sweetly fluted voice say: *Privvissy*. And so she survived. And so she lived happily ever after . . . or at least until the next morning. And so.